ALSO BY

IOANNA KARYSTIANI

The Jasmine Isle
Swell

BACK TO DELPHI

Ioanna Karystiani

BACK TO DELPHI

*Translated from the Modern Greek
by Konstantine Matsoukas*

Europa
editions

Europa Editions
214 West 29th Street
New York, N.Y. 10001
www.europaeditions.com
info@europaeditions.com

Copyright © 2010 by Ioanna Karystiani
Kastaniotis Editions S.A., Athens, Greece
First Publication 2013 by Europa Editions

Translation by Konstantine Matsoukas
Original title: Τα σακια
Translation copyright © 2013 by Europa Editions

Library of Congress Cataloging in Publication Data is available
ISBN 978-1-60945-090-8

Karystiani, Ioanna
Back to Delphi

Book design by Emanuele Ragnisco
www.mekkanografici.com

Cover illustration by Margherita Barrera

Prepress by Grafica Punto Print – Rome

Printed in the USA

CONTENTS

BACK TO DELPHI

THE SACKS

M
ay.
Ourtside, the sun brehind clouds, a brutterfly. Inside, the lirving room with no carpet, the borxes, two erggplants in the plattcr, half a canteroupe.

Anxious again. That's why the invasion of the r's into what she was looking at, the sun at dusk, the balcony, the floor, the household objects and what she thought of momentarily, having had nothing to eat since morning, eggplants and can teloupe.

For the best part of ten years she only cooked once a month, roast beef usually, and took it to Linus. On several occasions, he had refused to appear bchind the squarc of glass and she took the Tupperware back to her place, didn't touch it, the food was left in the fridge and forgotten.

She never put on a pot or pan for herself, her place shuttered down for all visitors as well, never did she wine and dine relatives, never invited a soul over for as much as a coffee, she made do with bread and cheese, a tomato every now and then, a piece of fruit.

A lack of desire for warm food, a voluntary deprivation of the right to pleasures, if negligible ones and, above all, frugality, for years she had not thrown out even a sprig of dried up parsley.

Thursday, May 3, 2007, dusk.

The wound up Vivian Koleva, who carried fifty-two years of weariness and seventy-eight kilos of sadness, shoved three white work robes in the washing machine; she poured a bit of the remainder of the plant food into the two pot plants, watered them, used a pair of scissors on the bits of the balcony tent that were frayed, called the Bulgarian replacement—the old woman's all right—went to the bathroom, finally, is now all cleaned and spruced with cologne, she'll go to sleep like a baby, she called the general's sourpuss of a granddaughter, Annie, darling, go to the Public Health Fund tomorrow, because you are entitled to free creams and nappies for bed sores, we can hardly catch up with grandpa, third bloody phone call to Castoriani about the milk from Alexandria, you go ahead, my precious, and have two spoonfuls and I promise you I will pray to the Good Lord in churches high and low for your normal ingestion, there's my career, right there, from tulle to turds, she thought.

She didn't feel comfortable leaving her clients in strange hands for all those days, she was hard pushed doing it, up till now she was always available, every minute of every hour, day or night, to rush to the side of those creatures with their mouths open like a pocket with a hole through which the money had fallen out, and their jaundiced eyeballs which at some time must have been like everybody else's, as cool and transparent as an almond flower.

She called the lovebirds at Exarcheia Square, spoke with the husband, be good, she asked of him, she also called the Cretan Methuselah, he had his improvised limerick all ready. *Make of your life a song and a delight, for death has you in his sights*, he wished her a good time at the wedding, and to give his best to her relatives getting married, and she thanked him in a way that pleased him, yes, my handsome, and when your time comes, I'll make sure to yell out, shit on your grave.[1]

She finished with the clients but didn't put down the

---

[1] A form of well-wishing, the Cretan equivalent of "break a leg."

receiver, she called the janitor of the apartment block for the
utility bill, it's not out yet, Viv, you the only one can't wait to
pay up, she also called Yukaris, everything's arranged I'm
telling you again, be there at seven in the morning, have no
fear, Viv, just keep yourself in check and keep your eyes peeled.

Yes, peeled all the way back, she thought and got up. She
folded the clothing and underclothes in her traveling bag, prepared Linus's knapsack, the hard part was laying hands on the
new shoes, she set the two pieces of luggage next to the front
door.

She took out the wallet from her purse, counted the money
again, eight one hundred bills, four fifties, change, the bank card,
her two ID cards. She put it back in its place, in the two side
pockets her sunglasses, the two ancient booklets, the three
receipts folded in two, the four photos inside their envelope,
some womanly tidbits and the small agenda with the useful
phone numbers, few that they were, she knew them by heart.

She went to the kitchen and fetched the iron pestle and the
cheese knife, put those in the bag, there was plenty of room for
both, but in the end, she only kept the one, returned the knife
to its drawer.

She had bought the pestle up north, in Komotini during a
three-day holiday, over twenty years ago, she never did make
garlic paste or roe paste, she'd set it along with two more
bronze ornaments, an oil lamp and an oil carafe, up on a high
shelf, no time to dust, let alone polish them, they'd gone all
motley. Though they were souvenirs of a happy outing, she
would have gotten rid of those as well in the general household
clean-out or while moving house, but they were saved every
time by a high shelf.

She went back into the hall, hung her purse over the two
pieces of luggage and thought, not for the first time, that
through all the years the coat hanger's four hooks only ever
bore her own clothes and knickknacks, her coat, her raincoat,

her umbrella, her bags, the worn wraparound for the cool night shifts on the narrow balcony.

From that position she now craned her neck and she gazed over her shoulder at her living room, a warehouse. The way things had turned out, there was no way she would lighten it up for the sake of appearances, embroidered curtains were out of the question as were flower vases.

Where does one, at this point, find the courage to steer one's life in a new direction, she thought and checked the time, nine in the evening, all set, now for the kitchen.

She put on the boiler, dipped in the scalding water the same tea bag for the third time, as she was in the habit of doing since the year before last, took the cup with the watery liquid and a piece of bread and went to the couch. In a low voice, diligently she recited the memorized phrases, a sip, a bite, a paragraph, the Amazon battles on the six decorative panels of the Treasure of the Athenians, the famous Sphinx of Naxos raised on an Ionian pedestal.

Possible questions: Who were the parents of the Sphinx? Typhoon and Echidna. Who were her siblings? Cerberus, the Lernaia Hydra and a coterie of other monsters. Very good.

She leaned into the back of the couch, brought her pinkie gingerly to her upper lip, there was the familiar business fermenting there, she would see the new day with herpes again. The blood was leaping through her arteries like a frog, her head a peeled cabbage, her mind eaten away by the caterpillar, she could feel it crawling, sucking away, getting fat.

She needed to give herself over to other thoughts, the mind cannot be emptied, it takes no days off.

So, then. From the Baltic comes amber. Twelve feet below the surface of the water there are transparent stones, yellow, red, brown ones, with enclosed tiny leaves or insects from the distant past. The pale ones always fetch a better price, one thousand five hundred drachmas for a good piece.

When the sea freezes over, the wild amber collectors drill holes and stick in hoses, the water pouring in at high pressure and dislodging the bottom layers so that the precious weightless sun stones are thrown up, that's what they call them. The Poles of the Gdansk thread them into necklaces and put those on their babies. Rhoda, the maid of honor at her wedding, had brought them one, there wasn't a place on earth she hadn't been to, seminar after seminar, journey upon journey. And truckloads of fucks as well, a connoisseur of dicks the world over.

Vivian Koleva's mind wrapped itself around amber at ten, unwrapped itself at ten thirty, chased after other alternatives, fixed for a while on the cost of getting a car serviced, a round two hundred paid up front, seized on changing the electric water heater, another two hundred for the plumber's fee, plus one hundred and eighty for the son's latest expenses plus fifty for the wedding bonbons, and, painstakingly, by means of the expense accounts, she expedited time.

Till two in the morning she didn't stir from the couch, rigid in the same spot, scrunched between cardboard boxes and bags, next to the silent radio, facing the switched-off TV, pinned to the silence of her own apartment and the scratching sounds from the one next to hers. The seventy-eight-year-old neighbor, with full-blown Alzheimer's, was struggling to let himself out the door to wander the streets. At one time a wealthy man in Africa, ivory and wild animal skins, then a business executive here, now with most of the big money whittled away, a widower, in the care of Juliana, a Ukrainian who, having grown tired of looking for him in the surrounding squares, put on security locks, hung the new keys around her neck and gave Tiger the old ones so he could scratch at the door, trying one after the other, again and again, for hours on end, days and nights, weeks and months.

It was always an issue at the building residents' meetings, Viv did not attend, from the first floor she could hear from the foyer fifteen or so irate voices berating the Ukrainian. Viv herself had grown used to the sound through the thin walls, like the woodworm eating through the furniture, a kind of company in her empty evenings when she got in from work, put her swollen feet up on the armrest of the couch and gazed at her belongings, piles of nappies, some fancy puff-sleeve outfits, leftovers from the *Titi* saga and a wealth of other objects, each hailing to a donator, the last that remained till she got rid of those ones as well.

A pink opaline vase, enormous like a pregnant belly, from her maid of honor, now in service as a carryall for small change, tacks, paper clips and phone cards, the handmade Cretan chair, a wedding gift from coworkers of his, she didn't use it because it gave her back pain, the Canadian lamp with the red leaf, turned upside down so the bump couldn't be seen from the punch, hers, the day before yesterday, during a solitary outburst, and a couple of knickknacks, a cigarette case with Saint Sophia and a cat-shaped ashtray, bequests from a client's heart failure, a fervent smoker who was bound to continue puffing away in the eternal pastures as well.

The trajectory of the gaze was the same tonight as ever, a little like a routine check to make sure the evidence of a forfeited life was in place.

Next door, the old man was getting his face slapped, the Ukrainian had a heavy arm, the night grew quiet and Vivian Koleva breathed deep. Before getting a blanket to throw over herself in order not to truss up the bed and waste time in the morning making it, she went into the kitchen, opened the cutlery drawer, trying one by one the sharp knives against her hand, the serrated bread knife, the razor sharp meat knife, she chose the small cleaver, took it to her bag, fitted it smugly in at the bottom, under the booklets, the tissues, the keys and the lipstick. Still, she didn't go back to the couch, she stood right there on the spot with her mind working at high speed.

Hold on, what if I stumble and take a fall and the contents of the bag spill on the floor, I'm done for, I won't have anything convincing to say, thank goodness I thought of it in time— there, she hadn't set up the five-day outing in every detail, after all. For a moment she thought of packing a plastic bag as well, so she could say that she intends to gather an armful of wild medicinal weeds, that get rid of white spots from the nails, wild oregano for dyspepsia, roots and herbs for cough medicine, on orders from her clients—old folks do require their elixirs and panaceas.

But, then, she had to change the cleaver for a common knife, she'd take the watermelon knife with the nine-inch blade. To be on the safe side I might as well change the bag too, might as well take the old brown thing with the zipper and make sure it's kept shut, she whispered to herself and then, while emptying the wide beige canvas bag, she got an even better idea. She went to the drawer and got a yellowing, uncut tome of Sikelianos from the terrible period when she had bought a dozen different poetry collections. There were three left, all uncut, thankfully, sometimes while rummaging for contracts, old bills or pens, she would stumble on the slim books, remember the accompanying circumstances, open one at random and read the beginning, the middle or the end of some poems. A few, the slimmest ones, she had read from beginning to end in fleeting moments, all forgotten now.

In five minutes, the brown bag with the zipper all set, Vivian sighed and returned to the checkered couch, to cover herself with the checkered blanket, to stretch out for a few hours, get her strength up for the five-day sojourn. Her courage, too. Enough of it for two people. Herself, she was an old hand at endurance, with any number of sunny days to waste still before her, but he, faced with the spaciousness of May, might lose his marbles and start banging his head against the ancient ruins.

The truth is that she had, in fact, entertained just such a

possibility. Several times. Sometimes fleetingly, on two or three occasions her thought got stuck there for days and nights on end.

The first unbearable year, whenever the phone rang, rarely, her heart skipped a beat—they'll tell me he's hung himself, she steeled herself for the news from an officious voice, slightly softened and wavering for the occasion, with an imperceptible stammer and appropriately compassionate.

She would grasp the receiver, glue it to her ear and, after putting it back down, she would virtually collapse in the armchair, deadened for ages, though the call may have been from the Express Service guy, asking when to come by for the renewal of the biannual contract, or from the diligent tenant of the office space in Pangrati, informing her that he'd put the rent in the bank.

She had asked herself, certainly, if she was afraid of such a turn of events or maybe even, deep down, wished it—suicide brings out people's pity and also acts as a detergent. It would be the only real end to their hell, an act of desperation and simultaneously of courage, of release when it's all said and done, and of justice, too.

The years kept passing, the hanging wasn't eventuating, that awful feeling in her of mixed dread and expectation faded, until in recent months a plan had again asserted itself in her mind for their joint redemption.

In order to decide on a destination and stay during the five days, she had used up eleven Sundays, January 7, 14, 21 and 28, February 4, 11, 18 and 25, March 4, 11 and 18, venturing in her dilapidated blue Fiat at one point in the direction of Nafplion and surrounds, towards the mountainous Akrata and Dimitsana, at another in the direction of Evia, towards Calambaka and Mt. Pelion, in order to oversee the environs, appraise the landscapes and hotels, spy on the people and their doings, and in covering several hundreds of miles, she had checked out the sharp turns thinking that, even unintentionally, due to the shakes she might get at the right spot, she could lose control of the steering, smash into a rock, send them tumbling down over and over till they ended up in pieces at the bottom of some gorge. Once she was back on to a straight piece of road, she would pull over for a while and bang her head on the steering wheel at her leisure, there was nobody watching, so she owed no explanation and no apologies, afterwards she wore a bandanna low on her forehead to cover up the bruising and the scratches.

Scented pine forests, verdant fields, hillsides with olive groves, orchards with citruses which she had no right to peruse with pleasure, years now with not a half an hour of ease and recreation.

No company, either. She could barely muster the courage herself to think directly of events in themselves, the routine, strictly, of consequences, the unfinished business of each day, the duties concerning the probably grim and hopeless future, how could she possibly share the burden, how could she voice the details required by third parties in order to get their fill of someone else's consternation and how stoop to the mercy they would halfheartedly offer?

On account of the creature, about whose misshapen form she still wondered out of what bellows and what anvil it had emerged, she'd had four changes of address in a decade, increasingly smaller, increasingly cheaper, from the four bedroom at Kato Patissia, to the three bedroom in Kypseli, to the two-and-a-half bedroom in Ambelokipi, to the two bedroom in Gyzi, a Spartan life in aged apartment blocks, not wasting money on herself and not bonding with butchers, hairdressers and supermarket cashiers, so that they wouldn't single her out and start getting intimate, what and how and whence, so, too, that she wouldn't feel the need to lay her load down somewhere, wouldn't let some half-word escape, wouldn't blow it.

Her scarce sleep, that strange sensation of her bones being constantly cold, dated back to then.

The poplar across the way signaled dawn, at dawn birds give their art form their all, warbles like piano scales and chirps like plucked guitar strings.

She got up before the alarm clock went off, sore and stiff-necked, folded the blanket, washed, pasted on the Cyclovir, had coffee, put on a colorful chemise to fool him and herself, loaded herself up with all the bits and pieces and was out in the street at five to six.

World of the morning. She walked around the back of the block, where she was parked, tried to unlock the car with the house keys, in the manner of her senile neighbor, the two hours she anticipated the special process to take with all the checks and signatures, were baffling her in advance, her anxiety over the five days which were now a fact was peaking, she broke out in cold sweat.

She put in the things in order, the luggage in the trunk, in the back seat the bag with the two Tupperware, treats of milk pie and spinach pie, snacks for the trip, she collapsed into the driver's seat like an empty burlap sack and started up awkwardly, she was in a hurry to get cigarettes and water and then be done with the bureaucracy and the procedures, put some urgently needed distance between herself and the buildings, highways and rows of cars because she suddenly got the idea that today, now, on her way to Linus, she might have her first car crash ever, all upset in this beehive of one-way streets, crossings and street blocks, she might bump into a car in front, veer into the oncoming traffic, even worse, hit some pedestrian and lay to waste all these months' preparations.

To pace herself and calm herself down she turned to her subject, the Sphrinx of Narxos, raised on an Iornian pedestal. Damn you, r's, until the age of six she said warter instead of water and she never did ask for mandarins or strawberries though she liked them, there were r's in them which could go wrong, she only ever had apples though she didn't care for them and in her small hand she always held a lemon, those ones didn't have any bloody r's. Now, here they all were, a barrage, blasting their way into all the needed words.

She gave up on the r's, took consecutive deep breaths, if nothing went wrong, in a couple of hours, tops, she could get some comfort from the straight lines of the national highway and the poppy fields.

After all, how hostile can flowers and grasses be?

***

Feckless world.

They were her mother's last two words early yesterday afternoon, in the short phone call where, apart from the high note at the finale, unexpected from the measured lips of seventy-five-year-old Stavroula Sotiropoulos, and Viv's thank you for the parcel with the spinach pie, the exchange was familiar, safe and beside the point, end of the season now for wild winter cress and radish, come tomorrow the old woman would be gathering charlock and grapevine shoots, waiting for May to end so she could collect rose petals for the making of rose-sugar.

For the two of them to pick up the phone once every fortnight or so, sometimes the one and sometimes the other, they needed an alibi: I called because, while cleaning out the wardrobe, I found the knitted shawl you said had been stolen, because the sleet scraped the bark of the lemon tree, because the plentiful rain has given us some nice sow thistle, on the mother's part, I called in case you want me to send some vitamins to help with your memory, in case you need to hire an Albanian to dig up the garden for you, on the part of the daughter.

For them to meet once every three years, always in Athens, for two days at most, the alibi had to be airtight.

The daughter never did ask, come, I need you, I am harrowed by loneliness, the old woman would arrange it tactfully, either because she needed a new prescription for her reading glasses, or because she had a buzzing in her ears and needed to come up to the capital, as if there weren't eye doctors and ear doctors half an hour away by bus from Alonaki to the city of Patras, they were both careful not to draw attention to the big city where solutions to ordinary problems could be found.

Viv Koleva no longer went to the village, how could she? And in 2001, when her father had sat like a vegetable at the intensive care unit of the University Hospital of Rio for twenty-eight days until encephalitis decapitated him for good, she hadn't dared show up at her native parts, she might be nursing strange old men but not her own, she sent some money and a pair of pajamas, she called the head of the intensive care unit, but absent she remained even from the funeral.

Had she gone, the leading part would have been hers even though it was the afternoon of September 11, with the sixty or so relatives and villagers following the coffin screaming themselves hoarse at each other and on their cell phones about the planes that fell on the Twin Towers, same thing over the freshly dug grave, with the priest among the interested parties, naturally, and as for the consolation coffee afterwards, there too, not a single word about the all but forgotten dearly departed, everyone glued to the cafeteria's TV, speechless before the fiery hell, the clouds of dust, the deranged Americans and Bush at the kindergarten.

Had Viv been there, her presence would have probably overshadowed both al-Qaeda and the President of the U.S.

She didn't go the village but she did buy a wreath which she hid under a blanket in her car, took up to her place in the dark and stayed up the night dislodging one by one the white carnations from the frame and hurling them at the window, the screen of the lifeless TV and the carved wooden chair, till she was left fingering the purple ribbon, *For my father, Vivian.*

Two weeks before her fortieth birthday, with the wind screaming at the highway, she went in her car to the village, alone, secretly, climbed the iron gate of the cemetery and spent half an hour by his side, plucking the withered flowers from the two wreaths laid out on the grave, her mother's and her sister's, and struggling to remember his hands, his shoulders, his chest, his mouth and his voice, everything a blur inside her head except for his eyes, always, whether near him or far from him, she could not put those aside. As a child she was scared of them, so huge, so black, later they kept getting smaller and more faded, washed over and over in life's laundry. One wondered, what happened to those eyes in the summer of 1997? And what about afterwards? His eldest daughter knew not, she had been away. High time for me to pass on to other hands, had been his last words and everyone in the village had heard of the thing he'd said and was in agreement.

You have now, Viv told him and got off the flower petals and the dirt, she didn't want anyone to see her car nearby, the village to get a whiff of her nightly escapade. Her mother had sensed it the next day when she went to light the oil lamp, she told her on the phone, I saw your traces, no, you didn't drop anything, that's not what I meant. She was like that, her mother, she drew out of thin air the words and deeds that couldn't be spoken of.

Yesterday's call had most certainly not to do with the charlock, but the anticipated five-day trip, even though it didn't get mentioned even in passing, what with the smell of fresh lime paint in the kitchen and the toilet and the smack with the slipper to the tomcat for trampling the herb patch.

Driving in the blue Fiat, Viv brought to mind her aged mother hugging the most precious object in the house of her childhood years, the bucket. With it, she drew water out of the well, in it she stuffed the leeks she unearthed from the garden, that was where she put the wild radishes from the fields, that's what she used to step on and reach the frankincense on the shelf with the icons, that is what she turned over to sit on in the courtyard of an afternoon, to have her coffee.

For Viv Koleva the sadness of her great grandmother, her grandmother—she had heard of their fortunes, as well—and of her mother, was her female dowry. It grew with the passing years and the colorless trivia of poverty, it swelled like a river that, from time to time, dashed her progenitors onto sharp-edged banks, their lives spoken for like every woman's of their time, though her it hadn't washed upon some turn but dragged her on through life, until in 1997 it drew her out into the open sea, far from any shore of salvation or respite.

Had she put in the small suitcase his camera, an expensive gift from his godmother at fifteen? No, she'd forgotten, she had probably decided his lordship would object.

This is what he'd say, Viv Koleva imagined the whole thing, she had to be right about some part of it. What exactly do you want to photograph? The wonderful landscape? Your wonderful son? Do you want to be able to show left and right what nice holidays the two of us had together? You want to give grandma my photograph to feast her eyes on? You want me to pose on my knees plucking a daisy? Lie in the fields on my back? Hug romantically a tree trunk? Give me instructions, Mom, and I'll do whatever you say, so you can get the desired effects.

She decided, play it by ear, if he was tame, they'd buy from the tourist shops one of those cameras that only take a film with twelve frames, so she can have something afterwards to look at of an evening. Plus, in case her plan worked, he too would have use for a nice series of photos from which to draw inspiration in future times.

Athens had been left behind.

To the left and right furniture dealerships, exhibition halls, factories of bathroom accessories, spare car parts, striptease palaces, garden furniture, Asopos Steel, Monyal, Fourlis home appliances, vacant lots, vacant hillsides and enormous advertising billboards, pieces of land in sixty no-interest installments.

It was nearly ten.

There's pies in the bag at the back, she said. And water, she added after a bit.

Linus on the passenger seat showed no signs of interest, he was leaning back with his dark glasses hiding his eyes from the front and the sides, like a hostage's blindfold.

Earlier, on this day unlike the rest, she had noted his eyes, had well and truly scrutinized them, very hollow now, as if they had moved farther back, half an inch deeper in their sockets. His whole look was terrible, the look of someone wounded, someone irredeemable. His cheeks pale and lifeless, as if run over by a bulldozer. Most of his hair gray already, grayer than hers, its blond light gone out, and not thick, either, like it used to be, its bulk listless, with no vigor to it, no spring.

She thought for a moment of caressing it, of turning her hand into a skullcap and cupping the back of his head, she didn't dare. It seemed strange to her that she could, if she wanted to, take his hand, she'd do that later. Still, she couldn't help making up two or three pretend awkward movements with the gearstick, just so as to momentarily brush his arm, live, cold and perfectly white, hanging down from the short-sleeved black T-shirt.

When earlier the two found themselves side by side, with nothing separating them, they didn't hug, didn't kiss, they didn't touch, either. They walked towards the car keeping a distance of six feet between them, with her leading the way, him falling in step behind.

Silent from the very start, constantly the cigarette, he'd

smoked ten already. She suggested music, she had brought along a load of CDs, she had paid up at a central music store for half a shelf-load of new hits, he didn't as much as cast a glance, only made a vague gesture which probably didn't mean later, but, leave me in peace.

Viv let ten minutes go by and, because she considered that every initiative was on her and that she ought to take some, she turned on the radio, searched through the stations, dialed past the high rhetoric about politics, Putin and bonds, drew away from some testimonials about the Sea Diamond's wreck a month earlier near Santorini, skipped jingles for air-conditioning and bank loans, hesitated slightly before an island tune of the kind that evoke pure joy for the duration of three minutes, though even a ten-second happiness would be an unrealistic ambition for those two, and finally latched onto a local station, a dynamic woman's voice, *Sleep, Persephone, in the earth's arms, never show yourself again on the world's balcony*, etc. They, too, were now heading toward an ancient lookout.

– Ah, nice, she said very softly, with some anxiety, but before the song was done, Linus abruptly pressed the button, silence again, a silence that was fearful despite the sunny day with the myriads of golden points of light shimmering on the expanse of cool crops, with joyous swallows dovetailing and the fallow fields studded with wildflowers, their playful colors surrounding the car and the scents traveling alongside them.

Spring, yes, but Viv's innards were two scoops of rotting yellow leaves and her mind a hand-grenade with the safety catch drawn, ready to blow up the Fiat in front of the Vlachakis egg farm, on the eightieth kilometer of the Athens-Lamia national highway.

Does he not want to see and to listen? she pondered. Does he not want his fill of buildings, streets, movement, hills that go up and down, rhododendrons and wild thistle, such nice sights to edify his way of thinking? Does he not want to avail himself of the generous possibilities of the numbered days ahead?

He might be afraid that all that will only make for a more difficult return, she thought.

That, too, had crossed her mind, last year, the first time she arranged for time off work but didn't use it, she changed her mind at the last minute, there were too many things she had been scared of. This year she did find the courage, though here she was, feeling like sighing and not daring. Her heart was beating furiously, she was driving at a hundred and twenty pulses per minute, she was a veteran of palpitations and, because of her work, could calculate them without even touching her wrist.

– Porppies, she burst out suddenly.

A forceful gust of wind was ripping the flowers off their stems and in the fields to their right a small red storm was rioting with thousands of red petals swirling against the May sky.

Poppies, she corrected.

Linus didn't blink an eye. The wind died down, the spectacle ended.

At eleven on the dot her cell phone rang. Yukaris.

– Much traffic?

– Middling.

– Can I talk to him?

– Later.

– Everything all right?

– I think so.

– I'm glad. Make good use of it. Seize today, do not trust the morrow.

– What are you implying?

– Me, nothing. It's Horatio who says so.

– Spare me, for once.

She didn't tell Linus who had called, he didn't ask, only lit up another cigarette.

– I bought you a carton, she told him almost sweetly, determined to keep up her morale, if one of the two had a right to fall apart, Linus was first in line and she would try by hook or by crook for that not to happen, but if in the end the meltdown did take place, she would do all she could to reverse the situation at any cost.

She had never slapped another person, had never raised the neighborhood with her screams, had not been driven berserk by any savage thought, or act or situation, to the point of tearing out her hair and beating her breast, nothing had thrown her off track, she knew that she didn't have the facility of most people to become sad for a while and then get over it, smash things up every now and then and get back to their normal self afterwards with no consequences, she was permanently immersed into pure blackness, weary but also experienced and enduring, and, above all else, obligated to remain upright so she could help out the creature she was now dragging willy-nilly through the countryside.

– Why don't you say something? she asked him with forced naturalness.

– Words are cheap.

– Why don't you look around?

– Pine trees move along, clouds sail together.

– What's that mean?

He didn't answer her.

Could May's feast be making him numb or, worse still, upsetting him? April, before, and March, before that, would be safer months, but what if they had cold and rain and were forced to keep indoors? The bright, smiling and lukewarm May was the final temporal frontier, so that everything could happen before the arrival of summer, before June's acceleration began, before July's lack of constraint and August's extravaganza.

She turned to face him.

– You haven't a bone to pick about where we're going have you?

A good question, timely, but that, too, was left unanswered. The eventual destination had given her much trouble. First off, she had looked into the possibility of the ten National Forests. Then, she had recalled and assessed random comments by admirers of caves, estuaries, artificial lakes and hot springs. A sort of colleague, one of those women with whom she did alternate shifts tending the infirm, whenever someone got sick or had other business to attend to, was waxing lyrical about her stay in the township of Orchomenos last July, during the celebrations of the trout season—fish cooked in the oven, fried and smoked, this last with a Golden Award in Germany—which took place at the spring of the Three Graces in tandem with a concert by the incomparable Kostas Makedonas. The spinster had a crush on the artist, great crowd, lots of spirit, she affirmed. Another colleague was committed to the yearly festival at her place of origin, the Prespes lakes near the northern borders, a free-for-all with a parade of musicians and ministers. The now deceased brother of the elderly Cretan swooned with nationalist fervor over Arkadi, in the Peloponnese, the niece of another client, even further back, swooned with revolutionary fervor over the Mikro Chorio, home of the heroic communist Velouchiotis.

Paros, Syros, Zagoria, which she knew herself from sneaky three-day excursions in the past, nice places, but they required planes and boats.

Crowds, holocausts, bloodshed, long distances and the sea were not suited for the Vivian-Linus pair.

Yukaris, the only one in the know about the whole endeavor, advised her, not an island, not impossibly far, keep it sensible, dear Vivian, Viotia, Phthiotida, Corinthia, Argolis,[2] take your pick, let's stick close by, just in case.

He suggested she should consider a quiet place, with open

---

[2] The prefectures closest to that of Attica, with Athens its capital.

views, comfort and cleanliness, with good meals to be had, and walks, for the sake of detoxing, even temporarily, from being cooped up, and from crowds and spittle on the streets, in short, a country pension at the beginning of May would be perfect, as the customers are few, usually mostly foreigners.

Vivian Koleva had been mulling it over, she'd grown unaccustomed to recreation, the past ten years she didn't as much as thumb through the pamphlets that were lying in wait everywhere, for everyone, with offers for unforgettable holidays in illustrated Edens.

Her final choice had to be focused. Be an investment for the future.

***

The parking lot of the pension Amphictyonia, buried in greenery, everywhere bougainvillea and honeysuckle, had six car spaces, only two were occupied, the bookings were minimal, thankfully, the crowds wouldn't pour in until a couple of months hence.

Not a soul in sight.

– Wait a bit, I'll go in first, said Viv, took her bag, got out of the car, shook her arms and legs to get rid of the stiffness, looked up at some birds frolicking from branch to branch, admired them, taking care that Linus noticed, as if prompting him to do the same, for the sake of a proper start in this beautiful environment.

For the sake of acting carefree, she walked slowly, even lazily, towards the entrance, went up three steps, looked inside and signaled to Linus, no rush.

A couple around forty-five was settling their bill, looking overjoyed as did the fat, middle-aged owner, a German woman, the fourth reason Viv had selected this hotel; that is, it was isolated, had a view, its décor discouraged depression and the receptionist was a foreigner, which definitely reduced the chances that she might be familiar with or remember Greek faces and events.

The couple came out dragging an overly sophisticated piece of luggage on wheels, personal articles at the bottom, computer on top, in a mood so jolly it verged on exhibitionistic, they both said good morning to Viv, have a lovely time, said the man, just like we did, seconded the woman, looking with some curiosity at Linus who was still sitting in the car, unimpressed. She drew a short step, thought of something, started towards the Fiat that was moored at the edge of the property, but finally turned back to Viv who was standing nervously on the lower step and opened before her the top button of her shirt. There were red marks on her neck and her cleavage was pasted with generous amounts of cream.

– Allergies have been the death of me. There's still pollen, the only drawback to this place. Make sure you get some antihistamines on time if you have a problem, she said, and acting youthful, she strolled sprightly towards the Golf.

They drove off to the accompaniment of classical music, at full volume at that, the piano bellowing.

In two minutes Vivian and Linus were inside the cool spacious hall, their luggage resting on the ceramic tile floor but the frau was nowhere to be seen, the reception desk empty but for a square glass vase chockablock with freesias, that's where Linus thought to put his cigarette out, and next to it a purple New Testament with a protruding piece of paper as a pagemarker on which Viv read a shopping list, soap-crème, insect repellent, air freshener, feta cheese.

They waited. He with his elbows on the bench, she with her gaze bouncing off the partitions with the keys, all there, twelve rooms, to the framed local flora, tobacco leaves, clovers and horsetail, then on to the shelf with the foreign titles, then to the Scrabble set on the low table in front of the fireplace, then the fireplace itself, made of stone and imposing, she hadn't managed in her lifetime, finally, to own an apartment with a fireplace, not even that.

– If you use the American kind of almonds, the cake breaks up in the oven and then it gets mildewy.

That's what the German said as she walked in with her mouth full, fine sugar around her lips, her Greek fluent, the heavy accent matching her body type.

She said hello, of course she remembered Viv, she even seemed glad, because she did like to chat, it showed, and a client the same age as her would be the ideal partner for a beer if she needed to play up the German side or an ouzo, if she was required to be Greek.

On her neck and in her ears hung handmade jewelry with strings, pips, screws, straps and tin tulips. Vivian Koleva had sold off all hers, four golden pieces, bracelet, ring, cross, brooch, had gotten rid of them for a ludicrous one hundred and ten thousand drachmas, after she had already stripped her living room of the silver. Five pieces, two candleholders, two small frames, a bowl, another seventy thousand, to get the money together for the deposit for the first piece of property in Pangrati.

It was true, certainly, that the lost treasure hadn't meant all that much, a fat lot of a treasure, too, more or less what can be found at every home, not at all priceless, emotionally or financially, wedding gifts that didn't suit her character, surrounded her and weighed on her against her will, she neither wore them nor polished them to a shine. Their remembrance, though, was more proof that she persisted in remembering everything unsavory, deaths, poverty and famine, her past was useful only as punishment. The happy memories were short-lived interjections, once in a blue moon, that dropped in like ghosts from thin air and then were gone.

The German drew attention to the fair weather, took down

two keys, to Viv's question, which is the room with the better view, number 10 at the corner, she said, let Takis have that, he's in need of a rest, a bit pale, Takis, on the delicate side, ascertained the foreign woman jocularly and handed him the key, first floor to the left, she called to his back, as he'd already grabbed his traveling bag and was climbing the stairs three at a time.

– My nephew, Viv spoke, she owed the clarification, from abroad, she continued nervously digging into the depths of her bag, that's where his folks live. He's finished his studies and is undecided as yet about the next step.

– Is he an archaeologist too?

– Something along those lines.

– So pale. Doesn't he get any sun at digs?

The German goggled her eyes in a funny way, shook, used her whole body to express herself, was after intimacy at all costs, sought to establish a relationship on the double, stumping the unprepared Viv, who put together an explanation any old way.

– He was sick for a long time.

– It shows. I could tell from the first moment.

Viv took her ID card out of her wallet and walked it along the bench to the form the foreign woman was filling out enunciating the particulars, two single rooms, four nights with breakfast.

– Your eggs are bought or your own? Viv interrupted.

– I adore chickens. The chicken and the horse are my favorite animals.

– So the eggs are your own. I'm thinking of getting him back on track with proper food, you see.

– In this place, he's sure to perk up, Mrs. Alifraggi, Xenia Alifraggi, the German spelled out the full name on the ID, as she wrote it down in her files. So, then, I'm Sabine, if I may introduce myself again.

– Xenia, said Viv and reached out for the handshake and to pick up the key for number 12 and the ID.

Sabine turned to a drawer, let me give you two remote controls for the TV, she said and Viv got the chance to pick Linus's soaked cigarette butt out of the vase with the freesias.

When she went up to the room it was twenty past eleven.

She flew into the bathroom and spent five minutes splashing cold water on her cheeks and neck, to freeze them, to anesthetize them.

She didn't open the balcony door, she hung no clothes in the wardrobe, she didn't take off her shoes, she fell to the bed on her back with arms open wide like a prone Jesus on the cross.

The simile was adversarial to her in its own right, she had no traffic with gods or saints that come marching in retrospectively, especially given that then, as events were peaking, the parish minister had knocked on her door, a stranger's unfamiliar face, a thirty-five-year-old terribly composed and mighty sure of his technique, willing to support her, even wash her conscience clean, she stoically heard through the introduction, according to St. Makarius, the sinners in hell are tied back to back so that they may not gaze upon each other's faces, she then listened to his personal spiel, full of poetic embellishments, installments of repentance and checks of forgiveness and then she decisively pushed him to the door and sent him on his way with a curt good-bye.

If there was a God and he had targeted Linus, let him grab the boy from her like so many who crash on motorcycles and die on the spot, making a clean exit rather than feeling life fade on their skin with every passing day and having this business drag on for years.

In the end, she did feel for Linus, she used his first name in her mind, ever since 1997, she hadn't once been able to think, let alone say before others, my son, and when they, either unsuspectingly or with a vestige of sympathy, said, your son, she jumped like some wild thing, the word alone affronted her.

Yukaris had weaned her from it after the second meeting, her father afterwards had never asked about anything to do with him, her mother was chomping at the bit for news yet very rarely in their awkward and summary talks about pills and wild herbs did she slip in out of the blue some epilogue about the poor wasted boy, and her younger sister, Xenia, barricaded with her family in Canada, she obeyed her husband who foi- bade any reference to the nephew, a condition backed by the threat of divorce, their two little girls, twelve and eleven, didn't even know they had a cousin.

Xenia's Greek ID had been mailed from Toronto, only don't let Spilios find out about it, her sister had moaned in her half-page letter, it was common knowledge that Doctor Alifraggis had on several occasions given her severe beatings and the last time, being an orthopedic surgeon, he had himself set her arm in plaster.

Viv considered the Kolevas surname as famous among Greeks as the surnames Karamanlis, Papandreou, Mouschouri and Onassis and she needed to guard the five-day excursion against any resurgence.

Neither Linus nor herself resembled themselves of ten years ago as they had been plastered across the pages of the press, he was half his size and had gone white, she was double and had molted.

While still in the car, she'd asked him to meet her outside the reception at twelve and he hadn't told her to go to hell, which meant he was amenable.

In his travel bag, there were new underwear, new clothes, new sports shoes. When yesterday afternoon at her house she took them out of the box and retrieved the bunched up paper tissue in their interior, she had replaced their black laces on the spot. As she was pulling them out through the holes and they snaked around her finger, she got short of breath, saw them elongate, turn into sleek, cool serpents and wind themselves around her arms, preparing to wrap around her throat, which naturally was instantly drowned in saliva and in r's, she started coughing and spitting again in the arshtray and on the morsaic floor, the words were being thwarted inside her head.

Just like last year when, during the general siesta, she heard from the apartment block across the street a voice, same as Linus's, rage, I told you, Mom, didn't I bloody well say, I need my running shoes washed?

The same distress then, too, the same craziness all over, even though she did at some point steal a glimpse at the irate bully, she nevertheless spent the whole afternoon in a tease over the damned sports shoes.

I wonder what happens to him when he lays his hands on a shoelace?

She couldn't afford to ask him, naturally, for the next few days' plan to work, the past had to be crossed out with an X.

Whenever she slipped out of reality, imagined things, grew fearful and was then preoccupied exclusively with fear, she felt contempt for herself.

Well, then, time to kiss the wasting of energy good-bye, time to focus.

Ten to twelve. She got up, rapidly skimmed through her two little books to quickly freshen her memory with the difficult names, she put some ointment on the herpes, redid her lipstick, pulled a comb through her hair, stuffed her bag under her arm and, clutching the strap, she went out.

On her way down she was welcomed by the local radio station with news from Livadia and surrounds.

The German woman at the reception hall was looking through the New Testament and she extrapolated on the Word to the client, though she hadn't asked for it, she favored a wide spectrum of knowledge, something of comparative religion,

something of space science, something of ancient Egypt, something of genetics, something of sea lions—they consume
twenty kilos of shrimp daily, she said, giving a sample of her
encyclopedic aptitude.

For her, Vivian-Xenia would become the perfect alibi for
uncontrollable soliloquies, Thanos who spends day and night
at the card table, brought me here while I was a flower and I've
now become a cauliflower, she mocked herself in impeccable
Greek, pitying herself with a warm applause, her thick arms
shaking like beams in an earthquake.

– We haven't been able to have kids, this in an apologetic
tone and immediately the question, you, Mrs. Xenia, do you
have kids?

– It didn't come about.

The client's answer imposed a short silence. Everyone car-
ries their sack and for as long as one lives, it will keep getting
filled with insults and sorrow, Vivian thought, waved good-bye
and walked out into the yard.

While waiting for Linus she took to examining the flower
boxes with the gaudy petunias though, at times like this, and
generally, in fact, she couldn't care less about flowers and trees,
the two flowerpots on her balcony in Athens were there
because any fifty year old woman on her own who doesn't have
at least two potted plants is cause for suspicion.

***

There they were trespassing on strange property, the navel
of the Earth.

They zigzagged among the increasing crowds in the streets,
tourists mainly who stopped to browse ancient souvenirs and
mock-traditional bric-a-brac on stands, benches and coffers in
small shops.

It was hard to evade a horde of seventy-year-old Scandinavians, some wore wide ties with piano keys, probably bought at the Salzburg stopover, on others ties with prosciutto, trophies from the Parma stop, and almost all the women had draped themselves in the folds of ancient-style chiton shirts, they must have bought out half of Plaka.

Tired faces, looks of incomprehension, it was more than certain that they didn't care all that much where they were travelling to, where they stopped on each occasion, to what sights the travel agencies dragged them, anything was fine, as long as they kept moving, simply remained in motion, in order not to get immobilized already in the familiar stillness before the end, visible in their case with no need for binoculars.

They overtook the tourist groups and they also overtook two groups of five folded canvas umbrellas each, standing upright, side by side and white, like groups of Arabs loitering on the curb.

Linus, with his dark glasses on, facing unwaveringly straight ahead, saw to reason to dawdle paying attention to anything to his left or right, followed Viv meekly, and at one point, as if asking for help or support in his uncertain progress, his feet released to a long walk for the first time in years, he even took her by the arm, for mere seconds, but their first bodily contact, a sensation long forgotten, like an electric shock, propelled them apart again.

Viv stumbled, but simultaneously sighed with relief, she had wanted that touch although at times the thought did cross her mind that she should avoid it in case she unwittingly flinches, in case some small cry escapes her and he gets in a rage and all hell breaks loose.

– No museums and oracles today, he turned to her and said.

-- Whatever you say. We're in no hurry. For five days, Delphi is ours.

Her choice of place was just right when the scales of her calculations and deliberations had shifted to antiquities,

Mycenae was declared off limits despite possessing a Lion Gate, Cyclopean walls and arched tombs, the clan of the Atreids was synonymous with a mayhem of murder and lust, same for Olympia, despite her prepaying two gym memberships, Linus wasn't the athletic type, the only one of his ilk who hadn't watched the European soccer finals and the Olympic Games, the social worker, the saint Mrs. Afroudakis, had noted his refusal, staunch and unexpected against the trend prevailing in the two months of July and August of 2004 when her bulls had turned to lambs, penned in front of the TVs and all the more effectively drugged with the national triumphs.

As a kiddie, Linus-Trampolinus walked on the curb to preschool hopping like a spring kid-goat and bleating out the numbers. He couldn't read the street signs yet, but he could broadcast, at 32 we have the bakery, at 34 the Lotto, at 36 the dry cleaner's, at 38 the vet, at 40 the barber.

Now, out of the corner of her eye, she watched him walk as if on a patrol duty, without harvesting the images he had been made to go without, the vibrant sounds that were offered aplenty, with no zest for the itinerary and impatient for its conclusion, his footsteps crushing heavily on the sidewalks, his shoulders sunk, his body derelict and old, sentenced at thirty to long-term punishment.

Tall and thin, he had his father's build.

Fotis was lucky, after all, she'd been right to call him a scoundrel on a bitter New Year's, he had exited on cue, with everything that happened afterwards, the preceding wreckage was negligible.

Sun that almost burned, light that almost blinded.

Let it also blind anyone obsessed with famous cases and the observant who might recognize them, any old acquaintance thereabouts on an excursion who might stumble on them.

In recent years, Vivian Koleva had the scenarios all ready

for such an eventuality. There had been certain instances to date when she had made use of them and they'd worked.

Mere resemblance, my name isn't Vivian, she had answered chummily to a man her age who had approached somewhat reluctantly at the Syntagma Metro station, I never studied, don't even know the whereabouts of the universities of Athens, born and raised in Argentina.

And, you are mistaken, ma'am, I never lived in Kypseli, I'm come from Thrace, here on business, she had cut short a woman waiting in the same taxi line as her, with whom she had once shared a grocer's, in the springtime one would be going in for strawberries as the other walked out carrying the same.

Every such emergency and the chance of being cornered again by some sharp-eyed and eager-nosed hound, necessitated frequent changes in hairstyle and sunglasses, avoiding rush-hour crowds as much as possible, carrying under her arm evidence from improbable places on the planet and renewing her stock of tales, ready to declare herself a resident of Hawaii, Bogota, Johannesburg, retrieving on the spot a tourist pamphlet from her overseas home.

Johannesburg had come in handy at a shopping mall, when, as she was paying for the plastic shower curtain, the cashier had given her a long, funny look, or so it had seemed to Vivian, who preempted her by explaining she was putting her mother's bathroom to order before getting back on the plane to South Africa.

Four years ago, one tenant at her building had bumped into her at the foyer while she was unlocking her mailbox at ten at night, saw in his look that he had an issue with her and gave him short shrift, a letter from my only daughter doing postgraduate studies in Sweden, she parceled out a ready-made fib and it worked, the guy shook his head and immediately concurred, yes, I know all about children leaving to study and never coming back.

The prearranged falsehoods were her armament against the unexpected, Viv saved herself any further ado while shamelessly admitting that she, who despised lies, was now issuing them forth copiously even if she did so with the sweat of her brow. She devoted hours, usually the early morning ones, to inventing new alibis, embellishing the old ones, rehearsing the words and gestures, stocking up on special renditions, gathering together a fresh crop for the five-day excursion.

She breathed in and caressed her own cheek and throat.

– Thank God you never had any allergies.

That's what she came up with, she was afraid of the prolonged silence, because the despicable carefree attitude of those around was driving her mad and because her bag was a heavy load and even more so was the thought of the things she had buried at the bottom.

But did she well and truly and seriously think that if a dangerous situation developed, she would be able to plunge a stabbing knife into him? That she could use the bronze pestle, which she'd barely ever used for crushing garlic, to crack his skull in two?

***

Beige wrapping paper bought by the meter and used as tablecloths, tin cans instead of vases, olive branches instead of flowers, the décor of the steakhouse Nectar, crowded with groups of mixed nationalities encircling platters with meat and bowls of Greek salads.

Viv and Linus had seated themselves at the table that was most remote, by the door to the WC, facing the wall with the National Tourism Bureau poster, savory marbles and digestive forests.

The waiter planted in their midst a kilo of chops, Viv put the fleshiest and best grilled on the honored guest's plate, since you were a wee thing you loved the white tubular bone with the lamb marrow, said she and pulled out with her fork the white tubing from all the rest of the chops and gave him the treat. He accepted it. The shadow of a smile, his thanks. She, too, was pleased.

– Beer? she said and got no answer but filled his glass anyway, a bottle for the two of them, no more, relaxation was desired and necessary, tipsiness was not, inebriation was forbidden and not only under the current circumstances.

How old was he when he'd broken every bottle in the house? At ten, fourth grade, and out of the blue. She no longer kept alcohol in the house and the boy had taken it out on the bottles with the cherry juice, the lemonade, the grape molasses and the vinegar, all in pieces piled up in the sink. A miracle he wasn't cut up, she sure got a scare, but that's all over, back to now.

Three lasses, lively and good-looking girls, thankfully were sitting seven tables away, yet the buzz alone of the tavern was by itself a devious stimulant, families that talked a lot, laughed a lot, groups of youngsters that teased each other a lot, *Measure in all things* was out the window and so was *Know thyself*, the overweight clientele were piling orders on the waiters, another round of souvlaki with all the trimmings, and, we're waiting on ten more mince patties and, buddy, grab another five mixed platters, and, bring us another two nectar carafes, good wine, evidently, locally produced by the owner.

The music abated the mood, fresh hits with no real longing, extroverted, trite and ephemeral, so that they fitted right in with the ad hoc staging of group revelry.

Viv and Linus were taking the hits of festiveness in the back, as they had elected to be facing the wall, the hanging poster wouldn't be in a position to remember them.

They hadn't decided whether to dine hurriedly and depart or to pretend, primarily to one another, that this was for them what it was for the rest, a meal in the countryside.

They had sought refuge in two or three awkward exchanges, this place must be raking it in, the bread's good, the french fries are precooked, she, they've left out the napkins and, let me squeeze you some lemon, he.

Twenty minutes later they hadn't had their fill, but they'd given up trying, their plates still half full, their forks laid down, the last remaining gulps of beer in their glasses, when the voice broke out in the hall of a three-year-old girl who was running among the tables like a spinning top, loudly singing the latest Eurovision hit "Yassou Maria."

The proud and tender dad was chasing after his girl, who was collecting applause and caresses, she was one of those creatures so blessed with gracefulness that you couldn't find it in you to call them annoying brats. Linus was listening, Viv had turned around and was looking at the child, a mirage in sea-blue swirls, her cheeks blushed a camellia red, her nails painted, her small palms two soft dates, she also looked at the father, a thirty-year-old, her son's age.

It upset her. She waited patiently for the chase to be over, but the jubilant little diva was enjoying her effect on the audience and the power of monopolizing her dad from the ten-strong family gathering, two babies plus grandpas and grandmas. For ten full minutes, the customers, even a couple of foreigners, became the chorus to "Yassou Maria," Linus kept his head down, right above the overflowing ashtray, and Viv, at the end of her patience and not knowing how to stem the obvious associations, his and hers, had a go at, Patriarch Bartholomew, I saw him on the news Easter Sunday rubbing up against Sarbel and offering his blessing, she said to Linus, hasn't been a single year without him showing up at that Eurovision circus, she added wryly, breaking in two an olive branch from the tin vase.

The barb got no response, the youngster was raking in acclamations, Linus was now surreptitiously following from behind his dark glasses the festive, luscious toy-girl that got a rise out of adults making them willing to play for a bit, even act silly.

The receipt under the salt and pepper read thirty-three euros, Viv left a fifty euro note, didn't wait for the change, a gargantuan tip. She stood up, Linus followed suit, they exited with long strides.

– My heard, she moaned, I got a headache she amended posthaste, as they took the road back to the pension. There was no need to consult among themselves to the effect that a siesta, some rest at all events, is a good thing after eating, they were both eager to be on their own, in their respective rooms, it was three and they had fought since just after eight that morning to make it unharmed through the almost seven hours spent together, quite a lot as a trial run at coexisting after years of sparse meetings of twenty minutes, a quarter of an hour, sometimes a silent five minutes.

A while later, as she sat at the edge of the bed, pressing down on her belly with her bag resting on her knees, she wondered how they'd make it through the next four days, the whole business felt like the beginning of a great adventure with an unforeseeable end.

Three years ago, too, she had been so driven to the ground that she felt she was running out of the energy needed for what had to be done. At that time, June, summers always a season of mortal danger, she would get rooted to the spot in front of a green light, without the wherewithal to cross the street, a journey of twenty feet. She would look at the shelves in the supermarket aghast, unable to lift her arm and pick out the chlorine or the sugar.

Days would go by without her washing her hair, she would get to work with crinkles in her skirt and her shoes unpolished. Those rare times when her cell phone or the phone at her house rang, she wouldn't pick up, two clients had her terminated.

The fridge had gone bust for a month, she didn't call the technician to fix it, it was July and she drank water from the tap and ate her tomatoes tepid.

As during that time, she turned on neither the radio nor her TV, filled with the festive furor of the Olympics, the objects around her protested the deadly silence and, in her mind, their commentary ran riot, the lunch tray murmured that pre-Easter feasting was long gone, the purple pillow on the sculpted chair was saying, I'm done for, the car keys were demanding, come on, let's go for a drive by the sea, the amber stone on the table declared, I want to go back to the Baltic, her ID card was not mincing words, you're on your way to fifty, the plastic chair in the balcony was complaining, you've forgotten about me lately, come sit and get fresh air.

As no others lived in the house or visited, so that things could hear their name being called out, bring the chair over, you're in my chair, and, wipe down the chair on the balcony with a wet rag to get rid of the rain-mud, several pieces of furniture and objects were throwing their weight around, were passing comment, were consulting among themselves, they scolded her, shared this or that with her, showed their affection, fought to give the apartment a semblance of life.

Especially the green glass shade around the kitchen bulb that had countless times shed light on Viv at night stuffing herself with stale bread, standing upright like a soldier at his post over the pot with Linus's beef, rummaging in the cupboards and unburying the old Donald Duck cup for his milk, his Batman eggcup and the colored straws for the frappé coffees of his adolescence, that were still being rescued from shelf to shelf and apartment to apartment, during those weeks of collapse, full of fruit flies from the wizened fruit, initially the shade would protest, I turn on and show the scum of the vegetables rotting in the plastic bag, then, later, it would whisper to her companionably, all I now illuminate is your fall.

Day before the seventh of July, feast day of St. Kyriaki, she spent the night circling the block in order to not fall asleep and, as in past years on this date, play the part again in her sleep of that mother with the all-white hair and the torn lining in her skirt, the one who, under different circumstances, would be celebrating the name day of her eighteen-year-old daughter. All told, tragedies aren't things that pass, they annex the days and nights and subjugate the future.

The finishing touch to the whole business was the visit by Charidemus. Charidemus who? Thirty-five-year-old, retarded, the lovey-dovey numbskull of Aigion and surrounds, the nitwit for some smart alecks, who rang her doorbell one late afternoon, came in, like he did yesterday, with the familiar milk pie in the round baking dish wrapped in a knotted dishcloth and sat, like he did every time, for half an hour, grunting and gesticulating with pleasure, proud of his blue suit.

Charidemus was a man of renown in his native land, a lover of the sound of typewriters, a daily visitor to the local law firms and accountants. They set out a chair for him and let him listen to the rhythmical sound of the keys, the dry tock-tock was his mainstay.

He did not speak, couldn't read except what was typewritten and in capitals, two rows, no more. With a note like that, with an address on it anywhere in Athens, he was capable of boarding the bus and arriving at the right place, let the specialists come up with the scientific explanation. The cousin of Petra, a half-mad fellow student of Viv's in high school, he had for years, starting in 1998, made the trip to the capital once or twice a year, just to bring her the milk pie. Viv had allowed her mother to give her address to Petra, hated milk pie, which she gave to the old folks, but she felt compassionate towards the youth, a delegate from the village of her childhood, and each time put a goodly tip in his pocket.

Charidemus with the baby eyes, the crookedly shaven

moustache and the black curly hair, had in recent years lost his bearings because the typewriters had been replaced by the comparatively silent keyboards of the PCs and the sound that filled him with joy was no longer to be heard. Someone had made a gift to him of a defunct typewriter and his cousin, single, compassionate and a loner, with no neighborly relations and fixated on her school years, would type Viv's address for him and escort him to the bus.

In the visit the year before last, summer of 2004, Charidemus looked around at the dust and the shells of the sunflower seeds on the floor and the coin-sized oil stains on Viv's robe and took to thrashing on the couch and yelling out at full volume his incomprehensible vowels. Right on top of his came hers, now brehave and be grood. The apartment block was up in arms, they called the police, the neighbors came out on the balconies, eyes and voices greedy for the details on which feeds the gossip of the contemptuous.

A trying afternoon. One trial among others, it was getting to be four months that she hadn't seen her son, on two occasions he hadn't wanted to, on the other two she hadn't wanted to herself.

Late that night, although in bed since seven, as soon as the policemen left with the milk pie and Charidemus followed in their wake, after spreading out on her bed six packs of aspirin and next to those three bottles of high-pressure pills, stock for her clients, she toyed with them, counted and recounted them, then put them away again saying, sorry, fellows, forget it, it's a no go, I have the strength but I'm not entitled, and she made the decision to at least try and escape by doing very different things, on the off chance she might be able to occupy her thoughts in some other way.

So she visited an institute of podiatry that solved the problem of ingrown toenails, though hers were fine, and let herself listen to the women, with her soles soaking in a tub, as they chitchatted about reflexology, cheesecakes, the perfect tan and Latin dance schools, a lot of tango, a lot of samba, she herself, despite her business at *Titi*, had only ever danced once, on her wedding day, and that was that. She paid and left knowing she would never set foot again in the pretty land of cosmetic parlors and nirvana sold by the hour.

She went to a lecture, too, with the projection of slides from the Galapagos Islands: Darwin, his schooner, his studies on the origin of the species, mounts covered in grass, sea elephants with their cub and birds picking the fleas off giant turtles; she left halfway through, her problem haunted every last inch of her body and her mind, didn't leave a smidgen of space for anything else, it throttled from the start all attempts at even a brief diversion.

***

Phone call, three rings, on the fourth she stuck the receiver to her ear.

– It's Yukaris again.

His voice against the background of other voices, a dutiful voice.

– Why, who else would it be?

– Anything worth reporting?

– The tour has been postponed for tomorrow. He wasn't willing.

– It's not the end of the world.

– As if he has no response to, takes no pleasure in, or doesn't recognize my effort. His indifference is alarming.

– Call it numbness, the numbness of the first day. He'll be right on cue as of tomorrow.

– Spare the irony.

– I'm sorry. But you are asking for rather a lot, yourself.

– I'll spend the night sleepless with worry.

– He will as well. Perhaps even me, he added after a short silence, then he put an order in for a jar of local honey and rang off with the admission, my girl, you are remarkable.

In two minutes he called back, asked if our boy looks left and right, Viv didn't answer, he apologized and ended the call leaving her even more uncertain about the afternoon, the evening, the day that was coming and the one after that.

On opening the balcony door, the pine tree forest appeared before her, dark, thick and silent, only some buzzing, wasps, bumblebees, carpenter bees, the expected soundtrack of any sunny afternoon in the countryside.

Viv rolled back her sleeves and leaned against the warm railing, to test if she was soporific, it would be a godsend if it came over her for half an hour. Besides, from that position, in every respect legitimate and expected from the tenant of an idyllic pension in May, she could stretch one ear to Linus's room and keep an eye on the terrain of the parking lot. If he elected to go out on his own, he wouldn't use the main entrance, he'd go out the back, even though Yukaris had personally pointed out to him in the morning, don't go anywhere without Vivian and don't put her in an invidious position, she has taken on a grave responsibility.

A grave responsibility is what it was all right, which was the reason why every five minutes she stuck her hand in her pocket, making sure the car keys were still there.

Linus didn't slip outside in the afternoon, didn't go out in the early evening, didn't even lift his shutters, he missed dusk and he missed the sweet nightfall, the sound of television was heard for about twenty minutes at around nine and his mother perked up somewhat and in order for him not to go to sleep hungry, she sent a double toast and fruit to his room with the frau, his lordship was unlikely to snap at a strange woman and send her away.

The strange woman, naturally, had been taken aback by her

two visitors who, instead of going for strolls and drinks, plenty of wonderful choices all around, opted for staying cooped up in their rooms, could Takis be suffering from a love affair gone wrong? she'd asked Viv who, standing by the door to the small kitchen, had shrugged, though love affairs have gone by the wayside with today's youth, they split up with one girl today and pick up another tomorrow, the German woman quipped as she arranged chips and three green leaves around the toast. Why don't I put some ice cream with that, my treat, no ice cream, no, he is not at all partial, Viv stopped her.

She invited Mrs. Xenia for a drink, let me treat you then, she renewed her offer, dark beer, very cold, she made the suggestion as appealing as she could, I have cherries, too, she upped the ante, and ten different kinds of pralines, she labored to hogtie the evening's live target, she failed, the customer had a headache.

– Mrs. Xenia you are condemning me to make do with some book, again, and it's a great sin to spend beautiful evenings on one's own.

Viv agreed, but she had sinned, she was sinning habitually and serially, thousands of evenings on her own like an isolated tree in the wilderness.

Many hours later, daybreak was fingering her shutters, horizontal stripes initially gray, touched in a bit by dawn with pink, then by the day with gold.

In bed, facing toward the closed balcony doors, she was counting the thin slices of the Friday morning, listening to the birds dynamically reporting for duty, smelling the honeysuckle that wound itself on her railing and rubbing her left arm that had gone to sleep, a casualty yet again of her sparse and anguished sleep, she began to think of people, random strangers, who'd never have to face a day like the one she had coming.

She pondered on how the heck one describes a smooth life

and of what it might consist. She came up with a few plausible answers as she washed, dressed, gathered and checked her things and her money, all of it in a hurry, seven minutes by the clock.

A smooth life is one where you open the window in the morning and have the luxury of wanting to gaze up to the end of the sky and where, at night, you turn the lights on feeling pleased to be back at home. A smooth life is that of people who eagerly buy a loaf of fresh bread, who enjoy a good haircut, who are talented at frying two eggs, who kiss and are kissed with some frequency, who give or receive a small slap without taking it to heart, who break their leg and friends come to write silly things on the plaster, who always cast their vote no matter what, who know the refrain to the golden oldies, who dream of an exotic trip and slowly put the money together for it, who play with their cat every day and remove one by one the ticks from their dog, who take pride in their children's engagement, who take their grandkids to Halloween parties, who bring the parental home up in the country back from the brink of collapse, who bury their parent with due honors.

***

– We see here a copy of the navel of Delphi. The decoration in relief on its surface represents the *agrinon*, a fabric made of woolen stripes which covered the navel and which in antiquity was placed in the holy of holies of Apollo's temple. According to the myth, Zeus let two eagles fly from Olympus in opposite directions and after they had circled the earth, the two birds met at this point. The navel symbolizes the belief that Delphi was the center of the world, that one you might remember from school, you were a very good student, Linus, up until, the phrase was cut short at that point.

There were no other visitors in Hall I of the Museum, the halls next to that were empty as well, Viv and Linus were the very first to arrive, at eight in the morning, after walking with comparatively greater ease along the still sleeping streets of the township and the tiled pedestrian walk that led to the site.

Earlier, at the small dining hall of the pension, while sitting still in their chairs waiting for breakfast, Viv had presented three articles she had cut from magazines with the mysterious E of Delphi and hieroglyphs, Lilliputian symbols and signs, ancient scripts from Minoans, Black Pharaohs and Easter Island, which wise experts on antiquity and linguists were still laboring to decode.

She had the forethought while in Athens of collecting a variety of materials, small surprises to break up the awkward silences and to simultaneously fertilize her offering at the Sacred Valley so that it might take root and bear fruit.

Linus would look over it in puzzlement and, surely, would comment on this or that, Viv had counted on two or three responses, like, where did you unearth this, mighty strange writing and, how long have you been involved with this subject?

In actual fact, Linus had lowered the dark glasses for a matter of seconds, just enough to pierce her with a chastising glance.

Immediately afterwards, she was given a different opportunity to improve the mood, with the freshly squeezed orange juice and the free-range eggs which were fully up to her expectations for a bracing breakfast, not for herself, of course, she couldn't care less.

Her first thank you for the great service, to Sabine, came at the serving, the second thank you at the gathering of the plates and glasses and alongside it came the prompting to her son, say thank you, talk with her a bit, to freshen up your German.

– You are mad and need to have your head examined, his response in a low, though not angry, tone.

The stroll to the Museum was made in peace, amid the unthreatening racket of the sparrows and swallows minus the unwelcome racket and presence of busloads of people, coming all the way here to have a closer look at the ancient celebrities. The guards were having coffee and tossing out short exchanges about real estate and construction, what with the antiquities and with the ski resorts in nearby Mt. Parnassus, moneyed folks were drawn to Delphi and to the adjacent village of Arachova from the world of show business, enterprise and politics, and putting up villas and setting up compounds for their weekends of luxury.

The navel of the Earth, the frieze in relief from the first century A.D. with Hercules against the Lernaia Hydra and the Giant Anteus and again Hercules wresting the horses of Diomedes and fighting an Amazon made no impression on Linus, who took the five steps to first this side and then the other, next to his mother, stopping wherever she did and listening to her recite the relevant information, memorized to a T since a long time ago, for his sake.

No questions at all, neither admiration, nor a second look, the dark glasses did not turn in the direction of the exhibits, as if they rejected them, at certain moments they might rest on the bases on which they were propped, at others they focused on his sports shoes.

– They're not tight, are they? Viv asked, staring against her best intentions at the white shoelaces. Linus advanced half a meter without a yes or a no.

The bronze sirens, the figurines of naked athletes, the small statue of the sheep in the same hall and the statue of the cow, the two bronze griffin heads, the three bronze shields and the remainder of statues in Hall II didn't affect the young man's mood, though Viv colored her reports with such zest and intensity that the guards glanced at her puzzled, a fifty-year-old, first thing in the morning, all fired up, pointing, insisting, comparing, parroting everything in the relevant publications for the benefit of the unspeaking and morose youngster.

In the Hall of the Sifnians' Treasure the mother sat the son before the Sphinx of Naxos and obliged him to listen to how that enormous marble statue, of a height of seven and a half feet, lion body and legs, bird's wings and a woman's head with braids, all in the color of dirt, was an offering to the Oracle in 560 B.C. by the citizens of Naxos who were then in control of the whole of the Cycladic Islands.

The Sphinx, an emblem of their island, as a votive offering, would safeguard the navel of the Earth like the python used to, until Apollo slew the dragon, or dragoness. Chances are the serpent had been female.

Like an elementary schoolmistress, Viv kept up the lesson in mythology, dragging her only student around the statue and pointing out that the fabulous sculpture was representative of the Greek spirit which humanized monsters, mythical beings with a demonic personalities, imbued with the capacity to avert evil.

– Fine, that's enough for now, let's go, Linus interrupted, but Viv had no intention of quitting her fight, she took his arm, dragged and planted him in front of the caryatid at the frontal frieze of the Sifnians' Treasure, the girl with the inward looking eyes and the half-bashful, half-sleepy smile.

– The indentations in the hairdo and the diadem indicate she wore metal jewelry, she pointed out with her finger the little holes, then lowered her hand and waved it before the bust, the white chiton is gathered in rich pleats, she concluded and breathed in avidly, she had ended up short of breath in order to say it all, there was barely any oxygen left in her lungs.

She stood pale and unmoving for a bit, Linus became aware of her discomfiture, gave in and walked ahead into Hall III, to stand in the middle of the room, dominated by two archaic kouroi. Viv's courage picked up, she followed him and mollified him, that's it, we walk along, we see, we marvel, with a measured step always and seeing everything through our imagination, like the archaeologist Andronikos puts it, the imagination is of the essence, especially in order to form the image of this place with the five hundred statues that Nero snatched and the many works of art that Great Constantine lifted from here, to decorate his new capital.

Before the barely awake hordes of tourists descended, the next hour was taken up with the porous stone friezes fronting the circular temple, the bull statue out of hammered silver, the gold wires from the decoration of the ivory and gold statues, the armless and headless busts, the elaborations, *aryvallos* is the small, lidded oil container for the athletes in training, *enagismus* is the offering of aromatic substances to the dead for the cleansing of the soul, with a five-minute breathless delirium by Viv on the column with the three dancers, the sacred ballet a gift by an unknown donor, marble from Pendeli, diaphanous clothing, column capital with acanthus leaves, another five minutes on the breathless beauty of Antinoos, marble from Paros, the evolution of the portrait in Hellenistic sculpture and, finally, ten minutes of a merry-go-round the bronze charioteer with the inlaid eyes of glass and stone.

Viv also cast a sideways glance at Linus's eyes behind the dark glasses, closed again, she didn't let on, nor was she upset, she pointed out the long priestly chiton, the strip holding back the hair, the reins in the extended right hand and, tireless, without forgetting the basics about the statue's origin, part of a complex with four horses and a child leading the chariot to the races, an offering by Polyzalos, winner of the Pythia Games, tyrant of Yela and one of Deinomenes's four sons who beat the Carthaginians in 479 B.C., she recommended short stops a little this way, a little that way and to the back and at quite some distance farther away, for the purpose of exalting in the multiple aspects of the masterpiece.

Linus lowered his glasses slightly, opened his eyes and, for a long time, stared flabbergasted not at the charioteer but at his mother, struggling and sweating with the effort of not mixing up the works, the deities, the artists, the donors, the dates. He felt sorry for her. The poor woman was stressed to the breaking point, she'd organized an entire operation that was meaningless, not possible to avert evil nowadays or to cleanse the soul, easily done, possibly, for certain ones among the dead, certainly impossible among the living.

Yet, the operation was still in progress regardless.

After two quick coffees at the cafeteria table that was most secluded under the umbrellas and as the throngs of Greeks and foreigners thickened and the place resounded with the voices of sprightly kids demanding cold juice, Viv and Linus, consistently wordless, fully morose and unwaveringly disbelieving towards one another, fled discreetly along the pathway that led to the antiquities out of doors.

It was almost ten, the sun was already burning and the rest of the tour loomed ahead scorching as well.

***

Tell the king that the artful flute has fallen to the ground, that Phoebus no longer has a residence, nor prophetic laurel, nor a speaking spring; for the speaking water has been silenced.

The final and very melancholy oracle by Pythia to Oreivasius, an envoy of the Emperor Julian, before the curtain went down on the ancient Apollonian worship, at the close of the fourth century A.D., Vivian Koleva did not recite it by heart, she'd rather read it from the booklet, after completing her presentation of the Castalia Spring, when it was engraved on the sides of the two perpendicular Phaidriad rocks, the one going by the name of Flemboukos, the other by that of Rodini, why it was called that, who bathed there, what Pausanias mentions, what it was that the oracles, the first professional psychics, chewed in order to give their ambiguous edicts, laurel leaves, Linus, the ones we put in lentil soup and meat stew, the same ones woven into wreaths on the monuments to the fallen.

All of this with a one minute pause, her cell phone, the instructions she gave, don't scratch your legs, you'll only draw blood, the itch will be taken care of with an Atarax.

Linus at a distance, his back turned to her, looking at the mountains while she went on with her soliloquy, she felt under obligation to not leave unfinished what she had prepared with hard work, rehearsals and fair expense, so, with a voice growing increasingly faint she finally arrived at the closing of the hours-long saga, *nor a speaking spring; for the speaking water has been silenced.*

This was at the end of three hours of walking under the full sun, with stops at every manner of ruin and ten or so speeches about the Gymnasium, where sophistry, rhetoric, astronomy etc. were taught, about the five-thousand-seat theater, the Pythian Games, musical contests in the guitar, the lute, recital etc., about the Recess of Crateros, the Rock of the Sibyl, the Rock of Gaia, the Stone of Lito, the Stone of Cronus, libations of oil, offerings of raw wool etc., about the treasures of various donors, the names Antiphanes, Onatas, Aggeladas, Vrasidas, Epameinondas, Proussias, Philopimin, Lysippus, Leocharis, were coming thick and fast and so were the mix-ups, who was who, where, when and what exactly they had done, Viv didn't get distinctions, that's not what she was after, anyway.

Some of it was the sun that had completely fried her brain, and it was also Linus's total unwillingness to take part in any of it.

– Touch the stones, see if you don't feel something, she had invited him twice, he had walked on.

– Why don't you read yourself the votive inscription, she had suggested before the pillar of the Athenian's colonnade, he had not.

– Stand next to the pillar, it's Dorian, being tall and thin you look like it, she had said at Apollo's temple, it has remained standing for centuries, don't you fall yourself before you make thirty, she had pleaded, that was no concern of his either.

Archeologists must be happy people, somehow, she had said at some other moment, they get passionate about a world that can no longer hurt them, she hadn't omitted pointing that out, and, I'm thinking of buying you some books, Greek, foreign, I'll get the best, doesn't matter what it costs because, Linus, pay attention to me, that is the window I thought of opening for you, you do need a large window, wide open, a light in your life.

– Are you dreaming of my future? Are you setting me up for a career? he had mocked, turning about at once and running away down the dirt road that led back to where they'd come from.

Despite the extra kilos, despite the heavy bag, overcoming, or short circuiting, her old cool demeanor, Viv had sprung after her son, had caught up with him, grabbed him by the shoulders, turned him around and was pushing him back up the hill, almost maniacally, heaving breathless words, listen here, you'll see it all, just be a little patient, don't close up like an oyster, open up your eyes, we still have the Stardium, we still have Carstalia, other things as well, your arms are all aflame for not putting any sunscreen on.

She bundled him uphill, some foreigners were watching openmouthed. Viv had seen them but she didn't care, her mental answer, call me anything you like, mad or not, you don't know, if only you knew.

Linus followed her through the rest like a prisoner who had no way of escaping.

He even meekly circumnavigated, staying close to his mother, whenever her eye, always on the alert, caught sight of those foreign girls with the shorts, moving statues, lithe like does, cool despite the heat, which she made sure they evaded by walking in the opposite direction in this place crammed with fictions, everywhere to the front and to the back, to the right and left, further up and further down, altars, temples, springs.

At about two, sitting in the thin shade of an almond tree, in Linus's pack the last cigarette, the butts of the expedition gathered in a tissue in Viv's pocket, the plastic water bottles without a single drop, the archaeological guide booklets serving as fans, certain things were said, she precipitated it.

– Don't the statues mean anything to you?

– No.

– Doesn't all this beauty make any difference to you?

– No.

– It makes a difference to everybody.

– I beg to differ.

– What did you think of the charioteer?

– He'd do fine as your new paramour.

– Can't you at least respect the willfulness of the ancients, that they're still commanding attention, after all these centuries? That's worth something.

– To you, for sure, that's your latest ruse.

– I didn't used to care about any of it either, Viv sighed after a few minutes of silence taken up with ingesting his insult, I've only ever gone up to the Parthenon two times total, the first as soon as I got into university, to save myself the embarrassment of not having been and the second with your father and you at four, I had put my broad-brimmed hat on you and ended up with sunstroke, if you remember. He didn't. Silence again, more diffidence. What more could she possibly follow this with?

She confessed that, some time ago, despite her anxiety about her mission, maybe even because of it, when she first saw the charioteer she was overawed, she was so moved that her bowels loosened and she started farting loudly and successively, she blushed the deepest red out of her shame but there was no way she could control her body, the museum guard fled the small hallpost haste and a good thing it was that a guide in the next hall was taking her sweet time with about twenty Russian students.

What she didn't tell him was that she, a woman who had knelt before no god and had prayed to no saint, had then begged the charioteer, save me, you who made it through the destructive earthquake of 373 B.C., take pity on me and my son and when I bring him here to you, do your best to impress him, win him over.

She was now thinking about that again, almost moved, after the million things that had transpired she was left with a sweet exhaustion, the pleasure that the day's program had at any rate gotten somewhere, and, then, she did also like the midafternoon in the olive trees, the cypresses and the wild grass.

She had her son by her side, nature and her child, the illusion of a lightning visit to Alonaki twenty-five, twenty, fifteen years ago, before their lives were derailed.

Time for the postscript.

– How can you not wonder about the ancients' persistence to still be in our midst? It's obvious, there's something they are trying to divulge, more will be revealed, she intoned the last prefabricated statement, that one was wasted on him as well, the son uprooted a tall mallow and crushed it, grabbed a stone and threw it at another one, rose slowly, gave her his hand so she could get up as well, moved to take her heavy bag from her, she didn't let him, he didn't insist and walking in front, so you can keep me in check, he commented snidely, led his mother through the five hundred feet to the exit and their little car, through lines of people on their way in or out.

– Nobody is looking at us, nobody expects to see me in a place like this, he reassured her with perfect conviction in his voice. Who would possibly get in their head what you got in yours, kidnap me and take me to an ancient army camp, he said to himself later, very softly, Viv was maneuvering out of the parking spot, she missed the pointed comment.

***

Indeed, under the circumstances, the whole conception, a five-day excursion at Delphi, would only occur and ripen in Vivian Koleva's mind.

The small Fiat was dancing. Green, green, green and lo! a purple tree, mountains, mountains, mountains full of hairpin turns and here and there a country chapel, a sheep pen. Far in the distance the township of Itea, steaming as it lay by the sea, others would visit it, they wouldn't themselves go down there.

They parked near the small restaurant Cheronia, which Viv had spotted when she came for a reconnaissance of the wider region, it was set apart, had a vine-tree shading it and a homely cuisine of cooked vegetables, which were on her list for the sake of variety. She had selected the place for a good meal there for her son, a good serving of horizon and to finish telling him about the Sacred Wars, the battle of Cheronia in 338 B.C., Philip the Macedonian against the Locreans, which of course needed to happen on Friday, in the late afternoon, before the weekend crowds descended.

They picked a table off to one side. A foursome at the other end, two pensioner couples, were picking at the apple slices of the dessert absorbed in two completely separate but simultaneous conversations, the seventy-year-old women in black were enumerating dead acquaintances and were scheduling in advance their preparations for All Souls' Day that was coming up, the men of the same age, one with the socialist party, the other with the opposition, were weighing up which of the leading parties was less full of horseshit.

As if by arrangement, or else telepathy, the old Cretan

called with his daily improvised limerick. *I voted Death for Prime Minister to get some peace of mind/ As all the rest have riddled me with naught but debts and strife.* Viv's resounding "well done!" could easily have sent a whole squad of Special Operations policemen fleeing. Terrorized, the elderly man rang off, the cell phone was placed at the edge of the table and lay there on the paper tablecloth.

Until the stuffed vine leaves and the meatballs arrived, which would aid and abate Viv in her serious and utterly decisive conversation, the woman repeatedly cooled her forehead and arms with bottled water, and attempted, as a start, to set the mood with a sprinkling of tales about unforgettable feasts, hoping to smooth the ground.

This needs us to be relaxed and intimate, she thought, filled up the two beer glasses, licked the froth off hers and, before even starting her stories, she broke out of the blue into a weird little laugh, syncopated like the code messages of old telegraphs or, even worse, like a school coach's instructions during a phys ed demonstration.

So she recalled the rare wedding banquets at Alonaki, the double souvlakia of the university days, and some birthday parties of his godmother, Rhoda, before she turned thirty-five, at a different apartment each year with a different décor and a different lover.

Inwardly, she was deriding herself for her uncontrollable prattle and the artlessness of her ruse. Rather than paying attention to her, Linus every so often turned his head in the direction of the barks of the restaurant's invisible dog, tied in the backyard. At one point, he picked up the bottle of water and emptied the rest of it on his hands.

– Good boys don't eat with dirty hands, right, Mom? He whispered, more as if reminding himself of old dictums of proper behavior.

Her mood plummeted, five minutes ticked by with her

unmoving and wordless. She became lively again, with some effort, at the sight of the dishes, they smell nice, she said to the twenty-year-old waiter, who deposited the order and left at top speed, his mind, too, on something else.

First she put salt on Linus's chips and salad, while he remained hidden behind the black shades.

– There are no people around, take off the glasses and enjoy the nature around you, she inveigled him, truthfully wanting him not to miss the greenery, grand as it was, and rare in the life he led, but also because she wanted to see his eyes while telling him the things she meant to tell him.

She started after the first forkfuls by chasing his gaze, which alternately descended to his plate and rose to her face, with an expression that feigned curiosity but couldn't effectively hide some anxiety.

– You must think I'm mad to have dragged you here, and Yukaris, too, though he didn't say so to my face, but I could tell he thought I was out of context completely, that I've lost it. I haven't. Your situation has been troubling me for years. I need to find you a redeeming interest.

She paused for a bit, a redeeming interest. She intoned again the formal title of the subject at hand so she could pick up her thread, then, with an expression and in a tone that no third party could tell for certain were sarcastic or agonizingly earnest, she wondered: Economics? Biology? Mineral wealth? Poetry? Model crafting? Stamp collecting?

Those were all out of the question, some due to circumstances, others on account of the cost, others yet because Linus had no such inclination, at least until his junior year in high school when he had collected his fair share of A's, and all of them together because they didn't provide the impetus needed to push him into a completely different world, solitary by necessity but intense, with triumphant enigmas, with mythic proportions and dimensions.

– Archaeology requires and provides knowledge, imagination, inspiration, adventure, it obliges a mind to take a reprieve from reality, to not go moldy inside four walls, she said with zest and disclosed that the idea came to her one night while she was watching a documentary on a national TV channel about the Incas.

She bit into a slice of cucumber so that their meal could move along with naturalness.

– The Acropolis, she exclaimed, swallowing. Eleusis, she pursued meaningfully. Vergina, Dodoni, Epidavros, Mycenae, Santorini, Knossos, she machine-gunned Linus with gusto, hoping, if not to ignite his zeal, at the very least to recommend her idea.

For his part, having lost his appetite altogether, immobilized, his body more wooden than the chair, his face soaked in sweat, he was listening to her arguments laid out in proper order with no supernumerary r's, with the flourish and conviction of a teacher preparing her student for entry exams.

The due honors were afforded to Evans, Kalokairinos, Schliemann, Andronikos, Sakelarakis, all top archaeologists, all well known, followed by dozens of excavation sites, descriptions of wondrous finds, museums worldwide, from New York to Bagdad and from Madrid to Berlin, each mentioned with a caption, whatever Viv managed to memorize in the recent months she had been applying herself to her program of enforced education.

She finished off with something more accessible, more attractive, the movie blockbusters about illicit traders of antiquities and the cartoon series.

All the while, they had no clue about the goings on around them, they didn't see the pensioners leave, the Albanian adolescents who brought two truckloads of flowering zucchini, and they barely glanced at the enthusiastic group of youths in green tops, their waiter among them, who packed into a Toyota and screeched off in the direction of Athens, to make the European basketball semifinals. The restaurant owner stood staring at the road, even after the car was gone.

It was nearly four, the oblique sun was now reaching Linus, drying the sweat that was running copiously but also shining into his eyes, which were half-closed and brimming with tears.

– Study will be effective, Viv preempted, next time you choose where we go and you be my tour guide. She had even dreamt of the possibility of studies via correspondence, it's not out of the question, one day it will be allowed, with a degree, too, awaiting in the future and, why not, with a book you'll write about antiquities, which always has a captive and passionate audience among the Greeks, you'll see yourself differently, others will too.

– You will see me differently, Linus whispered and with shaking hands, put his glasses back on.

The ashtray was filled with half-smoked cigarettes, three burning ones rested on its three recesses, still he lit a new one.

His mother's flow had been stemmed abruptly. Turned now to the view, every mountain an obstacle, every hill a hindrance, she was seeking a detour for an immediate return to the matter at hand and for a way to bring things again under control.

– A redeeming interest, she summed up the entire project with the one emblematic phrase, so that, if something happens to me, you have a solid anchor to hang onto.

She had him financially secured, two rents and the deposits in the Farmers' Bank from her work, but if she was to take sick and die suddenly, there was no friend on the horizon and no one from the family was going to take Linus on board, clean clothes, some proper food every so often, visits, a chat over the phone, a go-between with Yukaris. Everyone in the immediate family had written him off and had inadvertently taken their distance from her, too, her mother didn't figure in this, at seventy-five she was one step before the grave and, besides, Linus refused to see or talk to her, even once, he was adamant.

What was there left? What would give him courage, a little dignity even? In her attempted coup d'état at the valley of Delphi, Vivian Koleva was playing her trump card. Which meant that today and tomorrow and the day after tomorrow she was going to make it plain to him, whether you fancy them or not, these here antiquities are the only proposition that can buoy someone with a life sentence.

TAHINI

Her stride was still full and the past hadn't yet started getting wrapped in the cellophane of a weary mind's forgetfulness. Vivian Koleva realized that she had started getting old all right, the day she put tahini in her life. The dour taste and ready-made snack of moneylessness on the table of the paternal home and later, a daily cheap foodstuff, in and out of feasting days, for almost all her elderly clients, the familiar jar in their kitchenettes always caught her eye.

It was a rainy and cold Saturday afternoon, the first time she too bought at the supermarket the paste with the sad color and two hours later, as she dunked the bread slice spread with tahini in her tea, a birthday dinner for her fifty years, she brought to mind all of her past life.

Certain episodes were missing, they'd erased themselves leaving small or somewhat larger gaps. Some she omitted, some she passed over hastily, in others she wasn't in charge of the doses of reality, probably memory's familiar ruse of editing its notes when keeping track of derailed souls and derailed emotions.

Starting point, her grandfather's blurred image, the family provider, as he ritually emptied on the plastic tablecloth of the kitchen the paper bag with the few shopping items they could afford, usually two packets of spaghetti, rice by the ounce, lentils, sugar, coffee and invariably tahini which provided calories, was filling and also could be managed by old, toothless mouths.

Each thought drew in another, with every soaked mouthful and swallow Viv Koleva ran through the years, events and faces that surrounded her in childhood, youth and her adult years later on.

She'd been born on December 17 of 1955, first daughter of Sotiris and Stavroula Sotiropoulos, he forty-six, she twenty-two, disparate ages but well matched hands, for digging the fields, and well matched mouths, for sparse talk.

The two-room house in the village didn't resound with the liveliness of high spirits or quarrels, the communication was basic, you with the animals, me at the vineyard, you do the wood, I'll see to the cabbages.

The young Vivian, the name had been by decree of the godfather, it reminded him of an old fiancée from Patras, who ingested rat poison by mistake, was growing up unbeknownst to the adults, the men drafted in the many trials of poverty, the women, kith and kin, in black for three, five, ten years, or for life, for every one of the dead in the immediate or extended family, dedicated to the hereafter, with distinctions in mourning.

She was only a wee thing and life had already struck her with the triteness of a meager day-to-day. It didn't cross her mind to hanker after caresses, as children do, nor again was she in a hurry to grow up, she didn't distinguish between large and small events, no matter what was going on around her, she dragged her little feet impassively round and round the house, like a loose dog, a pale and silent seven-year-old who had been prematurely afflicted with boredom.

Nothing excited her curiosity, she wasn't impressed when the shadow puppet theater came to the village, nor when a car stopped at the square and a tall stranger of a woman came out to have a drink of water, dressed in a man's silk suit, she didn't liven up at the noisy city of Patras either, when her godfather had taken her there, before he left for Germany as a factory worker, and bought her a red synthetic jumper.

At school, she didn't trip over herself for a word of praise from the teacher, she didn't whisper incessantly with the other girls nor did she fight with the boys and at home she never cried asking for something, she never stole sweet quince from the tall shelf, she didn't even have a favorite dish or a favorite rosebush or chook from the pen.

They told her, go feed the chickens and she did, sweep the yard and she did, come here, and she came, get out from under our feet and she went, wash your hair, she washed it, go to sleep, she slept.

She did not plead, she did not quarrel, she did not negotiate, only silently complied with what the others decided, her elders and the grown-ups. The latter, in obeisance to their permanently bleak finances, credit at the grocer's, debts to the tax office, loans from the bank and lists of sums loaned to each other, had their work cut out for them whenever deadlines loomed, and, with the chronic fatigue of poverty, were relieved with the thin little creature that asked for absolutely nothing, an easy child, they sometimes said.

Only someone paying proper attention would have been puzzled and would have wondered, but no such person was around.

Besides, the grown-ups interacted exclusively among themselves, whether at their work or in the great feasts, three or four times a year, when they wandered in large groups from house to house. The men would start with an obligatory reference to issues of importance, each of them had to decide on three great tragedies, one for humanity, everyone agreed on the Second World War, one for Hellenism, here opinions were divided, half in favor of the Asia Minor destruction, half in favor of the civil war, and one for their lives, which is where the disabilities from old war mines were brought out, the birth of a sick baby, a knife wound over the boundaries of a plot of land. At the second round of drinks, they put their sorrows aside and hung from the lips of Theopisti, that old bag of bones with the sexual jokes and the fully perfected masculine cussing, also a local legend on account of her spunk to throw rotten eggs at every manner of politico.

Her foxy spiritedness was a league apart from the placid minds of the rest, but in order for her to lay out her goods and thus take the weight off her fellow villagers' sacks of sorrows—she was the one who'd initiated them in this theory—the family men had first to get rid of their children.

And they did send them off, finish eating the butter cake now and off you go. In those times, people lived extremely tamely and Theopisti's raciness was the only godsend reprieve.

At school young Vivian's ear caught from a distance the words cunt and prick, two boys were saying them, the one with the harelip and the priest's son, except she wouldn't go near her precocious fellow students to find out how the combination of those two fills out women's bellies and brings about babies.

Her sister was born when she herself was in the third grade, old enough to be assigned a host of duties, rock the baby so she goes to sleep, wash her bottom and, when later she walked, make sure she doesn't burn herself on the woodstove, doesn't eat dung, doesn't fall in the asbestos.

The little Polyxeni, little Xenia to her godmother, plain Xenia at nine, at her own request, with movies as her adopted religion and the actress Xenia Kalogeropoulou as her favorite saint, was one more domestic problem, as she peed herself until the age of five, spat the tahini on her blouse, and was willful about any number of things, the pretty face and the games with the kittens, notwithstanding.

Besides, regarding her grandfather, too, gray-eyed, a good singer in the church and generous with his blessings, the only thing she singled out was the large hairy mole between his brows, regarding her father who, despite his years, had a deer's tread, she directly saw his fingernails, black from the tar and mud, and as for her mother, instead of admiring her very long blond hair or, at the very least, her patience of an evening when she rubbed the dirt off a tubful of spinach in order to bake a pie, she persisted in unmercifully staring at her swollen ankles and the ash-colored cracks on her heels.

Growing up, she fine-tuned her predilection for the unsightly details, the unflattering aspects and generally the bad side of things.

Out of an entire green pine forest, her eye was drawn to the nests of larvae. Out of an orange grove in bloom, she spotted at once the torn chicken wire of the fence. Out of an entire mountain, her gaze singled out the dry turd at the base of a rock. At her teacher's doorstep, for trick or treat, she looked inside and instead of seeing the pleasing arrangement of the furniture that was the woman's dowry, she picked out the thick dust on the wooden surfaces. At Theopisti's windowsill to deliver the eggs, instead of relishing the extremely vocal goldfinch, her eye circled the hole in the curtain. Small wonder, then, that marriages of many years, in her mind, were marred by the man's one and only slap on the woman's cheek, her mother had been the recipient of one such, singular but effective, and as for the local chieftains, priest, policeman and mayor, they were deemed useless by her on account of losing their step on one or two occasions, at a wedding dance.

She wasn't, then, the kind of girl people would go out of their way to include in their company, she usually made her way solitarily with, occasionally, the rare, tolerant persons who didn't take her cold demeanor as an insult, and didn't interpret her temperament, closed-off and inaccessible to small joys, as arrogant, a thing which could on no account be justified by her family's social standing or by her looks, there was nothing about her that was exemplary, no pair of sea-blue eyes or blond braids, she was just a brunette in everything, like most others.

At fourteen she made up her mind that since, as a child, she hadn't happened to be the recipient of plentiful and gratifying endearments and, since her cheeks hadn't been covered in layers of kisses and caresses, she wasn't going to spare them, in turn, for others.

She knew that she herself somehow kept others at bay. She did it so that she wouldn't be crowded into the crammed space of their heavy lives. And the others never fought to keep her close by, maybe because they knew deep inside that their thousands of worries didn't make up attractive days for a secretly sad little girl, maybe because on top of it all, questions were the last thing they wanted.

Only because things aren't spoken, it doesn't mean they don't exist. Every person puts up a fight for silence.

In high school, there were another three silence fighters, Petra, Niobe and Eleni, all of them creatures blurred since birth, of mediocre looks, mediocre students, the broken stems in the verdant bouquet of the class. They didn't actually socialize, they communicated with rare but telling looks, maintaining the dignity of isolation.

Once in a while they exchanged a few words, those necessary for agreeing that there was no reason for them to be happy. In time, they restricted themselves to even less, and in their senior year they even replaced the good mornings and hellos with nothing, nothing, which was just perfect as a leitmotif. They were starting to be preoccupied with the drama of the body.

With the first indispositions of love, which boosted her breasts, rounded her bottom and lighted up her skin, Viv started the fight to not give in to the black eyes of Apostolis, then, to the perfectly spelled secret notes of Theodor and, later still, to the persistence of Michael with the irresistible blue jeans, who used to trail her to and from her village to the township, where the high school was, and pressed her for a night meeting at a place where the grown-ups would never turn up, the cypress grove by the cemetery.

She had unfailingly noted the jug ears of the first, the pimples on the nose of the second and the small, girly fingernails of the third, yet there were now unprecedented issues at stake.

Sometimes she felt sorry for the boys, melting away with desire. And sometimes she herself melted, which was a strange and worrisome thing, that uproar of the blood in the veins, but she did not feel sorry for herself, on the contrary, she felt satisfied when she would at last manage to impose her will over her body and concentrate again on the theory and exercises of physical chemistry.

Prudent, she heard around her the pronouncement of father, mother and the rest of the adults. She didn't much care for the title but at least they let her be

Nevertheless, the struggle of very prudent girls against fervid boys turns out to be an uneven match around fifteen, sixteen at most.

It was then, Christmas of '71, that Viv tasted the kisses of a George, which were not as fulfilling as those of the next George down the line, when she was seventeen. So from time to time, she would kiss and make out a bit but mostly she studied the despicable physical chemistry so she could get into college, which bore no attraction in itself but that was what most high school graduates did, at least once they sat through entry exams for some school or other. Certainly, it had already been said, at least three or four times, for the sake of you becoming a doctor, I'll gladly sell the old vineyard, words spoken of an evening by her father, who was pushing sixty-five, worn out by the sun and the bad prices of grapes.

Her mother was silently consenting and pushing her with her eyes, as if to say, make sure you get out, make sure you save yourself.

She barely understood how it happened that she was studying to be a doctor. Maybe in order to see what it's like doing your parent a favor, maybe because it was much harder than lawyer and teacher and she wanted to provoke, maybe because she got it into her head to take up wounds and traumas in case she could become absorbed in the wager of life against death, maybe the intensity of the subject would nurse a strong interest.

She was only an adolescent and she needed a way to make it through the rest of living, the many years that awaited her. She would leave the house and the village too. She had finally had enough of the people, the dogs, the chickens, the dirt roads, the fields, the weeds, the tahini.

She didn't make it on the first go, still, the need for extracurricular study brought her to the capital. Athens was decked with cars and apartment buildings, these were missing from the village and such differences did initially made an impression on the rural guest.

If I don't cook for my Kostas for one day, I will kill myself, Aunt Zoe was yelling all in tears, her father's sister, a cop's pensioner widow, whose base of operations was the kitchen of her three-bedroom at Kato Patissia.

Kostas was the thirty-five-year-old only son, who was obliged, the unfortunate, to drop in daily after work and pick up the Tupperware or the pot and take it to his wife, who was disgusted with the whole scene.

For the entire year, the aunt's daughter-in-law never once showed up. And through the whole year, at the top of the charts of the three-bedroom apartment was neither the junta nor the uprising of the Polytechnic, but the aunt's anxiety about properly stirring the egg and lemon sauce for her Kostas's stuffed lettuce leaves, making sure her Kostas's pilaf didn't turn muddy, her Kostas's fish soup did not congeal.

Viv hung on until the exams, passed them and immediately made it plain to her father that enough was enough.

The old vineyard went for two hundred thousand. Athens swallowed up another small vineyard with second rate yield. All that was left was a small useless stretch overgrown with wild reeds somewhere near the sea, nobody ever went there, just stones and mosquitoes.

The still few land buyers at the time secured for their country homes spots on golden beaches right by the sea without bogs of dirty water nearby, it wasn't easy to fool them. And I get the mosquitoes as my dowry? asked eleven-year-old Xenia. The doctor will see after you, old Sotiropoulos answered, evading his responsibilities and simultaneously feeling, for the first time in his life, optimistic, such a grand thing having a scientist daughter.

The last dusk at the village, after preparing the trunk with the sheets, the blankets, the cracked wheat fermented in milk and the icons brought by the village faithful for the one-bedroom of student life, was spent by Viv in the grove of tall, thick reeds with the half-forgotten George especially drafted for the occasion, the rest, young and older, were away due to the call to arms, it was the time of the coup against Makarius and the Turkish invasion of Cyprus.

The nineteen-year-old Viv was embarrassed to go to university a virgin. And she wasn't about to let the boys of Athens in on the news that, in this particular arena, she was lagging behind. The Greek junta fell, let's get the junta of virginity over with as well, she gave her guest the specific instruction.

George, with a serious cough though it was August, did the needed thing expediently, heroically and with gusto, though he was just coming out of pneumonia and, on top, had again bottomed out at school, not to mention he hadn't decided what was next, the army, Australia or Canada.

The definitive farewell was, of course, bloody but also very easy. Both of them were already thinking of something else.

Next day at the bus station, Viv's back and hips ached from

the stones and there were dozens of mosquito bites on her arms.

She scratched all the way to Athens.

***

Kypseli, 57 Eptanisou St., underground single flat in a twenty-year-old apartment building, Viv's first introduction to the concepts of light wells and communal backyards.

A fold-up bed, a fold-up table, two fold-up chairs, a small bookshelf with four planks, secondhand wardrobe, second-hand fridge and gas cooker with two elements in twenty-six square meters, where the bedroom, kitchenette and small bath-room hugged tightly, long overwhelmed by the heavy smell that accumulates at the bottom of things.

After she finished mopping and made the bed, set on the bookshelf the only photograph she had taken with her, of eleven-year-old Xenia in shorts with a kitten, she made herself a coffee and sat to appraise the effects of her housekeeping, medium, as for the reek of mildew, that was a waste of effort, it reemerged triumphant as soon as the chlorine evaporated.

She thought that her nostrils had been trained by village life, moldy mattresses and sheets stiff with sweat, dirt roads that stank of sheep piss and donkey dung.

She took up imagining her days and nights within and with-out the apartment, cramped inside, discomfited outside.

She had confirmed the thing that she had been suspecting since last year when she was studying nonstop, without allow-ing herself to waste precious hours in mental meanderings and luxury questions. From the very first day she set foot in Athens, nothing caused her to feel enthused or scared or even puzzled, just an enormity, an unwieldy heaping of bulky shapes with no coherence, unconnected architecture, unconnected thorough-fares, unconnected people, a vast junkyard of unconnectedness.

That suited her. She would be living in a city that wouldn't upset her, wouldn't introduce new issues in her life. She would study, she would read, she would circulate with no need to seriously heed her surroundings.

When she left the village, she knew there was no chance she'd miss it. When she first saw Athens, she knew there was no chance that it might ever feel like home. Steadfast to her principles, trained in locating defects immediately, she didn't remember, till the age of nineteen, having ever been attracted to anything at all on first sight and unconditionally, she was stocking up on reservation and objections about all things, she foresaw and simultaneously prepared, almost methodically, the disenchantment lying in wait in the future, whether near or far.

The fact that she'd managed to get into medicine was a victory, but victories do not make everyone feel better or even make a discernible difference.

Up until then, she had heard many people after some important event, a debt that was absolved, a lucky lotto ticket, the undoing of an ill-omened engagement, the end of an army service that tested them to the end of their endurance, being released after months of hospitalization, relay to relatives and to anyone listening that, the next day, I woke up a different person.

Sipping her first coffee at her flat, Viv analyzed the popular figure of speech and determined that nobody can escape their previous life and, especially, themselves, the skin is marked by scars visible and invisible, the shoulder is eroded by one's sack of dirty laundry and by trials, stolen sweat, poisonous words, sterile land, caresses that were never given, dreams that faded, oaths that proved false, guilt that festered with time. That's how she had learned to see people, laden with their sack wherever they went, in the street, the shop, the coffee house, the train, the church, the tavern even, half-full on the backs of the younger ones, overfull on the backs of the middle-aged and the elderly, some bodies bent at a right angle to the ground.

With the last sip of coffee she admitted, nevertheless, that the power of the expression, I woke up a different person, was not ever going to diminish, and calculated that in the course of a lifetime, a person will claim to have woken up a different person at least one hundred times.

Later, the first night on her single camp bed, with a wind that was driven mad by its inability to escape the stolid city, she thought of the wind in the village, which moved the darkness, the clouds, the pines and the grapevines and, listening to the banging of her next door neighbors' bathroom window that'd been left unlatched, to an empty bottle rolling back and forth on the first floor balcony above her and to the flapping of the derelict tent of the apartment across the way, she again resumed her ruminations on her new day-to-day, walls, faces, itineraries, activities would change but, inside of her, since she didn't have the gift of longing, since no sweet anticipation fermented her bloodstream, she would be preoccupied with much the same things, an excessive mistrust towards everyone and everything, a lack of motive to see the world more charitably.

That alone was what she excelled in and she almost fancied her prowess at swiftly burying new possibilities.

University was an ordeal, the classes reinforced her tendency to get distracted, the professors kept their distance and she let them, the students were bursting with the unforgivable self-confidence that they had the right and the guts to turn the whole wide world upside down, and she could not share in the absence of melancholy in their permanently excited faces, she could not find it in her to get in line with them with her fist also raised in the air.

Her own hands, Viv, when she wasn't in the street where she kept them in her pockets, or wasn't immersed in writing or housekeeping, she kept down. She had never raised them to ask, to smack, to applaud.

What's more, one November Thursday, looking flabbergasted at about three hundred fists shooting up in the air in the Physiology Amphitheater, she thought for the first time that often, when she was alone, both at her village and here, in her room, in cafeterias, she would twist her fingers for long periods, as if winding a piece of twine, or, stretching the palms straight out, she would look at the fingers one by one as if counting them to find out their number and sometimes patiently rub with one hand the fingers of the other, as if she needed to lengthen and slim them down.

She had spent more than a few hours of silence and loneliness occupying herself with her upper limbs. When, in addition, in order to throw people off her scent and forestall any questions, she whitewashed her expression with an unfocused gaze, unmoving eyelids and a protracted smile, the inner tension found another bank in which to flow, it spilled out into her hands which couldn't find a moment's stillness.

The palms played the part of the face, the fingers the part of the eyes. It was with the use of her hands that she made it through the obligatory great protest march on the first year anniversary of the students' slaughter at the Polytechnic. Everyone went, she couldn't not go too, she thought about it and she did it, she joined the tail end of the march on Stadiou St., the bellowing from up front and around her and everywhere was searing the heavens.

Entwined in the enormous crowd, thunderstruck by the uplifted faces, by herself among strangers, with her hands in her pockets struggling to keep up to the day's terrible rhythm, she poked a hole through the fabric, lost her key and her money, but she did cover a full five hundred meters, from before Syntagma Square all the way to the Parliament, at which point she desisted.

As for the rest, during the first months at uni, she frequently changed seats in the lecture halls and the labs, to avoid becoming familiar with those who made a habit of always sitting in the same place. That way she could be listening to the lecture at the downtown campus, the Old Chemistry Building, the New Chemistry Building, and simultaneously scrutinize at ease the crowd of freshmen, some of them lively creatures with the air of being born and raised in the capital, and others timid, bearing the marks of their native Hepeiros, Thrace, Crete, Cyprus, on their cheeks, their speech, their posture.

In the hours between lectures, she sometimes determined to sneak in among one of the groups in the hallways or the yard, just enough to get a first taste, but she was derailed by the phrases she plucked off the air, the groups of Athenians mainly spoke about political organizations, avant-garde movies, and abortions, whereas those from the countryside again dealt in politics mixed in with expectations and ambitions of all kinds and Viv just wasn't up to either of the two.

All alone in her apartment building as well, after she had expediently checked out several tenants and had with pleasure given them bad marks, a family of three who meowed in succession, one of four who came in and out as one and barked in unison, a well matched couple of sixty-five, both extremely well versed in excerpts from the Bible, an unmarried cop with a nose like a dried-up meatball, covered in more than one hundred zits, who came down to the communal backyard on two Sundays to pick up underwear he'd dropped, a philosophy senior with a double chin like a bag of lard, who was waxing philosophical about her situation while frying frankfurters on a daily basis, and so on and so forth, not a single one to upset her because she couldn't find something repulsive about them, or sad at the very least.

After a few weeks, she circumnavigated them with ease, a curt, good morning, at best, until she gave that up as well, none of them was capable of making her feel guilty over her disdain.

The physics and chemistry textbooks on the table, on the

camp bed, on the chair, on the breadbox and on the laundry basket in the bathroom, circled her like snakes, bit her with their many unread pages, paralyzed and dragged her stupefied into a mental void.

The sum total of unfamiliar things in the first trimester that withstood her critique were, firstly, the taste of ham in a sandwich and, secondly, iced coffee, she saw three young girls order it at a fashionable bistro, so she did too, she ordered it again for four Saturday evenings in a row, and then she'd had enough of it.

The third relatively good thing were a week spent with her sister. At Christmas, in order not to go down to the village, which was preparing as one to welcome her as a doctor, she hosted the young Xenia, took her to the pigeons and the change of the guard at Syntagma Square, to the Royal Gardens, to the new multiplex of stores, on the electric railway, to a fun park with a Ferris wheel and bumper cars, to two movies, to a ballet demonstration at a neighborhood dance school, saw her eyes burn with passion, heard the words come out of her little mouth like a punch, Daddy is really old, several times and apropos of nothing, while enjoying a Chicago ice cream or while continually shifting the position of her colored hairpins, above the temples, behind the ears, then, at the top of the head, her hair dark and wavy, just like Dad's.

Death was staking its claim on her, it had already tunneled into her mind and was doing its work, you could hear the crackling as it eroded, piece by piece, the child's fragile sense of ease and safety.

Viv, to be sure, was now properly a grown-up and, for her, death's address was at the morgue where she would be welcomed in second year by cadavers receptive to manhandling and vivisecting.

Her father's age was prompting other observations, too, to do with the uniform of old age in general, dentures, baldness, the skin sagging, the bones corroded, the gaze slowing down in reverse to the rapid progression towards the end and her parents' age difference, one over sixty-five, the other under forty-five, obliged her to think often that when the husband enters old age, the much younger wife must follow suit, she is drafted into old age urgently and as a rule, she obeys, that's what her mother did. She was racing on the heels of her husband's old age, she was fighting her robust arms, her still upright posture, her eyes which defied her will, their flashing and quickness would not be halted.

Mrs. Stavroula was commandeering her age, her pillow and her table, oiling and polishing the rifle of patience.

She would give herself a break by playing hooky from the house of an afternoon. She would stray out into the fields, farther and farther away, gathering edible weeds, more and more of them, which her family ate less and less of, they'd had their fill of them, boiled and steamed, as for pie, they were well and truly over that.

One night in a student winter, Viv had seen her in a dream, in her convict's accessories of the black button-down house robe and the bucket, soaping money, then changing the water and soaping down the slimy surface of the broad pebbles down where the reeds were, changing the water again and carefully bathing a dozen naked male infants, including the Holy One, before it was a year old, intoning the while, poor women like us are given a goat's horn as dowry when we marry, and we chew ever after on our trials as if they were milk and honey.

And you feed your daughters the same, Viv added next morning, before dawn, gazing at the policeman's undershorts on the cement of the inner courtyard.

***

Fotis Kolevas's first kiss was thrown at Vivian Sotiropoulos's mouth like a punch and it made her gums bleed.

– You are so soft, he told her after two minutes of silence, as he was caressing her elbows.

They were standing still in a minuscule park, a handful of trees, just enough for the necessary décor.

It was a Saturday evening and Saturday evenings, even with mild weather, even on dry land, bring on a sea storm in people's inner hearts. Just previously, they'd had schnitzel, they had each downed two glasses of beer and, past eleven at night, they were walking uncertainly, zigzagging in the narrow streets of Kypseli, the kind of slow meandering of two people who expect something more to eventuate and are gauging the moment when they ought to take their chance.

The island carpenter Fotis Kolevas landed on the platform of Viv's student days while her life's second pale decade was about to expire and speared the girl with his clumsy kiss under October's faint stars.

The Peloponnesian youngster had gotten through the first year with a passing grade in all her courses bar two, biology and chemistry, toughies that were left for September's exam period.

The year had rolled by with heavy textbooks and mild unrest in the school, especially as she stood at the entry to the Physiology Amphitheater and listened to the rapid fire of arguments and counterarguments and more especially when, from the back of informal discussion groups, she watched the debates on all things political, shifting the students into two groups in her mind, roughly, the loud ones who considered, and probably worshipped as the country's most significant events, the Split, the Asia Minor disaster, the Occupation, the Civil War and the dictatorship, and those less loud who passed over the tragedies with distaste and counter-proposed as watersheds, though without much conviction, the liberation, democracy, truces, ceasefires and peace processes, things in general that didn't smart.

Herself a stranger to such passions, inclined towards personal rather than collective failings, she had no place in the aforementioned rumpus and resorted to less boisterous gestures of collectivity, glances, how you doing, a wave, a nod, mainly with other girl students from the countryside, until she allowed herself, on entering or exiting the lecture halls, to walk a short distance, gradually getting longer, with Eleftheria, Martha, Dora and Rhoda, all pretty, none of them a knockout, and all of the same height, about five foot three.

By degrees, they turned out to be almost pleasant, almost charming, certainly intelligent and Viv could take occasional breaks of mundane interaction from the spectacular upheaval of her loneliness, the underground flat, mildew, silence, long faces and the cop's boxer shorts and tank tops.

In January she went out with them for pizza downtown, in February for spicy meatballs in a central suburb, in March for shopping at the open air market of Monastiraki, where they bought corduroy trousers and sandals.

Each of them had entered the scene with an impeccable pedigree from Crete, Samos, Parga and Serres, armed with their families' poverty, which they turned à la mode times five, sunless rooms were à la mode, loaning sums of money was à la mode, and so were the smoked pork and stuffed vine leaves from their villages, the halvah and lettuce pies and their hunger, too, for a boyfriend, industrious and romantic, just so they could refuel for their long hours of study.

The affairs faded very quickly because the boys were insatiable for adding notches to their belts, they competed for conquests, the times did not favor romance and the girls had difficulty adjusting to quick developments, the period of grace was six months.

During that period they had figured out a fair amount about the student crowds and their coats of arms. If someone entertained doubts, the others said he lacked coherence, if he expressed objections, he was branded a reactionary or a wuss.

Every so often the students would ride on all-night political conversations, staying awake making dreams and listening to Theodorakis, they dismounted from the songs at dawn and left in couples.

The group of five attended, sometimes in full, others by proxy, on a few occasions only, as if by chance.

Martha and Dora had slept for two, three nights with members of the school's Communist Youth party, Eletheria had been too embarrassed not to sleep with the rich and voluble liberal leftist who was raking the girls in, indiscriminately, truth be told, self-confidence crackled in his eyes and jingled in his pockets.

Rhoda was a different kettle of fish. Her lit teacher in high school, a lover of the arts and a progressive, had taken his vocation in earnest and produced, as a result, cultural devotees aplenty. The girl from northern Greece was one such. So she went to plays by Carolos Koon, listened to the composer Mamagkakis, read the poetry of Anagnostakis and was godless, except she had deified the working class with industrial workers first on the list of martyrs to social injustice and construction workers at the forefront of the class struggle, who were also her favored love interests. She had been with a builder, a painter and a carpenter and she exonerated them when they'd had enough and dumped her, she liked been rejected by a worker.

She spoke with awe about their banged fingers, their bubonic hernias and their lumbago, and with genuine admiration about asbestos, crushed rock and bricks, her chosen specialty was cardiology but you'd think her an expert in pouring cement, tiling, and hanging gypsum ceilings.

They are good people and they know how to live without hope, she said about all three, words from an old letter of her dad's, a cog in the automobile industry of Munich, she mentioned him often.

Viv's score was slight, a scrounger from Medicine and a whiner from Dentistry, ungraceful creatures whom she gave short shrift on day one without insulting them, they weren't even worth that.

What did she think of all of last year's and this year's events, till very recently? The junta felt unreal, the liberation unreal, and so did Athens, the university, her interests, her socializing. Her way of thinking about life and putting her views into effect wasn't enough, there were too many unfamiliar subjects, who was there to put them in order, how to define the priorities, how to ignore them.

At the end of March she skipped class ten times, hopping on bus routes in random directions, forgetting herself in her seat for hours on end, looking out at everything, continuously, and retaining nothing, absolutely nothing, as if her gaze pierced the asphalt, the apartment blocks, the stadiums, the factories, the billboards and the sky of Attica and travelled miles away to a safe and unimpeachable void.

In the evening, she would take the bus tickets from the back pocket of the olive-green corduroys, throw them in the bin with the loo papers and not remember where she had seen what, which place was which, how she had frittered away another whole day.

Rhoda was the only one who came looking for her. It was almost midnight when she rang her doorbell and as soon as she came into Viv's hole, you crazy fool, you tell the owner of this place to install a phone line, so as not to scold her outright about her disappearance. It was the first visit, she'd asked for the address from the registrar's office.

They stayed up the night. With small green apples and raki. After the first two glasses, they took an inventory of their melancholy. With the third, Viv enriched the talk with dark predictions about the future, not the vocational future but the rest of it. After the fourth, Rhoda, who liked things to be event-

ful and hated disappointing those who asked her, have there
been any developments?, set out her program of resistance,
she'd start tomorrow with some movies about which there was
ongoing controversy and she'd follow that in time with travelling around the world. After the fifth, the half-drunk Viv traveled back to her childhood years, girls never omit this part, and
was surprised to listen to herself pay retrospective attention to
small things, such as that as a child, she braided the quinces
and pears and hung them up to dry, as an aperitif for the men's
winter drinks of tsipouro, and also how she spread ashes in the
home garden, a trick to keep slugs away, they were blinded and
retreated.

Equally half-drunk, Rhoda, the daughter of migrants to
Germany who'd left her with Grandma at five, was enchanted
by the rural life, it had been an omission not to fall for a retired
farmer. After the last two shots they also found nicknames for
themselves, Viv was anointed Sourpuss, Rhoda was Highbrow.

They fell unconscious in each other's arms on the red
woolen carpet. Ever since, on those Saturday nights when
Highbrow wasn't dragging some unfortunate house painter to
Ionesco or Arabal, their bottle was waiting for another round
in the championships of sorrow.

They kept control of their relationship, not too close, occasional allies against the hostile, solitary Saturday nights. They
were aware, too, of the ludicrousness of their pronouncements,
Sourpuss with her trials at Alonaki, the insect bites and the
Georges, Highbrow parading her mottos, those who have one
eye want a second one, those with a lightbulb demand a night
to go with it.

At the end of June, after exams, all the girls, fed up with
intestines, neurons and, mainly, the school's invertebrates who
accosted them for a free fuck and to sell them coupons for the
political parties or to get their vote for the school elections,
went out as Rhoda's guests, with proletarian dates, handpicked

by Highbrow for their manliness and forthrightness, she'd met them at a construction site downtown.

They did naturally talk about the Soviet Union, the Attila operation in Cyprus, the crisis in construction work and the demeaning wages, but also about the golden voice of Rita Sakelariou, the soccer team of Piraeus and the comedian Kostas Voutsas, while working their way through a whole lamb in a tavern off the Hill of Pnyka, the immortal working class were as liberal with their appetite as they were with their money.

The five lads, a bit awkward with the girl students, a bit stiff with the effort of keeping their tongues from straying to unseemly expressions, courteous, filling the girls' glasses and emptying their ashtrays, ages up to twenty-eight, all of them likeable, the more talkative among them were Panos, very tall and handsome, Asimos, rotund and green-eyed, Manousos and Michael, brothers, Cretan through and through, they improvised a couple of limericks, too, about the value of education and the beauty of the dames, the girls felt properly appreciated as women and got tipsy and rambunctious.

The fifth one spent the night virtually silent, bar a here's to your health, and a long live here and there. Viv, faithful to her principles, first off noticed and jotted down his defect, the youth would suddenly jerk about for a few seconds for no apparent reason. Then she took in his slight smile, full of sweetness, and had the thought that it's nigh impossible to be matched with someone unless you like their smile. Finally, as she had made up her mind to be attracted to enigmatic types, she studied his gaze, full of stories, though they didn't make it to his lips, who knows why, the beer glass was the only thing that made it there.

He was the construction team's youngest, twenty-year-old Fotis, with his shiny black hair, the cleanest hands and the best ironed shirt.

After the tavern, they went for drinks and political songs, some among them sang a little, touched each other up a little and paired off a little, if only for that night, eventually Fotis, glued to his seat for three hours nonstop, turned to Viv and asked for her phone number.

She didn't have one, she said, but a short while later, as they were coming out of the boîte and dispersing, she called him and handed him a piece of paper and a pen to write his if he had one,

He did.

She was going to her village the day after tomorrow, should she see him or not the next day, Monday came round, should I see him should I not see him today, she wondered, but the very next thing she knew was she'd jumped in with both feet, she called him at seven and met him at eight.

On the way, moreover, to see him, as she crossed a main thoroughfare in the slight summer breeze, she noticed that the tree leaves were twirling on their branches on both their sides, as if to remind her of the inevitable downside of all things.

***

– On April 21, 1967, the junta arrested both my father and mother, that's how the date started, with Fotis slowly unraveling his family credentials, pausing for a sip of coffee and a drag on his cigarette.

He might have thought that Viv was with the student movement and they had political misadventures in common.

The description of that morning, with their small dog barking enraged at the invasion of the house by the five members of the Secret Police, whom everyone knew perfectly well, the fritters turning to charcoal on the gas stove, and himself running out of the toilet without flushing, numbed Viv somewhat and contributed nothing to the anticipation about what was to come next, all the more so given that one or two couples at nearby tables, perfectly carefree and completely in tune with the mellow evening, were rejoicing in sweet nothings, my duckling, you doll, you gorgeous thing, and so on and so forth, at the advanced stages of flirting.

– They carted them off, dumped them in the car and disappeared, Fotis went on, not omitting to turn red in recounting that he went back and flushed the toilet, got out of his pajamas and into his short trousers and put a semblance of order in the disarrayed home, drawers ripped open, mattresses overturned.

That image, of a shocked boy who is putting to order a ransacked house and all the rest that followed, finally got Viv's attention because, in a different manner and for different reasons, the unbearable loneliness of childhood was to her familiar and unforgettable.

Fotis Kolevas was left completely on his own at twelve. In town lived only his two much elder sisters, Kiki, twenty-six, married to an employee of the electricity company with two babies already, and Melpo, twenty-two, just married to a teacher and pregnant. They declined to take him in, their husbands were against it and they brooked no opposition.

An aunt from his father's side also refused, for years she'd kept her distance, not wanting to rub shoulders with the communists, to avoid repercussions for her own family, his godfather likewise, a jackass whose second wife had spent a lot of money and energy to consolidate relationships with the wives of powerful locals, and the neighbors lay low as well, those were times when most everyone was shitting bricks expecting mass trials and concentration camps to crop up everywhere and death verdicts.

The terrified boy made the parcel with the blankets like he had been told and took it to the prison barracks that same morning, they received it with scowls, sent him away with a shove, he did the rounds of the homes of relatives, heard everyone's miserly excuses for not putting him up, I'll lose my job, they'll start watching me too, I've unmarried daughters, my husband has a heart condition. Each hoped that the next one along the line would do it. He finally went back home and spent the day hugging Gagarin, who was barking disconsolately.

The next day was spent pretty much the same, it was Lazarus Saturday, and the one after that, Palm Sunday, the whole of the Holy Week and Easter and ten more days after that.

In the tin box with the painted kumquat there was some change, in the fridge there were seven eggs, yellow cheese, apples and two bottles of ginger beer, in the kitchen cupboard there was rice and pasta, on the shelf sugar, coffee and tahini. Tahini? Viv interrupted for the one and only time, as if that was the most memorable thing in his story.

The twelve-year old Fotis, prideful and angry, did not go out in the neighborhood to ask for loans, he shared the food with the dog, cooked for the first time in his life, washed his clothes twice, watered the potted plants five times, drank endless coffees and stayed up through the nights, he just couldn't sleep and was afraid into the bargain of having dreams even worse than the terrible days he was going through.

His mother came back the Sunday after Easter, he found her on his return from school at the grocer's across the street having a fight on the phone with her daughters, then swearing at the neighbors, bitter words in every direction, if they kept me for a year, you, would you still have left him on his own? Was there no pity in your hearts, these holy days, for a little kid? You mongrels!

She buried him in her arms, rained kisses on his hair, called him her little man, told him the good news, too, your dad is fine, he'd been sent off to a desert island in the Northern Aegean with good company, each one of the men on the ship with him was the best, they all knew each other from previous times of trouble.

Those two spring weeks riled Fotis inwardly, not just because he was left alone, in a rehearsal of orphanhood, but mainly because he was abandoned by his sisters, his brothers-in-law and everyone who had been around him till the age of twelve.

So he chose to grow up alone, not to let his sadness come to an end or his anger, not to spare any forgiveness.

Now, he had lost both parents for good, had been out of touch with his sisters though they did chase after him, when it was too late, being themselves chased by guilt, that is how he completed his story, spoken in a soft Corfu accent and with the full stop, he relaxed in a smile, maybe a Corfu smile as well, wide and unstinting.

This was a strange attempt at kicking off an idyll, or even an exploratory meeting. Fotis, more comfortable now, patted down his shiny hair with both palms and asked for her story, or whatever she chose to tell him, come on, it's time I heard your voice, he prompted her.

Vivian Sotiropoulos didn't start on her family's politics, they didn't really talk about that stuff much, she was only now realizing that the family in Alonaki were leaning to the right, not so much because they feared communism but because they feared what its supporters were being put through. She wisely avoided the drama of the tropical poverty and the arctic muteness of her childhood years, she delved into things with greater entertainment value, starting with something someone from the Ionian islands would probably be familiar with.

She remembered that at the village coffee shop, when the radio tuned by accident into an opera, the grown-ups chortled and the younger ones brayed, arias and screams were one and the same to all of them, until the café owner's wife, distressed by the ordeal, grabbed the closest stick and chased the children out, shut up because my head's about to split in two, find something pretty on the radio to sing to, if you must.

Viv herself was not part of the braying, she was sitting across on the sidewalk, she made her position quite clear, by herself as usual, she added meaningfully.

She hit the mark with the opera, Fotis's communist dad, a tailor of furniture fabrics by profession, in the princely city of Corfu with the velvet-covered living rooms, when not in prison or exile, never failed to attend a choir of lyrical singing, to catch up for his many absences.

However, now, the young girl had to volunteer something more personal and so, in a while, as they were walking down Patision St. without paying attention to the shop windows, in an uncoordinated, yet almost comradely step, she did.

She couldn't pronounce the "r" till she was six, mothel and fathel, ailplane and tlain, tlee and load. It was one more reason, she made no mention of the others, that she was a child of few words, she was inwardly counting the words with "r" in them, and they were too many.

She was afraid to speak spontaneously. At nights, she made sentences without "r"s and the next day she served them up out of context, the postman is fine, the dead feed the things that live below.

When, finally, the "r"s entered her mouth, thankfully just as she went to first grade, for at least three years, all day every day, she whispered to herself, for her own pleasure, difficult, complex words, drenched in "r"s, rarely, railroad, repertory, rhododendron. As she was relaying all this for Fotis's sake, she wondered at her own volubility, at the fact she was, for the first time ever, taking so long to reach a full stop.

At a square near Omonia they each had a souvlaki and they must have been inwardly in agreement that a good time was had because, while they didn't make out or kiss, and their good night was accompanied by a simple handshake, with no rubbing of fingers, they said let's keep in touch and they both meant it.

Their meeting, three hours from beginning to end, had integrity.

The day after, the bus brought Viv to her native land, wrecked roads, wrecked villages and wrecked people in the treadmill of life.

She ascertained that she'd probably missed the dust of the dirt road in front of the house, she'd probably missed the drenching of the village in sheep piss.

She attributed her placatory mood to Fotis, she thought that even soldiers at war every so often need a ceasefire and considered it a temporary mood, just till she was firing on all guns again.

The neighbors welcomed her awed, they thought the world of the medical profession, especially the elders who only had a rudimentary education, had lost people on the way to the hospital and suffered on an average from three different ailments each.

At the table, her mother served pasta and her father, overcome with pride, was sipping the food and chewing the wine.

The thirteen-year-old Xenia, who had brought home straight A's from her first year in high school and was cashing in on her diligence by going out every chance she got, came in fairly late and didn't give Viv a moment's rest with her prattle, unless they had the money to send her to English and French language classes, she wouldn't clean out the bird shit in the chicken coop anymore, unless she became an actress as well, she wasn't going to become a pediatrician, unless she fell madly in love, she wasn't going to do all of the mad things she dreamed of doing for the sake of the future heartthrob.

The following days and weeks were spent on futile missions of nostalgia and civility, a coffee here and there with the classmates Petra and Niobe, a day's work on Sunday memorial services, where the local women, in the permanent employ of the dead fathers, fathers-in-law and husbands, kept on as servants of their tombs.

The two-month period from July to August passed her by in a hurry, the summer slipped through her fingers with the exception of the few times she went swimming with Xenia, with the now ripe breasts, perforce taking on the role of chaperone, and then she could let herself relax a bit with the gurgle of silliness on the beach, adolescents in the waves, kiddies on the pebbles, dirty words bubbling up, eroticism boiling over.

She had seven phone calls with Fotis, she called Athens when she went down to the township of Aigion on her father's errands, Farmers' Insurance Fund, Farmers' Bank and pesticides for the crops.

The carpenter had no time for holidays, he wasn't the partying type anyway, he mustn't have let it rip even once in his lifetime.

They were suited in that, as well. He was her age, too, and Viv, encumbered by her parents' age difference of twenty-four years, chalked that one up in her deliberations in order to conclude that the boy did interest her.

In the seven calls, rather brief and certainly proper, she had dared ask him if he thought she was too short, if he minded that he wasn't in school, as well, if he was seeing anyone else and who was ironing his shirts.

People, she contemplated, often hesitate to ask something face to face because they can't control their expression as they put the critical question in words, they think that their eyes, their whole demeanor, might be saying something else. That's why they leave any number of volatile issues for the phone, best to struggle with the wording and tone of voice and leave their facial expression in reserve for another time.

Fotis Kolevas did not think she was too short, didn't have a girl, did his own laundry and ironing, envied her for being a medical student, the lucky thing!, and as for himself, he wasn't planning on spending the rest of his life knee-deep in sawdust.

His answers made her think that she had miscalculated and had missed out on the expression of his face as he answered her honestly and directly.

And she did miss his gaze, she was hankering for it, no question about that.

The punching kiss took place forty-something days after Viv's return.

In the space of six weeks, with both of them on Athenian soil, they only met three times, a quick ice cream, a couple of awkward exchanges, the affair was going bad against their will. The need to study for the two courses was the pretext, except not from her side, from his. Don't you neglect study for the sake of merrymaking, there'll be time later, he would say to her, but he seemed to doubt the possibility of a relationship with a future woman of science who wasn't Rhoda, laying on her back and harvesting in succession the sweat of an entire workers' union and then thinking nothing of it.

Rhoda, Dora, Martha and Eleftheria passed all classes with A's and B's, Viv got one D and one F.

Now, the lecture halls only ever rarely saw the petite brunette who was starting to be attracted to the idea of behaving insensibly, getting rid of prudence, finally striking a fatal blow to her own best interest to breathe freely for a bit, cutting herself loose from the circle of doctors. She was resisting ever more robustly her incorporation into student life, the aim of graduation, clear-cut aims in general.

And that tentative young man was to her taste, not only because he was familiar with life's obstacles and had no intention of circumnavigating them, but mainly because he was so confused and inspired no trust in her.

On the November night when they made love for the first, second and third time and destroyed the springs of her aluminum camp bed, Fotis again came up with a couple of his father's communist ditties and seemed to be irresistibly attracted to the thought of Siberia, perfectly distant and frozen.

His descriptions, loaned from the lyrical, now dead, tailor, humid loneliness, colorless steppes, interminable expanses with conifers of the deepest dark, dead colors, rotten apples and leaves, gray-black, eroded wooden planks on the fences, rusty tin sheds, factory floors in the midst of snowstorms, the bell of the freezing northerly tolling day and night, all indelible impressions from three months spent there in '46.

Under the cheap blankets, with their exhalation visible in the cold room, the couple reached a joint conclusion as far as the vast and frozen continent was concerned, melancholy crossroads to confuse you, unknown townships to exile yourself to, forests to get lost in, snow to bury yourself under.

Viv slept like a bird, sweetly lulled by the male breath against her neck and the sound of the bathtub from upstairs as it emptied and the water was sucked in big gulps down into the sewers of Kypseli.

A year followed of love and roses and much absenteeism from the second-year classes, studying by force, pitiful grades. Viv had now discovered the use of the lower limbs, opening them up in welcome to the warm, male body.

In March 1977, the pregnancy was certified, all this time they'd done nothing to avoid it, they were drawn to the inevitable. And in May, while everyone was taking out the short sleeves and the bare-backed dresses, Viv wore the heaviest of all garments, the wedding dress.

***

On the night she turned fifty properly, Vivian Koleva had finished her tea with two slices of bread and tahini, but was far from finished with yesteryear, with all the basics of before. She dipped the teaspoon in the jar, she needed a few more spoonfuls of this emblematic pulp with the worst of colors, that stuck thickly in the palate and blocked the gullet, in order to complete at a run her life's exposition.

No matter what she brought forth out of the pits of her mind, it was evidence of her retrospective conviction, now that the crime was a done thing.

Wordless images from her wedding in the church of St. Zoni, five of her relatives, five of his colleagues, her father's outraged gaze, her mother's disappointment, Xenia in tune with the others' overcast mood on such a sunny day as this, the benumbed friends' awkward attempts to support the couple with funny faces and gestures of courage and the best woman, Rhoda, enthusiastic, moved and self-critical, against everyone's expectations, she wouldn't have the guts to get knocked up and tie the knot with a carpenter.

There was no wedding feast, they'd eat each other alive, how to raise a toast, what to wish, how to pretend.

On the first night of the wedding, the kitchenette at his rented bachelor's flat was thick with cigarette smoke, the best woman had already enlisted the pregnant bride to the smokers' club and the bridegroom was a full-timer as well, half a pack since he was thirteen, a whole one since fifteen when, in the evenings, after school, at the shop of an acquaintance of his mother, he started getting the knack of cross-beamed oak floor paneling, a pack and a half since seventeen when he'd come to Athens and encountered Swedish wood doorframes and cypress French windows, two since the day his sweetheart announced the state of things to the Peloponnese homeland and her old man had told her she could go hang herself.

It was almost dawn when they peeled off the formal clothes that reeked of cigarettes and, leaving them on the floor, trampled them on their way to the bed, to nestle in Siberia and fuck themselves blind upon the snow.

They drew added inspiration, too, from the gray fur cap, the *shapka*, a memento from Russia, hanging on the back of the bedroom door.

The day after that they started making some plans, why delay, the new bridegroom was exempt from military service on account of being an orphan. Fotis's savings, sparse as they were, were the kickoff fund for a small shop, he would also take out a small loan, he'd start a business of his own, to be sure, she would help too, she would study and she would bear a child on top of everything.

They consulted as many clueless friends as they could find, were showered by brilliant ideas, open a cheese pie shop, an underwear shop, a flower shop, they trekked around half the city, answered ads and got involved with crooks, finally they came across the Dream Corner, a semi-underground hole downtown, going at a very accessible price with all the stock, toys and knickknacks. He wasn't into it, she, with her rising belly, was in earnest, anything that's going, she cut him short, this is no time for dillydallying.

This is just the first step, when we're able to we'll set up your shop, she promised, we're not getting rid of your hammer, your chisel or your jigsaw, she sweet-talked. She had their best woman backing her up, too, an unremitting third presence in their midst, who was looking forward to tasting the adventure of a small family business.

Fotis Kolevas vacillated from the carpentry shop to the gift shop, the opening was at the beginning of September, the construction workers all came and bought picture frames decorated with little hearts, the neighbors weren't to be seen, evidently they didn't need any picture frames.

The dud decision was a blow to the marriage, they celebrated their first fight, in financial terms they were now short on joy and rich in troubles.

November, as soon as winter muffled the city with rotting

clouds and threw up its muck on the streets, the baby was born, more fragrant than myrrh, more angelic than all the cherubs of heaven and so smiley that it seemed unnatural, coming from such a long-faced couple. And his hair was gold. The renowned golden mane of Mrs. Stavroula had skipped a generation, that of her daughters, and reappeared as her bequest to the grandchild.

Viv breast-fed her son for three months and during those hours, with the baby's little face so close to hers, she was contriving ways and means to scrape some money together.

The little shop came into its own with ballerinas from porcelain, clay and papier-mâché, was rechristened to Tutu, from the ballet dancers' short skirts, both ideas of Rhoda the theatergoer, mothers had started enrolling their girls in dance schools en mass so they could turn out to be the next Margot Fonteyn or Maya Plisetskaya. In the afternoons, Viv went from school to school hawking her stock and the mothers, grandmothers, aunts and godmothers found out about the shop and bought Carmen and Degas's little ballerina for the birthdays and name days of the young girls. Her till was greatly remunerated, choked with bills and a grand moment it was when she sent her father the check with the four digits.

Fotis was generally embarrassed, he felt uncomfortable in the exclusively female universe, he did not do the rounds to attract a new clientele, did not manage to attractively set out the shelves and store windows, did not know how to pick up the starched tutus and delicate limbs without pulling them apart, did not, unlike Viv, who had been tutored by Rhoda, have handy a couple of good lines about the London Royal Ballet and the Bolshoi. So he took on the transport, the packaging, the bank and the liquor store and he started to drink. To drink and to remind Viv of a drunk in Alonaki who started out by beating his mother-in-law, went on to the wife and in the end, left his ten-year-old boy a cripple. At home, so her husband would sleep and leave her be, she did away with the baby's rattle, then she took down the musical Tweety that was attached to the baby's crib and later took the horn off the kid's tricycle so that it wouldn't go off in the middle of the living room.

Nobody heard her voice, either, as a child, she never bothered anyone, that she remembered fully well.

"Be quiet" became an order to the little boy, the two words he heard most often from his mom. His dad, too, on the grounds that she needed to find her peace and quiet so she could take up studying again, though she never did open her textbooks and hadn't been to the university for many terms.

The three fellow students of the former group of five put in one appearance, at the christening. And his name before God was neither Spyros nor Sotiris, neither of the grandfathers' names, but Linus on account of the boy's day of birth, November 5, feast day of Episteme, Galaktion and Linus. Rhoda was the godmother, to her pride and joy. Linus was also one of Apollo's singers, and the artistic name would usher the couple whom she'd married into *The Sound of Music*.

The construction workers were more effective in their support even though their comrade had withdrawn from the common struggles, or, to be precise, had been withdrawn by his wife who was slowly turning his head and curbing his red flights of political fancy. Come back down to earth, will you? she would often say, here's the landing strip, our home, your friends are daydreamers from outer space. Those cloud-treaders, according to Viv, in order to give Fotis a breather, sometimes booked him as helper for fitting door and window frames on constructions away from Athens, so he could get some fresh air. Whenever he came along, they got into trouble. They came to the house once every three months to see the boy and make their presence felt but, with such different lives now, the visits kept going from bad to worse. They would eat the peanuts, drink the whiskey, talk about workers' accidents and insurance and then get started on the jokes, one after the other in rapid succession, a bunch of guys maniacally picking on the Pope and Brezhnev and Tito because they couldn't find anything else to keep them close.

Viv would invariably run to the toilet to throw up, the apartment was tiny, the wall thin, they could all hear her and they no longer asked if she was expecting a second child, already she'd made it plain, in the very words, I'm not making the same mistake twice.

The first one, at all events, like every child, had turned things upside down. Its needs, its expenses, its future, were all gaining momentum together and required a quick mind so that the tulle kept shifting from the shelves. The young mother moved accordingly.

In two years they'd paid off the store loan, in three they'd bought a little car, in four they'd moved to a new place, still a rental but in a four-bedroom, they'd found out the ins and outs of loans, porcelain couples in tango poses were entering the Tutu, black and white swans from *Swan Lake*, framed images of Nureyev, miniature ballerinas on tiptoe, pyrographic engravings of Zorbas dancing, attracting a stream of clients, the ladies were asking for one item, Viv convinced them to get two and three, to order for the special occasions, leave a deposit and your address and Fotis will deliver, Fotis, go deliver.

– I'll go Viv, I'm going anyway, only don't order me, you remind me of the colonels.

Really? Is that what she reminded him of? She would make no answer but she inwardly considered military discipline a compensatory award for the disgrace of poverty, everyone was awarded where she came from, in her family, in thousands of homes everywhere, one pair of shoes every three years, one pair of trousers every five, a jacket every ten, this year one of the daughters will have a skirt made, next year the other one, Mother will adjust the old one, Mother at the war of the pot with insufficient ammunition, the daily bread never enough, the plates never full.

It was unfair of her husband to make her feel bad for steering Tutu successfully.

– We're doing swell because you don't get weak-kneed at the prospect of installment payments, she flattered Fotis one night, as she counted off bills, I wouldn't have made it on my own.

He answered her, after some consideration, I don't want gratitude from you, just like I don't want pity.

He was one hundred percent sure that he had bowed to making her life choices his own, Viv was convinced that she had made concessions in order to fall in step with her husband's potential for the daily struggles and so they felt inwardly at peace, there were moments when they admired themselves for their adaptability and self-sacrifice in the name of a harmonious coexistence, they never ever went at each other in front of the boy.

The Peloponnese wasn't apprised of the new state of affairs. In fact, her old man had to bow before his son-in-law for begetting a son where he hadn't been able to, and afterwards, they sort of found some common ground in anti-Americanism.

Sotiropoulos disdained the sound of the word "America" because when he'd come back from the army he hadn't found any of his age group in Alonaki and surrounds, four had left as migrants to Chicago and Detroit and, immediately, another two or three who'd just left the army with him also made their papers. The American melting pot was sucking in the best men to labor and sweat for the sake of strangers' fortunes, reason enough for the father-in-law's curses and teeth-gnashing.

– Your old man's all right, after all, Fotis had told her, if only I had mine around, as well, was the part he hadn't voiced.

Not that it would have made any difference if he had.

Recently, whenever he referred to his father, in moments when he needed to say something about him and say it out loud, so that he could really feel it, relish it, that the dead man used to speak in a quiet singsong, his every word a spoonful of holy communion and a hymn wrapped in one, or that he was keeping him at the top of everyone who crowded his thoughts, always in his white shirt, like a small mountain chapel, Viv no longer shared in his longing, her indifference burnt him like hot oil from the frying pan, her silence scorched him.

Twice he had suggested going to Corfu for a few days, so he could take the kid for a walk on the cobblestone streets of the old town and shout him the local treats. Next year, was her response to both the first and the second request.

Now, their interchanges were short and tight, in between the silences which dominated, as Fotis, after being dumbfounded, had now made a habit of lulling himself in the jelly of protracted silence.

At least without in-laws in Athens and with her parents all mellowed out, grandparents, now, sending eggs and chooks for the boy's soup and wine for their son-in-law, they were saved the additional tension which usually goes with the presence of an extended family, they could rest at ease, mutely, each in their private world.

They lived in the house like snails and made a snail of their boy, as well, who under the threats of, don't let me hear you whimper, not a sound out of you, and, I've told you once to be quiet, withdrew to solitary games, blocks, puzzles and broken figurines, leftovers from the shop.

Meanwhile, the orgasms in Siberia also grew few and far between, Viv considered that normally she should be able to remember by heart her husband's heels, his toenails, the direction of the hairs on the inner thigh, but, in truth, if he wasn't right in front of her in the flesh and naked, she wouldn't have been able to recognize his thighs or his arms.

She sometimes searched on his head, the thick, raven black, shiny locks of renown that had imprinted themselves on her mind and saw that they were thinning at top speed, ever less lustrous, ever less inviting to touch and to gaze upon.

– Stop thinking all the time, you only do it as a put-down to me, he would surprise her out of the blue, as she'd take up ironing in the small kitchen where there wasn't space for him or clean up with a vengeance, in that same space. When she cleared the table, she wiped the leftovers from the dishes so meticulously that they looked practically washed. She'd run them under the tap once so they wouldn't smell, place them inside the rinsed salad bowl, rinse the cutlery and place it like an upright bouquet in the likewise rinsed jar where she'd stirred the oil and vinegar, next came the water and wine glasses, one inside the other and all together in the thoroughly prepped baking tray, to wait for her in the sink till next morning.

Fotis was unfailingly already in front of the TV with a drink in hand, absorbed in a movie which, chances were, did not actually interest him. She never did interrupt, he would say, I'm in the middle of watching something, she was positive that if she asked what, he wouldn't be able to make an answer.

He'd become the kind of viewer who lived for hours across from every manner of show without absorbing a single thing, just as if he hadn't been informed of the invention of the tube or of its existence in their home. Once he'd turned towards her suddenly to say, let me like you, please, let me like you.

While Rhoda, Dora, Eleftheria and Martha had virtually graduated and were setting sail for their traineeship before embarking on their specializations, cardiology, microbiology, microbiology and neurology, respectively, Viv, with the takings from the shop as her only asset, was rapidly orbiting her old haunt, depression, and her old skill, undermining life, except now she had a kid. Two enormous eyes watching her all day asking for help and explanations, why is Dad sad, why does he cuss and throw up on his clothes?

Rhoda was overseeing, analyzing and concluding that the new Fotis who had emerged revealed the root of evil, the junta was to blame for everything, the right wing in power and the cruelty of society were the reasons he'd become his wife's helper, the home's fifth wheel.

Once, the interested party heard this though he wasn't meant to, and although drunk he didn't strike out at them, he'd never raised his hand, he only struck them with a withering gaze and then finished them off with the well aimed saying, a bitch-whore needs her snitch.

That same night, blind drunk by then, he grabbed Viv while he was stumbling about, and yelled, we've carved our life out of worm-eaten wood. He screwed her by force, calling her names, while she stroked his back to calm him down and get him to quit his yelling, so the boy wouldn't hear.

In the morning, five-year-old Linus refused his milk and bread, looked his mother in the eye insistently, picked up his small kindergarten pack and left for the school bus, unwashed and disheveled, banging the door shut.

Fotis was snoring. From that day on, her marriage sounded to Viv's ears like a death rattle. He didn't fight the drink, she made no effort to reclaim him, they exhausted in a flash all the good things of a common life and hurtled into the senseless recycling of time, the mounting towards finality. With one stop. The purchase of the cocker spaniel, which morning and night took the father and son out for big walks and then brought them back with their ears drooping like dumb pups.

The woman had fully taken on herself the shop's maintenance and various responsibilities. It could be no other way since the one bottle became two, the two became three, with Rhoda coming around in the middle of the night for a cardiogram, or to babysit while Viv ran to the hospital to collect her husband whom, she was notified, they'd picked up off the pavement, after he'd consumed more wine and/or whiskey than he could possibly handle.

Viv did not wonder how things had come to this, she was perfectly aware of all the intervening stages. And if, even after ten years with him, she couldn't seriously answer what positive feature the man had possessed, really, for her to be with him, she knew what negative thing he did not possess: pretense. Always heartwarmingly true, proud of the small, and too small himself, in the end, for anything more than that.

Fotis died and left her mourning, guilty, lonely and indebted for an exorbitant amount in unpaid installments and taxes, which he had liquefied.

Her sack was heavy. But so was Linus's, it was no negligible weight to be orphaned at eight.

✹ ⅄ ⅄

The violent gust tore off thatched roofs, fences and sheds, sent flying hats, umbrellas, plastic bags, seaweed, empty Styrofoam cups and children's buoys, puffed up the paper tablecloths around the oil-and-vinegar stands, blew on the dry dunes and blinded the bathers, the waiters and the clients at the restaurant who left off their calamari and tomato salads because they were doused with sand.

Viv Koleva and Harry Margaritis had just had a dip, their first swim together in Marathon, and had been sitting at the tavern for a small bite, some wine and the first attempt at a serious discussion of the possibility of living together.

Harry had come into her life about three years after Fotis's death, at a period when the shop was raking it in big from nuptial gifts. The twelve-year-olds of recent years who had, with their mothers' prompting, dreamt of careers as prima ballerinas, at twenty-two and twenty-five were working in beauty shops, electrical appliance stores, travel agencies and were bidding farewell to classical dance with a souvenir on the living room shelf. A ballerina doing the splits, her delicate neck upright, her painted eyes trained on what her hands held aloft, a wedding bonbon wrapped in tulle.

Dora, a relationship nowadays consisting of a phone call every New Year, had married a doctor in Nikosia and alongside the mandatory photograph, Cypriot glamour, dedication and some news, Yannos and I will be doing lab analyses of Cypriot urine, she'd sent the airy-fairy thing, one single bonbon tightly wrapped in gauze on the wire stem of a mini purple rose. That gave Viv the idea, the engaged sylphs were all notified and within six months she had sold out the two hundred pieces she had ordered, her shop a regular marriage outfitter's.

One evening, just before she closed and having had enough of hearing about eternal vows, church decorations and furniture, she passed off the last piece to Harry Margaritis, he was marrying two friends and the girl, of mature age, was still entranced with ballet, she even planned to perform one last time for a live audience, a wedding dance choreographed by herself.

The best man, with a sizeable zit on his neck, admired unstintingly, shopped without bargaining, helped Viv pull down the shutters, they were heading in the same direction and in the course of about two hundred meters he found time for the essentials, divorced, no children, thirty-nine years old, accountant in a big firm that installed air conditioning units. Viv went back home one hour later than usual, having downed two whiskies and having admitted to the best man her difficulties and her loneliness.

The affair, a welcome oiling up of her rusted body, it was that rust that precipitated the involvement, started in May and ended with the first winter cold, end of November.

Only Harry himself favored the approach he had taken to

get close to Linus. Why call your dog Buddy, you should call him Bobek, was his first mistake. He spoke to Linus exclusively about the Panathinaikos soccer team, waxing nostalgic about the unsurpassable Bobek and the line of legendary trainers from Puskás on to "Jaws" Gmoch, on to Bonev, go, Rocha, go, and there were replays of the goals of Zajec and Saravakos and frequent gifts, a poster of Warzycha, a green soccer top, a white and green mug for his milk.

No poster ever decorated the wall above the child's bed, sports tops and mugs received scant attention, the kid remained coldly indifferent to the team colors and to soccer worship in general, he resisted the accountant's attempts to score and kept the goalposts of his world unassailable.

Soon, his mother's lover was at the end of his tether, it didn't cross his mind to look for another point of engagement, he was probably having second thoughts about the whole thing, anyway, a sour orphan makes a love affair trying, not to mention he couldn't enjoy his whiskey, served by Viv in a teacup to camouflage the consumption of alcohol.

Some nights at the house he had sat listening, from the room of eleven-year-old Linus, came a voice repeating rhythmically zdoop-gup, doop-kraf, this for such a long time that Harry would prompt Viv to have a listen as well, but what on earth's your son on about, he would ask, chastising her indirectly.

– Encourage him to take you seriously, she tried suggesting a different way to him, encourage me, too, to take you seriously, she implied, though she never said so out loud, the physical connection was wearing thin, moving in together kept being postponed, Harry's chapter was on its way to foreclosure.

It hardly matters who finished it, if it was Viv or Harry, the thing is that the night Viv closed up shop to walk back to the apartment alone and with no detours, she was shivering and enjoying it, she found the array of naked trees reassuring, she could look at them without them sizing her up, could mutter without getting comments back, touch them and the trees wouldn't get goose bumps, she could lean against the trunks without them running away.

It took her a long time to give herself to another man, another two years went by, she made a couple of one night mistakes, until she hit on something bigger that lasted for nearly a year.

She fell for Eftichis Athanasopoulos not as a lover but as a human being, this was a phase in her life when she deliberated about reconsidering her values, her faithful service by the till and the victories measured in bills had no real exchange value, she could see that her home was being eaten up by sadness and her kid driven mad with it, whenever she tried to talk to him or turn up the radio, he threw the old "be quiet" back at her and locked himself up in his room, to him a refuge, to her, forbidden territory. She was in dire need of support, of a volunteer, a good Samaritan of some denomination.

Eftichis Athanasopoulos, in partnership with his two brothers in a company importing frozen vegetables, had taken on the sector of distribution to supermarkets and he first noticed Viv when she called out to him that his station wagon, parked in peak traffic, was blocking the street, already, behind her car, a mayhem of honking and swearing was erupting.

They exchanged the essential glance, wordlessly he left her a paper carton full of frozen mushrooms and corn, the firm Green Garden, the address, the phone numbers were printed on every bag and when she used up the last one, she called, looked for him and found him, thanked him and made him confess how much he had anticipated her getting in touch and how much he had liked the miniature ballerina that adorned her windshield. How is it, then, that there are five Holy Mary's dancing about in yours, she thought of asking, she had counted them that first instant, during the altercation. She refrained from putting the question to him and a good thing that was.

Within six months he proposed, after having already told and shown her enough to have him under her thumb for a lifetime. Unremittingly tender, gullible to a fault, with an other-worldly integrity, the sucker of *Green Garden*.

Viv had met his sly sister and sly brother at a dinner fit for the Holy Inquisition, she hadn't liked them and they hadn't liked her, not because she was a widow with an almost grown son, then thirteen, but because she could see a bit further than what they were comfortable with. The two siblings had barely picked at their pasta, and the intensity of their curiosity was already replaced by the intensity of fault-finding.

The kindhearted Eftichis was paying no mind, he had long known he was different from his sister and brother, he wanted neither to be like them nor to part with them, a share was enough, and out of the four people in the middle-class restaurant, he was the one beaming, with his arm protectively over Viv, not letting her out of his sight, sticking up for her with comments of endorsement about the prudence of her only son, a homebody, with a dog for his pal and keeping right away from bad company, no small thing that, he addressed his brother and more so, his sister, who had the body type of female gorilla.

Why, such brotherliness, such generosity of spirit in the face of their sourness, such kindliness, such exemplariness! Should she perhaps be suspicious of the all holy one?

That evening, alongside the blissful Eftichis and the two stiff-necked vultures, Viv realized that innocence can disturb and honesty can terrorize because some people might get weak knees right at the critical moment when they are supposed to slaughter the lamb. She was those people. There were times when she was overpowered by Eftichis's guileless face, this was no creature you could harm without guilt. So she'd best leave him to his joy, to the gypsy violins, sold on them since he was twenty, no other music touched him, he was only moved musically by the violin strings of the virtuosos in the genre, saccharine sweet to Viv, increasingly more intolerable and maybe a fair explanation for the inexhaustible mildness of the prospective bridegroom. He would be listening with eyes closed and would soften up, mellow out, turn saintly. She, of course, didn't love him, she found him useful.

At home, Linus, even more withdrawn, stared at her sharply from head to toe, meaning, I know fully well what's going on.

She decided not to put them both through the ordeal, her body had had its dose of lovemaking and masculine proximity and her ears, exempting the syrupy gypsy tunes, had enjoyed the tickle of courtship, so she might as well return with renewed forbearance to her unblemished life, widowhood, child, shop, tax office. She made herself scarce, very gradually and gently she put Eftichis on ice and he, with a mind to her household, filled up her freezer with lima beans and brussels sprouts, as garnish to her son's pork chops, full of vitamin C for a growing kid, he had said, and had thanked her on top of everything, ever faithful to the vice of superiority.

The men of your life, all with happy names, Fotis, Harry, Eftichis,[3] the Bridegrooms of Happiness, was the final pronouncement of Highbrow, as they were enjoying the movie of that title on TV, she could still crack jokes, collect boyfriends and have sex here and there, she had no child to drag along.

Vivian Koleva foresaw what was inescapably coming, her routine that would grow mangy, her loneliness that would thrive like a jungle, the waves that would creak against the rocks of her mind, she knew about those things and, in the end, she did prefer to go through them alone and with dignity. Up until then, especially in front of her son, she had never shed a tear, had never allowed herself to lose it big time, her anger's gunpowder was by and large unspent.

[3] The names signify, respectively, "light," "gracious," "blissful."

She would go on, strong, proud, hardworking.

She didn't want to try out another affair and she did let Linus know that none of them were important. By 1997 it was all a moot point, where to draw courage, how to rise above herself, if ever she had, how to steal time from the days and nights of work and who wouldn't run a mile as soon as they found out about her son.

Scraping the bottom and the sides of the jar with the teaspoon to get the last of the tahini, on that night of turning fifty, she also put under lock and key all reminiscing about the men who entered and exited her life, while touching her cheeks, her breasts and her bottom, upstanding at one time, now about to collapse, and counting with her palm the folds of her stomach, as many as those of an accordion.

Still, she could listen to the last of the underground explosions, her neglected body, running on empty for years, was asking again tonight, was asking in vain. And since the hours were in no hurry, the night still in place, here was the familiar, the three-minute acidic monologue that set her head on fire.

Why couldn't I have the life of so many others, who look into the eyes of the same partner for years on end, who go driving out to Evia for an ouzo to help them bear up, who are the first to turn up and help friends moving house, who illegally put on the roofing to an unauthorized room with a large group of family and friends, who give blood to strangers and their kidney to a relative, who play pranks and make jokes at work just so they get a laugh out of their coworkers?

She knew that she had no part in such a movie, she never did imagine it when she was young, had never looked for it once she was older. Some folks, one fine morning, suddenly brace up and decide to turn their life from drama to comedy, to have fun, to spread their wings smiling and go out, into the fresh air.

That wasn't her. She didn't have what it took. She was

aware, fully aware, and there was no place for waxing lyrical about life's hardships. No song will be killing us softly, she neighed at herself, there'll be no memories lighting the corners of our minds.

***

The terms were succinctly spelled out and nonnegotiable. There was to be no picture of Linus in Viv's home. No running shoes forgotten in some corner, no sports jacket on a hanger, no laundry drying on the balcony with items from a young man's wardrobe. Attention to be paid to shelves and random surfaces where a magazine might have been left to do with basketball or racing cars or anything of the sort.

His room needs to appear like a guest room for relatives, his mother-in-law from the village or Xenia, a pair of fluffy slippers might be parked in the corner, an icon of the Virgin Mary might do well on the wall.

Every trace of Linus needed to be erased from the apartment, the little girls didn't even know they had a cousin and, as they liked digging into things and exploring, they might unearth some piece of evidence or other and start with the questions, note their awkwardness and realize there was something fishy going on.

For the two days they'd all be spending together, Viv was prohibited from mentioning her son's existence, taking phone calls from the lawyer, she was not supposed to take her sister aside for whispers and sobs, above all, she was supposed to be pleasant.

That was what Xenia's husband had decreed, they were coming for a family holiday to Greece, two days in Athens for the aunt and the Acropolis, two days in the Peloponnese for Grandma and ancient Olympia and then Zakynthos for swimming and the loggerhead turtles.

To start with, there was no more a room of Linus. Viv, then in a small two-bedroom downtown that had been stripped, anyway, of her son's possessions, did the last of his laundry, sent it off on the next visiting day and then searched again every corner, cupboard, drawer and shelf and all she came up with were the Donald Duck mug, the Batman eggcup, those she exiled for the crucial days up in the loft, a bead against the evil eye with a blue bow and the amber sunstone, neutral and unthreatening though they were, she shoved in her bag all the same.

She emptied the living room of her work things, piled them up in boxes on the balcony, in the loft and under the double bed. That's where the couple would sleep, the girls she would put on the living room couch and she'd spend the day in a fold-up bed in the hall, she measured it, it just fitted, it'd be all right for just the two nights.

On the day she was expecting them, she made pasticcio, Xenia's favorite, bought cornflakes, fruit and sweets and set out on the purple velvet pillow of the carved chair two blue velvet queens she had ordered made, not to sell but as gifts for her Canadian nieces to play with and, if they so pleased, they could shred the dolls to bits.

She wanted to hold her sister's little daughters in her arms, to kiss silken braids, to ruffle frilly dresses, girls are nice, Xenia was luckier as a mother, despite the fact that her husband stayed away for twenty days right after the birth of their second daughter, he had wanted a son and there was none forthcoming.

At the airport she waited for them trembling.

It was the fate of Sotiropoulos, now deceased, to live the elopement of his second daughter with the hated America, even if her luck set her down in a doctor's arms.

Xenia had married Spilios in '93, four years before the bomb went off. Her second marriage. The first, a hasty decision, to a colleague, a professor of English, had lasted two years. She had taken him and left him willingly because she wanted kids but the only thing he could get up was his mind, she had confessed to Viv, sobbing.

Spilios Alifraggis was a darling, hot-blooded, tall, handsome, generous, humorous, rich and an orthopedist, in other words, the family's opportunity to at last boast a doctor, even if it was halfway around the world, she had playfully needled her older sister, pinching her bottom, after she'd first introduced him to her, then waxing lyrical about his gray temples "like in the movies," those were the words with which she skirted around the age difference, he was fourteen years her senior.

The darling, generous humorist etc. had been orphaned as a child. He had been taken up by a childless uncle, who took him along to Canada, put him through school. It was there he had specialized and done his postgraduate studies, had found a job straight away, first at the university hospital in Ottawa, then in Toronto, where he quickly established himself and, with his uncle's support, was soon showcased as a distinguished member of the Greek community, with a rich record of professional and social activities, a member on the board of a dozen organizations. All that was missing was a marriage and a son to name after the beneficent uncle, Diagoras, so as to make sure he was sole heir to the colossal property, a glut of real estate properties along central thoroughfares, it'd be a crying shame for the Church to gobble them up.

They met with Xenia during a short vacation on the island of Kalymnos, they roomed next to each other in the picturesque hotel, adjacent balconies in the gold-red sunset, him leafing through medical journals, her reading English poetry, darkness falling, the two switching their light on simultaneously, looking at each other.

Now, with the two daughters, levity was out of order. And what happened with Linus had radically transformed the husband, or showed him up for what he was, Xenia was nowadays getting thunderbolt-glances and their kiddies were getting preached at in a fashion that made no sense whatsoever for preschoolers.

On second thought, it might also be fated and inescapable for an event of such magnitude to shake up the people who are closest, to uproot their attitudes and way of life from their foundations, a man of medical science turning into a bully and a stalwart, professional woman allowing herself to be beaten.

Only once did Viv make it to the evergreen Toronto, summer of 2001, Spilios had broken his legs in a car accident, two months in the hospital, in his wing, Xenia needed help and she demanded, sobbingly, her sister, after she swore to him there'd be no talking in front of the children, there was no cousin as far as they were concerned, nor would she blurt anything out in phone calls with his colleagues and clients, plus she wouldn't take her sister visiting or to church, it wouldn't do to bump into someone apprised of the events, and then have to run for cover.

Their house was made up of the two paternal homes together, the wife's wooden rack for the china, wooden chest and woven rugs from the Peloponnese, the husband's island dresser, island sofa and island mirror from the Dodecanese.

Xenia pretended she was happy, her life full, she taught Greek, translated, published clever articles on current affairs which were popular, was the heart and soul of the amateur thespians and cultural activities, went skiing and sleigh-riding with her children, bore with panache the legendary cold of the Canadian winter.

Viv, still a wreck from the three years of mire treading, went apeshit, from the second or third day, a changed person. She was in seventh heaven with the stammering, curly-haired kiddies, then six and five years old, for the first time ever she adored childish prattle and childish cheating, she stood perfectly still while they pulled her ears and spattered her with lipstick and taught her English singsongs, she told them with pleasure stories she made up, applauded with even greater pleasure their joyous screams and made them mountains of french fries.

It was a good break from the bleakness, Greece, the old folks, and it lasted just as long as it should, three weeks later she was replaced by a student from Rhodes.

The return trip, over the Atlantic and all of Europe, was a ten-hour shriveling of her heart over the many "don't"s doled out to her own child by herself and by Fotis. Linus had been preparing since he was a wee thing for his mind's somersault.

For the two days in the summer of 2003 that the Canadian denizens stayed over, Viv was practically silent, out of fear, it doesn't take much for a blunder to happen.

The little ones didn't understand why the knives and forks of the grown-ups stayed put next to their untouched pasticcio, why when they told their aunt she, too, should make some kiddies, Dad got in a huff and said not to talk while eating, why they didn't take her with them at the museum and why, at home, their mom and aunt held each other's hand like they used to in Canada but when Daddy turned up, they let go as if they'd been doing something wrong.

End of stay. Viv wouldn't forget in a hurry the two nights she spent with them, cleaning their reading glasses thoroughly and feeling as if she was hatching them in her bosom, with kisses on their cheeks and noses.

After that, a repeat performance in Alonaki, the grandmother was to take down the one and only remaining photograph of Linus, at seven months at his christening, and to spread word that her son-in-law was recovering from pneumonia and that's why they didn't want visitors to the house and let there be no offense if he didn't drop by the village coffee shop for a drink and a chat with the local men.

After they left for Zakynthos, Viv's mother had called, probably to ascertain from her eldest daughter's voice if she'd been able, finally, to take all that pressure, though, of course, no question was put straight out, she said she'd just brought in a load of freshly cut peppers from the orchard and they've stunk up the kitchen, that her granddaughters are a joy to behold, that she went with Xenia and held a small memorial at the grave.

In a call several days later, she added the rest, that the doctor put the small plot with the reeds up with the real estate agent, he had no intention of bringing the family back to Greece again, he needed to protect his daughters and his wife, Xenia had taken the situation very hard and the visit did her no good, he was going to have her put on medication. The phone call ended with a sigh over her second daughter and the phrase, that was the end of her, then.

Many nights then, and ever since, Viv Koleva thought about her sister, mixed in with the other accoutrements of her every sleeplessness, Linus, walls, Yukaris, money, but no longer wondered about the reasons why, nor did she expect relief, she had acquiesced to the oncoming march of calamities, to life as one long death rattle.

What a birthday, her fifty years uncelebrated, tahini instead of a bloody cake or even a couple of Christmas walnut-and-honey pastries from the bakery. And it was still only eleven-thirty.

Time, may it be cursed for all eternity, is plentiful at night, same as the weird light that turns on of its own accord, automatically, and searches out everything that does not breathe under the light of day.

In the past, she wouldn't have minded if there was only the night, forever and a day, she had in her record about ten starry skies spent kissing someone and as many again calm in solitude.

Things, though, had changed radically since '97. She couldn't stomach the night, she didn't have the stamina for her mind's scaling the heights in the small hours, following on her son's heel in the boulevards of his heroics, the time when a black shoelace suddenly shows up and she freezes like a hare caught in the headlights of an oncoming truck.

Also she can feel it in the air that it's high time, too, for the r's to rise up from the trenches, and rush her, ever willing to enhance her discomfort and pilfer her distress.

Come right along, then, there's a nice sorfa, here's some nice tarhini. And they do come, another ten minutes of uproar.

In the wake of that, she looks at her hands, arms, elbows, wrists, palms, fingers and begs them to move, to get her up, put her to doing housework and keep her madly busy till dawn.

As she got up to throw the glass jar and the tea bag in the rubbish, the phone rang, the only one who remembered her, Canada.

At first a chorus of mother and daughters, happy birthday, dear Auntie, they were late calling because they'd been out Christmas shopping, then kisses, then the two sisters on their own. Xenia asked her again how many years ago her period had stopped, scolded her again for not having had a pap smear and a breast scan, encouraged her again to take up computers, empathized once more about her having been left behind in the phase where one goes through life in her house slippers, confused her again with her high tech kitchen, reassured her that, thanks to the antidepressants, she'd regained her good cheer again, told her she had the leading part in *The Shepherdess' Lover*, with the local group of thespians and, after she'd said all that, she cried about it all.

That's as much as poor Xenia was good for, her own troubles, if that, she wasn't up to much more, Viv couldn't count on her sister, not even for something as small as this from far, so very far away.

Who or what would take her place in a time of need?

There was no one and nothing on the horizon.

In the grim dark of December 2005, as she rounded half a century of living and was taking her turn in the slide of old age towards the final pit, she sounded an alert.

The other one as alone as can be. And stupefied. And faint-hearted. And a walking corpse. This is an alert, all right, reinforcements are wanted, new ideas are wanted, a new direction is wanted. She had to think ahead. Come up with a solution that did not depend on people, in the absence of people. But in order for the mind to jump to a different orbit, some kind of fuel is necessary.

For a start, she thought she'd spend some time sowing warm and bright colors in her mind, even by force of will.

So she started skydiving, bomber fashion, the blinding snows of Siberia. The pale blue froth of a large corps de ballet. The red posters of Fotis's comrades. The yellow tide of spring daisies spilling over the fields down in the Peloponnese. The blinding outburst of October on the elk tree forests, up in Hepeirus.

And all those waves of beauty ushered her into the Alonaki of a time without a criminal record. She let herself remember Linus's naked little body turning turquoise on the beach at Akoli, at dusk on the road her child and his bicycle turning orange, at the dead of noon in the harvested fields of the village, always her precious boy running with the cocker spaniel, lying on his back, a golden pup that dug the dirt with his little hands and spoke to the sun in his incomprehensible code, zdup-zdoop and khrup-khroop.

THE SHOVEL

Fuck her and throw her away. That's what she needs. She's wearing the clinging low-slung pants in order to shove in our faces the top half of her ass and the bottom half of her belly. On the straps of the blouse are hanging bits of back, bits of tits and tanned shoulders that shimmer and flash whenever the lights from the shops are reflected off the broad that's passing by.

This one loves to suck and fuck and get splattered in cum.

She walks and she sizes men up and counts in how many men's trousers the telltale stain shows, endless back and forth on the sidewalks to turn us on just so we can't concentrate on anything.

The twenty-year-old Linus Kolevas was selecting the phrasing and gradually shaping the speeches—his private monologues—on the spring and summer nights of 1997, as his breath was knocked out of him by the dirty cunts that took the streets by storm, in their white heat, grenades with the safety catch off, ready to explode and tear to pieces the males who ran after them salivating and trembling, with their minds already moving rhythmically, in and out, in and out of their heads, until the final explosion, their skulls in shreds.

He was following at a distance of three meters one who was wearing tights, whose ass was quaking at seven on the Richter scale, then left her to follow one with two frisky braids, *Hey, little rabbit, where is your rabbit hole*, she was in a hurry, had a date with Mr. Rabbit a bit farther off, within five minutes the next target showed, wearing half a skirt, her thighs like a schooner in high sail, her shoulder bag whistling, the heels lying in wait in her sandals for the guy who'd grab them and suck them dry.

He wanted to hunt down all the partridges that had been let loose in the dark, and pluck them for good, so as to rid the night of the shadows that impaled themselves in his eyes and froze up the blood in his veins, so as to reintroduce order on the sidewalks.

There were moments when he would lose control, break into a sweat and turn white, stumble and groan. They lasted as a rule for five, ten, fifteen minutes, the women caught the danger signals and had the time to step up to areas with other pedestrians, families and couples, and he had the time to become himself again and get back home, having erased the damned quarter of an hour from the evening, eat his mince steaks and devote himself to some movie on Star Channel that'd already started, American cops taking bribes and cars flying over bridges.

His mother would collect the tray with his plate and, ostracized by his persistent silence, would disappear in her room, leaving the door half-open and inelegantly calling out the news during the ad breaks, the tax commandoes are zeroing in on gas stations, the prime minister and his ex-wife are fighting it out over the villa in the northern suburbs, some group has gone berserk and is slaughtering civilians in Algeria and this is the fiftieth anniversary of the beginning of operations on the rock island of Makronisos, your grandma was in exile there, you know which of the two.

It would be almost dawn by the time he went to sleep and getting on to noon by the time he woke up in the empty house, Viv was away at the shop and he could easily not study, not so much as think about exams or computers, and even more easily crawl on his belly in the black pits of his mind and enshroud himself in darkness, hugging the dead Buddy.

His mother always treated him like the dog, Linus, and she would slap her thigh to call him to her in order to cut his nails, Linus, here's your chocolate wafer, and she'd throw it on the blanket and he would eat it and return the wrapping paper in his teeth, she put his boiled rice in a pale blue plastic bowl the same color and almost the same design as the dog's, she arranged for the boy's and the dog's inoculations on the same day, she stroked them at the same spot, the back of the neck, never long enough, and she was probably a bit afraid of dogs and children, he could see it in the quiver of her eyelashes when, startled, she would take a couple of steps back.

When he was little, he would hear her on the phone, shop, kid, dog, laying out her troubles to his godmother and, ever more troubled with the passing years, say wryly, I'm off to feed the two beasts.

He would see her sitting at the table with envelopes, receipts and paper bills, you're always counting money, he'd speak to her, no yakking, kid, I'm insanely busy, she'd answer, but it's really, really late, he implored, be quiet so I don't lose count and get in trouble, she ordered and he was quiet, same as his little brother Buddy, a dog that was forbidden to bark.

He was quiet all his life, that's what his father and mother had asked, they raised him with motions of the hand to be silent, not so they could talk among themselves, but so that each could think alone of everything he or she had saved up for the other, a tension, a coldness, a hostility he wasn't even allowed to temporarily interrupt, let alone dispel, he would be watching on television some film with Roman emperors, she'd be putting the price tags on the dollies for the shop, he would be filling his palms with sequins then emptying them for three-hour stretches, she would be starching shitty stuff made of tulle, he would stuff by force the batteries into the twirling dancers, she would polish two stupid candlestick holders, he carved a piece of wood, she looked murderously at the shavings, he spent half the night brushing the Russian hat, gazing at the wall, he hung on to the bottle until he'd drained the last drop, he was at the balcony afterwards, chain-smoking and putting out the butts in the potted plants.

One time, when his mother was away at the shop, some woman named Kiki came by the house, the same Kiki who had phoned a few days previously and who his father had hung up on after saying, I have no sisters, ever since I was twelve I've made it my business to forget about you, for your own sake, Kiki, don't make me remember you again.

When the bell rang and his father answered the door and saw her there, something came over him, I'm not going to lend a hand in your making peace with your conscience, Kiki, you are welcome to suffer some more, be my guest and torment yourself, go back and take it out on your suckass husband, he was yelling at her, she was standing on tiptoe and looking at little Linus over his shoulder, please, let me in, she was saying over and over again, her pleas in vain, Foti, you've had too much to drink, Foti, you're drinking, her last words, he sent her away.

Afterwards, he took Linus in his arms, hugged him so tightly to himself that it hurt and told him a story about a dog, the only true friend not only of kids but of grown-ups, too, who didn't get along with other grown-ups, he'd had Gagarin who danced all the time and leapt high in the air like a bird and he wished he still had him, only dogs deserve immortality, and he even promised to give him a fluffy puppy for his birthday.

That was Buddy, a two-month-old black cocker spaniel who was also raised without being heard.

Sometimes, his father took them both out to the butcher's, the small-goods shop, the liquor store, the walk of the silent trio. If Mom wasn't home, they went back straight after. If she was, he would drag the kid and the dog on, doing the rounds of five or six blocks, steps of muted anger, as if he didn't want to go back any time soon and Linus, to give himself courage, and keep from crying, memorized the numbers of the shops, 44 for medicines, 67 flowers, he didn't dare say he was going to miss his favorite TV show, *Bolek and Lolek*, he had managed to follow it even with no sound, so as not to disturb.

He was growing up and had no firsthand experience of what it means for a child to shriek, had never turned blue from crying, had not once heard his own voice trying how far and loud it could get, but he was intimately familiar with exhalations, whispers, internally spoken words, drunken "go-to-hell"s, with talk that started out loud and veered off or was switched off mid-phrase, the obedience to silence.

That's what he was taught, and got used to, and kept up, scoring with a soft fabric ball into a plastic hoop across from his bed, sometimes he got ten out of ten but never once broke out in a self-congratulatory yell, making do with silent applause and the tail wagging of Buddy as his fan and audience, not a squeak out of him either.

Silence was the largest thing he could imagine, wide as the Sahara, tall as Mt. Everest, deep as the Atlantic.

When his father died he was in third grade. There were no other orphans in the class and he felt distinctive, important, grand. The bell would ring for the end of classes, mothers waiting at the front gate, he paid those no attention, but if there were a couple of fathers out there, he didn't leave them out of his sight, he minutely scanned them for their unattractive traits, yellowed fingers, red noses, but he fancied them, too, figuring out their ages, heights, watching the way they held their children's hands.

How is it that you can fear and hate someone so much and yet be mortally afraid they might die and, once they're dead, instead of letting them sink away into forgetfulness, need them in your mind all the more, the sadness constantly growing and the fear never going away at all?

Thin drizzle, fifty or so umbrellas, dark suits and dark coats in the world's whitest neighborhood, a row of marble houses at St. Anthony's, at his dad's funeral, some familiar people, some not, everyone pushing through the rest to get near the boy, bend down and stoke his head, Linus shook it off annoyed, he didn't want to be touched, be spoken to, be distracted.

He was wedged in between the diggers, with eyes riveted on the two shovels that dug with difficulty into the frozen earth and ears diligently saving up each and every zdoop and ghupp as the dirt was loaded, every fraap and khraff as the dirt was emptied into his dad's grave. At one point one of the diggers leaned his shovel against the nearby cypress tree, took out some tissues, used up three to blow his nose, then zealously rejoined his colleague, the shovels again paired up.

The shovels, which ever since a cold Wednesday in February 1985 never left his thoughts. Nor did his mother's dry eyes, she had never cried before, didn't cry at the cemetery, didn't cry afterwards. And in forty-one days, which is to say, the very next day after the memorial service, she took off the black blouse. Eight-year-old Linus was terribly hurt by her beige shirt.

He almost told on her to his black-clad grandmother while the two of them were eating the last of the boiled wheat-and-pomegranate mix. He checked himself, he didn't say it, after two days the old woman and Xenia went back to the village because Grandfather had taken a turn for the worse, a heavy cold and delirium, Viv grabbed him, took him to the National Historic Museum, made a stop in front of the headdress of the revolutionary hero Kolokotronis, another in front of the heroic Lambros Katsonis in the uniform of a Russian fleet commander and, that same night, she rolled her sleeves up and made a plan of action to deal with the new situation, disorganization is deadly, she said to herself out loud and she repeated it, in those exact words, on her phone call to Rhoda late that evening.

Orders, deliveries, sales, distributions, she worked like a horse, fifty hours a day.

There was no one at home to whom Linus could complain about the beige shirt, a good thing probably, because that kind of pain and certain other things that happen cannot be fitted into words, you need to go through them alone. One time there was something choking him up for weeks and he stammered it, you keep saying all the time that you have a headache, the grown-ups pretended not to understand, shooed him away and that was that, for them, because Linus's choking inside got worse.

Eventually he did speak about the beige shirt and the green blouse after that, and the even brighter colors that came next, to Buddy, the two of them started then their hour-long conversations without loud words and exclamations, complete understanding through the eyes and, to signal the end of the session, the muffled sound of the shovel.

And what the heck is all that zdooping to the dog for? Viv had asked a couple of times, he made no answer. There was more that he didn't tell her at the time and more would be added in the future which he wouldn't tell her about either.

He would watch her eat her eggs in a near panic straight from the frying pan, the boiled maize straight out of the Tupperware, bang her forehead with clenched fists, almost wallow in her guilt towards him, especially when she let some man into her life, always a wrong choice so she could expeditiously cast him off, so quick in her disappointment, so willing to be wrecked.

Old Buddy was run over by a bitch in a BMW, April 1 of '97, a cursed Tuesday. His mother was walking him because he was with a fever.

The next day, Viv threw out the dog shampoo and dog food, soaped the upholstery of the sofa, washed the rug in his room and mopped the entire house five times to get rid of the dog smell.

You gave yourself away, Linus thought as he watched her take the detergents and the bucket to the bathroom, you really didn't love Buddy one bit. When the floor was dry, his mother closed the windows, stood in front of him and said, time to get over this abnormal dog worship, girls are a much better toy.

In the last year, she kept making comments, on two occasions she'd even come right out and told him off, why did Margarita leave you, why were the night calls of that other one cut short all of a sudden and why, for three years now, has there been no mention of another woman's name?

On that particular day, though, Linus, gutted over the loss of brother-spaniel, didn't talk back. At any other time he would have loved to contradict her, as if you really care what happened with those girls then, or just ask her, why are women so sure about everything, but it was impossible to open up to his mother, to trust her, to discuss anything with her calmly and normally and gratifyingly, his father hadn't been able to, either, nobody measured up to her in talking, she closed the subjects without delay, in three clipped sentences, her mind moved on faster than the others', she completed her husband's phrases, her sister's, her deliveryman's, her accountant's, the soccer fan's, the gypsy violin lover's, she was the first to locate the requisite words they needed, or confused them by interjecting her own, and she drew the final conclusion having arrived at the epilogue at top speed, while all the rest were still laboring on the introduction.

Only that slut, his godmother, could stem her, she brought to the house heavy books or foreign newspapers to read a couple of paragraphs out loud, doing off-the-cuff translations about imperialism and cultural affairs, to show her off as half-literate or completely uninformed and gain the upper hand.

That slut, his godmother, who christened him Linus so the kids could make fun of him in high school, who, since the age of ten, when they had taken the dog out together on a couple of occasions, would point out in shop windows things she intended to buy, bloodred sheets for king-size beds.

That slut his godmother who once, at her house, when he was about twelve, shot down in flames over the phone the young doctor who had cheated on her with an even younger nurse, his skillful assistant in surgery, and skillful cocksucker when their night shifts coincided.

That slut his godmother who came on to men whether at the height of their prowess or half-dead and, for every man she cured, gave a heart condition to another three.

That slut his godmother who, ever since he was fourteen, would corner him and pressingly ask, have you done it? How many have you tumbled in the sack? How many times have you done it in a row? Do, pray tell, give me reason to be proud of my spiritual offspring. You still haven't done it? Why, when do you plan to? Jerking off is sweet, but now you need to get set and go right at them, no female's too good for you, you'll be doing each and every one of them a favor, by the time you go in the army you need to have lain waste two platoons of women in the battlefield.

**

In May and June of '97 everyone at the school and the kids his age in the neighborhood had plunged headlong into kissing and fucking, the park benches turned into beds, the parks into whorehouses.

For Linus Kolevas the previous month had been disastrous, Buddy and archbishop.

A standard April afternoon, the pridefulness and self-assurance of spring generously dedicated to young and old.

Every man with a quiet head and a relaxed attitude would take pleasure in the creation which sparkled, would admire the foliage of the trees that shimmered like silver hankies in the breeze, would relish the clouds undulating like silk curtains and when the expected afternoon shower arrived, would feel lucky to be witnessing myriad Swarovski crystals raining down on everything with their festive, otherworldly shimmer.

Linus Kolevas saw everything differently, the spring sun to him was a trap, the sky was unwinding barbed wire, the clouds were a shoal of huge, shiny dogfish and the thick raindrops were tons of scales that fell on the city in waves, dirtying the houses, the cars and the asphalt.

He was walking and feeling as if he was slipping like when he waded in the shallows and stepped on flat slabs of rock covered with the slimy green cotton from the bottom of the sea.

He started to run in the direction of his neighborhood, but the street ahead of him was becoming more and more narrow until it turned into a dark tunnel barely twenty inches across, with the building walls rising to his left and right, full of thorns that tore at his clothes and pierced his sides.

It seemed like forever by the time he was turning his key in the door of the apartment block. When he finally got into the house, he went straight to his room, lay on the bed in his wet clothes, ran his palm against the wall, there were no thorns, turned on the lamp, checked his clothing, no holes anywhere or scales, lifted his T-shirt, not a scratch.

He brought his knees to his chin and lay curled up with his heart beating so fast that the pulse, like heavy hammering, jumped from his chest to his knees, the pandemonium resounding in his temples, his palms, his heels.

I have been struck by every version, every kind of fear, he thought and recapitulated, shovels and dirt, waves and leviathans, nights and blood.

Outside, darkness had fallen. The tenth day in a row that he wouldn't be setting foot at his school, ICS, Institute of Contemporary Studies, fuck them sideways and then some. And how to dare turn up, after that slime-bucket Elina had told her best friend who had told everyone else that she'd kidnapped the silent blond who was mourning his dog with the intention of seducing him in her car and the weirdo had thought she was an archbishop and spent two hours kissing her hand.

The very next day, two sluts by the entrance stairs proffered one hand to be kissed and, with the other, made the sign of the cross over him, may the Lord bless thee, as he turned about and fled he could hear their nonsense, come back here, you, we're just kidding, can't you take a joke?

Now night, nothing behind the windowpane but jet black.

If only he was another. Somewhere else. With others.

But can I become other? he wondered with a spasm first in his belly and a second in his eyes, which were torn up and burnt by tears, sharp-edged and sizzling.

His mother came back late, opened his door softly, Linus pretended to be asleep. He felt her standing still to listen to his breath, he obliged her by perfectly controlling the sound and frequency of his breathing.

Viv, well trained in treading lightly, approached soundlessly, took off his shoes, threw a linen blanket over him and went out again, carefully closing the door.

On his own again, he opened his eyes, fixed his gaze on the ceiling and kept on wondering when he would grow less afraid, when he would be rid of his chronic helplessness, when his head would stop hatching those millions of misery eggs.

It was almost dawn when he came up with an answer. The best known wars are the deadliest. Nations that haven't been through fire and brimstone get no glory. The meek are the clowns in the cowboys' lasso. Nobody mourns for the whiners. Only violence has spunk, only evil works endlessly, unstoppable, that must be the way to get in sync with the way others behave, to get in the swing of the times, to get into the spirit of things. Those who are decent are few and far between, the beasts are plentiful, so there's your solution, right there, if you want to be someone in order to exist in the crowd, he thought.

Well, then, since I can't be powerful, unfazed and unflinching in the face of fear, I can be evil, he determined and said it silently and in a whisper about a hundred times like a spell or a punishment. And, finally, as a lullaby, too, because at a quarter to seven in the morning, he didn't hear his mother's alarm clock nor did he register her coming again into his room to find him sleeping like the dead on his back, his socked feet sticking out of the blanket, his head thrown back on the pillow as if decapitated, his Adam's apple hopping like a frog and his mouth crookedly open, ugly and dark-colored, trembling with every one of the few weak snores that swelled up from the depths of his chest.

– Where are you, you little fuckers? were his first words when he woke up, past eleven, and looked for the barbells.

He located them eventually on the balcony, in the plastic basket under the plastic chair, along with the torn net of a basket hoop, a holy box glove, a deflated ball and a child's table-tennis racket, gifts all of them and mementos of his failure in sports.

At eleven, thirteen and sixteen, his mother and godmother had coughed up for him to join three neighborhood gyms and sports teams, he went to each a couple of times and then quit, no more discipline, no more orders.

He washed the two blue barbells in the bathroom, wiped them dry, hung them on his thin arms and started exercising full steam ahead, from today, from now, he was boarding a different train, the express to a Stallone-type body, to a build that would be proof to plenty of guys and girls that he could, retroactively and in one fell swoop, make a big splash, get a piece of the action and a share of the limelight.

Next day he was stiff, his arms ached and burned but there

was nothing else in his mind, I'm on a training schedule and I'm getting on, he told himself and that is what he said each successive morning through Easter week and the week after that, while the other one labored night and day with ballerinas inside red eggs and chocolate bunnies, musical boxes with Easter hymns, popular jingles and Fred Astaire tunes.

In about fifteen days, he saw his muscles more defined and he could, with his mother out of the house, lift the heavy living room table high above his head.

***

First thing in the morning, in a manner of speaking, of Wednesday, June 18th, Linus Kolevas found on the kitchen table, next to the aluminum foil wrapped sandwich, a note, some cash and the notification from St. Anthony's charnel house, that Viv hadn't paid for the six months of storing his father's bones and she was asking him to go take care of it, the deadline was expiring that day.

– Screw you, mommy dear, he muttered and stuffed the note and the money in his pocket.

On his way there, while he was paying and on the way back, the business with the shoveling started, which got him straight in the head, in twos at first, then by the dozen, then a nonstop avalanche. It had happened to him before, in the fifth grade and in high school, on the way to school some winter mornings, to suddenly see the whole suburb under attack by millions of thundering spades that struck the mountains, overrode the resistance of the hard earth, shoveling balls and crumbling knots of frozen mud, tons of it, a dark-colored flock of dirt tornados that fell resoundingly on rooftops, on cars and on the asphalt. People fled, looking for somewhere to hide so they wouldn't be buried alive.

It wasn't real, he knew that already from the second time it had happened to him, but he, too, fled, regardless, so as to get a rise out of his lungs and his heartbeat, to air his head and save himself from his imagination, so adept at producing scenes of terror and devastation.

Was that the same thing happening all over now? Did he have to close his eyes and walk with a stoop? Cover his ears to stop the rockets of zdooping from flying? Feel like it's freezing cold in mid-June? Flick his collar to stop worms from getting in? Wish he had with him the fur cap from bloody Russia as a shield?

Powerful arms weren't enough, finally, to defeat the chaos in his mind, that's where the enemy was.

He got home in the early afternoon, breathless and stumbling, and lay on his back on the hall carpet. His head kept him pinned down, heavy as a rock, unmovable by even an inch.

He only got up in the evening, as soon as his mother came in, to take the car keys from her, while she threw the question at him, where are you off to in such a hurry, is there someone new?

He was going to leave without answering, except he felt like giving it a go.

– I'm going to roam the streets like a madman.
– If that's the case, give those back.
She pulled the keys out of his hands.
– Then I'm going stumbling about in the streets.
– You're acting like a baby.
– To carve up cars and put holes in tires.
– You're asking for a good hiding.
– To beat up little kids.
– You are as harmless as a hummingbird.
– To swear at policemen.
– Now, why do you say things like that?
– To get on your nerves. I've been too quiet for too long.
His mother was tired, in no mood for having her nerves

tried. She stood for a bit, heavy and sweating, still except for her eyes, those were never quiet, never still in their orbs, they scanned endlessly to the left and right, up and down, every second her gaze was on something different, flighty, pecking at every inch of the small hall where everything, mirror, coat hanger, wall color, was exactly the same, unmoved and unchanged since day one.

The son still there. Mother, look at me, in case you see that I'm on the road to nowhere, he wanted to say but changed his mind, her rotating gaze was true and tried and so was the other kind, steady and interrupted, sometimes looking straight at him for quite long, except he could see the line of her gaze was being interrupted, there were momentary lapses, as if she were seeing in him something else as well, as if she were facing him interpolated with this person and that, and the many and various things that preoccupied her.

– Did you take care of the payment for the bones?

Viv changed the subject, in her opinion, and did so in a motherly voice of caring for the affairs of the house, of putting things to order as was appropriate, so they could be over and done with.

He didn't answer her.

Impatient to be done with this unpleasant reception at the end of the working day, she took out a handkerchief and daubbing her neck and forehead she said, you please yourself, then.

– It would please me to get you mad.

– And why is that, pray tell?

As she was asking the question she was jingling in the air and handing him back the car keys.

– On the off chance you might cry.

– Some other time, right now I need a shower.

She left her bag on the table and making her way, finally, to her room, she turned and called out, bring me a bar of chocolate, and added, take a bill out of my wallet.

Linus stuffed the keys in his pocket, ran to his room and grabbed his backpack, put it on, went out, spotted the red Mitsubishi at sixty feet across the street. He sped along the lit up boulevards, Patission, Aristotle, Acharnon. He turned into the smaller, half-dark streets of less central suburbs. He would stop, get out, walk a bit, rummage through a construction site, take a piss, get back in, drive some more, finally he parked somewhere near the small park of Lykovrysi, steeped in darkness. He left the car, roamed around a bit, checked out the lanes, the trees, the branches. He sat on the ground and smoked a whole pack. He picked up a dry two-pronged pine needle, split it in two. He split a second one, then a third, he kept it up, fifty, one hundred times two equals two hundred single pine needles.

It was almost midnight, twenty to twelve by the clock, when he emptied out his backpack, it wouldn't do putting it off anymore.

For the past ten, or was it more like twenty days, he'd been putting off from one day to the next. Let there be no new day with more of the same, getting constantly confused, getting chaotic and weighed down, building his muscles in the mornings and going out purposelessly roaming by himself at night, walking till he could no longer walk, in the wake of lively pretty girls without daring to make a proposition, even something as simple as, girl, you look great in white and, hey, gorgeous, yellow really is your color.

Fallen on his face on the dirt, the tree branches, his cigarette butts and his things, he saw what time it was with a twinge of despair, twenty past twelve, Thursday was here, the bitch had already arrived, yet another day trailing a host of ills.

He opened a second pack, one did go through these quickly, inexplicably quickly, and cigarette by cigarette till the twentieth and last one, he succeeded in putting together an inimitable monologue about the two-pronged cunts which at nightfall open automatically, via a photosensitive cell, to release the chemical gas which spreads out and hypnotizes and traps in the fork escapees from their momma's regime, words that shook up all the squished, transparent little bags with his brains and in the corridors of his mind and on the very last phrase, fucking lethal bitches with the toxic heels and panties, though he was still, no facial move, locked jaw and tightened lips, his tongue bit itself to shreds all of its own, the blood filled his mouth, he swallowed it, it quenched his thirst, it strengthened and aligned him with the words that lifted him up and out and away from himself.

As a warm-up, he made crude passes at a couple who were unaccompanied, he cornered one who sneered at him, go jump, you jerk, you and your stupid hat, and that one he took care of in the bushes. Unfortunately for her, she drew his eye because she shone with joy, her high spirits pierced the dark, her flower-patterned dress made her look like a shimmying plant and Linus was veritably affronted by such visible happiness, the variously happy people made him fume, he growled, the hell with everyone except for those who are desperate, and he went after her.

The day after next, the newspapers wrote about the beast, about the nineteen-year-old's bravery in reporting her mishap and about her courage in noticing several details. So, then, they knew about a tall young man with a strange dark hat who had gagged his victim with his sports shoe and, in the course of the act, was growling something that sounded like dupp-dupp. They didn't know and they weren't going to find out, the reporters, the policemen and the victim, the mother, godmother, or anyone else, that an hour previously, the young man had tied a chain to a robust tree branch, had circled it around his neck, had kicked at the four double bricks which he had stolen that same night from a construction site in the suburbs and which he had been carrying in his backpack to use to stand on, but at the critical moment instead of hearing his neck cracking, he heard the crack of the branch that sent him sprawling to the ground, alive and a failure.

***

Junk, is what he said to his mother when she asked how come he got into a housekeeping mood. She'd come in on him emptying the contents of drawers and shelves on the floor of his room and ripping out pictures and postcards stuck with tape to the inside of his wardrobe.

All mixed in together in two large plastic bags, he stuffed old comic books, faded and at one time hallowed T-shirts with spaceships and pirate ships, shapeless socks, videotapes, expired markers, broken triangles and rulers, a kid's snorkeling mask, two anti-flea collars, four plastic bones and three of Buddy's old name tags, last year's flip-flops and last year's sports shoes.

– Why not throw out the poster, too? Viv suggested, Linus didn't answer and he didn't take down the shiny poster, yellowed and torn at the edges, with the dog breeds and Buddy's breed circled with red marker and red sequins stuck all around, from the remaining ballerinas, four in number.

– Throw the fur cap, too, or the moths will get it. Why save it, who wears things like that anymore? He heard his mother's voice from the kitchen.

I do, he thought to himself.

He grabbed the bags and went out. It wasn't the clothes and the magazines he urgently wanted to get rid of but the shoes, not that anyone would find them or that they had teethmarks on them or that they were special, it was just an ordinary pair of everyday plasticized white shoes and the size wasn't a 14 or 15 so that the strange girl might remember a big foot, he took a 10, the most common size for a man's shoe.

The shoes inside the house made him fearful, all day Thursday and all day Friday his thoughts and his eye kept being attracted to them, they were a challenge.

He took to the streets and started emptying the stuff in out-of-the-way rubbish bins, a little at a time, he threw out the shoes at a distance of several kilometers, the left one off Omonia Square, wrapped in one plastic bag, the right one two suburbs away, wrapped in the other.

It would be nine when he got home, Viv was watching the news with her feet in a tub of water, from time to time she complained about calluses, phlebitis, swollen ankles, I've turned out a prima ballerina of sorts myself, she had told him some months ago, dancing the daily grind till I drop.

Tonight, she only came out with the absolute essentials, how come he was in so early, how come he doesn't get a haircut in this heat or, at least, pull his hair back with a rubber band, and that the green beans and feta cheese were on the kitchen table and next to them was money to go on Saturday morning and buy a new pair of running shoes, proper ones.

Linus didn't touch the money, for three days it lay on the edge of the tablecloth while he went about in his winter boots and, as he had cut off all communication with his mother, Viv, having had enough of his silence, and of her attempts to break or interpret it, she acted of her own accord, in the interests of practicality, and on Tuesday evening she brought home two pairs of new sports shoes, one red and white and one white and blue, with black soles and black laces, and she emptied the lot, along with the receipt, on his bed for him to find when he came back, at God knew what time.

Past midnight she heard the key, then his footsteps toward the kitchen, the opening of the fridge, the glugging of water, he must have emptied that bottle and now he's not going to fill it up and put it back in its place.

In a bit the noises transferred to the bathroom, a two-minute torrent, then shifted to the living room, the TV was switched on, a quick zapping, it was off in three minutes.

Linus knew that each night his mother kept her ears pricked to catch his familiar, well rehearsed motions and Viv knew that he intentionally made a little extra noise to facilitate her tracking his course through the house.

Steps now heading to his room, the rustling of papers and then dead quiet.

In about five minutes he appeared before her in his boxer shorts, barefoot, holding in his arms the four new shoes.

– Don't they fit? she asked, lifting the sheet to her chin, then went on, don't just stand there like a midwife presenting quadruplets.

Linus looked at her full in the face, saw her hand turn over the opened book on her belly, her toes fidget nervously under the white sheet, went back to her eyes and stayed there, as if wanting to transmit a signal that couldn't be put into words.

Viv waited and waited, don't they fit you, she asked again, he nodded, an incomprehensible nod, is there something the matter? You must be wanting some money, that's what she surmised, that's what she said to him, her son was standing graceless and speechless, rooted to the spot next to her bed, except she didn't have the patience to look for a way to loosen his tongue, he was too grown-up now for her to undertake such obligations, she didn't much care for his look either, his red eyes, the hanging lower lip, the Adam's apple roving in his throat, and she didn't much like the time of night, questions at nighttime have a way of turning unpleasant, so she sent him off with an, I'm in the middle of my book now.

Linus let the shoes drop to the floor and disappeared in his room, the key to his door was heard turning twice.

There wouldn't be any reading and then going to sleep for him. Like yesterday and the previous night and six nights before that, the frightened eyes would jump out from all over the place, would instantaneously multiply in the room, would sail along the walls and the ceiling, would swarm into an army and walk straight at him, would attach themselves tightly around the circumference of his head, their moisture clinging to the hairs on his neck, his cheeks, his mouth and, from there, the irises would eject rounds of hundreds of black lightning rods to disintegrate and scorch everything.

He wasn't afraid of getting caught, he wasn't afraid that Buddy's chain, which he hadn't thrown away, would again become a noose, he was afraid that by the time they caught him, the shoes would have made him march again.

And the first time that the words and the shoes picked him up and teleported him towards evil, when, instead of turning him into Stallone and Jackie Chan, they had drained all his power, it had happened at his home, with the power supply cut off.

He picked up the left boot from the floor, the left was the shoe he'd used that night in the small park, and he shoved the front part of it in his mouth. Within seconds, his body started shaking, his arms flew out and pummeled the sheets, his legs gathered up and stretched out spasmodically again.

His ears were filled with muffled sounds of "don't" and "don't" and moans and alongside them, confused phrases piled up, stammers, random syllables that puffed out and swirled in the darkness of the room, golden mane, in your panties, coupons with the hammer and sickle, the zit, the cheeks of the calf head, how cute, and in order not to miss out on the words and their meanings, he bent his ear to the sizzling whispers in order to latch onto the ribbons of the phrases, to clear up to whom each voice belonged and what they were saying, to get the threads in order, weave them thickly into a long, sturdy rope which he would then wind twice around his neck.

You've got me living inside your panties after all, he'd heard this phrase at age seven, his father had said it to Viv one night, after they'd put him to sleep in a hurry, they'd practically pushed him into his room and shoved him under his coverlet, because it was their day to fight, they'd made the relevant preparations early, had sat wordless around the kitchen table, no bread had been cut, the glasses stood empty, the food cold, he smoked three cigarettes in between mouthfuls, she cleaned the plates before they had finished, they were all choked up, they would have to let things out any minute now, but not before they'd ushered the kid out.

The kid, to be sure, had half opened his door, he heard things, he didn't retain much of what was said out loud except for his father's sad, broken voice saying that thing about the panties. The panties that grew in size, they grew as big as a burlap bag in his grandfather's storeroom, a doghouse for an oversized dog, a lion cage in the circus. The panties which, sometimes white, sometimes black, on their laundry rack, pretended to be an innocuous little chit, but, it seemed, at nights swelled up and became an enormous sack that could swallow up a full-grown man, his poor father.

Years later, he must have been eleven, while thumbing through an album with Russian landscapes, his mother found inside dozens of coupons from the Communist Party's fundraisers and, nostalgic for the good old times when she had the deceased ready at her disposal to chastise, she rang out, as loud as a church bell, I was right to suspect he was too embarrassed to ask people for money and was paying for these himself, a truckload of money, he singlehandedly made the Party rich, the silly fool.

Right there and then, Linus came up with the unforgettable phrase about her panties, hoping for an explanation and conveying the message that when he grew up himself, he wasn't going to let her lord it over him.

— Best you remember other things, was her first, abrupt response, though after a while, half in regret and half in confusion, she afforded the eleven-year-old a synopsis of her defense speech, unhurriedly, taking up half his evening.

– I left medical school because I got pregnant with you, we were looking for ways to make a living, your father had been sold short by his boss and I'd no time to wait until when, where or how he would open a business of his own, with my belly out to here I found three reasonable little shops, one with underwear and nighties, one with pet accessories and the one I eventually went for, which he didn't like, he only contributed his savings halfheartedly. I didn't like it either, didn't give a damn about ballet, but it was the right decision, for our means. We didn't get rich and we didn't go without either, plus I'm saving for you to study when the time comes, anything you fancy, whether doctor, architect or astronaut. You see, because of my forethought, you will be able to do what you choose. He, poor soul, wasn't. I do think of him. He loved strong woods. I handmade window shutters. He was born for carpentry. Only he crafted the window of his own soul crooked and ended up a lost cause. It wasn't my choice to make decisions on behalf of others, life forced me.

Next day, life would force her to bring home the soccer-loving jackass.

On that distant night the kid understood a fair bit, because it all dovetailed right in with his fathers' friends, two bearded Cretans, another bald guy, another fat guy, faint memories from increasingly more scarce visits, until his pack, as Viv called them, was defeated and no longer had easy access to the home, they showed up en masse for the last time on his father's name day, one week after Easter, many happy returns, friend, stay strong, comrade, a good year to all, why, Linus, how tall you've grown, one whiskey each, dried nuts and out the door in half an hour.

Another three appearances, at the funeral, at the forty day memorial service and at the one for the one year, and since then, a phone call and a toy car by post each November for the orphan's name day and birthday until eleven, then nothing, his mother must have kept them at bay.

For a young child, Linus had a great predilection for memorizing sad events, his mother's mouth helped, which insisted, when on the phone to her sister, or having coffee with that slut his godmother, or with her clients, on recapitulating every trial and tribulation and doing it in words that were bitter and sour, she really did much prefer them.

All these details leapt out again from that now very distant evening. For this one here, the one at hand, inside the buzzing room, the phrase with the panties was more than sufficient, almost emblematic.

And next to it, the mane.

A pointed church and a black belfry with a golden areola, the postcard Margarita sent from Germany and at the back, in red ink, Leipzig, July 17, 1994, and nothing more, you blond-haired chicken-brain, with a golden comb on your silly head, he had wanted to tell her at the time, except it was a farewell card.

The last date in her room had been crowned by failure, he was kissing her for half an hour, even after she'd had enough of smooching, the appetizer before the main course, she had called it, impatient for what was next, on that particular weekend when her parents and younger sisters would be off to Corinth visiting relatives, she had dreamt of a feast that would last till dawn. So she had made Linus put his hand first in her bra and then in her panties, the pink transparent ones that scared him half to death, she had pressured him to take them off her, he was worried that the lace would snap on his fingers, panties are sly, in the end she took them off herself and stood before him, bare-assed and impeccable, milky white thighs and blond bush.

Linus didn't really want to make love, not just with her but with anyone, he didn't feel desire and that scared him. That night it was the same all over again, he apologized a dozen times to his fellow student about the throat ache, the bellyache, the upset stomach, he left bowing low and while roaming the streets as if he were homeless, he was still apologizing to her prepped body, her pert breasts, the navel bud and the golden hairs he'd scarcely touched.

He was in trouble because in movies, normal ones not porn that made you want to throw up, and in random readings he was fixated on images or descriptions of a male arm resting over a female shoulder, on two hands tightly held, on a cheek gliding on long hair, on a kiss which there was no doubt both wanted very much because it was a great thing on its own right and not because it would propel them onto the bed at top speed. Moaning was all right, and so were the bare-assed bodies and all the rest of it, but no matter how original they were, what with all their minutely worked out lustfulness, Linus only felt that prickling in the heart with what were called tender embraces.

This particular saccharine description, stolen from a magazine, was top secret, locked away inside his head. To the rest of the world he pretended to be cool, even threw out a cynical comment every now and then.

Margarita, Sylvia and a couple more had no time to waste, not for movies or wordless strolling at night, they were on a schedule, down to the minute, school, private classes, English, German, home study and, in between, either a hamburger or a screw with a chalking up of aptitude, a cataloguing of experiences, rating and ordering by number.

Some girls, spoiled by their beauty, turn bitchy if you don't fuck them, Linus couldn't get it through his head that the girls in question got horny, he himself didn't, to him bodies weren't important.

– A zit, you have a zit on the back of your neck, Rhoda had

whispered in his ear, renaming him on the spot, you curly-haired, white-blond little horse of Patisia, tickling him with a lock of her hair, as you can see I went and had my hair dyed in your color and, playacting the godmother all along, putting around his neck and twirling the amber piece of shit she'd bought him from Poland, put it on for me to see, just for a minute, for good luck, and like a tarantula, kept sliding her hands along his bare back, pressing her fingers along his sides, sneaking her palms into his armpits, putting them at the front and pulling at his chest hairs with her lips stuck initially on his shoulders, each one in turn, then descending to his waist, each kiss twenty inches long.

This was the time of making up between mother and god-mother after six months of curtailed diplomatic relations, because Viv had had enough of Rhoda lording it over her and one beautiful Sunday morning she'd let it rip, stop sucking on our lives, go to someone else's, stop acting so high and mighty, you, too, get your bribes under the table when you can afford to, what do you know about the troubles of a difficult son, you barely have time left to have a child of your own and then you'll know what is what and, to top it all off, what business have you with the under twenties, stop hitting on your trainees, get it on with someone your age and unmarried, your years are starting to show, words which cost her the ripping out of the door handle and of the entire door as Rhoda slammed it on her way out, just as she slammed out her answer, Viv, you think you know me but you don't.

The alibi for the reconnection was Linus, Rhoda had taken up an obligation towards him, she said when she sailed in with-out warning at past midnight, with a state-of-the-art computer, a jacket, a huge box of Belgian candy, a collection of English dog food cans and a few one-liners, sentimental but also direct hits to her friend, laid out on the couch with ankles the size of tin drums, Vivika, it's beyond me to not forgive you, it's simply out of the question not to care about you, so, then, dear heart, don't you move a muscle, I'll give you a miraculous massage and, while rubbing and caressing the swollen feet, she served up the rest as well, Linus who was feeding Buddy on the balcony heard it just fine, you and I raised that kid together, I'm speaking to you as a doctor, he needs to get over his timidity with the silly girlies, he needs to be rid of his inhibitions, find a man's sure-footedness, I worry because I've been around and I see many boys at the critical age lose their sense of orientation, if you see what I'm getting at.

The threat worked, it allowed them to make up and to reclaim the comfort of their old relationship, the grand dame arriving loaded like a mule with myrrh and frankincense and art and sweets and political news, all of it cream of the crop and, as such, to be unwaveringly subscribed to.

One bloody Monday she went too far.

Rhoda and her seventeen-year-old godson in his room, Viv had left them to their chat, about his future, what to study, what openings there were, she'd drop thirty dollies off at a dance school and when she got back she'd fry some choice hot dogs and lay those out in the platter along the cheeks of a calf head, the treats were a gift from the latest admirer of the elegant arch-slut, a pig farmer or something near enough from Thessaly, she had picked him up on an excursion she'd been to at the nearby lakes and she didn't pass up the chance of getting to know the world of the animals.

Her trip had been made in the middle of a bad spell, a sixty-year-old patient had died on her who reminded her of her dad, by his side she had again seen the eyes and heard the voice of the deceased, but, then, all the talk about cows and pigs had cheered her up and perked up her appetite, upon her return, the good godmother was of a mind to devour her godson himself, the kisses turned to savage bites to his neck and belly button, oh how cute, what awesome adolescent flesh, we're having us an initiation, don't be shy, lovemaking requires a free spirit.

Later at the table, Linus wouldn't touch the goodies of the pork man, wouldn't answer to the two porkies, mother and godmother, who kept on his case, eat and talk and drink and speak and why don't you go to parties and why don't you go out with friends, bars are great fun, you're keeping yourself at a distance on account of your father.

That hoover his godmother, now sucking in the beer as if dying of thirst and sucking on her cigarillos as if nicotine-starved, was reminding Viv, as if he was absent or deaf, how she had fought with albums of painters, and tapes of classical music and biographies of the great in general, to train the kid artistically, to kindle his spirit, to awaken hidden talents and, blind drunk by now, was answering in a child's voice, no, god-mother, I don't like it, no, godmother, that's scary because to be a great painter you need to have one ear cut off, to be a great musician you need to be deaf, to be a great poet you need to have committed suicide and to be a very good person, you need first to be imprisoned in snow and rocks.

He left them when the drunk one starting checking her image on the underside of the spatula and the sober one observed, the blond hair hides your age, it does that, blond hair hides age.

He went back to his room, got into the sleeping bag and pulled it over his head and was then thrashing on the bed, that single bed which only ever saw this kind of triumph, arms and legs quaking, chest and mouth in synchronized spasms, the grunts of high fever.

**

– Do they dig into you?
– They do.

– Why didn't you say so, I could take them back.

– They'll stretch.

– How are they going to stretch if you only ever wear the Gestapo boots?

– Leave off already with your shoes.

– But why not change them and not waste good money?

– Fifty, seventy, what's my price as far as you are concerned?

– Linus, you aren't in one of your moods, are you?

– Instead of the shoes, you'd better take me back and get a refund.

– What'll it cost you to stop talking nonsense? Have you ever heard of positive feelings?

– You should have taught me those when I was young. You're too late now, it's not going to work.

Linus in his blue-and-white shoes was playing back the memorized dialogue during his two hours of street roaming, doing his juggler's walk, throwing up in the air and catching Buddy's green plastic frog, first with the right hand then with the left, all wound up into mechanical motions, the fear burrowing in his heart also mechanical, as was the hammering of anger at his temples.

He'd stayed up and then gone out before dawn, July deposited its heat everywhere though, to him, everything remained pale, blurred and cold like a November dawn lasting for twenty years.

He searched for help in his pocket without leaving off his frog juggling, his hands still at the balancing act, his eyes still looking up but his mind to his wallet, not for money, which he hated, for his father's mug, the face squashed against the small wooden frame he held in his arms, the mouth kissing the carved wood surrounding the lock, a smudge on his cheek, the picture of the guy who went off to get some peace among the cypresses leaving his only child to his own devices.

Sometimes he fought desperately to remember him, he was

only eight when he'd lost him, he hadn't had enough life with him and he wasn't old enough to clearly make out and hold onto the many sometimes strange impressions from the gestures and events which a child observes for the very first time.

He remembered him coming into the house holding up high, like a lit torch, a paper funnel with roast chestnuts, he remembered him peeling a grape and feeding him, looking incensed for his lighter which he'd put inside the cigarette pack, going through papers and receipts in a drawer, reading some old poems and shaking his shoulders as if he'd been electrocuted, barking at Buddy on all fours, blind drunk, leaving the house abruptly in the middle of a meal, but coming back very soon to help with the dishes, not holding his own in conversations with Viv, getting knocked out already in round one.

He remembered two awesome, horrible wordless fights without anything at all being spoken, his parents moving like spinning tops from bedroom to kitchen, from living room to balcony and back again, each in a different direction, pushing against one another in the hallway and the narrow passages next to the dresser, between the sofa and the big table, chairs being overturned, doors slamming, windowpanes creaking.

Crouching behind the carved chair, Linus was whispering in fearful obeisance, I'm being quiet, I'm being quiet, even before being told by the grownups who were, at all events, causing the whole ruckus by themselves.

The things that finally remained were quite a few, if they were actually true, but even if they weren't, he'd thought about them so many times that they'd become regular memories, massively enforced by the things he saw in his dreams, all mixed up together, a healthy savings account, a till overflowing with shadows.

When he was younger, some nights when he was asleep, or half asleep, he dreamt that he and his dead father were going in and out of shops and dealerships with gardening tools, they admired and haggled over new and used shovels, some red, some yellow, with wooden handles, with metal handles, short ones, medium ones, painted, unpainted, many together standing against the wall, in eights and tens and dozens, like spears, like bayonets waiting for the soldiers to come pick them up to go to battle with.

In his half-sleep they always bought two rusty ones, costing next to nothing, splattered with dried mud and on their way back home, bouncing along as happy as larks, the dead man and his kid banged them on the sidewalks and the sewer grilles to shake the mud off.

For the first Christmas Linus had asked for a shovel as a present, Viv was puzzled but she nevertheless bought him a red one along with a watering can and a guidebook for young gardeners, my weird child, her endearment as she delivered them and then, sit still, you're giving me a headache, as the shovel-bearing kid assaulted the living room with the war cry of zdoop and gupp and targeted his mother, dueling and shoveling air.

And at the village, during the first summer of orphanhood, he kept right at it, scraping and shoveling the dust from the stone hard dirt of the yard, he'll be a digger, an orchard tender, an agriculturalist, Grandfather proudly commented on his devotion to the earth, to him the earth was the paramount blessing, like for every poor farmer, he'll be a gold digger in the Far West or even an oil miner in Texas, his godmother upped the ante, a weekend guest at the village to flirt and parade her graces around the countryside.

Viv refrained from comment, even though she constantly watched him, her mind's eye was trained somewhere else.

The new white-blue shoes were a perfect fit, of course they were, nice and snug, the soles light as a feather.

He spent the day with no food or drink covering on foot half of the city of Athens, zigzagging among Datsuns loaded with cantaloupes, bike riders in army shorts, double-parked cars, scooters on pavements, piles of cardboard boxes and rows of fossilized old men, more encumbered by the sun with every hour, deeper and deeper and ever more lost in the vast desert of strangers, white noise in his ears, flies before his eyes, ants on his skin, wasps in his belly, snakes in his mind.

When it got dark, he started on his night patrols, stumbling back and forth along the main streets and, around ten, he withdrew to more remote neighborhoods, until, breathless, he nailed himself, a lonely piece of driftwood, on a bench at Attica train station.

The air was hot but he shivered, he couldn't make heads or tails even of the weather. And the head couldn't make sense of the body, a constant scrape, a feud that was years old already, ever since he put on long trousers.

He didn't want it to happen to him again, the torment of the last few months, some nights when he felt his body shrink like a piece of fabric in the wash and then, in a confusion of complaint and anger, helplessness and violence, everything inside him changed and he managed to finally muster his courage and become bold, to get up some steam and get horny, it took him months before he got his shriveled tongue to unfold, turn it into a sword that ejected the panegyrics about cunts and cum.

The trains pulled up in front of him, they emptied and filled up again, people in a hurry, full shopping bags, plastic water bottles, crumpled newspapers, laughter, see you soon and hi and goodnight, many lit up cigarettes as soon as they came off, an Albanian asked him for a light, a junkie for some change, an elderly woman asked him what the time was, Linus sat with eyes of cement and sealed lips, though inwardly he was talking nonstop, sometimes to some stranger, sometimes to his own self as if he was looking at him from a few inches away or as if his left eye was spying on the right. His stories were hundreds, in slices, mixed-up settings and mixed-up years.

He needed to make the night stop, to stop it from advancing and overtaking him, needed to put up some resistance.

With the frog in his palm for company, he leaned against the bench, a beat-up dog, shoulders scrunched up, ears drooping, eyes bleary from the thick tears, head swollen by the assault, like hail, of successive outlandish scenes, ballerinas exploding, staircases breathing, alcoholic drinks sleepwalking, apples biting, loaves of bread keeping their silence, hair fainting, pianos sinking, forests swimming, the dead giving birth, streets frothing, barley and pomegranates creaking, shovels having hysterics, the dirt tasting bitter.

***

Little baby Christs who are sprinkling snow.
And snow that is sprinkling little Christ babies.
Christmas trees that sing lullabies to ghosts.
And ghosts that sing lullabies to Christmas trees
Marmalade biscuits giving birth to puppies.
And puppies giving birth to marmalade biscuits.
Birds that are strangling clouds.
And clouds that are strangling birds.

In the late hours of the night, Linus Kolevas returned home barefoot, locked himself in his room, sat on the edge of the bed, snuck into the heart of winter and the heart of his childhood years with Buddy, who had been waiting for him like always, royally sprawled on the sheets, they took up their whispering repartee, careful to not disturb.

From patient listener, the dog, after death, had evolved into a skilled practitioner of the post-midnight simulations of holocaust that his master, friend and brother Linus sought, scrunched up into a ball, befuddled inside the overturned days and nights and crushed by the bedlam of events, the human gold and the human filth all rolled in one, and the mind springing up and veering into crooked rainbows, billowing rivers, fields sailing off, cities stammering, crowds shimmering, New Year's Eves afflicted by old age.

Leaping off the bed onto the floor, Buddy licked the dust from Linus', soles and softly growled his contribution, blind people taking aim, deaf who answer back, cripples parading, one-armed men making the sign of the cross.

The small cocker spaniel had watched unremittingly the developments sparked all these years by the faces coming in and out of the house, and Rhoda was his number one dislike, he'd bitten her in the calf twice but unfortunately she had been vaccinated and he failed to turn her rabid and pack her off to the hereafter.

Every Maundy Thursday, the madam, torn between atheism and the observation of certain traditions, brought her godson Easter candles with the badges of organization for the protection of nature, of every manner of minorities and of those victimized by plutocracy and, in addition, she delivered them with a thirty-minute discourse so that the child knew at four about Pinochet's bloody coup, at five about the crematoriums at Auschwitz, at six about the persecution of the Palestinians, at eight about the embargo to Cuba, at ten about Chernobyl and the defunct nuclear reactors that will blow up and thousands of people will die from cancer and by twelve or thirteen he hadn't missed out on any source of misery, any occasion for mass destruction.

Every year, Buddy's young master was starting to turn pale already from Holy Monday, unable to figure out a way of getting out of the trial of the imminent Maundy Thursday. His godmother had the officious air of a harbinger of ills and the status of an intellectual who didn't allow anyone not to be terrorized by her statements. Along with the shocking candle, she always brought gifts, all purchased overseas, a large drawing pad from recycled paper decorated with fish and seabirds dead from Exxon oil-spills, a T-shirt with a logo against furs, a poster by a famous photo-reporter full of dead people, a pair of ecological footwear with silk-screened images of the nearly extinct Red Indians of the Amazon.

Linus would have been about thirteen, first year in high school, when one night, alone at home, he stuffed it all in an old suitcase, along with his mother's beige shirt towards which he still harbored a resentment, and went and left it at an isolated bus stop, the suitcase could travel where it pleased, as long as it was away from him.

The night was slowly fizzing out, sleeplessness and exhaustion were slowly getting the upper hand. When Buddy, the much loved ghost, rested his head and softly rubbed his cheeks and ears on his pal's knees, he heard him repeat words by the ignominious godmother in three installments, unforgettable audio documents of the loss of his virginity.

First installment, I like the way you turn your body towards the door. Second installment in a bit, I like the tone of your voice when you say don't, godmother, hands off, be proper. Third installment, a couple of minutes later, she was licking her fingers at the table and moaning, what a great-tasting, big, juicy sausage this is.

When did three years go by? Why didn't he fill them with something worthwhile?

Dead tired, Linus lay on the floor and went out like a light for five hours, a sleep without dreams, without nightmares. The previous night, Wednesday July 2nd, 1997, was never going to be erased from his mind but it was as if it had happened to someone else, the protagonist was a stranger, he himself had nothing to do with the white ankles that shone in the dark, unmoving on the single pine needles, no trace of himself in the second rape.

In the night, at the small park by the Hill of Strefi, in an alley with sickly trees, hidden behind a tree trunk a strange, frightening guy with a fur hat, standing dead still for two hours, soles without footsteps, a walker without a path.

In the yellow light of a distant streetlamp, he checks the late passersby, first some middle-aged men coming home one by one, then three young boys running and giggling, later two heavy sixty-year-old women prattling, all moldy necks and rotting breasts, melting underarms, the apocalypse of aging flesh and, finally, by herself, a girl with a Walkman in her ears, hurrying along and as sprightly as a young horse, the stripped black-and-white skirt split up the side, the T-shirt short, the hairstyle modish, the nipples puckish, the belly button churning, a body at boiling temperature.

She didn't see the man, he let her pass by his tree, then sprang after her, grabbed her from behind, gagged her mouth, dragged her deeper into the copse of trees, threw her down on the pine needles, covered her face with the fur cap and ejecting two coarse zdoop, he did his business in three minutes.

The girl was so scared that she didn't utter a sound, didn't muster the strength to scream even when he took back his hat, got up and waltzed off, like a true gentleman.

This was the same guy who, a few hours earlier at Attica Station, as the last train was pulling in, got up from his bench and silently hurled himself into the railroad tracks, more than willing to be crushed to a pulp.

If it wasn't for the two damned Albanians who, at risk of their own lives, jumped in and dragged him off at the very last instant, with one of the two then forcing his beer down his throat and the other fanning him with a flyer for a pizzeria till he was able to stand on his feet and silently go off to wherever, the zebra at the park would have been spared the brutal fuck.

***

As a kid, he spent a lot of hours at the ballerina shop, his mother had nowhere to leave him after school. He did his lessons behind a curtain and never moved an inch, he then went on to Mickey Mouse, picked through *Lucky Luke*, drew fortresses with Chinamen, handled some of godmother's books brought by the half dozen to refine and educate the uncouth Sourpuss, novels of the sort that are read or, equally, left half-read for months and years.

He didn't show himself, he was embarrassed to be seen planted in the midst of all the pink dollies and at Christmas, when he had to help out because of the great crowd of clients, he kept the till, being good at arithmetic, he didn't fancy being seen by the girls winding and packing the tulle-wrapped trinkets.

Of course, he did hear their wheedling and cajoling, he knew about the massive orders to the importer, he knew well the hits among the stock, the white Odette and the black Odille, the swans of the pas de quatre, Prince Siegfried, the Sleeping Beauty, Clara with her gaudy costume, the Sylphs, in the blue tutus, the netting on their hair-buns which Viv loaded with extra beads, sequins and butterflies to bring the prices up and bolster her gains.

He did not like ballet, did not like training ballerinas, did not like any kind of dancing, it was out of the question going to any of the dance school shows, where his mother showed up unfailingly to applaud with fake enthusiasm, give fake congratulations and pass her business card around.

He'd pleaded with her countless times to change the sign *Tutu*, just make it *Dance*, pure and simple, or take it right off, everyone can see what you're selling, at school the teasing was merciless, greetings to your mother's tutu, and as for her, it was always, yes, later, next week for sure.

While growing up, he remained unswerving in his disdain for dollies, pirouettes, curtsies and dance figures, including those of folk dancing and rock, that's what he would say to

Xenia, a working student who had opted for sharing an apartment with two fellow students and later, as a graduate, for living with graduate boyfriends. Whenever the young aunt came visiting, she would bring him two or three music tapes she had made herself, being equally a fan of the traditional countryside clarinet and the drummers pummeling their instruments as if possessed.

Her visits were few and far between but for the while she was there, two hours or a whole evening, her time was devoted to the morose nephew, in mad earnest to let into her sister's house a draft of jollity, to draw the boy's thinking along a different route, full as she was of ideas for fun and progress, during exams you must combine study with the right music and the appropriate food, ancient Greek with Vangelis Papathanassiou and fish soup, mathematics with light pop and pasta, history with ballads and lots of french fries.

One historic Halloween, his aunt and his godmother visited in tandem and turned him into the disputed trophy, Rhoda was jealous of Xenia's attentions and started deriding her, kid, you talk too much and your advice is long like green beans, it's like you take the seeds out of the words one by one to fill up the tub of your lecturing, only to get the young girl's prompt answer, both green beans and yourself are out of season.

When Xenia got married to her first one, her savior's zeal visibly dropped, her visits grew rare, she mostly turned up on the phone and that, in a way, was a good thing. For Linus, to be alone in the house with a woman, his mother, was bleak, with two it was sheer disaster, with three, pure hell.

Nor did he have any friends. How many kids had come to their apartment? Nine, all together at his birthday, fellow students from the first grade. Linus had wanted a chocolate cake, Viv ordered vanilla, Linus had wanted lots of bags of salty chips, she forbade them having laid out the clean carpets the day before, as there'd be parents coming in and out of the liv-

ing room to bring and come get their kids, she finally brought
out coconut tarts, which she herself approved as nutritional,
the kids didn't go for them much.

It was the first party of his life. And his father finished it off
by stumbling around drunk, crowning by force one kid after
the other with his fur hat and singing the revolutionary songs
his own father had taught him, *Black crows with sharp talons
upon the workers are falling.*

He didn't want to have another party and he didn't go to
anyone else's. Twice he brought Tolis home, lively and mis-
chievous, he broke a lamp and wreaked havoc, Viv said he's
out. In the fifth grade, a Yannis would come every so often, sit
for a couple of hours unspeaking, reading the *Lord of the
Rings*, he carried the tomes with him. And Socrates, three visits, came only for Buddy, took him in his arms and they rolled
around the floor delighted, his own parents didn't want a dog.

Linus knew the whole story of his fellow student, the fat kid
of the class, who wanted a golden retriever above all else, but
would sing for joy over any dog at all. He'd found for free a
female griffon, then a young Labrador crossed with German
shepherd but his father, mother, sister and grandmother were
adamant, they didn't fancy animals. Do you want to own the
cocker half and half? he suggested on his third and last visit,
because Buddy's boss didn't invite him again, he wouldn't
mind sharing his mother by halves with some orphan, his food
and his pocket money by halves with some underprivileged
kid, but not his dog, or, to be exact, his dog's love.

With Yannis or Socrates, whenever Viv stuck her head in
the room, Linus would say, we're being quiet, and sent her
away with his eyes. His mother, overly busy all the time, overly
fed up, looked on all kids like a middle-aged teacher who's
been burnt out by many years' exposure to the students' anni-
hilating liveliness and wishes never again to have to lay eyes on
any creature under twelve, not ever.

In high school, Linus neither invited anyone nor went over, he had steeled himself for savage loneliness.

Viv, periodically weighed down with her own stuff or completely focused on profits and expenses, rarely commented, for the sake of appearances and with the standard formulas, why don't you go out and play some basketball, why don't you invite someone over. He'd seen her sitting listening to Rhoda about how adolescents, in a group, have a nuclear energy and a radioactive libido that can cause successive explosions, with the shock wave slamming grown-ups against the wall like swatted flies. Probably his godmother, in amongst her many interests, medicine, politics, tourism, men, also cultivated an active interest in the automatic dicks of boys, you touch them and they rise up, you squeeze them and they take off, you grab them up in midair and you swallow them right down.

He loathed her. He would have liked to tell on her but she was good for getting his mother out of a tight spot with a loan, and kept her company so they could get overwhelmed together by the stress of how best to manage their affairs, the Cyprus issue and their woebegone heads, so he didn't have the guts to parade her dirty laundry out in the open. Someday, though, he would and he was going to keep on the lookout for that day, work up to it and he would settle with her, even if it took till the Second Coming.

In the court-martialing of his adolescence, Linus didn't manage to clash with anyone, Viv would just not oblige him, his relatives had labeled him an orphan and were unwilling to concede any further rights and his father had indebted him with a void, palpable and solid, which nobody else could fill, another could not play his part, good or bad there's only one dad and if the fucker goes off and dies early, the mourning then grows along with the child, alive for as long as the memory lasts, the unbearable anger and the unbearable pain.

Around him, the kids of his age wasted time in cafeterias,

went apeshit in concerts, exchanged millions of kisses, used up condoms by the bucketful, studied for university, fought about offsides and penalties, went through the city on protest marches about this and that.

Himself, at a distance from it all, faithful to his indictment of living, obsessed with the shovels. Untouched by small joys and positive events, excluding himself from the good and the beautiful, dutifully imprisoned in things unpleasant, seeking them out. Being sent a fabulous watch from Canada and never wearing it once, instead taking it apart to the point of no return. Getting two A's in Physical Chemistry and in the next exam knowing the answers but turning in a blank paper. Having the mini-market owner's daughter giving him the eye and him turning sour and never stepping foot in the store again. Swimming in crystal clear waters and fearing that the crystal would shatter and cut him to shreds. Climbing a staircase and freezing halfway up for an hour, having forgotten the mechanism that makes the feet work, not knowing anymore how the knee bends, the sole lifts and touches down on the next step, three inches higher. Lying in bed and, just as he's about to turn his bedside lamp off, getting suddenly short of breath, forgetting the mechanics of breathing, how you suck in the air and expel it, his mind short-circuiting and him asphyxiating for Lord knows how many minutes. Having his grandmother bless him over and over, may the Virgin Mother be by your side, and it not working.

Linus was certain that from time to time, Viv was stewing in the same dark juice, turning her back on opportunities, organizing defeats, practicing her talent for frustration and long-term despondency. Mother and son filled with energy for misery.

If only he had one . . . two . . . three siblings to help carry the heavy nothingness and the abundant loneliness, more kids should mean smaller portions of orphanhood for each. If only he had three . . . two . . . one brother or sister as his ally in fear when facing the outraged or worn-out or absentminded Viv, in the courage needed to stop looking back all the time, in the appetite required for the coming day, so that a new day might arrive without him sitting with arms folded, waiting for the sky to crash down on his head.

***

Damn it, another sunny day, again the sunlight drenching everything, summer with no reprieve.

And the city full of girls called Amy, Lena, Aliki, Violet, Marina, Chryssa, Sylvia, what might be the names of two girls who get out in the heat wave, stroll this way and that, are still out in the streets at nighttime and at a late hour are crossing small parks by themselves, one in the suburb of Lykovrisi, the other on Strefi Hill, girls who have thin arms that can't throw a punch, thin legs that can't land a kick, whose hearts must skip a beat or two as they lose their bearings in the pitch-black alleys, few are unmindful of danger, few are unafraid of the dark.

– Get me some kitchen gloves, thick scrubbing wire for the pots and, what am I telling you for, it's all on paper on the table, it's a bunch of things, I haven't got the time myself, I have a delivery coming in today. Don't you forget again, it's not like you're studying or anything, you didn't even show up at the exams, I know all about it.

Viv had had enough of getting angry and pressuring Linus about his courses at the school, she had queried him a couple of times specifically, he'd made vague answers or none at all, you do as you bloody well please, she'd finally say to him, though her expression indicated she was giving him a bit of time to rethink his choices, it was just that she just couldn't modify her style and speak gently, her tongue had a will of its own. As she handed him the note and the money, she stood watching him button his shirt and thread the laces in his shoes, he was wearing the red-and-white ones.

– I threw away the other ones, he said straightaway without being asked.

– Why?

– Fungal infection.

He let her see the reddening in the heels and in between the toes.

– Fungus, already?

– I sweat.

Put some socks on.

When his mother lifted her shoulders to indicate his eccentricity was beyond her, he stood in front of her and said, slap me.

She picked up her bag in a flash, as if she hadn't heard, as if she didn't know what to do or was scared, and she fled.

Linus took to the streets a while later after soaping the red marker off his feet and, strangely enough, cleaning the bathroom, making his bed and washing the morning coffee cups.

Would he go to the supermarket to get the orders? He had the money and the list in his pocket, above him the sun zapping everything and around him the heat refugees, with bags and hats, guarding their eyes behind dark shades, looking dazedly for cool water in the kiosks or for some shade under the awnings of the shops, at 17 the silverware, at 29 the glassware, at 43 the frozen goods.

The girls, one by one in the to and fro of work, in twos looking for a cafeteria to sit down in and dissect their love interests, in groups of four and five at the bus stops with the wrapped straw mats under their arm and the large bags in which could be seen the multicolored beach towels, made for nakedness and for lying on the beach.

Should he also go to one of the city beaches: Varkiza, Vouliagmeni or Sounion? He went round and round the same streets of his neighborhood till it was afternoon, went into ten coffee shops to use the toilet and get a drink of water, bought an ice cream, ate half of it, if that, at around seven, worn-out, he made a stop at a children's playground.

He shared a bench with a grandpa looking after two grand-children, the kids were few, almost all of them fat, the children had started putting on a lot of weight, they slammed them-selves on the seesaws which couldn't lift under their weight, their bottoms barely fit in the swings, half of them broken.

He went behind a bush and retched yellow-green bile, went back home without the shopping, locked himself in his room for two days, drank water out of a vase, Grandmother had sent him cheese and roses from the village and Viv had put a cou-ple in his room, like big pink cabbages.

His mother didn't notice a thing, she thought her son must have been out and about while she was at the shop.

– Where were you and how come you're so beat-up, did you get into a fight and is that why you can't be reasoned with, you forgot the shopping again, you ate out again, so all my efforts to feed you properly are in vain, you could at least have put the okra back in the fridge.

For two evenings and three afternoons her phrases could be heard from the kitchen or outside his door, one per hour, or even a couple in succession, although she didn't insist, she'd toss them out and then go about her business and would leave again or turn on the TV, so there's some semblance of life in this house, she would say to herself out loud, the Greek and the Turkish prime ministers in Madrid, the pharmacists' strike, concerts and ads, until everything and everyone was giving her a headache, she turned down the volume, I'm going to read, she would loudly declare, she would go to her room again to fondle her books, the *Memoirs of the Eunuch of Abdul Hamid*, with the book marker on page twenty-seven since last year, Umberto Eco on the mass media, page thirty-two since the year before last, some title by Ernesto Sabato on page sixty, Chapter IX, since time immemorial.

Linus watched them creep from her bedside dresser to the kitchen table, to the small table in the hall, to the shop, to the car, always the same titles plus the new charters of wisdom which Rhoda dumped on her girlfriend in vain, the covers divided into two categories, on one side, high speculation, genocides and pogroms, on the other, female characters, alone, sometimes in a deserted square, sometimes on a dock, always in a wilderness of some sort. His mother's mottos, don't lose my page number, and, let me read my book in peace.

On the second night of his self-incarceration, the phone rang, after a while she called out, come over here, Rhoda wants you, he neither came over nor answered, but he could hear her for some time chatting away to her girlfriend about him, I'm at a loss with Linus, about her finances and her blunder with the tax declaration, next about the new car tires, then about the *Glory of Byzantium* at the Metropolitan Museum and the Highbrow's triumphant visit to New York, and then about men, and he could make out some of what she said, there isn't a single one worth giving the rest of my life to, telling him with all my heart, even asking, come on, you, get me old.

His mom was a natural, she could both deliver a lecture and sum it up, always hit the final word on the head, make the strongest impression.

Detestable and trite women, the vile Highbrow and the vile Sourpuss, misery and company, he sealed his ears not to hear them infest the nooks and crannies of his mind, but he couldn't save himself from the thousands of dry pine needles that appeared out of nowhere and started burning in front of his eyes so that all of him sizzled and smoked, a burning bush.

He was thirty and in pain, in pain.

He stayed in his bed for about two hours with the light off and the evening noisiness of the neighborhood invading the open window, TV's set outside, musical shows and hits and applause, small talk across balconies, irrepressible snickering on the terraces, children's screams on the pavements.

Past eleven he got up, dressed, put on shoes and on his way out he called to Viv sitting still at the balcony door airing herself with the TV program, don't you pine, mother dear, I'll do you the favor, I will get you old, even before your time.

***

I'd say she's getting it out of her system. Because when she was little, we never got a squeak out of her. As if she wasn't in the house. As if she didn't live with us. I look for her with my mind in those times long ago and I can't find her. I almost don't remember her.

His grandmother's words about his mother, one afternoon, over a month ago, after two hours of fire and brimstone, Viv's lungs were trumpeting the paeans of wrath and her tongue was unfurling the papyrus of the maternal commandments, all aimed straight at him, isn't it about time you cut out the adolescent atrocities, time for some sense to start gelling, to get some training, plan ahead, get on your feet as a man?

Nowadays, he saw right through his mother's yelling, her anger about her hollow power, her worry in case her words meant nothing to him, sometimes uncertainty, too, in case she'd chosen the wrong way to sound the alert, to open his eyes and, simultaneously, prove her affection. From time to time, she seemed to realize she was overdoing it, carried away by her love of criticism and her sharpness of vision when it came to others' defects. Thus, she would make her feelings plainly known at the end, lighting a cigarette, taking two or three puffs and slowly spelling it out, I forbid you to doubt that I worship you.

That afternoon, as soon as the old woman left and the abrupt silence in the apartment foretold of yet another hard evening, Viv had approached Linus gingerly, in case he pushed her away violently, reached out her hand and stroked his hair as he sat there, gazing at her wrist. There were several white splotches, small ones like lentils and smaller ones like pinheads, she'd spent Sunday painting the railing and the iron table on the balcony.

After a while, he pushed her arm away.

– I'll go and shower, then get you some watermelon, she told him. This summer's first, it turned out red and sweet, hail to the gypsy I got it from. It should be cold by now, I put it in the fridge in the morning.

In twenty minutes when you come back, all freshened up, with the watermelon platter and two forks, your son will be gone, again without good-bye, that was what Linus decided that Sunday dusk and as soon as he heard the bathroom door close and the shower running, he got up.

Spending Sunday evenings at home was fraught with danger. With the store shut, his mother considered she should make use of the available hours to point out his laziness, which she did unremittingly, but on that day she outdid herself for the sake of her mother, she'd fucked his grandmother's Sundays as well. Poor grandma, for your own good, hurry up and die, get a heart attack, the old man could get it from you, too, you could both snuff it, better not be around when your grandson's great hour arrives.

Every piece of earth has its own sky, the old woman's weird farewell comment, the elderly couple keep coming up with stuff like this, it's their bread and butter, it takes two millstones to make flour, whoever doesn't have old folks buys them, blood sings true, no end to that shit.

He was hovering like a ghost that night over the familiar ground of his suburb, mountains of rubbish because of the strike and the blonde TV presenter loved by all of Greece screaming at him, *Welcome to our show*, chasing him from street to street out of the TV screens of the ground-floor apartments and him making his getaway and hurting mightily somewhere inside of him, one hundred meters down into his body. He leaned against a wall, took some breaths, thought about what his grandmother might be thinking about her daughter, he thought of her leaving in a cab, like a stranger, taking the bus for the village on her own, she would have arrived by now, she would have fed her old man tea and lies, everything's fine in Athens, she'd be in bed by now, lying awake on her back.

He tried to get himself to miss the village, the two mammoth rosebushes, his grandfather's pride and joy, the fried eggs straight out of the chook pen, the strolling under the citrus trees and the frolicking on the beaches, he tried to be a thirty-year-old with his own job and car, a forty-year-old family man with a perfect wife, two perfect children and financially secure, all his efforts in vain, he didn't have the infrastructure for good as others understand it.

You can have your perfect lives and keep them, dear relatives, acquaintances and assorted fuckers, he was the plaything of evil, which at first drew him against his will but was slowly turning him into its lackey, he'd be walking the streets and his own piece of sky rained bile, his own piece of earth, the whole city, an ignominious stench, hey, godmother, why don't you get pregnant yourself, Rhoda's odious rodent.

The next watermelons went uneaten as well, day in, day out, under the sweat of the hostile house, night after night under the dictatorship of summer, June ended, the immodest July in full deployment, full of female mercenaries of lust, tourists and locals with their lethal shorts.

What did he have against those girls he didn't even know? They might even not be real, it might be his imagination constructing the bodies and the flimsy clothing and pushing them at him in waves when darkness fell on the neighborhoods and night sank into his chest.

Sunday, thirteenth of the month, a five-hour pointless meandering, with him buying water, cigarettes, ice cream, pissing in cafeterias or against walls, with his eye roving wherever a solitary female was to be seen.

At ten at night he left the main street, crossed the next busy thoroughfare as well, went past white women and black women, young ones and old ones dillydallying at street corners and blocking the narrow pavements.

He once again took to the narrow streets where there wasn't a soul.

– Your ID card.

The cop appeared in front of him very suddenly, he must have stepped out of the patrol car that had pulled up a few feet back, the bored driver looked on, stroking the circumference of the steering wheel.

Linus presented his ID, he asked nothing, nor was he asked, he remained still to be scrutinized and heard the two policemen say, he's Greek, let's go get a coffee and then get back out.

The ID check took place at a remote intersection, the police car turned right, Linus continued to the left, unperturbed, with his backpack on his shoulders and hands in his pockets, in one, along with some paper bills, the green frog, which couldn't care less about the money, hopped out and started its leaps in the air, with its owner's palms for springboards, rhythmically, just like the juggling of the two shovels, and numbered too, he had counted the shovelings then, there had been thirty-seven, one every five or six seconds, he'd even noticed a long white worm squiggling in the dirt in one shovelful and a piece of yellow wire hanging off in another.

The kiosk in the small triangular square was open, he paid for another two waters, drank one, put the other in his waistband, it fitted fine, he had lost weight. He turned into another side street, nobody, followed a pack of mongrels, became one with them, he barked at the black leader, barked at the gray second-in-command, they, too, barked at him, he whined at them, they whined back, he ran with them for three hundred feet, they got away, alone again, he walked along streets named after the school poets, Palamas St., Polemis, Filiras, Krystallis, his father's favorite, Ritsos, was missing, you are a snob when it comes to poetry, Kolevas, that was his stupid literature teacher in high school, go take a hike, you moron, he made himself comfortable at somebody's doorstep, the house was all shut and the garden dry, they must be on vacation, Mykonos has opened, Sifnos has opened, welcome one and all.

Why not leave forever, somewhere far away, where he wouldn't know anything or anyone? The unknown is fearsome but not painful. He lit a cigarette and went to the other side of the world, to Peru. He lit a second and was over in New Zealand, on the third he stormed the Sahara, on the fourth he swept over Siberia, every drag one thousand versts, he tunneled through the forests, lost himself in the tundra, burrowed in the snow.

He was shivering again. Around him the outlines of buildings, trees, a few parked cars, were all flickering. A two-story house bumped into a three-story, a white apartment rolled into the garden next door, a dusty kindergarten bus was dancing with a stone fence, the poplars were sailing on the walls, the dead cigarette butts were swaying around his shoes. All those moving surfaces made him dizzy, the night's motion destabilized him. His chest creaked, he felt his own heart come unsheathed and slide to the left and right, felt it scuttle across his belly. He heard his blood pumping forcefully through his veins, tumbling inside him with a whoosh.

At sixty feet to the left a stray dog evaporated in some bushes, at eighty feet to the right a bicyclist was being pulled back and forth by an invisible string.

He shut his frozen eyelids and inside the suffocating small space of his eyes, two holes half an inch across, the party started again, gorges flipping sideways, waterfalls overturning, vineyards barfing, lakes staining, quarries getting soggy, mud reeking, an orgy of foul smells that turned his limbs to stone on the steps of the strange house, an Armageddon of piss and shit that soaked his head, making it droop on his chest, as heavy as an iron barrel, dripping on his shirt.

Why was this happening to him?

He got the idea into his mind that he had no mind. The box at the top of his neck was hollow, there wasn't anything there that might offer an explanation, might resist, whoever felt like it could walk in, then walk out whenever, leaving there their kids, their horse, their cigarette butts, a head that was an unsecured place, a stable and a garbage dump.

He took the fur shapka out of the backpack, caressed the soft fur, ill-suited to the summer of everyone else, perfectly suitable for his own freezing temperatures, the snowy Himalayas in his gut. He put it on crookedly, leaning to the left, so it at least kept one ear warm.

He stayed like this for a while, alone, the dogs and the cyclist gone, no one in sight, no cars coming through. He pulled the plastic bottle out of his waistband, drank all of the water down and threw the bottle over his shoulder, heard it crash and roll a bit on the verandah of the house. Then he bent, undid his shoelaces, pulled them off, scrunched them up and shoved them in his shirt pocket and got up.

***

Stars, shadows, asphalt, marble bust, jasmine, *Eva*, windowpanes, locks, Papadiamantis St., mailboxes, meowing, street signs, uphill, church, downhill, lottery shop, Polydouri St., iron railing, shutters, watering systems, climbing plants, insects, panting, vertigo, the night is climaxing and I need to move cautiously.

Linus, disoriented, felt like he was being watched from behind, not by cops or by a couple of unsleeping mongrels crawling along on the cracked cement and worn-out flagstones, but by the houses which turned towards him as he passed, the cypress trees which machine-gunned him with their cones and the closed kiosk which started following in his wake.

His was a familiar face, they had caught sight of him in his previous night patrols and they were suspicious.

He walked on, took a turn, turned again. Arched gates and more arched gates and, behind them, four- and five-story buildings. Their rooftops sixty feet up in the air, that should be enough, he estimated. He tried one, two, three front doors made of glass, they were locked. Maybe break one? It'll be noisy. He picked out a wooden one, heavy and imposing, eight squares with brass hoops, his father could have carved it. He rang some bells, no one answered, they were probably away. The last one did answer. Who is it? A male voice.

Linus made himself scarce, he saw from a distance two lights come on at the third floor balcony and a chunky guy in boxers leap to the railing, bend and scan the ground, call in an angry voice, who's there at this hour? light a cigarette and patrol back and forth while he smoked it.

He went farther up the street, cautiously. He saw himself climb on the balconies of all the penthouses, Linus times twenty, two dozen copies of him letting go, floating like feathers, waving good-bye to one another, a school of wind-borne Linuses on a reconnaissance flight, until they settled down on bushes, pavements and the asphalt to sweetly sleep for eternity on this never-ending night, night forevermore, everywhere and over everything, darkness recycling itself invincibly.

He pissed on them and left them behind.

Going to sleep wouldn't help, on waking he wasn't going to behold what he deeply wished for, a brand new city, buildings, streets, places and people that would not confirm his life to date, that would not carry anything over from yesterday and the day before and last year and the year before and ten and twenty years before that.

Not again the number one question, what the percentage is of kindly souls and vile ones, and question number two, how many today are bosom buddies with how many.

He pressed a button in his head and everything went blank, the place emptied out, he walked on for some time in a void, a dot on white paper, a cursor on an empty screen. After a bit, he had the sensation that his shoes were sinking, his course on the bare expanse was a trek on the surface of gigantic, swollen gums that was taking him to an abscessed hill, the ugly smell of pus assailed his nostrils.

He hadn't had anything to eat, his stomach and innards a knot, two mosquito bites on the face, aching, skin irritations in the back of his neck and armpits, itching, unwashed hair, his scalp tingled.

I'm going for my first swim, it flashed into his head, I'm going on holidays, right there and then Piraeus lay before him, it was Friday afternoon, two months previously, end of May. Cars and motorcycles in line for the ships' holds, a crowd heading off to the islands and him, with no suitcase, yet another day of playing truant from his exams, the course was Information Systems in Private Business Administration.

He didn't have his father to say to him, this is one big water, like that time when they'd swum together in the sea of Akoli, he didn't have a girl or friends to go with him for three days or three weeks or three months to an island, he bought a ticket to Paros, there, he was going to suck in a ton of seawater, till he reached bottom, riddled with problems as he was, suddenly, the sea bottom seemed like perfect freedom to him, weeds dancing, fish strolling carefree, a lovely documentary. He got on the boat, in the lounge fifty-year-old women on the decline were fanning their wrinkled necklines, on the deck horny teenagers were rubbing up against sickly sweet dorks, all the uncouthness of the pleased, he bent over the railing and threw up, yelled out, you motherfuckers, and got out in the nick of time before departure.

So much for the refreshing sojourn, so much for swimming and plummeting into the deep of Paros, full steam ahead now for the homeland, where he would be welcomed by the money for the charnel house, Buddy's collar without Buddy, the phone that didn't ring, the house that wouldn't cool down and, unfailingly, the stupid rituals that went on and on, every Monday night he would eavesdrop on the two hags, mother and godmother, mulling things over and over on the balcony, first subject himself, orphan prince, baby boy, sweet wee thing, one of a kind, ragamuffin, charmer, lazybones, good-for-nothing, wonder how many he's done it with, mark my words, boys need to be pushed towards women or they turn queer, it won't do for our pretty boy to gallop around at night without bit or rein, second subject how much garlic and how much onion in the summer diet of veggies in the oven, third the curtains, curtain rods and assorted accessories, fourth Marlon Brando and his lecture in Athens about the environment, fifth Highbrow's announcements about the upcoming tragedies in Epidavros, sixth bonsai, which is to say poppycock in miniature, they identified completely in their disillusionment, his mother's with the Magyar violin player, his godmother's with a Kurd construction worker.

He would slam the door and off he'd be, out again, alone.

All night and all day he walked around delirious, sidewalks, train cars, buses, his ear picking out triumphant cries about the fucks of the century, about community funding and community programs, about graduate and postgraduate diplomas, about country houses and second country houses and, week by week, noting everywhere the decline of stamina, the sun more bent, the clouds discouraged, the darkness a burlap bag for the dried-up city, the neighborhoods with no pulse, the women without the guts to resist, swans that can't be bothered spreading their wings, zebras that can barely drag their step along.

The blue-purple abscess ready to burst, an evil inflammation covering everything like a lid, even over the ones already six feet under, even over the sovereignty of the dead.

Where was he now? Who's the jackass who's printing those maps without gums? What irresponsible motherfucker isn't sweeping up the stench?

His shirt reeked. He unbuttoned it, took it off and threw it away, went back, took out the laces from the pocket, held them tightly in his hand, walked a bit and suddenly he stopped, his antennae were signaling.

At sixty feet was an orange phosphorescent dress.

The lucky one was walking through the night alone, in a hurry, was giving a solo performance at a slight trot, one-two, leaning to the right, pulled by the weight of two red plastic bags.

The colors attracted him, a bird of paradise and the hair blond, hateful. He stood up straight, picked up his shirt, smoothed out the creases, made it presentable, in half a minute he was hurling himself onto center stage in the lead role, he found his rhythm and the pacing and forged ahead for the hat trick.

THE SHOELACE

The victim, eighteen, had finished her shift at the ice cream parlor where she worked at shortly after midnight and had gone out with a girlfriend for a drink. She was found in a clump of trees off a main thoroughfare at five-thirty in the morning by three Albanians, a father and two sons, on their way to their daily wage. Round her neck a black shoelace was tightly wrapped. On the ground, next to her, were a small purse with her wallet in it, intact, and two red bags stamped with the name of her workplace, Alaska, in the one, packed ice cream cones in the other, two dirty aprons and a book with recipes for sweets. The police had sent out search parties to hunt down the dangerous murderer-rapist.

That's what they said on the TV before the sports news and Viv Koleva chalked the event up to merciless July with its mean heat waves, the infuriating stolidity of public servants, the shop's drop in business and her brother-in-law's outright refusal to discuss the possibility of Linus's going over there on a trial basis, to change his surroundings and look for a more attractive course of studies, she'd pay for all expenses, naturally.

– First, get him to settle down and finish his school, then let the army iron the rest of the kinks out of him, and then we might look at a visit to Toronto, Canada isn't going anywhere.

– But orphans don't get drafted.

Sir would not budge. He stated that it was the worst possible moment for him to take on a guest for two months, or even for one. At home, the two babies were continually hollering, and so was her sister. Viv hadn't prepared the ground by first talking Xenia into it, her brother-in-law brooked no wheeling and dealing behind his back, he had a habit of turning rabid.

She wasn't even going to tell her sister about the phone call, Alifraggis's tone and his nerves about his wife's nerves disallowed her to make worse an already tense situation. The guy was a cannibal and a clown, Viv had a stack of evidence that her younger sister hadn't fared well.

– Vivika, at first he swept me off my feet with his lovemaking, battle ready morning and night, not like the one before who was forever blaming the political situation, was driven to anxiety attacks by the illnesses of his beloved prime minister, was wrecked by the backstabbing within the Socialist Party.

Later on, the things Xenia divulged about her husband's sexual practices took a dramatic turn, he bounded on the bed, he stood up rotating like a helicopter that's lost its propeller, about to crash to the ground and go up in flames, or he fell on her like a tractor and excavated her insides till she was turned inside out while, after her second birth with the known outcome, he crashed into the house like a truck with faulty brakes and fell in a swoon on the bed as if in a ditch.

– Does he drink? Viv had asked.

He didn't drink.

– Does he beat on the babies?

He didn't beat them.

– Has he made peace with having daughters instead of sons?

He was reconciled with the situation, he loved the girls, they were, perforce, his life's guiding principle but, according to Xenia, having had his peace and quiet till the age of forty-five, he needed a period of grace to adapt.

It was probably better that the beast declined Viv's request, Linus, beast number two, wouldn't see eye to eye with him for even a week, Canada would end up in tatters, in any case, she had inquired into that possibility as well, had given it a shot, had done her duty. So much for Canada.

Now how was she to pass the rest of the bloody evening?

Again the TV with *Everything you wanted to know about sex*? Again on the balcony drinking by herself a lemonade or a beer? Again polishing the pewter Giselles and the tin Presleys? Again waiting for her son and revving for a stylish argument or, better still, a grand confrontation?

She wasn't feeling hungry but, standing still in the kitchen, in front of the small window, she started thinking of pumpkin recipes, not because she was fond of that winter vegetable or of cooking, that's just what happened to come to mind, the trick of multicoloredness, spending some restful time among the crates with vivid colors, bright yellow pumpkin, bright red tomatoes, bright green spinach, it's a proven fact that no food is gray.

She decided to do some laundry, went to the bathroom, emptied out the basket, picked out the dark ones, there were more of those, mother and son were predisposed toward the deathly colors, no flower children those two.

Turning shirts and T-shirts inside out, on the inside of the collar of Linus's black T-shirt of yesterday, she found three tiny spots of blood. Her son wasn't hirsute, had no need to be shaving his neck, she thought mosquitoes must have got him and then he must have scratched. She went to his room in search of more dirty laundry, she first plugged in the mosquito zapper with a fresh tablet on it, she gathered a dirty pair of jeans from the chair, turned those inside out as well, emptied the pockets, small lighter and bus tickets, a melted piece of candy, a wafer wrapping, four blue tops from water bottles. Her palm filled with refuse. She made to go but didn't. She went down on all fours, peeked under the bed, sometimes she found there stray socks and crumpled underwear. She lifted the bedsheet, there you go, two empty cartons of chocolate milk, more rubbish, looked further in and her eye caught the weights, she would see them in the balcony basket whenever she raised or lowered the tent or mopped outside, always under Linus's specific order, don't mess with my stuff.

She pulled them out, they'd been washed, another season, or half of one, of exercise and bodybuilding aspirations, ha! ha!, she thought, pushing them back to their place and then noticed, right behind them, his sports shoes, even better hidden than the eight-ounce weights. She tried to reach them with her hand, failed, then reached and dragged them out with her foot.

On part of the length of the right shoe were stuck bits and pieces of some dry weed, some kind of a bush-leaf and two wheat fronds.

On the left shoe there was no shoelace.

Just then she heard the key in the apartment door, leapt to her feet, barely had time to lower and smooth out the bed-sheet, her son didn't like her to look through his things and spy on his kingdom.

Holding his jeans, she bumped into him at the hallway. He had a silly brown handkerchief wrapped around his neck, evidently bought today, he had never ever worn anything so dumb.

He noticed her puzzled look and she his, eyes like caves.

– Are you going to lock yourself in the bathroom or should I go put some washing on? she said to him in lieu of good evening.

For half an hour she listened to the water run, endless quantities of it, so she knocked on the door, just do the body for now, will you, leave your soul for later.

Waiting for an answer, any kind of an answer, she looked down, Linus had left his Gestapo boots and his socks outside the bathroom door. She stood gazing at them deep in thought till his lordship came out, she squeezed past him, stuffed the jeans in the machine as well and pressed the buttons.

In a bit they were sitting wordlessly in front of the TV, he with a Greek salad, she with an untouched peach, she was looking at him as if he were a time bomb and every two minutes checked her watch. For one whole hour she and her son competed in who was going to stress the other out most. An intense word-fight gives you a headache, a prolonged silence intimidates.

They so studiously avoided looking at each other or speaking that the evening became leaden, virtually terrifying, as if they were about to do each other harm.

Linus caved in first, left the tray on the table, had only had two slices of tomato. He ran to his room and locked himself in as if fleeing from someone with murderous intent.

Viv turned up the volume, again the winter serials, again the news broadcast, she mechanically watched it all again. She couldn't find something to think about, to plan, to remember, her mind, used to digging things up and keeping busy, was searching for any old subject but, rather than leaving it unfettered to bring her bad tidings, she might as well dictate herself its nightly program.

It's July and we haven't been to the sea once, neither of us, she thought, and immediately amended, "us" is used for couples, the party in question was neither me nor my son, the fruit of my loins.

So, then, not even one swim, wet bathing suits, reddened shoulders, dry salt, seashells and sea breeze, splashing and revelry, this and that and right there was her subject for the night, the wondrous children's questions, summer at the village, fifteen years ago now.

This is a great big water, her boy astounded and a little intimidated, refusing to wade into the endless sea for Fotis to teach him how to swim, after trying everything, Viv bodily carried him into the water and delivered him to his father's arms.

The world above is empty, another of his verdicts about the

sky, which had no houses, grew no grass, presented no movement of people and cars. The silence is very great, bigger than a mountain, his hesitant comment some nights when the grown-ups, scattered in the yard and at a distance from one another spoke neither to him nor among themselves, each bent to the plate with their slice of watermelon.

The sea's gone, a phrase that told of his relief when, at last, they were on their way back to Athens.

Willfully affixed to the village years, she protracted her stay there for quite some time, garnering images from her own childhood as well and, for the first time, she realized that she went through them tightly clutching in her palm a small unripe lemon.

She'd picked out a bushy lemon tree, she drew lots or she chose the companion lemon with eenie meenie miney mo, cut it and, until it got too scratched, rotted away or turned watery, she went about in the yard and along the dirt roads, to the grocer's, to funerals, to school, always clutching the lemon in her small hand.

Often in class she stuck her head in her schoolbag and in a whisper informed her little green mascot, the teacher has three drops of piss on his crotch, Eleni just farted and accused Petroula, I purposefully broke the priest's umbrella, I secretly dug up the priest's wife's two climbing ivies, they won't suspect me, they think I'm so proper and quiet. At home, she lifted her blouse over her head, stuck her hands in, scratched with her nails the green peel and inhaled the fragrance.

Other times, she made her coat or the blanket or the curtain into a tent, carved eyes-nose-mouth on the lemon and, hidden from the grown-ups, the two of them exchanged long conspiratorial looks.

There were times when the lemon in her palm was enough to make her feel that she lacked for nothing.

My childhood was three hundred lemons or thereabouts,

she summed things up, my dowry of sourness for a lifetime, she surmised, subject closed and the night still held out, copious.

Seashores and pebbles, piss and climbing ivy, priests' wives and lemons, what else was there, for heaven's sake, that she could summon to keep at bay the missing shoelace from her son's sports shoe?

***

She was sitting in the driver's seat but her hands weren't touching the wheel. Viv Koleva was driving the car with her breath, going at medium speed along a road that cut a dry flatland in two.

Caravans of clouds were catching up with her, drafts of air were pushing her along, freezer-freighters overtook her, trucks with hay, semis loaded with apples, Datsuns with potatoes, busloads of people with special needs, motorcycles with helmet-wearing leather-clad drivers and schools of birds, long and narrow like arrows that whooshed and pierced the horizon straight ahead.

Suddenly, the car turned to dust and she was at the entrance of an unknown city, at night, with no lights.

The houses without bells, with no doors or windows, tightly packed, small and white, like candy in its box. She walked the narrow streets for hours, in a great hurry, anxious and out of breath because she had at all costs to be somewhere at a specific time, except she didn't remember where that was supposed to be. To the wake of someone dead? And who was that? To a name day? Whose? At a store opening? Which belonged to whom? At a play? But where?

Meanwhile, in her palms had sprung a bouquet of white roses, except this gift was of no help in remembering her destination because it fitted most every occasion. Whom could she ask about funerals, parties, premieres or other city events?

The streets were bustling, though empty of people, not a soul anywhere, only snatches of talk, dry coughing and the dragging and shuffling of shoes that belonged to no bodies, walking empty, with their shoelaces properly done up.

She woke up with her mind short-circuited and herpes on her lip. She dragged herself to the bathroom and heaved down on the toilet seat hating the day in advance, it wasn't quite day-time yet.

It's decided, the battle of life is won by those with inspiration. Everything requires inspiration, practicing a profession, balancing your bank account, whether large or small, making a relationship work, setting up a home, raising a child, rounding off the past, orchestrating friendships, weekends, Easter, every single phone call, how you'll make it through your day with integrity, how to have a nice nap.

She wasn't one of those.

Others taking it easy and Viv on the daily grind and in the vise of the Tax Department.

Others reserving a touch of mercy for the defense of this or that thing from their childhood years and she beating things to a pulp.

Others conceding to reminisce, for instance, over some fervent nights with an Ionian islander at a student flat downtown, she keeping her distance.

Others receiving succor through heavenly embraces, she making do with mediocrity.

Others celebrating children that were state-of-the-art, Viv getting near heart attacks over her one and only dismal son.

The same scenario, over and over, since she trained her sights on trouble the way others train theirs on a jeep or a yacht.

She put the laundry out to dry, got dressed, left without eating.

At the shop, later, she had five coffees. The shitty thing on her lip tripled in size, it burned and smarted. From nine till two, the only two clients who came in the store to buy gifts for their young nieces at the country didn't find Viv's service of the usual standard, herpes is an alarm bell that your immunity is down, the first and eldest gently chastised, the second one, sour-faced, messed up all the thingamabobs on the shelves, turned the store upside down and, having whiled away her morning, left with a ballerina on a key chain, cheapest item in the store.

The noon paper was bought but left folded on the table, next to the cheese pie also bought but left to grow cold, untouched in its paper bag, while Viv watched in a daze the few midday passersby, a short, proud big-assed woman strutting like a partridge, a poor black carrying two bundles, his head hung in the heat like a lamb's head on the spit roast, two baby girls watching in awe an old man winding his old-fashioned watch, children are mostly amazed with the past, as far as the future goes, they have no questions.

The afternoon was highlighted by a flamboyant fag who bought a heart-shaped pillow silk-screened with two ballerinas, by two kids, bosom pals obsessed with wind-up Michael Jacksons doing the moonwalk and where could they find such a thing, and by a call from Rhoda, another three-day cultural retreat, the Nile, river boats, Crocodile City, oasis of Fayum, the savanna of Antinoos and an Egyptian lover breaking his own records in bed, night after night.

How is the devil's lamb, how's my godson? she asked in the end, she had brought him posters and videotapes with camels, piranhas and serpents, we have in our hands neither communist nor artist, it remains to be seen if his body's central circuitry is wired like his father's who did make you swoon, Viv sweetheart, that much he did do. Of course, Rhoda was well apprised that Linus was over his childhood whim of exploring jungles and living in the tropics but anything to do with Africa is just the thing, especially for wild young men's summers, that was how she put it.

After Rhoda's bye-bye, girlfriend, talk to you again soon, Viv didn't replace the receiver, she called the gym, she'd found the number in her old agenda earlier, should I call or should I not, she kept changing her mind, eventually she did, just before closing shop. Kolevas hadn't been in two years and if he hadn't been satisfied then, new pieces of equipment had been brought in and there were special offers on membership programs plus a brand new handpicked trainer, a Bulgarian, expert in building godlike bodies.

On her way home Viv brought three kilos of giant broad beans, she didn't cook those even in wintertime, went to the kitchen and emptied them in a large tub of water, as if she intended feeding a platoon after a day's march on snowy mountains.

Her son wasn't there but his boots were, the sports shoes were missing from under the bed.

She took out two steaks to thaw for him, she boiled him some corn, herself, she made do with an eggplant from the day before yesterday which she ate standing up, with no bread and no Parnassus feta cheese.

She brought in the dry laundry and set up the iron in front of the TV but didn't turn it on, she deliberated, she could afford to miss the news, besides, what news, it was the middle of the summer, boats delayed in their departure and how much hotels cost on the islands.

Placing the ironed clothes in the cupboards, she counted Linus's blue boxer shorts, five in royal blue, the color appropriate for encasing his family jewels, five, she'd bought half a dozen and she was sure her son wasn't wearing the sixth, he only ever bathed at night and she had given him a change yesterday with khaki boxers and a sleeveless top.

She searched the bottom of the wardrobe, caps, scarves and

gloves. She turned the laundry basket upside down, there were only whites, dishcloths, towels, her bras, his white socks with bits of dried weed. She loaded the washing machine, emptied the toilet bin, went to gather the kitchen refuse too, stale pieces of bread, peels, fruit pips, milk and fruit juice cartons.

The metal tip of the lace stuck out of a can of Coke, she pulled it and the whole of the black shoelace came out, with the fronds stuck to it.

Why had Linus shoved it inside the can, he who was so untidy, always leaving a trail of rubbish in his wake? She wasn't going to ask him. And she wasn't going to use it to tie the overflowing bag of rubbish with.

She saved the lace in her pocket, took the rubbish out to the street, and there was the prodigal son in the flesh, with his hankie, wearing his running shoe with brand new snow-white laces in them, they came up in the elevator together.

While he washed, she fried his steaks, turned on the TV, skipped the nightly news, found a spy movie, set the stage of a normal evening at home.

While he ate, distant and subdued, Viv avoided looking at him, she feigned being absorbed in the movie, at every explosion and shootout she even jumped in her seat exclaiming, God Almighty, and, will you look at that. Her thoughts, nevertheless, were on the ominous night before last, and on that ominous night before last, her son, probably without a girlfriend, certainly with no friends, had been out till dawn.

How could she even be thinking of something like that? Imagining atrocities about her own son, the very one who, as a child, was upset because the grown-ups beat up on olive trees with long sticks, pinched the poor sheep's teaties hard and didn't give the piggies proper food but their leftovers.

She reached and stroked his hair, he let her. She then walked her fingers gently through the hankie and touched a hint of a scab, at the front of his neck.

– What are you doing? Let me be, Linus bent abruptly in the opposite direction, where his mother's cloying fingers couldn't reach him.

– Your nodes seem a bit swollen, you're thin as a rake, she said and left the medical at that, rising urgently to carry his tray to the kitchen. On her way, she sneaked a peek into the bathroom, at his dirty clothes, the khaki boxers were there all right. The thing on his neck could be a hickey from some love-crazed widow or wife who saw her chance, gathered him in her boudoir, tore up his blue boxers, sucked him dry and then sent him on his way.

You don't say? And what about the lace, then? What was that there shoelace? What color? It hadn't come off a pair of moccasins, had it, now?

From the living room came the sound of ads for ice cream, insecticides and cockroach bait.

Viv slipped into the kitchen, put the tray down, stuck her hand in her pocket with the black trophy and stood looking, as if hypnotized, at the broad beans soaking.

Even when she heard her son go to his room, she stayed right where she was, staring at the pulse for hours, waiting for it to soften.

It was almost dawn when she started peeling and counting them one by one, she knew you're not supposed to peel them before baking but, at long last, her hands sprang into action, they'd found a way, the only one, for the night to pass.

And it did. At a quarter past six, she opened the garbage bin and emptied into it the white mound of skins and the four hundred and twelve white-fleshed broad beans.

***

Noon. The morning passed with cleaning the store windows, disinfecting the toilet seat and the small sink at the WC, soaping the small fridge, madly dusting the shelves' five hundred bits and odds and with a group of three idlers who came into the Tutu, took up Viv's time asking the prices of the flamenco dancer candlesticks and the belle époque aromatic candles and left without buying a thing.

Viv Koleva ran a disgruntled eye over all her ethereal ballerinas, stretching their limbs in unnatural poses that made you think of dislocated limbs and heads in deadlock.

At half past two, she turned her key in the lock, she was in no mood for home, sleepless and worn-out from the general cleaning, she felt her body defeated and succeeded in thinking only about her swollen toes and stiff back. She let herself wander, looking at shop windows to get ideas for more attractive merchandise, maybe beach towels with Travolta's mug on them, maybe sorbet glasses with ice-skating champions, she still had time to put an order in for some pieces, cheap stuff, gaudy and low quality, in case it worked in the massive heat and moneylessness of summer.

But how come she was saddled for all these years with such stock? What had come over her in her youth to get a store like this? Why didn't Fotis put his foot down? Why didn't they leave Greece to go live somewhere else and make their fortune? But then, what did the deceased know about business, he was perfectly capable of opening a fireplace business in Africa and selling swimming pools in Greenland, of importing wood to the Amazon and sheep to New Zealand.

Streets and more streets, the place churning under the stifling heat, the buildings shimmering before her eyes, the city a cooking pot of food that was turning to mush and was in danger of its bottom singeing.

She crossed paths with a big hirsute fifty-year-old man who looked like a German shepherd, she overtook a minuscule old lady with an off-white dress full of pleats that made her look like a poodle, she was given right of way by two youths dark and robust like Labradors, she pulled to the side to let pass a short-legged Filipino nanny who resembled a Chihuahua, dragging two kid-puppies, everyone reminded her of the poster with the canine breeds, the poster reminded her of Buddy and, naturally, Buddy brought Linus to mind with a vengeance.

Where was the masterless mongrel roving day and night? He didn't go to any kind of job, didn't go to the school, had no bosom buddies and there couldn't be a girl around since his face didn't shine and no smile appeared on his lips unprovoked, as when you are courting.

A square, two kiosks, three cafeterias, five trees. Completely worn-out by this time, she sat on an isolated bench under a straggly bitter orange. She lit up, counted the few pedestrians, the red cars, the black motorcycles, the dog turds on the flagstones, the occupied and the empty chairs under the tents, the Nescafés on the tables, until she was struck as if by electric current by a group tumbling from a side-street, six turquoise, yellow and orange miniskirts. The girls in the square were like fresh fruit in summer's platter.

They took an adjacent bench by storm, they straddled each other's laps, a heap of colors and thin limbs, a tutti-frutti of their interests, six mouths yakking at once about concerts and parties, bikinis and discounts, city beaches and island beaches, a George and a Tolis, they finished off about one Alex, took up one Danny, from there to the proficiency diploma of English, then a short round of personal deodorants, that's what young girls do, they tell each other everything, down to a T, they get all worked up and they settle down with the telling.

There was no chance, damn it, that they might mention one poor Linus, the girls had never heard of him. She wondered, was it him who'd sent Sylvia and Margarita off or had they been the ones to say, fare-thee-well? Did he fall in love with someone else, young, old, divorced, married, and who? And if not, will he ever fall in love again, and when? Why is he taking so long? Let him not delay further, the age of twenty needs plenty of lovemaking, the central switch needs to be permanently on.

The six lasses had now gone back to the chain of boys, Jimmy, Petros, Vaggelis, Leo, madly excited, they were going at it full steam ahead, teasing, stroking, kicking and kissing one another.

Viv Koleva turned her head away and her eyes skyward, another sight, another subject, balconies were something that might occupy her attention, perhaps immediately, perhaps very shortly. At the apartment building across from her, two narrow balconies were proper open-air galleries, tableaux with flower compositions, one dotted with gazanias like the mayor's flower beds, the other seething with basil and marigold, in the Peloponnesian style. Her own was how? Plain dismal. Tomorrow, she'd go at the crack of dawn to the open-air market to buy three flowering potted plants and, then, come October, she would take on the balcony as a whole with ten hanging jardinières and forty bulbs, tulip, hyacinth and daffodil, she would orchestrate next spring's surprise.

Is this me? she wondered. She didn't recognize herself.

Return to the gray house. Shops were closed for the afternoon, so she bought a newspaper and headed home as if this were her life's last itinerary, to the gallows.

She went up to the apartment, her son gone. Had a quick shower, swallowed two spoonfuls of marmalade, opened the paper, forced herself to become interested in international finance and Parliament's summer sessions and eventually turned to the two-page centerfold of local news.

Unsolved cases of the rape and murder of women, the Albanian girl who was identified by a birthmark on her elbow, the unforgettable bride-to-be, dead and surrounded by wedding bonbons that had spilled out of a box, the beautiful mother of twins, a nurse, on her way to her last night shift, the tragic incidents abounded, Viv devoured the article and, line after line about strangled prostitutes, carved up migrants and unsuspecting girlies found dumped here and there, she was greatly reassured.

The first of the nine open cases occurred thirteen years ago, when Linus was seven years old, and then when he was eight, ten, twelve and fourteen—except for the last one with the damned shoelace that had planted in her mind such horrific suspicions about her child.

Coolly now, she went over the common threads, all the victims were blonde, all the rapes and murders had been committed in summer, all in tree clumps and small parks, no beaches and no rocks, and happily, if not overjoyed, she, like the policemen and the psychiatrists putting together the madman's profile, arrived at the conclusion that the evidence pointed to one perpetrator who had been around for years, wreaking havoc.

The shoelace did confuse them somewhat. The crimes had not been committed in wintertime, when the man might have used a pair of pantyhose on the women, and in the last incident, probably, some noise made him flee before he had time to untie and retrieve the murder weapon, his own shoelace, since all the victims wore heels or sandals and the latest one wore clogs.

From old and recent statements by women who'd gotten away with their lives, and some who had escaped the rape as well because they'd run like hell, the descriptions of the veteran were understandably contradictory. The brute was both of average size and big, both thin as a spider and strong like a bodybuilder, his ample hair was both full of curls and straight, both blond and jet-black, and as, according to one witness, he roared and snarled incessantly, there was the possibility of him being a deaf-mute.

For Vivian Koleva it was now a child's game reading

through the smaller columns devoted to infamous perpetrators, to master rapists and to dilettantes of rape, and the statements of women who were working late and had to pay a cab to take them home since they didn't dare walk alone even for short distances. One of these, a natural blonde, said she was forced to dye her hair black. She finished with the call by police for more information that might contribute to the maniac's arrest, left the paper on the small table next to her and wondered, at long last, who those poor souls might have been, what names the mothers of the dead were calling out, maybe some of those mothers had set up small votive stands where their girls had been martyred, under the trees, their death preferred greenery, didn't much fancy the seaside.

I'm sending Linus for a swim in the sea whether he likes it or not, she said out loud, it suddenly seemed to her terribly important, we simply can't disobey the laws of summer. She wondered why whenever we think of rocks we always think of them in the range of gray even though, she told herself, there are rocks the color of wheat, of green almond, of unripe plum, rocks with scales of rust and with sardine skins.

She felt heartened, got up, pulled back her sleeves, mentally arranged the house chores in order of importance and counted them off on her fingers, first she would put chops and potatoes in the oven, second she would put music on, she would set out the table properly with the immortal turquoise tablecloth and her good set of immortal plates and glasses, and fourth, she would welcome her son no matter what time he came in, in a chatty mood, they could relax a little, shoot the breeze a little, enough already with the silence that was running amok.

With the potato peels, finally, the shoelace was also thrown in the bin and good riddance.

The imperial sunset touched the house with gold and Viv decorated the throne room for the imminent arrival of his highness, methodically and in high spirits. Her bones, normally a pile of rusty iron rods and corroded springs, unhinged and creaking at every awkward move, responded to the maternal alert like a brand new electrical appliance.

It must have been about ten-thirty, the music was rioting, tambourines and flying notes, when her son came home, filthy dirty and, evidently, having had a good cry, the tears still shone on his cheeks and there was a shiny trail of dry snot on his upper lip.

– What happened? Did you get beat up? What have you been up to?

He made no answer. He was standing in the middle of the room and his sorry state promised anything but the unfolding of the perfect dinner as planned.

Viv noticed his gaze, distressed, the irises tracking haphazardly left and right inside their yellow-white nests, enlarging like black stones and being hurled at the unexpected preparations and the lugubrious setup. But also at the open paper on the small table. He rushed over and stood above the paper's main spread.

Now, Viv didn't much like this development, it had been amiss of her not to put away the newspaper with its varied atrocities, she did so now, closed it, folded it, the two needed to focus on their stuff, to find a way to breathe easy.

– I've turned the hot water on, she told him.

– Give me the car keys.

– The chops will get cold.

– I want the car.

– There's ice cream as well.

He looked at her dumbfounded.

– The car, he said again in a faded voice.

– No can do. I need it.

She came up with an excuse, despite the late hour, she would be making a delivery to an aged client whose daughter-in-law was picking her up in the morning to spend the summer day at Sounion, she had promised she would drop off a feng shui ballerina.

Some packets around the house were proof of her claims, normally she'd take those to the indisposed and those accustomed to being taken care of in the next few days, there was time.

Nevertheless, Linus didn't stick around to be informed of the details about feng shui and Italian porcelain, he'd opened her bag right there and then, had lifted her six fifties, and was out the door, Viv heard the elevator going down.

She went out to the balcony, just in time to glimpse him turning the corner. She stood frozen, till the music gave up on her, too, CD over, dead silence. She lit a cigarette staring at the windows across the street on the off chance she might forget herself in others' lives.

A mother was combing the freshly shampooed hair of her baby daughter, a fat forty-year-old guy, the Cypriot dental technician, was putting up a mirror.

She had the last drag and went in, looked at the food and the plates all set out, left them there.

Went to the rubbish bin, stuck in her hand, pulled out the shoelace, shook it, wound it up and put it back in her pocket.

She returned to the living room heavy, the wings she had spread earlier now withered.

She turned on the TV.

Bat-fish, cabbage-reefs, the oscillating frequency of sharks and striped pajama-squids.

***

Can't even get the coffee down. What coffee? She'd been making them by the dozen, at home and in the shop, spent all day and all night bent over the cup and the phone.

Her son had been gone three days now, hadn't called her, wouldn't pick up his cell phone.

From day two she'd been calling him nonstop, she memorized his number again which she had forgotten, Linus had forbidden her to chase after him, if the reason you got it for me is to be on my back all the time, you might as well keep it yourself, he had made himself perfectly clear.

Had he gone off just like that? He had. For how long? For twenty hours or thereabouts. The trip to Hepeiros and back on the bus, the first time he'd skipped school, at fifteen, the train to Salonika was the second one, a little after, on the way back he'd brought her a box of chocolates.

On the afternoon of the second day she called the Orthopedic Hospital, the Laikon, St. Olga's, and every other major hospital, nothing. Should she call the police? She rejected the idea, she was too frazzled, the words that might escape her could cause damage.

A coffee cup or a coffee glass? Sugar or no sugar? Viv Koleva began to know less and less, she was giving herself a headache as much for good reason as for no reason at all.

At some point, she swallowed her pride, called at Sylvia's and at Margarita's, she never threw out the old phone numbers, she played it cool. Their mothers surprised, almost annoyed and certainly abrupt, informed her that as soon as summer rounded the corner, the daughters had taken up island hopping with a vengeance, they well and truly needed it after all the studying, the former had demanded it after all the philosophy, the latter after all the German.

Whyever was she calling them? And whyever did she also call two old fellow students of his and then a third one, everyone whose number she had. One father confessed utter ignorance about his son's whereabouts, everyone else was away.

She called the village, fat chance that her one and only would run into his grandparents' arms, Viv did not ask specifically, she fished around, we are alive, her mother said, they exchanged greetings to those there and those here, they rang off.

And then, there was the newspaper buying at the kiosks, rifling through the car accidents in the countryside, dead and injured from motorcycle crashes, pileups, drunken driving, every one of those had a first and last name, no Linus Kolevas, nobody unidentified in case her son didn't have his ID with him. Did he?

She closed the shop early and ran home, looked through the pockets of his black jacket which had, by her son's decree, to hang winter and summer on the hallway rack, she went into his bedroom, found the ID in the desk drawer under tabs of anti-inflammatory pills, expired vitamins and loose batteries. Still, after making sure to lock the front door to the apartment from the inside, so the prodigal son wouldn't catch her in his room if he appeared suddenly, she continued her meticulous rifling through his videos, books and papers. Among the pages, the stub of a cruiser to the island of Paros, the date recent, an attempted holiday, which is to say wasted money, a bunch of cutouts of cartoons by famous satirist KYR and sketches by Arkas of pigs and roosters, pamphlets of foreign universities, a washed out black-and-white postcard from Stalingrad, verses about the dog, a photograph of Fotis, the one with the eyes swollen from alcohol and sadness and two mysterious letters from one of his sisters, when had those come and why wasn't Viv told? Why had the kid saved them? Why had his father given them to him or else where had he found them?

The first one, March 14, 1984, my beloved brother Fotis, only two lines this time, just so you have the time to read the following, I love you very much, in case you even glance at my letter before you throw it out—Kiki.

Which was to say, more letters had been sent. Had they been kept or thrown away? And to what address had the woman been mailing them for Viv never to have seen any in their mailbox? Under different circumstances, she would devote some time to weighing the matter up, though it was a frayed thing of the past. But this, now, was of no interest to Viv Koleva.

What was she trying to find? She recalled that a few days ago, Linus had thrown out two large bagfuls of stuff. Could it be that he was getting rid of evidence? Such as what? If it was him, he certainly wouldn't be holding on to mementos. No, it wasn't him, he wasn't the wanted veteran, he was barely twenty and besides, the room cleaning had taken place in June, it must have been June, yes, June it was, before the shoelace.

She lit a cigarette and scanned the pigsty. The hawk mother trains her chick, the bear her cub, the cat her kittens, herself, a bitch that taught her pup nothing worthwhile.

There was no denying it, her son didn't have the foundation for a normal development, the plaything of a terrible, silent rage, buried under a ton of mistakes, hers, his father's, grown-ups' in general.

She took the car keys, didn't know where to go, she drove around at random, found herself in the vicinity of the airport and fell on a hundred soldiers in camouflage gear, about to fly out to Cyprus. In groups, they were smoking, unwrapping sandwiches, softly singing, cracking jokes. Why couldn't her son be among them, the army edifies and smoothes out the rough edges.

She turned about and encountered another group, a dozen girls around twelve, lithe and porcelainlike, a team of synchronized swimmers, traveling to some competition. Why not have a daughter instead of a son, and she wouldn't even have to be like one of these heavenly creatures, she could be fat and awkward, girls are less trouble for a mother.

She went back home posthaste, the living room seemed arctic to her, she was shivering, she sank into the immortal couch, the stench assailed her from the perfect dinner that had been rotting on the table since the day before yesterday, in the immortal platter.

At midnight, she called Rhoda, with the surgery and the house calls and the rest of her activities, the Highbrow never went to bed before two. What could she say to her? The vileness and terrors that filled her mind? How do you utter such things? She whined about having had a fight and about her godson having given no signs of life for three days now. You didn't happen to talk? But we don't call each other up anymore, Rhoda started, cool to the point of insensitive, as every woman would be who does not have and does not wish to have children, she suggested not keeping him anymore, a grown-up man, so close to her skirts, to give him space and time to roam and act the barn rooster, come to terms with himself, and, at all events, to run out of the money he'd taken.

Good thinking, Viv put the phone down and went straight into a dead sleep, that was the only way to cut short the mind's milling about. At dawn, she had a one-minute dream which was inundated by the smell of rock melon, she got up saying out loud, as if delivering a speech to an audience, that to veer off course so unexpectedly, so dismally, was out of the question for the grandson of a martyred communist and son of a guileless and honest craftsman.

She cleaned up the sour food, put the house in order, wrote a note about where the Mitsubishi was parked, and left it with the keys on the hall table, just let Linus come back and he could have them and go wherever he liked with her blessings.

A good thing she took a taxi or she would have missed that fascinating cabdriver who cheered her up with his drama, in his first youth he boarded a tanker for a year, came off and got onto a freighter truck for two years, came off and burrowed into the taxi and ever since, one and a half million kilometers in thirty-four years, his whole life was taking place within two square meters.

The day was sparkling, the bouquet of the miniature red

roses she bought off the Indian vendor looked just perfect in the ballerina vase, the music boxes added the Tchaikovsky, she put up the lids of all twelve, there was her symphonic orchestra, the concert began and the shop took off.

Around eleven, the fugitive called, are you all right? he asked her, where did you disappear off to? she asked in turn, he said "bye" and hung up, at the very least she'd heard his voice, fine.

Having had her spirits restored, she sold a client who came in looking for something fancy as a courting gift to a belly-dancer, a gaudy bra with silver bells on it, left over from old stock, gave him a discount as well. Next was a sixty-five-year-old English-woman with a walking stick, barely managing her rounds of the shops in search of a Queen Elizabeth doll.

She had brought three over from London, given them to neighbors, now some other acquaintances were keen, the long velvet royal blue gown, embroidered with pearls, on a dresser or a cabinet always made a winsome display.

During the midday break, Viv did some accounting, since the Queen of England was popular, she decided to look into it, even though it had nothing whatsoever to do with dancing, she might be able to get a small production line going with some cottage industry somewhere.

In the afternoon business slowed down to nothing, her mind started to stray towards the seventeen-year-old blond daughter of the minimarket owner, the newlywed, white-blond baker's wife and the equally golden-haired Moldavian girl who made sandwiches at the corner fast-food place, she checked herself, there was no reason for her to poison her life with far-fetched and paranoid scenarios, it was established fact, our guy was a veteran.

She found the phone number of a sign-maker and asked how much a sign would cost, say sixty inches by fifteen.

She closed a little early, shopped royally for the house, filled the fridge with bacon, chocolate spreads, peanut butter, sweets and ice cream for when Linus showed up, it wouldn't do for him to come back unexpectedly, say, tonight, and not find all manner of treats.

But it seemed that the son who railed against money, calling it unconscionable but, in practice, had no issue with pocketing a handful of bills, was keeping track this time round and making his money last. Was he sleeping in a hotel? In which city? How much was he paying for a room? Single or double bed? Who with? Was some woman putting him up? Was he secretly frequenting her home and had now taken to sleeping there? And till when?

He came back after five days which weren't easy for Viv, who went through her ups and downs, especially when she was rifling the papers, thankfully no new incidents but no news either about the perpetrator's arrest, that's the police for you, instead of apprehending that unknown public menace, so she could get a reprieve from her mind's torment, they'd apprehended an ounce of cigarette butts at the locale of the assault.

It was past eleven when he unlocked the door and came in, his scalp shorn to the skin, a piece of burlap on his shoulders, like some Somalian or Nigerian border fugitive, his clothes stinking, extremely thin, with a piece of string holding up his trousers in place of a belt. He looked finished, old, and apparently the color of the eyes does also age, their once vibrant black had degenerated to the gray of mold.

He looked at her for a while with a weary expression, left on a chair his cell phone and five of the six paper bills and dragged himself off to his room.

In a bit, the zdoop and ghup sounds were piercing the walls, more and more rapid and sharp, a regular pneumatic drill of wretchedness.

***

Next morning, as soon as Viv heard her son heading to the bathroom, she lay in wait and when he came out, she took hold of him firmly by the arms, immobilized him and looked him straight in the eyes, all at once pleading and challenging him to talk.

No need to form the questions, they were self-evident, why were you keening for three hours last night, why wouldn't you open the door, where were you all these days, what did you live on, how come you spent no money, why did you shave your head, who's giving you trouble, what have you done?

Linus evaded all the questions and, closing his eyes, whispered.

– Mother, say exactly and directly what is on your mind.

Viv was taken aback. How could she utter exactly and directly what was eating her alive? If she was wrong, which she was 99% sure she was, having been duped by coincidences to do with the infamous shoelace, the remaining 1%, far from negligible, was shattering, Linus would never forgive her for suspecting him of something so barbaric, they weren't in a stupid TV serial, for him to just fluff up his bowtie, burst out laughing, pinch her cheek and scold her, why, you, silly little woman, best you went to a doctor, have some sedatives prescribed.

So she didn't speak. She went to the kitchen and spread out on the table everything she had in the fridge, eat, she called out in a booming voice, the whole apartment building must have heard.

Forget the shop and forget the business, Viv Koleva decided she wasn't going anywhere, in order to tie up her son in the house as well, he was bound at some point to break down and confess the nature of his trouble, some rival, maybe some woman's jealous husband, must have cornered him, some cheap twit must have insulted him for not getting it up, he might have been proselytized by some sect for the featherbrained, surely something out of all these, which for solitary and spoiled single sons would be the end-all, but for experienced adults is not quite to keel over and die for.

So, then, at home and later, if the kid had to go anywhere, she would drive him or, if he just wanted to get some fresh air, she would join him.

When it's all said and done, difficult children do need a helicopter mom, rushing to their side for emergency assistance and constantly hovering close by.

Then, she reconsidered the spoiled part. The truth was her hands didn't often touch her child, not when he was young and not when he grew up and her lips didn't kiss his hair much and her eyes didn't enfold him tenderly and her voice didn't come out in stories and gentle words.

The spoiling was done via her wallet and the deep fryer, a generous allowance and lots of french fries, till he finished high school the deep fryer was working overtime

The morning passed with Linus dramatically quiet in his room and Viv on guard in the living room, indulging in an orgy of businesslike efficiency, phone calls to two seamstresses, to a fabric warehouse, to the little shop-in-a-hole that sold trimmings, tresses and pearl beads and to a self-taught Pakistani Picasso who said yes to everything, he would take twenty plastic little heads, would attach gray hair and paint on the features of the English queen, he already had in his folio a successful Charlie Chaplin, a Mao Tse-tung and a Kissinger in figurine, bust and Halloween mask, respectively.

It was dusk when Linus washed, dressed and in the middle of the living room said out loud to himself, I keep imagining I'm someone else, someone I don't want to be.

In the hallway he read the note, threw it along with the keys to the Mitsubishi to his mother and opened the door, the yellow light from the corridor fell all at once on his bald pate.

Viv moved towards him.

– Don't you need some money? Shall I make you some french fries?

He pushed her out of the way and was gone.

Late that night, the two curtains of the balcony door paid the price.

Viv pulled them down forcefully, pulling and unhinging the curtain rod, an elegant handcrafted piece of Fotis. She took the large scissors and for two hours, with jaws so tight she almost pulverized her own teeth, she cut up the voile fabric into strips half an inch wide.

Past 3 A.M., knee-deep in a mire of white rags, she put the scissors aside, lifted her head, looked outside and concentrated on the moon's imperceptible march across the dark.

She didn't have the strength to get up. Or the will. She held her breath and closed her nostrils and her eyes to dive into the deep, till she reached the bottom of the night.

***

The dark extracts a high interest from daytime anxieties, those who've had a rude shock are likely to lose their bearings and get way out of line.

At midnight the next day, driving the Mitsubishi around neighborhoods with fenced or unfenced woodlets.

Viv Koleva was driving slowly, with one eye on the parked cars, up and down the narrow streets, watching her driving and the other, more lively, eye scanning the few pedestrians, couples and solitary men. No woman was out on her own.

Twice she went over to the hill of Strefi and the wooded parks of several adjoining suburbs, then back again. Large areas, a multitude of streets, several all-night places. She slowed down in front of cantinas and coffee shops in case she made out her son, she looked for him, she rounded three clumps and scoured his playground, to no avail.

She crossed paths with police cars seven times, the cops were probably out patrolling for pretty much the same reasons as she was.

If they are careful and smart they'll single out my car, she thought, if they stop me I'll say I couldn't sleep, chronic insomnia and a love affair gone sour, she put on a tape, a gift from Rhoda from the two months she was besotted with a gorgeous gypsy whom she'd saved from a heart attack, and whose family had inundated her with tapes and kilim rugs. At times like these, she wasn't interested in any song, there was no space in her ears for the lovelorn words and notes, as they were jam-packed with a stream of questions broadcast by her brain at breakneck speed.

She changed her course, different suburb, all-night kiosk, purchase of a pay phone card. Then, the next suburb down in the direction of the sea, back and forth in main streets and side streets, a park, a walking distance of three hundred feet to a phone booth that stood alone, no all-night shop or a park bench nearby, she wasn't a fool to be overheard by anyone, nor, certainly, to call from her home and have her number and address traced.

– I can't tell you my name, she said to the policeman that picked up when she dialed the number for emergencies. She mentioned the reason for the phone call, waited for a bit, the first line she was put through to was wrong, the second was right, to someone who was dry coughing as if he'd swallowed on the wrong side.

She stated that she occasionally worked in bars, here and there, she didn't name which ones. She stammered she had something like a relationship with a foreigner, gave no name, was afraid of him and of getting involved with the police, she had no intention of fronting up at the police station. Her man was an adventurer, out at nights, into drinking, into women, he had a soft spot for blondes, then he would go back to her with gifts of fur coats. The night in question he was out, came in at dawn, if they look for me you'll say I was with you the whole time, he ordered. She hoped it wasn't him. Am I in danger? she asked.

The officer asked her to meet him immediately, anywhere she chose. It can't happen, she repeated.

There were two coincidences. The passion for blondes and the guy's absence on the night of July 13. Probably the foreign nationality as well, no Greek had been spoken at the incidents.

– What else do you have? Viv asked in a shaky voice.

– You tell us. I'm not on the case. I am merely taking notes. His age?

– Thirty-eight.

– Hair?

– Blond, non-Greek.

– A lot of it and curly, by any chance?

– No. Starting to go bald. Are you looking for blond hair, lots of it and curly?

Of course he didn't verify it, he moved on to the rest of the questions.

– Does he work out? Does he wear sports shoes?

– The black shoelace that the papers wrote about was that from sports shoes for certain?

– Flat and long. Does your man have shoes like that?

– No.

– Fine. Furs you said. Russian?

– I cannot say.

– Does he own one of those Russian hats like Gorbachev and Yeltsin?

– No.

No? She put down the receiver with her heart thundering away and the blood shrieking in her veins. No? She made herself scarce before any police car turned up, in case they'd already traced the booth. No? Flat long lace, rich blond hair and now a Russian hat, the cherry.

Was all this the veteran's or his successor's?

When did she get home already? When did she look through wardrobes, drawers, cupboards, to locate the shapka, the damn communist cap of her poor father-in-law? She didn't find it. She found yellowing books with poetry by Ritsos and Rotas in a plastic store bag. She took them down, dusted them and threw herself into reading, certain that there were no verses there about rapists and no splatter poems either.

She needed to escape from the abysmal, the worst reality in which a person can find themselves, and if novels are not recommended for people with a lot on their hands and on their mind, poems are just the ticket, they can be read quickly, the words do not rile, their speech the opposite of Viv's and the way they spoke at her home, even the bitterest things are said considerately, and the somewhat unintelligible bits also have their place, nothing at all like the helter-skelter and the crossed communication of two people who could not even synchronize their "good morning."

The *rotten half-lemons shining like small suns*, the *mountains, lower yourselves, ridges, move back*, the *slaves have me as their beacon, the disenfranchised as their flag*, the *let me kiss your smile one last time, while I still have lips*, the *sunflowers that run, dance, gesticulate with cyclical fires*, and the *cut up the bread in even potions so that the sun rises*, landed her safely on the Sunday dawn.

She slept for three hours and woke up with ideas.

She washed, did her hair, made a double espresso, set up the slim tomes in prominent places, the small living room table, the shelf next to the couch, Linus's small desk, so he would bump, upon his return, into the labors of devotion to the good of humanity.

A new beginning, this was what was required for both, as a mother, she ought to support the venture, a 180-degree turn which would draw on verses of noble thoughts. Come tomorrow, she'd go into a bookstore and fetch down a whole bookshelf of the stuff.

Quarrels, bitterness, suspicions and evidence would be bygone, the past would no longer be an issue, and let the police numbskulls chase after Russians

Vivian Koleva even imagined her son as one of the zealots of the Communist Party, leading extended strikes and militant protests in front of the Parliament, and derided herself for the previous years of belittling his grandfather and father as suckers, the major one and the minor one respectively. From now on she would shut up and pay any price to see her son advocating for fundraisers and spending day and night selling buttons and putting up bill posters with the sickle and hammer, it would be a reprieve for her peace of mind.

Would you like us to become grape tomato growers? That, too, was an attractive proposition which she could put to him, enough already with the bloody ballerinas, she could close shop and sell the apartment, more than willing to fund an exodus to Evia Island, to the prefectures north of Attica, Fokis or Magnesia, to rent or purchase fertile lands and take up innovative and lucrative farming projects. They, too, could milk the infamous European Union funding programs which for a long time so many with acumen had been feasting on, she would set up the business for him within a five-year period and then she would discreetly retire and Linus, with a 4x4, would manage the fields and the bank accounts.

Why, oh why, did she poke fun in front of him, of those who suddenly discovered nature and left their law firms and advertising agencies in favor of hillside farms and the hoe? She again derided herself for the thoughtlessness with which she rejected, mocked, judged everyone and everything without ever considering what prompted people to sever their ties with their past.

She would be oblique, Attica is saturated now, Athens is

finished, the future has left downtown Kolonaki and moved to the mountainous north, to Roumeli, twenty thousand square meters are waiting for us somewhere there to get into action, you choose what suits you, whether oyster mushrooms, grape tomatoes or asparagus, they were all a great success at the vegetable stands, they would make him a man to be reckoned with. He could even become involved with local soccer, setting up games for amateur competition in the Fourth Division, she remembered how the boys in primary school were transfixed by the amateur groups of Panachaiki, Ikarus and Thunderbolt and derided herself a third time for being sarcastic with Fotis's soccer-loving comrades and the other soccer fan of Panathinaikos whom she used to entertain in her home and whom she had forbidden to infect her son with his soccer mania.

She had declared everything lacking, she doused the orphan's mind with disdain about this, that and the other thing and this was the result, a Linus without a part to play.

The house needs to become a home and for it to become a home, the walls require certain family photographs. She had never before framed progenitors and descendants, never put an album together, she didn't favor reminiscing while rifling or rifling while reminiscing as a pastime. She mistrusted every sort of immortalization, poses bothered her, the politicians' warm handshakes in front of the reporters, the philanthropic tycoons' next to people at death's door from bombs, epidemics and famines, the models' with the electric fans twirling their hair and their silks.

She didn't change her mind about the few of her own family, inside the shoebox she brought down from the loft where it'd been exiled among the spiderwebs and mouse droppings. In front of the lens, one, two together, three and five and fifteen at weddings and meals, she knew their lives, their trespasses, and their miseries inside out; none of the smiles could be justified.

Nevertheless, she singled out three, one the father-in-law, one the husband, one the dog, she emptied three frames from Plisetskaya, Makarova and Baryshnikov, a canceled delivery, and in ten minutes, grandfather, father and dog went over and stood on Linus's desk.

Did she have self-adhesive bandages and iodine in case she needed them later? Gauze? Aspirin? Viv Koleva checked the medicine cabinet and elsewhere too, she had what she needed to clean and bandage minor cuts and wounds, there was a full bottle of shampoo, two intact bottles with bubble bath. What else? There were food and poems in the house.

Sunday went by with no phone calls or TV. In the evening, eleven sharp, she went out to the balcony, leant on the rail and looking alternately down and heavenward, she reviewed scattered verses that were still in her mind. *To starry feasts and moonlit revelries, let the white sheets wear the dreams, oh, this exile within our own clothing that is fraying, this house can no longer carry me, I can no longer bear carrying it on my back.*

When she saw her son arrive, she finished her recitation with, *an ash-gray hat, empty, with no head.* The gray shapka, she said out loud and shivered, the curly blond hair, the shoelace, she added.

She went back in. Her chest hurt. She started a massage, soft circular motions which within a minute turned to scratching and punching. The poetry collections got their share, too, of shoves and kicks, books and picture frames ended under her bed.

They didn't so much as say good evening. She didn't dare come out of her room and he made his way to his, after having his shower as usual, mumbling out loud about the fucking stale bread.

***

She woke up sweating with her left arm numb.

She'd gone to bed having wrapped and tied around her upper arm the lace which was hidden under a long sleeve, just in case, she'd put on a winter nightie.

She couldn't afford to lose it, to misplace it somewhere in the generalized chaos of herself, a mind at times shapeless and distracted, at others in overdrive, combining a thousand thoughts, examining a thousand possibilities, and a body sometimes insensate and others overexcited, the hands spinning propellers inside drawers and chests, the feet spasmodically pirouetting along the length and width of the stage of those days.

Above all, she could under no circumstances afford for Linus to see the shoelace, if he came into the night to wake her up for some emergency, if they lost control and fought, if she left for work and he searched the house for money, for old letters from unknown aunts, for fatherly traces and all the ancient and twisted things that haunted his terrible head.

Her own head hurt. Did she or didn't she have a nightmare? She surely did. A nightmare to end all nightmares. She had been called to the morgue to identify her body. Cause of death indeterminate.

Formalities, a cold room, cold lighting, metal table and on it, covered entirely by a creaseless sheet, herself, naked and dead. She uncovered and observed that self from head to toe. She was not convinced by the selfsame face, the hair with the inch of gray, the selfsame stretch marks on the breasts, the sunken belly button, the chubby fingers and short nails.

The positive identification came about by means of the chapped heels and the callus on her pinkie toe. I am the dead one, she confirmed to the man in charge, I haven't taken good care of myself for some time, I need to start doing it again, she promised, embarrassed.

Getting up was a Herculean task. Monday will have no meaning, the days aren't doing me any good, she thought.

She showered without undoing the shoelace from her arm,

put on a long sleeved chemise, did not even go near her son's
door to eavesdrop, he must be in, she could see the boots
abandoned in the hall.

Was he still asleep, she wondered. Could he have heard the
water running in the bathroom and was not getting up on purpose, so that they wouldn't have another frontal collision,
either with insinuations or silently? For weeks now, maybe for
months, maybe even for years, each spied the other's every
sound and competed in the sports of stubborn silence, threat-
ening gesture, murderous look and the banging of doors.

One hour later, after she spent everything she had on her at
the first open bookstore she came across, books of poetry worth
twenty-two thousand and seven hundred and thirty drachmas,
she went into the Tutu and, while the coffee was brewing, she
called the sign-maker, suggested the name *Salome*, he counter
suggested *Let's Dance*, she agreed, she could pick up the new sign
within a week. Drinking her coffee and munching on a packet of
crackers opened days ago, she jotted the rest of what she
absolutely needed to get done in the day, she made arrangements
over the phone, she apologized on a couple of occasions for not
being able to personally play Santa Claus because of something
unexpected, called a radio-taxi, gave the driver two parcels and
the delivery addresses, got that done, opened the packet with the
beach towels, the print was a failure, Travolta looked like an ape,
she priced him at four hundred and hung one behind her so she
didn't have to look at him, besides, even the American presidents
have their flag standing upright behind their chair.

As no passersby were lured in by the shop's attractions, not
a single soul, she decided she'd read some poems, short and
convenient, ten lines are perfectly capable of keeping you
occupied for ten hours, just as long as you put your mind to it.
She changed her mind, she'd give all the books to Linus, intact.
So she checked the deadlines for the bimonthly tax payment to
her fund and for the utilities, put the sum of money aside, went

on to balance her accounts, prepared the accountant's envelope, she dug out of a small closet the four ballerinas with the
broken legs, casualties from last Christmas, the time had come
for her to fulfill her orthopedic duties.

She would expertly stick the broken off limbs back together
and would sell them half price, maybe give them away to the
down-and-out sods that stood gawking at her shop window
from time to time, it was through such things that she kept her
good name in the neighborhood.

A relatively simple task for her capable hands, still, it took
her nearly an hour, at first she felt kind of sad holding on to the
sole of a misfortunate invalid ballerina, then she didn't feel all
that comfortable pawing calves and lifting short tulle skirts.

Meanwhile, since morning, just as soon as she'd opened the
store shutters, the radio was playing in low volume its nonstop
stream of jejune commercials and summer hits, live yogurts
and pop anthems, air-conditioners and soppy ballads.

She was enduring it for the sake of the news bulletins, let
her hear the glad tidings that two and three and a million and
three Russians had been arrested and, along with them, their
shoes and hats had also been arrested, their mass-produced
shapkas, and both the people and their clothing had confessed
to everything and the avalanche of coincidences toppled down
and her home was pronounced innocent again.

No mention of the subject, at least there were no new victims or assaults. Unless they hadn't been reported, Viv contemplated, by Jove, for a woman it would be the stations of the
cross, starting with the stripping by the attacker and on to the
stripping of the police statement, then answering to women
cops, medical examiners and assorted assistants, what exactly
the monster did to her, confessing to her father or her husband
what went down, shutting herself up in the house to avoid the
neighbors' looks, turning a deaf ear to the underhand comments about the way she dressed.

What might the victims have worn? They wouldn't be dressed in the regional costumes of the islands or in prudish school uniforms, they would be making their way through the night in the minuscule and transparent fabrics that leave the thighs bare and show the nipples pointed.

She wouldn't be having these lowly thoughts, would not be looking for excuses high and low, if it wasn't for her son's shoelace wrapped around her arm, black and long and flat.

At half past three, when she got back home, she found Linus laid out on the living room couch, throwing in the air and catching his green frog. He turned his shaved head, his eyes met hers for a few numbered seconds, long enough for Viv to promptly lift first the one arm with the plastic bags, saying, poems, then the other with the netting bag, presenting two kilos of tomatoes.

They shared a salad and an omelette, but it was impossible for them to speak, it was as if each was beseeching the other to muster the courage to start a conversation on anything at all, from the sweet onions of Thebes to the thirty-seven degrees Celsius, even the canaries of the Cypriot across the street, waxing triumphant despite the afternoon's unbearable heat.

Were there, really, that many chances that they would in time have quiet conversations about small things and insignificant subjects, onions, birds and suchlike?

This suddenly seemed to Viv direly necessary, in fact, absolutely vital, it ought to be included in their future.

As soon as they'd finished eating, mother and son separated again, each to their appointed planet, until eight when Viv pummelled his door with her fists hollering, why don't you listen to some songs, what young person nowadays doesn't listen to music?

Linus came out about fifteen minutes later, ready for an outing, he bent down in the hallway to put on his boots.

There, his mother grabbed him again, shook him, yelled at him again, you need at all costs to go into the sea for a swim, you need to breathe some sea air, get in the waves, get some salt on your skin.

He threw her off him, not paying attention to the beaches she was listing at the top of her lungs, ordering him, you must go at all costs for a swim in the sea, are you listening to me, I want you to go and cool yourself, I want you to go for a swim in the sea, if only the once, tomorrow wouldn't be too soon.

***

Wednesday noon at the shop.

Linus Kolevas was standing on the sidewalk looking at the bric-a-brac in the window as if waiting for an invitation by the owner to step in her house of commerce.

With her elbows sunk in the tresses and beads on her small desk and her head in her palms, Viv scrutinized him, a bold, ugly skull, a pallid face, a ghost in a midsummer's noonday. He was wearing black jeans and a T-shirt.

Yesterday, Tuesday, in the back pages of the newspaper, a single column about the case, with a delay of all those days, a blue shirt had been found in a bush thicket twenty feet away, maybe belonging to the perpetrator or maybe not, the DNA test results were not yet in.

One look inside Linus's wardrobe ascertained that the dark green, the gray and the brown flannel were in their places and out of the other three in various blues the darkest one, acquired two years ago, was missing, the son didn't wear it often, at all events, he preferred T-shirts. The blue shirt was to be found neither in the washing nor stuffed in some drawer or traveling bag.

The night was taken up with that, the color of the fabric and that of the dark were one and the same, and so was the one phrase she kept repeating over and over, as if the needle was stuck, just till dawn, just till dawn. How much the weight and how deep the shadows, how much forbearance till dawn.

Linus, absent till now, a wreck outside the shop, loitering on the sidewalk like a beggar.

She tortured him a fair bit by making him wait, eventually, after checking that the edge of the shoelace wasn't hanging out of her left sleeve, she raised her right hand and invited him in, well, well, here's Bruce Willis, she sprinkled him with the pointless and facile comment, though she did offer him an orange juice as well.

He drank it down like a thirsty dog whose bowl had been left empty for days and had been filled just in the nick of time before he collapsed.

Here, wipe yourself down, she said and handed him some tissues for the drops of the refreshment and sweat spilling from his face and neck down on the glass top of the small desk.

From up close, in the perfect light of day, sitting across from her and newly quenched, he didn't look dangerous, did not carry the aura, the mark of the killer, there has to be such a mark, visible without fail to their mothers.

It was beyond her asking him straight out and she didn't have the presence of mind to corner him indirectly, not yet anyway, her heart was skipping beats, an engine without fuel.

Still, they needed to say something this time, they could at least try, though her offspring had taken after Fotis, he either didn't get into conversations, or quit them halfway, of this Viv was positive, like a sudden storm in her head gathered all the vital conversations left inconclusive, her deceased husband getting up and walking away leaving questions unanswered, doubts unresolved, burning issues unfinished, his son was exactly the same.

I'm gathering mementos from your dad in a little chest, she started gently. I'm saving them for your children, she added meaningfully and, given that Linus had no intention of waking up and showing some interest, she went on to describe the treasure, a wood carving of a bunch of grapes with three leaves, a wooden farmer woman with a bunch of wheat and a sickle, a Russian Red Army harmonica and some poetry books of that period, all with passages underlined and exclamation marks by your father's hand.

– Are these poems not fit for minors and is that why you haven't given them to me all this time?

– Would you have as much as glanced at them? The ones I got you the other day are still in their bags.

– All poetry is repentance, is what he came up with after a few minutes of silence.

It's now or never, Viv thought, took a deep breath and forged ahead unstoppable.

– I've been looking for the shapka, your grandfather's ash-gray fur cap and I can't find it. It belongs in the chest.

The son unspeaking and unmoving.

– So, then, where's our shapka? Some weeks ago I'd seen it on your bed, her voice now clipped, decisive, a clear sign that she would brook no evasiveness.

– No more mementos, I don't want to remember so much, my mind is sore with that business.

That was his answer, while his eyes started brimming, his Adam's apple started pounding like a drum, and his arms flailed like the wings of a shot bird.

– Careful, you'll damage things, she yelled at him, got up and pulled aside some porcelain things, everything in here is fragile, she pointed out to him.

Now, why had she said that, since at times like this, she couldn't care less about even the costliest miniatures, she inwardly chastised herself.

There were prospective clients, too, checking out the anti-mosquito dancer-candles in the window. Thankfully they decided against them, even if they'd come in, even if they were willing to lay down a month's wages, Viv would have said, we're putting on the discount price tags right now, come back later for better prices.

She focused again on her subject and resumed her questioning.

– Where have you left it? Have you taken some things, some shirts, to another house? If you're staying with some woman, you might as well tell me.

He didn't enlighten her so she asked the other thing, had he fallen in with any anarchists and is he in and out of any of those filthy dirty communes? Is there electricity? Is the bathroom clean?

Viv Koleva might as well have been talking to a wall.

– I know, she stammered suddenly. Like your father, you're probably going off to drink. That's just what I needed, she told herself with her voice turning falsetto, and kept on, for five years after he died, I didn't even allow liqueurs in the house, and I only ever drank water in front of you. I was wrong to start up on the beers again, with your godmother and with whomever, and allow them to creep back in. Are the beers doing you in, my boy? Are you drinking? she asked, longing for him to confirm that he'd become a raging alcoholic.

– He drank everything there was to drink.

– What then? What is going on?

– You pretend not to know, but you know everything, you don't miss a single thing, these were Linus's last words, spoken slowly, word by word, before he got up and left.

What else could she possibly do with that child? How to get on his good side, how to talk some sense into him? Should she buy him a piano, which they say is good for a child? Should she get him a large, comprehensive encyclopedia, the *Britannica* or the *Papyre-Larousse*? Send him for a holiday to Amsterdam? Enroll him as a student in Bologna? Take him for manual labor to some kibbutz?

She hadn't been able so far and it seemed like she never would be a good actress like most moms, who give their all for the family performance to succeed and the audience of the house to be happy.

She remembered several of them from the years of kindergarten and primary school, chatting as they stood, patient and smiling, next to walls with every manner of insect and livestock in monstrous enlargement, cicadas as large as chickens, chickens as big as goats and goats like panthers. And she remembered five or ten from high school, those ones also relaxed and self-assured, satisfied with the carrot cakes, the parks and the weekends in mountainous Corinthia.

She snuck her right hand into the left sleeve of the chemise, moved it upward, touched the lace, you, she said, you and your two accomplices, the blue shirt and the shapka, will be responsible for what happens from now on.

The rest of Wednesday went by with difficulty. She got rid of one Travolta, two Zorbas and five small Degas prints, collected eleven thousand altogether, and then, with shutters closed, she sat jotting on a sheet of paper questions and answers from the hard quiz which kept her hostage.

At nine in the evening back in the Mitsubishi, again the reckless itineraries virtually scraping against paralytic buildings and bellicose streetlights from the far-flung sea suburbs back to the center and up to the northern ones of Chalandri and Aghia Paraskevi. At around eleven a stop somewhere in the north, in a dark spot where stood the right telephone booth for what she had in mind.

Second anonymous call. This time she stated she was almost a rape victim. She would not go to the police in person, absolutely not, she hadn't even told her husband, he muttered over her going alone to the cinema, didn't like it himself, wouldn't take her.

In short, five days ago, leaving at 12:30 A.M. from the

Amaryllis, she had stopped at an all-night liquor store and bought two bottles for her husband, a vodka and a rum. On her way up to her house corner of Trikalon and Chlois St., where there were some open fields with pines, in Aghia Paraskevi, someone jumped her from behind, put his arms around her and one palm over her mouth, gagging her, and pushed her into the pines. The only thing she remembered clearly was getting him a good one on the shins with the heavy liquor store bag and making her getaway. I was scared because I've heard about the maniac still out and about, she finished her report with remarkable speed and with her eye on her watch.

What attracted her to the police and made her set up scenarios was the hope of finding something out that would place her son out of the picture, being told by the cops that, according to latest evidence, the rapist had a big prominent scar or a missing ear or that they'd just caught him in the act, a pumped up Russian boxer who confessed to everything and the blue shirt was in his size and his shoes match as does his shapka and that's the end of that.

– Aghia Paraskevi was the last thing we needed, the officer allowed himself the liberty, made a comment about women's risky night walks, and weighing up the event with the bottles, had the presence of mind to ask, so, then, he might have a bruise on his knee or his shin?

– He might.

– Should we then be looking at men's shins?

– Do you have him?

– We have Russians and Poles and Romanians all of whom have alibis and bring as witnesses truckloads of fellow nationals whom you wouldn't want to meet alone in a dark alley.

The cop told her she had a duty to go and try and identify the attacker, Viv wouldn't hear of it, she was afraid of her husband, he proposed that she talked to a female colleague of his, a psychologist at that, some of the victims end up severely traumatized, a step away from being admitted, and who can blame them, since, as the fellow is having his sport with them, he stops them from yelling during the rape by stuffing his shoe in their mouth, one of those ones worn by basketball players.

The conversation was going on for far too long and Viv put down the receiver so they wouldn't locate her. She reached the Mitsubishi with large strides and turned on the engine. She didn't know where to go. She didn't want to go back home. It was her turn to stay out one whole night.

Her son's previous shoes, the sports shoes Linus had thrown out, traveled with her for six hours around Attica, in her mouth, unhinging her jaws, in her mind, trespassing in every thought, dragging her into the dark forest, into the pitch-black tunnel with the keening of the unfortunate girls.

☆☆☆

For the sea. That's what she wrote to him on the paper, the letters orderly, peaceful, and the distance between words correct, the marker pale blue. She left it on his pillow, next to the presents she'd bought him, the black bathers with the red stripe on the side, the sunscreen, the thongs, the beach mat and finally, as a kind of self-evident signature, the two self-evident bills, all of them in a straight line on the light summer blanket.

Before setting out the display she'd changed his bedding, the bed was a mess, on the sheets again a hodgepodge of crumbs, ashes and leftovers of sweets.

All this in the afternoon, Linus was out, Viv alone in the house.

She searched everywhere in case he'd left her a note, where have you been, Mother, where did you spend the night, are you all right? Nothing.

He hadn't tried to call her, nor had he been by the shop.

Despite her emotional and physical exhaustion from wandering all through the night, Viv was at her post and she even collected a little money, hair ribbons, a hair netting, three mini posters, the dough was handy, not even misery is free.

She took an ice cream out of the freezer, went to her room, lay down, ate it and slept, a deep sleep, no resemblance to the afternoon siesta it should have been.

It was ten past five when the bell rang, Viv opened her eyes, grabbed hold of the sheets and lay low like a wild animal sensing danger.

Who can it be? They've come already? Did they track him down? Did some acquaintance point him out, who'd seen something by accident? Should she open the door? Should she play possum? What if they smash their way in? Should she treat them to something? Should she cover up for him? Should she provide him with an alibi for the night in question, the young man had a fever or colic pains and hadn't moved from his spot? Is there a mother who doesn't cover up for her child, no matter what?

– Viv? Vivian? Viv, baby? Rhoda's voice. After the third ring, she was banging on the door with her palm, she could make out the sound of her large ring.

She opened the door and got an earful. If you weren't in the bathtub why did it take you so long to open up, and, you sly fox, sleeping out and not sharing the good news so we might get a bit of pleasure out of it, a telephone call wouldn't do things justice so I came over to get it live from the horse's mouth.

The best woman called the house over and over the previous night. Viv's cell phone was off.

At something to two, her godson had picked up, he'd just walked in, had no idea where his mother was, he sounded fuzzy-brained, never the chatty type as was well known.

Saying all this and other things besides, a reprimand for the missing curtain, a reprimand for the dust on the windows, she dropped off the promised Egyptian souvenirs, the piranhas and whatnot, went to the kitchen and put on a coffee, filled two mugs, sat Viv down for a quick chat before the sourpuss returned to the Tutu and the Highbrow to her coterie of refined acquaintances.

Nothing came out of it. Not, at long last, a love interest, not a night with live bouzouki at one of the spots by the sea, a fiesta at someone's house somewhere, in celebration of the name day of a Paraskevi or a Pandelis.

The sudden visit wasn't like past get-togethers over erotic or political impasses of the kind that don't actually arrive at a conclusion, don't solve any problems, nor do they cause any hurt, they just sit two people down in the living room until the coffeepot is empty and the ashtray full of cigarette butts, so that, afterwards, the hostess has to air the space and that is all there is to it, no miracles and no dramas.

Of the visit's thirty minutes, twenty were eaten up by silence.

Rhoda backed up, put on the hand brake, desisted from her interrogation, realized she was not welcome under the current circumstances, hermetically private and ill-omened, something again to do with the devil's spawn, her godson.

She gave a short soliloquy about her affairs, her dear old mum who was well advanced on the way to senile depression and she had to look after her, caressed Viv's shoulder and got up saying, whenever you're up to it, give me a call to go out to a restaurant or a movie, cheer up a bit.

At the last moment, as she was letting herself out, she issued her statement of support, we're all in the same boat, you know, if you think that I'm happy as a lark myself, the answer is, no, not by a long shot.

Out she went, in he came, ten minutes apart.

Mother and son exchanged the same look they'd been giving each other over the past few days, they'd both been well schooled in it.

– Linus, Viv asked hesitantly, almost breathlessly, if someone asks me where you go at nights, where you were on the night of July 13, what must I say?

No response on his part, only the quiet and methodical retreat again into his warren. She waited for a bit outside his door in case he said anything, even about the bathing costume and the sea, nothing, nothing whatsoever.

Time for the Tutu, a business is a business, it does not open and close according to its owner's moods, she went, she sold, she came back.

Her son was still holed in, but declared himself present in his own way, the squeaking of his chair and his desk drawer that shut noisily.

He didn't answer when she called out, shall I order some pizza, nor when she tried with, how about souvlaki?

Now, past ten, there was no light in the crack under his door, yet the son wasn't asleep, some whispers were audible that gave the evening an added dimension.

Oh, he has visitors, oh, he's got some girl in, how I wish, whoever it may be, single or married, smart or dumb, wise or a fool, Greek or foreign, white or black.

Walking on tiptoe, Viv approached the Berlin Wall-door, like a spy, in case she could make out one or two of the words that had been in such short supply in this home, something along the lines of, come, my love, let's hug some more, and she overheard one whole phrase: Buddy, out of the way, the shovels are attacking, dirt's about to heap.

– Are you all right? she called out. Is there something wrong?

He didn't open his door, he let her walk around some more like a blind woman on tiptoe by his door, before announcing to her with much ado:

– All you care about is that night. Well, for your information, there's plenty more, there's a whole bunch.

Viv Koleva grabbed her bag and went out, she was afraid of staying with him, afraid of what terrible things might be uttered or done.

Now, she didn't want to hear his confession, he was perfectly capable of coming out with ten unconscionable crimes.

Would she take him in her arms to console him, to say bygones are bygones, but things would be better from now on? Would she suggest that he flee on the spot, on a night flight abroad? Should she join him herself, wandering through the insignificant townships of insignificant countries till their traces were lost? Would she finally slap him? And what if Linus strangled her using the length of his foulard?

What is better? A plain rapist and murderer or a matricide as well?

Her heart was beating loudly and irregularly, volleys that unhinged her limbs from their position, her hands gaping, her feet quaking, her head revolving out of sync and ending up facing backwards, in case her son was following her.

An empty mind, a small little mind, yes indeed, without suspicions, without indications and proofs, that is what she needed for a carefree evening stroll, like the others who slowly ambled and paused in front of storefronts or traffic lights with a soda at hand.

She was encircled by the signs of an ordinary evening, ordinary people in an ordinary neighborhood.

If only she could change there and then the traffic signs, the street names, the store signs, the plants in the flower beds, the children's voices, the newspaper titles at the kiosks, the stations of the TV and the radio that could be heard near and far, the business of people, if only her suburb of Patissia could be radically changed, if reality could be gotten out of the way.

She wished she was in Germany with the thousands of rail tracks, as if each man had a train to himself, like Rhoda's dad used to say, so she could get on a train all of her own, trailing boxcars, overtaking cities, passing through industrial complexes, leaving landscapes behind.

She went round and round the same old ground without reprieve. Her footsteps didn't obey her, didn't take pity on her, brought her before accomplished facts, in front of a tavern where groups of people were feasting and telling jokes, behind a couple being all lovey-dovey, next to a group of women her age, all of them coiffed and perfumed, enjoying the outing.

Eventually, they led her to the corner of Thiras and Drosopoulou streets, in front of the police station.

She looked in surprise at the guard post in the entrance with the lit sign, froze in place for a few minutes, turned about, walked away. She covered several more kilometres, five and ten times around the same city blocks.

Every time, on approaching the building of the police, she turned back or crossed the street. When she realized that the guard had noticed her, the same woman visitor over and over again, Viv Koleva went up the steps and asked to see the officer on duty.

Now her heart was beating like a window shutter in the northerly, her innards were draughty, her blood was freezing like a mud hole in the mountains at wintertime. She felt her feet hit turbulence and dip, her knees shortened by three inches, her soles sinking in the floor of the police station.

She dragged herself to the office she was led to, standard furnishings, standard face. Holding the receiver the officer, you are not in a hurry? he asked good-humoredly, he gestured to a seat and went on with his spiel, who knows to whom, a woman at any event, philosophizing according to his profession and the time of night.

– Every city with thirty, with one hundred thousand residents, with half a million or one million, let alone the countless and diverse crowds of Athens, gathers to itself angels as it gathers every manner and type of being, sinners and demons included. A city with five million people needs both unhappiness and transgression. There is a wisdom behind the robberies and the murders, it makes householders be careful, lock up, watch out for the wanted, scrutinize the newcomers. Otherwise, what use would the patrol cars be, the lockups, the sleuths, the tear gas, the Port Police, the Vice Squad, the Drugs Squad, the lawyers, the courts and the decorations for honorable conduct? And, dear lady, where would your channels and newspapers be without deviants, defaulters, white slave merchants, murderers, rapists and pedophiles?

He was keeping notes, he said, after he retired he'd write a log of events and meditations, he considered it his duty.

He finished his call pleased and replenished, he had a lot of night ahead of him as well as the pale, despondent lady sitting quietly across from him with her right hand stuck into her left sleeve.

– A break in or a disturbance of the common peace by the neighbors? he hazarded a guess, with a friendly, reassuring smile.

Vivian Koleva could not find the appropriate words.

– I've lost my ID, she muttered eventually. I've come to have a new one issued.

– At 3 A.M.?

The officer was now looking at her dumbfounded, even though, in his line of work, nothing should really strike him as strange, his doorstep was often visited, particularly after dark, by the drunk and the deranged, the loners and the worse for the wear, the night's sorrowful denizens.

– You'll need to come again tomorrow in the daytime, he suggested, treated her to a glass of water and saw her out himself, bid her goodnight and watched her go down Thiras St., to the right.

He saw her again before him two hours later in her nightie and a shirt thrown across her shoulders.

She was holding a bag.

He again motioned her to the chair across from his desk.

– What is your name?

– Korleva.

This was her first illegal "r" ever.

**

He did not resist, did not ask them anything, did not delay them. He followed them like a dog wagging its tail because it was now the time for its walk, at eight o'clock in the morning.

Viv was out, she'd left for the store at seven thirty, it had been arranged, she did not want to witness the scene.

Just in case, she had given the police a key.

We opened noiselessly, they told her the details afterwards, though she hadn't asked, two had stayed in the hallway outside, two were under the balcony, three went in the apartment, went with every precaution to his room and found the door unlocked with him in bed, on his back with eyes open, fully awake, if he had slept at all, he was in his jeans and boots.

– You need to come with us to the station for a short chat. There is something we need to discuss. If nothing comes of it, you'll be free in a few hours to go where you please, that's how the one in charge spoke to him.

Linus got up like an obedient child, put on a T-shirt that sat folded on the dresser and stood before them, ready.

My child doesn't have a gun, he's not one of those bullies with the pistols and the Kalashnikovs, he detests guns, I took him to an antiwar rally when he was younger and, as for his dad, he used to lead right at the front in peace marches, Viv had pointed out to the policemen and had made sure on her way to work to take along in a big bag all the kitchen knives, the sewing scissors and Fotis's tools, hammers and screwdrivers.

It had been quite a trip that day, carrying ten kilos of armaments in the elevator, the car, through the parking lot, dragging them into the doll shop, sticking them into the small WC, in between a carton of detergents and the mop, and covering them up with eight roles of toilet paper in their packaging.

The police chief called her at seventeen past nine, no client had walked into the shop in that time and she was wishing that nobody would, after watching her clock minute by minute she had even, at nine past nine precisely, turned over the paper sign on the glass door, *Closed*, had drawn the shades across the store windows, had turned off the standing lamp on the small table that doubled as a till and was pacing in the minuscule space, barely ten feet across, back and forth, as weary as if she had covered whole miles, as if she'd crossed the desert of a biblical destruction.

– Mrs Korleva, everything's fine, we thank you, you did the right thing. Let's hope the young fellow is the victim of diabolic coincidences.

– His cigarettes? Viv asked, she'd thought ahead about that, too, in the night of her second visit to the station she had left a whole carton, they'd give them to him a pack at a time.

– Did he ask after me?

– No.

– Would he have known?

– Not a chance. Please trust us.

– What if he finds out?

– He's not going to, don't worry, we know our job.

– What does he think about his arrest?

– That we had been watching him for weeks.

– You didn't hurt him? You didn't flog him?

– Most certainly not.

– Shall I bring him fresh clothing?

– He hasn't gotten dirty. Later. We'll be in touch.

That was it, curt questions and answers, for the first instalment they didn't say any more. The policemen had patiently heard Viv through in the night, after she handed the lace over, telling them a bunch of dumb things, that it seemed inconceivable to her that her child was sexually deviant, that once she even came across him by accident watching a porn video and he might as well've been watching a documentary on Charles de Gaulle, that her son has a fine upbringing and patriotism as well, given how distressed he was last summer by the incidents on Cyprus and the killing of Solomos Solomou, climbed on the flag post, cigarette in mouth and, given the laws of statistics, we may have before us a tragic story like the ones we see in the movies, extreme coincidences leading to the electric chair a man whose innocence isn't proven until much later.

Now, the hours passed with no news, for better or for worse. Perhaps, none of the victims recognized him, this might be the day when, finally, they caught the real guy with a dozen witnesses and a dozen pieces of evidence.

So, Linus would turn up suddenly, pale and outraged with the misunderstanding and the hardship, swearing at the cops in earnest, she would join him, the this, the that, the scum, the imbeciles, drawing a wage to no good purpose.

And he would surely tell her his story now in every detail, where he was on the damned night, where and why he'd shaved his head, where he'd lost the other lace, what happened to his shoes, who stole the fur cap from him, to what needy soul he had given his blue shirt, in accordance with *ye who have two chitons,* and so on and so forth.

Late in the afternoon she was called by the central police office, went over, did not see her son, saw a police chief, and was briefed about the basics.

Out of the seven women who had been called in for the identification, Greeks and foreigners, young and mature, whores and not, from older and more recent cases, six had said no, not him, no way, they insisted on someone larger, more muscular, shorter. One was not too sure either way, the telltale blond hair was missing but the eyes and the body type kind of matched.

The identification happened in reverse, as if this was a joke, by Linus himself through a series of gestures, he wouldn't open his mouth to courageously confess, he bowed his head every time silently confirming that yes, it was him at Lykovrisi, yes, it was him who had gagged the girl with his shoe in her mouth.

The police chief seemed relieved and proud with the outcome as if it had been his own work and not the mother-Judas's.

The interrogations had a long way to go, he was naturally not at liberty to divulge his planned course of action to Viv, he didn't have it in him either, he said, to torment a mother by keeping her on the premises longer than necessary, despite the fact that both he and all the policemen that were coming and going, in uniform and out, scrutinized her and swapped among themselves glances which signaled they also thought her guilty over the upbringing and the negligent watch over her only son.

Viv Koleva couldn't see Linus yet, thankfully, it was the last thing she wanted.

She wished she never did see him again.

That same evening, under lock and key in her house, she didn't pick up the phone to look for a lawyer. She wandered through the rooms, gutted by the police. Linus's computer was missing, his wardrobe a mess, the poems spilt out of the bags onto the couch, Ritsos and Rotas on her bedroom floor, the cops had even looked under the beds.

She lay down. At 35 degrees Celsius, the inside walls were burning and the sheets were lukewarm but, on them, her hands and feet were frozen, her outbreath a cold breeze, no sweating at all, her body a fridge, her body an obstacle. The body is to blame for everything, the head a mere fixture, the mind a pawn. Bodies with their autonomy and self-will are continuously preoccupied with themselves, finding fault with their shape, finding fault with the skin, the breasts that need rubbing, the shoulders that need polishing, the calves crossed in lust, the lower area churning, the testicles scheming, the male back in a show of strength, the female belly in search of a pump for the nine-month fiesta.

She placed her palm on her cold stomach and struggled to understand what had gone wrong with that boy from the outset, from when she was pregnant, the mother's belly is the cradle of every good thing, the cave of every evil, the headquarters of every future uprising, the coffer that holds the treasure or the ashes, the nest with the bits of thread and the sprigs that become the loom where the child's sack is slowly woven as it grows.

Pinching the skin and pressing down on her intestines which were making gurgling noises, hadn't eaten all day, she tried to recall the frequency of throwing up, of bloating, the kicks, the foodstuffs, the constipation, the sweats, the obsessions, the nerves, the bad sleep, had she slipped, stumbled, overeaten, drunk too much, gotten too frightened and marked the baby ever since, as if she could turn Linus back into an embryo and wall him inside her womb again, an egg in her ovary, and perchance leave him there for good.

How did the night pass, how did the day break, how did she drag herself again to the central offices to see from a distance, down a corridor, what she would not even be able to imagine in the past, Linus in handcuffs, an extraterrestrial thing?

Her eyes got stuck there, it didn't even cross her mind to look at his face, if from a distance, it was secondary, she was abstracted and riveted by the metal shining on his wrists.

She felt that from that moment on, no other kind of unhappiness would ever make an impression on her.

***

In life everyone has a poem they have to say. And Viv was

saying hers, the one allotted her from birth, and she had to say the rest, too, all the verses till the last line.

The jailing and the hearings, the trumpeting of the media, the chorus of the neighbors' excelsiors, the ostracism up and down her suburb were now all past and she had made it through to their aftermath.

The latest events became a whole armada sailing unsinkable in the ocean of the coming weeks, the coming months.

Rhoda in a hurried phone call, she was over her head, ever so pressed for time, recommended a lawyer, a client of hers with high blood pressure who, it turned out, was dreaming of TV interviews where his pronouncements would be given due attention on the way to being appointed a parliamentary candidate with the New Democracy Party. At his very first appearance on a channel among pensioners and detectives, Viv dismissed him, she went at random in and out of a dozen small law firms and finally hired someone who was not, and did not wish to become, a TV star. Please pay mind, she was perfectly straight from the start, keep away from cameras and if some director or writer turns up wanting to turn us into a movie or a book, make it perfectly clear to them that we are not fond of playing lead roles in the arts, and just proceed with what needs to be done.

Menios Yukaris, a small man of fifty-five, equipped with the armor of experience, four thousand hearings in all, asked her the difficult questions discreetly, not expecting an answer at all costs, drew inferences out of the half-finished sentences, correctly understood the content of her silences, and didn't hold it against her that already from the first minute her eye had noted his threadbare carpet, the missing corner in the wooden border of his desk and the worn edge of the plaster frame of his diploma. Entirely focused on the matter at hand each time, a devotee of specifics and of essential words, he preferred all narratives and events to be succinctly expressed and to reach a relevant conclusion. Whenever he found himself in a tight spot, he had recourse to some quote, Marcus Aurelius, Voltaire and Nasser were always on standby to lend a helping hand.

Day by day, the amount of documents and notes from the hearings grew larger in his briefcase as did the list of his appointments. He briefed his client, gave her instructions, empathized with her predicament, he knew with all his years in penal courts that in every crime, along with the accused, society also tried the mother.

In his eyes, Viv Koleva was an apple that had started to rot and her son a crabapple that had slipped through her hands and rolled on his way, leaving her holding the stem.

The stem wouldn't open his mouth, but in his own way, he didn't deny the acts ascribed to him during the interrogation, he wouldn't have defended himself even if they'd blamed every case on file on him. The police search through his computer hadn't turned up any sex goddesses giving blowjobs or portraits of great womanizers or serial killers, no orgies or Satanist rituals, nothing but idyllic landscapes and information on steppes, taigas, tundras, bio-plantations, shamans, martial arts of ancient China, Braveheart and Irish methods of malt fermentation and drinking, there was a list found, too, titled *Dates*, where Viv recognized the dates of Fotis's death and, Buddy's death and the cops identified the dates of three rapes.

The television, newspapers and assorted publications were having a field day with the case, a godsend in the summer media limbo. On-site reports, articles upon articles, interviews with sleuths, statements by feminists and specialist exposés about sexual perversions, orphanhood and the sinister underside of the city, were dedicated to the subject. In the scandal-mongering press Linus was a star, his picture was all over with an inch of block-out in lieu of blindfold across the eyes and the surname Kolevas in capitals.

For his mother, time, which had flowed minute by minute,

slowly and terribly, until the confirmation of his guilt, now was of no interest, it passed of its own accord, scattered in the courts and in the neglected house. The days had lost their cohesion once and for all, they no longer followed their established routine, the Tutu, decorative minutiae, the paying off of loan installments, cooking and housekeeping of the mind, their hours would suddenly break up in unexpected directions, like a shoal of fish whose unified swimming is disturbed by a stone thrown in the sea, scattering them this way and that.

The events had her on the run from the lawyer's office downtown to the central headquarters of the police on Alexandras Avenue, from the courts up at Kypseli to the tactical interrogations office in Omonia Square, from Annas to Caiafas, starting the day with help me, Christ Almighty, and ending with Mother of God, have mercy, because the way things had turned out, she did wish there was a God if only so she could tell him point-blank: since you made him in your image, you can now take over and do with him what you will.

The hours were many, too, that she spent shut off in her home, she gathered them around her chair like cats that purred away the minutes and the seconds without her resisting such a prodigal waste of time.

The shop closed, how to put in an appearance, what to explain to the other shopkeepers, how to face any mothers who might demand amends, we were bringing our little girls into the dragon's lair, where to find the presence of mind for business deals, she went once and picked up the Queen Elizabeths, didn't even open the cardboard boxes, merely kicked them into a recess. As for the new sign, she never did pick it up, despite the advance payment she'd made in hard cash.

Her apartment building was unbearable and so was the neighborhood. The manager bumped into her at the entrance, she was going out, he was coming in, and far from saying even a cut-and-dried good day, his clenched body and stone face indicated she was no longer welcome at the five-story building with the twenty-two peace loving, Christian families. Next day, his wife came face-to-face with her in the hallway, took two steps back and turned about.

The mini-market guy, who was usually a prime candidate for a chat, said not a word for the first time ever, not the silence of compassion or awkwardness but of disapprobation. He gave her the little net bag with the milk portions and the lighter, took the money, pushed her change across and then turned his back to her, ostensibly to arrange the soda drinks in the fridge.

At the baker's, too, as soon as she walked in, the owner, his wife, the Albanian worker, a filo pastry expert, and the clientele, all familiar faces, cut their talking short and stood about like pillars of salt. And what might they say? Well, hello, and aren't you right on time, the spinach pie is just out, take a couple of pieces over to the boy to keep his strength up? Maybe pat her on the back and soothe her with a "God is great" and "It's all going to be all right"? Maybe tell her, these things happen, my son, too, my nephew, my brother did the same? Nobody's son, nephew or brother had done the same.

Viv left without getting bread. Ever since, in order to get a few basics, just to keep herself going, she had to go out of her way, change grocery stores and mini-markets, make sure she did not become a target.

She kept thinking the pavements would buck and throw her off, the trees would wither in her wake, the rubbish bins would overturn to cover her with shit-paper.

The poem also included the page of the psychiatric assessment. Her son did not want to collaborate with the doctors, not even for his own good, as he had no interest in his own good or the future or anything of the sort. Viv didn't like that stage one bit, nor did she like the psychiatrists' eyes, like the rays of ultramodern CAT scans, cutting up people's soul into slices. And that's supposed to be a good thing, is it? Being emptied out like that, no bones made about it? Who are those who decide to do this monstrous, Peeping Tom job of undressing everyone else's insides?

Viv Koleva wouldn't mind nearly as much going around buck naked, the saggy flesh and flaccid buttocks in full view, but she didn't want her soul stripped down and poured out all over their desks. At the prearranged appointment with them she felt trapped, as if facing a terrible agency of power whose job was the retroactive lynching of mothers. The woman doctor in her smart linen suit and her colleague with the thunderbolt in his tie and his shoes shined to mirror-like perfection, seemed like interrogators whose questions were measured but who had in their eyes the assurance that eventually they'd find out everything they needed to know, nobody slips through their grasp. To be precise, in her mind the psychiatrists were an evolved version of inquisitors, same system, you'll spew every thing up, you'll all break.

We're already shattered, for all time, Viv was thinking, experienced, ever since a wee child on a trajectory to contrition.

The examination decreed that, overall, Linus Kolevas was of sound mind and in a position to be charged. In other words, not enough of a schizophrenic nor enough of a manic-depressive. When his mother lost the vague hope of madness, she thought a lot about that one.

She exhaustively scrutinized of her own accord her family and the family of Fotis, from what little she knew, everyone was all right in the head. She thought it through some more, and reached her own conclusions regarding the myth of the progenitors of the young man in detention being in fine health.

Who wasn't fit to be put behind bars? His bard of a grandfather, half his life spent making up songs, the other half in the nationalists' prisons? His father, hankering for destruction, throwing back every type and brand of alcohol? Her father, who took as his wife a woman who could've been his daughter? Her weeded out mother, all day, every day, in the fields kneeling before thorny burnet? Herself, a lifetime in the Sunday school of ballet and the dance classes of despondency?

Her son had been assigned to manage their stock of ammunition and he had deployed it in the familiar, epic manner.

The most revealing verses in her poem concerned the infamous family and a select assortment of close relatives.

The rapes suited them down to the ground. With a small dose of exaggeration, or cynicism, that'd be the conclusion of a third party studying the way Viv's relations treated her.

The relationships with her father, her mother, her sister, her brother-in-law, the best woman at her marriage, shallow, with all the essence having fizzed out, were a net full of holes, they were waiting for the event that would bring them undone, the merciful blow that would finish them off, so that the list of cumbersome obligations could be crossed off.

Her father, not even a phone call. Her mother, at his command, didn't come from the village for even one day. Her sister and her brother-in-law dug themselves in, in Canada. And the bitch Rhoda, not a single visit to her godson, she asked Viv over the phone what Linus had recounted and had admitted to, the psychiatrists didn't discover anything, did they, she sent a check for two hundred thousand and she disappeared.

Viv Koleva weighed the many people and things that had passed through her life and was left with nothing. She had nobody to share a coffee or a phone call with, nobody's hand to hold.

The only one who picked up the phone was the old Theopiste, past ninety, sick and close to death and more fearless than ever three days before she died. Wishes for bearing up, swearwords at bloody life and an observation, the news turned out the most world historic event for Alonaki ever: two of its renowned offspring who had been distinguished, the first as general secretary in some ministry during the junta, the second as something or other in Strasburg, took second place, Linus became the number one name in the vicinity. So, Alonaki, out of bounds as well, even as a mental stroll along the map.

Highly accomplished at one time in cover-up operations, unsuccessful as a rule but, nonetheless, an integral part of her routine, Viv all at once gave up her attempts to review the past with the intention of bedimming it, everything had better be up front, everything crystal clear.

At such times, retrospectively she did assess correctly a thing her son had said, you're taught love and positive feelings while you're young, or something to that effect—he had tossed that at her during the fight over the shoes.

She now saw him in the brief visitations behind the glass, giving him counterfeit regards which he wasn't buying. He was listening to her expressionless, quiet, amenable, asking for nothing.

The times were gone when he would slip out the door setting her on edge, I'm going out ripping out windshield wipers, breaking things, going to beat somebody and get beaten up, and she would answer, on your way back get me some cigarettes, take money from my wallet, and take a jumper, it's getting chilly out.

Every time, after the prison, she'd spend three hours wondering, did he maybe cry over his victims? Does he get red eyes at night from crying? Do his eyelids get puffy? Will he be crying for all the rest of his life? And what if he didn't cry? What if he never does?

That seemed wrong to her, it made her feel confused.

With the cunning of guilt and the inertia of despair, she who loathed sentiment and never prayed to Mary and the saints for miracles, bowed and prayed for even a single tear to roll down her son's cheek, the first, the difficult one, for the machine to get started, so then it could accelerate to the voluble wracking and sobbing.

She, herself, didn't cry even once, not in front of third parties, nor, most importantly, by herself, because grieving washes one clean and, at its summit, offers relief, solace even. In her case it wouldn't work, she'd made her mind up that events had pronounced her guilty for a lifetime. Nevertheless, the amount of sweating she did, at odd moments and on completely unexpected occasions, seemed to her at times unnatural, her body would be soaked out of the blue, as if, instead of by the eyes, tears were being shed by the arms, the breasts, the palms, as if even the backs of her knees were crying at the joints.

With one thing and another August passed, and September too, summer was at last finished with its blinding turquoise and canary yellows advertising tanned flesh. The bathing suit for the much desired swim in the sea-slash-pool of Siloam was stashed away.

October came in its faint gray and went out in its dark one, out in the streets long sleeves and thick jackets appeared, it was getting nippy, the weather was changing, if that mattered in any way.

**

She started with the easier stuff.

First, she got rid of the red Mitsubishi, so she didn't have to fantasize about her son driving around casing the dark woodlets, so it didn't remind her of her own sprees to secluded telephone booths to call the police. For weeks, she couldn't even turn on the ignition, she had it towed to a dealer's yard. She scored a beat-up old Fiat, from now on she would be saving with a vengeance.

The house was next. The four-bedroom at Kato Patissia, its mortgage paid off four years ago, was sold on the last week of

November for nineteen million drachmas, that was the best price it would fetch, on account of the age of the apartment block, the real estate man appraised.

Viv Koleva needed to rid the neighborhood of her good self but also to get away from the icy stares of one and all since, in such cases, no one remains uninformed, the whole suburb was abuzz, the news stormed every house and shop in the area with vivid descriptions, both real and imaginary, some folks relished embellishing upon the abhorrent details.

Rented housing again, in Ano Kypseli, second story, three small rooms, fifty square feet if that, why did she need more, who and how many would be coming in and out of her home for the rest of her years, she agreed with the real estate agent without even seeing the apartment. She saw it on the day she brought her things over, decimated by a merciless elimination, several pieces of furniture, paintings, lamps and carpets were sold off for a pittance to a gypsy who filled up his truck, got as a bonus all of Linus's clothing plus a number of oddities from the cupboards, hibiscus and mango teas, last year's offerings by the Highbrow, all untouched, plus two wooden boxes with Fotis's implements, plus a bagful of novels, after she'd fist turned them over and shaken them in case some historic document was slumbering in their pages.

Three sheets fell out with Linus's childhood paintings, Chinese dogs with slanted eyes, convict dogs with a ball and chain, acrobat dogs in a circus. It had been a mistake of hers not dragging him to some visual arts school, anywhere at all, they were all over town, so he could learn to express his feelings on paper, using paint instead of words.

She went into her new home with the bare necessities like a thief, at night, with a rush of winter stars glimmering at her through the window and the moon stalking her from behind the folds of the curtain, new though cheap, it was the first thing Viv put up to isolate her from the world outside.

At the doorbell she stuck a piece of paper with her maiden name, the notorious Koleva would be too much of an affront.

Viv seriously contemplated reverting to her unknown maiden name on her police ID but she didn't pursue it. She remained in the bonds of a common surname with her son and it wasn't an act of support, but of complicity.

On the first night at the small apartment she slept with most of the boxes around her still unopened, herself a sealed box in a storeroom, the thoughts packets in her mind and parcels pressing down on her chest.

What might have happened had she not snitched on her son? Would they have put some poor Russian sod behind bars? Should she have been clear to him about it, I know, here's the black shoelace, stop already? How could she have said that since, prior to his confession, she hadn't been one hundred percent sure? What if he did away with her as well? Might that not have been the best scenario, so she would be spared all this hell? If she hadn't turned him over to the police and Linus had kept on unhindered, would that have been a new victim per week? Would she sit by keeping his score? How could her conscience bear that? Should she have taken him by force to a doctor in the know, plied him with chemicals, bound him up, locked him up inside himself? Should she have swallowed three bottles of pills herself to get things over and done with? And what if, afterwards, he went completely berserk? Should she have killed him with her own hands? Would that have been better for him since, that way, his actions wouldn't have come to light? Would she even be capable of it, she wondered. How? Suffocating him with his pillow? Slipping him rat poison? But what's this madness she is pondering and why after the event, when it's no longer possible?

In yesterday's visit, at the beginning and at the end, he had told her word by word, so that not a single syllable was lost, Mother, all your life, you have found ways to be at ease with your conscience. He was looking at her over the glass, a distance of twenty inches and yet she felt that Linus, blurred and disembodied, was millions of light-years away. Maybe through her whole life she'd been looking at him from very far though he was next to her, a bird watcher with her eye on the binoculars watching a strange bird grow wings but unable, finally, to take to the blue sky.

When at last she fell asleep, she dreamt of her child sitting bunched up under the shelter of a red mushroom which dripped poison on him, drop by drop. Either Linus was of normal size and the mushroom as big as a beach umbrella or the mushroom was normal and Linus was as small as a beetle.

Both in sleep and wakefulness, Viv Koleva had lost perspective on the proportions of things, real sizes were waging war at her, actual images misled her, correct responses were beyond her. The next day, in the afternoon, on her way to an appointment through an ad to sell off her few bits of gold and silver, she saw one, or rather, one hundred flocks of locusts, she had never seen so many thousands of tiny black dots darkening, piercing, nibbling at the sky while heading maniacally her way as if by arrangement, to crush over her in waves.

Are the Pharaoh's seven plagues coming alive? she pondered. They were starlings. Wonderful little birds in a heavenly corps de ballet, each one a wish for a Merry Christmas, a prayer for an abundant crop. Her thoughts, though, trained invariably on ill.

Later that evening, the estate agent clinched a luxurious office space close to the inner city, at fourteen million, he'd also find a tenant for her, the rental would go in the bank and Viv Koleva wouldn't touch a cent, a sum would be collecting for her son, in case anything happened to her.

By December 15, with lightning speed and to the great joy of the realtor, the Tutu sold as well, after she finally cleared the bloody debt to the tax office which had tripled in the meantime, she invested every last remaining penny in yet another office, same area, same sacred cause.

The ballerinas moved in temporarily with her, housemates in the three-bedroom, twenty-six cardboard boxes piled one on top of the other.

She paid for contracts, commissions, property taxes, settled with accountants and with the state, and counted her change.

During those days of the endless to and fro she again had for company a small lemon in her pocket, from the same lemon tree of her childhood years, her mother had sent a humble basket with edibles, olives, lemons and oranges from their orchard. They'd exchanged a couple of words over the telephone, the daughter, thank you, the mother, I light a candle every day to Mother Mary to have pity on us.

Xenia called every so often, unbeknownst to her husband, she would start with a question about Greece, the seventy-one dead from the crash of the Ukrainian Yakovlev, and would go on, always in a dolorous tone, asking for information about the property buying, about the overall health of her sister and nephew and about the extent to which he had benefited from the two photo albums she'd sent him, without dedication, it goes without saying, the first one of polar bears, the second of Indian tribes of Northern Canada. Viv was reserved, she'd say two and three times, kiss the babies for me, and always hung up on the same pretext, the pot on the stove. She had made her mind up that she would go the length, or rather the depth of the fall, without allies, everything on her back, all on her own, and, she did, finally, prefer it this way.

The holidays were already drawing close, the first of many seasons that would follow with her son in prison and herself doing time as a murderer's mother.

At times, she would forget herself, a single being among the crowd of the main streets, looking at the glass buildings prideful over their size and their smeared glass panes, watching the traffic-jammed trucks, trolleys and cars honking, stampedes of outraged elephants in the Athenian jungle.

A new week was dawning. The Monday wind dusted, the Tuesday rain washed down and the Wednesday sun polished the city, a sparkling day does no harm, it cleans out the mind, it provides a semblance of order to the unfinished items of business that seem to multiply like rabbits and never come to an end.

Once back home, she dealt with the merchandise. She needed to get rid of it so it wouldn't take up space in her narrow house and her narrow life. She called a small production factory and three gift shop owners from the old days, offered it at half price, they weren't all that amenable, finally they said yes, she made the year's rent and her cheap cigarettes, she'd changed brands and her throat was scratched.

She also opened Picasso's two cardboard boxes to see how the artist had fared, spread the twenty Elizabeths around the room, the place turned into Buckingham, her hovel filled with velvet and tiaras. When they'd been delivered, she had taped on one of the boxes the card of the English old lady. Mrs. Judy? She called her up, thankfully the nice lady hadn't a clue about the interim developments, she was enthusiastic and moved, the monarchy holding up splendidly, the Windsors undying, by New Year's Eve, she had scored five hundred thousand, untaxed what's more. New orders for another fifty pieces, Viv would arrange it even without a shop, a peddler with a flowering trade on the side under the auspices of Her Majesty.

The Elizabeths paid for half the cost of the trial.

***

– Where did you disappear to? Why have you made yourself so scarce?

Phone call to Rhoda. She did pick up this time and said what she did halting, dry coughing and sighing. She was racing to vacate her surgery, pass her patients on to other cardiologists, mandatory leave from Athens, a whole lot of formalities to be gone through in order to establish herself elsewhere. She was babysitting her mother, the two of them were leaving for Serres up north, so the aunts could lend a hand, the old woman had grown unmanageable, she kept crying, kept getting lost in the streets of Munich, as she said, no longer remembered who she was, where she lived, her old age was turning vicious.

This was Highbrow's wreck, she even made reference to parallel dramas, precious sorrow, infertile labors, fertile despair and on and on with the diamond studded talk and the gold-and-ivory bullshit.

– Aren't you coming as witness to your godson's trial? There's nobody else.

– I'll be up north.

– So, come down. It's a half hour flight.

– With all this stuff, I'm on antidepressants.

– Your mother's lost her marbles, why are you taking them?

– I'm losing mine, too.

– Rhoda, does my cry for help have to be in a voice that would split the heavens asunder?

The useless friend, silent.

– Have you no compassion for your godson?

The useless one answered with snivelling and mewling.

That same afternoon at Yukaris's office, Viv was informed that her son did not want his godmother as witness to his trial, her especially, not on any count, he wanted no one, he demanded from his lawyer and his mother to not drag unwilling relatives or acquaintances by force, his exact words, don't put up a fight, it's not worth it, I'm not worth it.

– Is that all he said?

In essence only that, Yukaris served a coffee to his weary client and mentioned that Linus opened his mouth and said things out of rhyme and reason, that when swallows return next March and find their nests taken up by sparrows, they build them up inside, he knew this from his grandfather in the village, who took pride in the empty swallow nest on the eaves of the outdoor toilet.

That was the extent of the grandfather's help to his grandson at a time like this, the memory of an outhouse story, a village shithole, thought Viv and glanced hopelessly at the lawyer. As in every meeting, they boarded on the five-minute trip around questions such as, how can a human being do something so horrific, how can some people spiral downwards, when does the crucial switch fall in their mind and if there might be an adequate and indisputable explanation, which there isn't, we read through all the paperwork in the files and get the wiser by 50%, then we go on to trial and only 30% of the truth comes out.

Then, by necessity, Yukaris and Viv turned more practical, they set the facts down.

At the lawyer's office two volunteers had turned up, proud Cretans, brothers and sworn friends of Fotis, putting themselves at their disposal, they would with all their heart put a good word in at the court for the Kolevas family, and they'd help out a bit with the costs of the court, too, they had left an envelope for Viv.

We looked for her, the store's no longer there, we found you through your colleagues by asking who had taken on the young man's case, they had told the surprised penal lawyer, this was not something he would have expected.

– I don't require anyone's financial assistance, what we did, we'll pay ourselves, was Viv's first reaction.

However, when Yukaris called the willing Cretans in her presence, first the older one, Manousos, and then Michalis, his client, she did, finally, speak to the latter, declined the money, thanked him and submitted to his insistent request for a meeting after all these years.

The outcome was that the two brothers painted for free the two offices to be rented, filled in with silicone the cracks in the kitchen bench and basin at her house, got the collapsed balcony grilles unstuck and straightened them out, polished the Cretan chair that had been their wedding gift, changed the rubber tubing in the faucets and several broken tiles in the bathroom, they were jacks of all trades.

One afternoon, while having a cigarette at the narrow balcony, the three were watching an old man who'd taken his dog for a walk, an aged collie. Every neighborhood has one of those, said Viv, and the Cretans thought about it and they agreed, they'd worked all the neighborhoods of Athens and everywhere a grandfather with a collie could be found.

By the third drag they were close again, had shed the old coldness and the old resentments.

Manousos and Michalis with their blue eyes aflame, like pieces of cotton doused with blue alcohol and set alight, rolled out again the nostalgia for the red brotherhood and the times when they all brimmed with tears at the sound of the revolutionary songs, along with their lost companion, Fotis kept turning up in their talk, he patched the holes that threatened every time a stray reference was made to sons, they had three apiece, a half a dozen good in school and at basketball and at Cretan folk dancing.

Viv learned things about her husband she hadn't known, that he gave generous discounts and extended the number of payments for those who weren't managing, that he made gifts of doors to newlyweds starting up a household. The Cretans, as human beings and as party members, had their conscience burdened by their failure to pull him away from the road to perdition and were now seeking with their screwdrivers and wire brushes to repair the damage that God himself could not undo.

They invited Viv to go out with them to a small tavern in Pireas, somewhere out of the way, their wives, comrades themselves, born and raised Cretans as well, from the mountains, at that, really wanted to. Viv didn't. She had no right to entertainment, she ought to stay concentrated on her destiny, faithful to the consequences, cut off inside her four walls, not even a single painting anymore.

In this game, people and things were taking part. When she got back to the apartment alone, she had the impression that the carved wooden chair ceased her conversation with the old checkered couch, the few bits of furniture and objects were quiet, some were afraid to take her on and others were in no mood for her. Wordless herself, along with her trable and her brookshelf, the r's, especially at nights, a torrent spilling over everything.

After that came the hours of the toasted bread. She sat in the small kitchen in her robe with the holes at the elbows, a five-year-old garment, who would see her, it would last through the winter just fine, and held before her gaze all through the night the piece of toasted bread on the plate, scrutinizing minutely the grains of rye, counting the tiny bubbles of the baking, gathering, subtracting and moving around the crumbs with her finger on the porcelain, until another heavy night was bloody well over and done with.

She had learned to make her way under the threat of time, to defend herself with crumbs, she could give classes on that one.

***

February, the offices were rented out. March, the branches budded. April, the two Easter buns came from the village. May, the mass media took up position, they'd sold out with the many-page spreads and the inserts about the deceased Karamanlis and the night-flower of Patissia promising merchandise.

The day before the trial started, Viv Koleva watched television, two hours standing and unmoving as if she was at a crowded movie house. They can do as they please in the movies, they stab with ice picks, saw people up in pieces, take out fifty in one night and they get an Oscar.

Then she slept like an ox for six hours straight and had a dream, again with an awful lot of trekking. She was walking along a dead-end alley, a labyrinth of low, old houses, like dentures with teeth broken off. She was looking for the disappeared Fotis, but she couldn't call out for him because she couldn't for the life of her find the middle consonant to his name. She was consumed by the anxiety of completing the *Fotis* in order to call him and find him so she wouldn't wander blindly on her own, but it was impossible because the t had gone missing from her mouth and from everywhere as if it had up and left this worldly existence.

In the morning she recovered, girded her loins, fortified herself with a double coffee and set out for the courthouse.

Her son took up his position and not on that first day, nor in those that followed, did he move his head or hands, did he flicker his eyelashes or cough or lick his cracked lips, he seemed like a taxidermist's bird. His eyes looked twice as large as normal and his hair, much of it again, enough for two and three heads, looked like fake riches on his skeletal and twisted body.

His mother had counted on his wreckage entering the courtroom well preserved inside a suit.

Eighty thousand, expensive flannel and impeccable tailoring, dark blue with a white shirt and a black tie with diagonal gray stripes, so that he would appear civil before the judges but also before the victims and their relatives as well as the curious crowd and the reporters who had descended like crows in the hall of the Penal Court.

– Put on a suit, for what? So that my victims take a liking to me? To show respect towards the ceremony? To feign remorse? For you to show me off to good advantage? So that people don't think you a miser?

These and then some, Mom, you're throwing your money away, and, forget your stage coaching, and, best if you stayed at home, and, I don't want you in there, God damn it, he had delivered them the day before, as eloquent as it gets, his spit flying, volleys of it on the floor, smashing his hand on his knee with a zdoop resounding at every punch and for the finale, dropping his head to his belly button and speaking to himself, I don't know them, I don't remember their faces, I don't want to look at their eyes, I covered them with the shapka.

Yukaris was listening to him patiently and a little abstractedly, he'd dealt with several tough cookies accused of every manner of transgression, there were other trials he had lost too.

During the hearing, the solemn suit was absent but so was Linus himself, though he was present, as if the goings-on did not concern him, he was not surprised, he did not react, his reddened eyes fixed constantly on the bare wall opposite, every day on the same exact spot.

Against her son's will, Viv Koleva in dark glasses and clothes was every day at her post, in the back seats and to the side and usually alone, Manousos and Michalis had come along separately one time and for half an hour each, they had held her arm for a while and then they had split, on the pretext of the day's wages, how to behave and what to say to her, how to listen soberly to all those testimonies and all the detailing by the consultants and the experts which bounded from wall to wall in the hall, imposing on the crowd sometimes a deadly silence and sometimes a susurrus of rage.

Viv herself, with her head buzzing, made no effort to listen, to combine, to comprehend, to anticipate, on the contrary, she struggled to miss the salient points of the depositions, to not catch sight of the two girls, to avoid the spectacle of their parents, the mother of the dead Koula, as youthful as they come until last year, she had seen her photographs, now, within ten months, an old woman with sunken cheeks, dishevelled, snow-white hair spilling over the black clothes and unkempt, the ripped lining was hanging from her skirt.

Scrunched up in her place, Viv Koleva was pressuring her mind to leave that place, go anywhere else, to the medical classes of the first year, to the scenes of Kurosawa's *Dersou Uzala* in the boreal forests of Siberia, to paragraphs with fire-flies in the lush fields of foreign novels, to the compliments of the famous choreographer Yannis Flery who'd chanced into the *Tutu* once, when he saw a poster of one of his shows on the shop window.

Her ear caught fleeting phrases from depositions and testimonies, although there were some instances where she didn't miss a single word. I'd just said goodbye to my girlfriends, I'd shouted to them to celebrate my new, well-paid job, I was happy and wasn't thinking of any danger, this from the first victim, I crossed through the park to save some distance, I was in a hurry to get home so my stepfather wouldn't get mad and take it out on my mother again, this from the second victim, the third could not testify, she wasn't alive.

The details about the modus operandi took up hours and days, dozens of questions about the shoe in the mouth, the Russian hat, a headrest or a face cover for the victims, the blue hairpin, the torn up skirt with the side split, the pink panties, the pubic hairs in the mouth, the throwing up, the hemor-rhaging, the bruises, the nipples, the nail-marks to the perpe-trator's neck, to his genitals, his shit-smeared underwear, the genetic material.

This is where he faints, now he's going to faint, Viv was

waiting from her son to at last do something right, eventually it was three others who fainted, one of the girls, the mother and father of the dead girl, the latter twice.

She was watching the accused as if seeing him for the first time, examining his shape, his apathy, his rigidity, not someone she knew, a stranger.

In the taking of a human life apologies don't count, there are no miracles, the dead cannot be resurrected. Still, with years, people can forgive on their own not just thieves and robbers but killers too, during a fight, a pursuit or for reasons of honor. There is only one unforgivable crime, rape. For all the women of the world, half the earth's population, the rapist is an animal and will remain so for the rest of his life, the stain, even if he hasn't killed anyone, never wears off.

During the breaks in the trial, Viv listened to people comment on her son, a clear-cut killer, a sick bastard, scum, needs to be shot, hung at Syntagma Square, castrated, and some wondered where his villainous mother might be, she, also, ought to be toppled into some gorge, everything is the mothers' fault.

Reporters looked for her, too, she covered her face, refused, evaded them. One photographer pursued her all the way to the toilets where Viv sought refuge, she shut herself up in there for an hour, the nightmare in full throttle.

All those days she didn't turn the TV on, bought no newspaper, didn't want to see, nor, certainly, to save any clippings. At nights her phone would ring several times, the indefatigable hounds of the media, just one statement Mrs. Koleva, her mother with a thousand sighs, Xenia, and, overwhelmed and terrified by the furor, Rhoda from Nevada, yet another medical conference, that was the cherry on the cake, impatient to be told what Linus had said up to now and what he intended to say in his defense.

Linus made no defense speech.

Menios Yukaris, without any great arguments that he could

use as ammunition to shoot down in flames the evidence of guilt, didn't put on a performance and he probably disappointed the court aficionados who only live for a good trial. He did his duty, fairly modestly, did not speak for very long, did not overstate his case, he wrapped up, within a quarter of an hour, the orphanhood, the trauma due to an alcoholic father, the past of the honest family, the unceasing struggle of the working mother who, let it be noted, did not proceed, as is common nowadays, to look after her own life by means of a second marriage, he improvised a small lie too, about how the unlucky Koula offended the masculine pride of the accused which is how the tragic end must be explained, and he interpreted the young man's refusal to ask for the Court's clemency, on the mitigating grounds of post-adolescent confusion and as acknowledgment of his responsibility, acceptance of the acts ascribed to him, and as silent amends. He made a little bit of a splash only toward the end, which was intentional, by revealing that in his private meetings with the accused, he had repeatedly expressed the wish that the death penalty would be reintroduced.

Viv Koleva didn't doubt it and she didn't think it was such a bad idea, what kind of life could he expect, what kind could she expect herself. She was even thinking that a court of self-punishment was needed, she would go of her own accord, the prosecutor of herself for ruinous acts of omission and the judge, too, giving down the harshest conviction, exile to some hell or other.

She was rollercoastered by the proceedings and mainly by the unanswerable questions that had, for some time now, been jostling in her mind, do I love or do I hate my only child, did I ever love him, was my heart ever truly warm to him, did I mollycoddle him, my precious and my lovely, did I ache for him, can someone who hasn't loved their parent really love their child?

The nights promoted her to the highest echelons of sleeplessness, they barely allowed for some ten-minute snatches of sleep, just enough for the nightmare to fit in that she was the white-haired mother of the dead Koula, who storms the place where the accused sits and strangles with her bare hands the killer and tormentor of her daughter.

Linus Kolevas went in for life with no ifs or buts.

The jurors' decision was as expected and it was hailed by the audience with a mixture of applause and curses, may you rot in that cell, here's your one-way ticket to hell, the other jail-mates will do right by you, hope you die like a mongrel dog, hope you get cancer, all together like a marching war band striking a paean of hateful spleen against Hannibal.

Viv and Linus looked at one another for seconds only.

The son's stare was hostile, so that his mother would never forget it. But the mother's was no less so. In a way, the trial mainly concerned the two of them, they were the opposing parties, simultaneously accusing and defending. So they judged and convicted each other of the highest penalty.

This was a just decision, too, and it was taken wordlessly, at the moment when the father of the dead girl raised up and held above everybody's head, like a flag, a large framed photograph of his hapless daughter.

Yukaris did not submit an appeal, Linus did not allow him, his refusal was staunch.

Later that afternoon, Viv rolled into her chair as heavy as an old olive oil pot with all the muck at the bottom. As she could no longer think and could no longer bear bringing to mind her son's face and looking at him even in her imagination, she brought to mind his toenails, precisely because they were the farthest away from his eyes and his gaze, especially that more recent one, the courtroom gaze, so she raced stricken to his nails, five little horns on one foot and five on the other, longish and a little curved, often with a small gray edge at the end when Linus neglected to trim them on time.

She now wondered if the toenails were properly kept, if nail clippers were allowed in jail and if at night shoes were left inside the cell or just outside the metal door to air. She wondered how many have holes in them, if they steal each other's shoes and if the guards mix them up as a joke. Straight after that, a more general question occurred to her. Was she so voluble in her thoughts when she was a little girl too, or was she as silent as a sphinx back in her village of Alonaki? She did not remember her little head prattling so, besides, what can a little kid have amassed in the space of seven, ten years, how could it be practiced in this dark, cursed art of holding its tongue, like they say, but then unleash it inside the mind and work it nonstop? Still, even now, in these trying times, Viv Koleva was not too sure that the echoes in the chambers of her brain were always those of her own voice and not the externally dictated elaborate pronouncements by some unknown overseer of her existence, observer, exhumer and judge, all in one.

Life inside the head is always harder, more painful and long lasting, my head, she thought, will be concussing with the reverberations even after death, it will become a skull in delirium.

Just then the doorbell rang abruptly, the sound hit her in the back as she sat, it jerked her upright, she stumbled, nearly fell over.

This was Charidemos's first visit. She heard the inarticulate cat like little cries behind the door, saw him through the peephole, let him in without a second thought. Her dumb, cross-eyed and deaf-mute compatriot, the cousin of her schoolmate Petra, was holding in one hand the paper with the typed address of Vivian Sotiropoulos and in the other the tray with the first milk pie—in the years to come others would follow.

His broken syllables had an immediate impact. They brought into the room the village with all of memory's dung, the old voices tied into a knot, the old looks tied into a bunch, all of it together, the detritus sunk forever at the bottom of her life's story.

Unsuspecting of this particular home's unhappiness and the hardships of the whole wide world, happy as a lark to have seen his mission through, Charidemos was pleased with the cold water and, later, the three pieces of toast, was ecstatic over the Queen Elizabeth Viv gave him and he cried with happiness when she dressed him with her son's unworn blue suit.

He sat on the couch like a debutant, back straight, palms folded upon his knees, well mannered and grateful, as was appropriate to the quality, the price and the kind of his attire, a formal, robust, manly outfit.

Viv Koleva was looking at the retarded boy and couldn't get enough of him. His saliva, the crooked mouth and black beady eyes trained on her, didn't bother her one bit. When, eventually, he grunted his concern over the time, and picking up his doll, got up to leave, he had to take a taxi to the bus station and make the last bus to the Peloponnese, the directions for the return on a second note, the woman hugged him tightly, stroked his head and even kissed him on the cheek.

– Better if I had you as my son, she whispered, yet another verse out of the poem of her life which she had to recite bit by bit to the end, there were probably still many verses left, her sack was heavy. It was heavy, all right, because her sack was her son himself.

THE WALL

The *old door of old people*, a recent verse so that her life's poem could draw on at length.

It was a subject Viv hadn't thought about before, despite her apprenticeship, via Fotis, to many kinds of wooden casings and frames.

Old people, when they happen to be moved elsewhere, know they cannot start a new life, they carry along with them the old walls, saturated with everything that's happened to them. Even in a newly erected building, in the most modern or renovated apartment, their door is old, not to mention it could easily be said that most of them, people of a humble and humiliated youth, have spent many decades waiting silently behind the world's door.

Viv now crossed those old doors daily in the exercise of her new duties, home care for the elderly who needed someone's care and reassurance, especially before the terrible onset of evening.

She had asked from Rhoda the one and only favor of introducing her to a couple of patients for a start and to provide relevant directions, she wouldn't encumber her with the rest, she would read up, get equipment, look after things by herself.

A few phone calls were made and the prize patients were located, Viv had said outright she preferred those over seventy-five, the more over the better, who wouldn't set much stock by the reporters' mongering, wouldn't be into current affairs much and would not, at all costs, have large families, especially not nearby, she couldn't take the extra stares, the old wretched patients' stares were more than enough for her.

Up until then, she saw old folks as the pedestrians of life, without money for taxis, no knees for buses, slowly doing the rounds—bakery, pharmacy, Social Health Fund—or resting on peeling, unhinged park benches like half-eaten bagels in a crushed paper bag.

With such as these, four loners and two couples, as the first crop, her brilliant career took off, creatures that had met with need as time rounds the bend, with the memory gaping, the thoughts blocking, the tongue stumbling, the body collapsing and the offspring beating a hasty retreat.

After May '98, her life drawn out, empty and simultaneously full of arthritic fingers like bunches of tangled intestines, feet disfigured by swellings, broken veins and myriads of tiny vessels like handfuls of purple threadlike kadaifi pastry, with old women like old-fashioned cartoons, rounded swollen bodies on toothpick calves, aged lungs that coughed green mucus, old asses that farted like trombones or raised a tsunami of shit when some grandfather's intestines didn't mean to dry up.

All of this in an environment of partial abandonment due to helplessness and lowly pensions, worn two-seat sofas, sheets with the flowers faded from all the laundering, flattened pillows, towels with their fluffiness corroded by overuse, showers with rust around the nickel-plated pipe rings, sponges half eaten away with black muck in the holes, wounded plates and glasses, the cups and pots without handles, but everywhere lots of color photographs of the grandchildren at the pianos, the karate classes, the birthday parties, on the destroyer warship in a sailor's uniform, at the military pilot's training school, put up like submission forms for an extension on life, over all the objects and pieces of furniture, around the edge of the prewar picture frames with the black-and-white relatives, on the plastic St. Panteleimon, healer of bodies and souls, the laurel-wreathed Eleftherios Venizelos on the TV, the gilded Andreas Papandreou and his wife Mimi on the dresser, stuck with scotch tape on the fridge, pinned on the inside of the wardrobe and next to it, on the bedside table, back-to-back with the bottles of cough syrups and alcohol, so they can reach for them, so they can caress them at all times.

Viv herself would never get a daughter-in-law or in-laws or grandchildren. She had told none of her clients that she had a son and what kind he was. How could she come out with it? In what manner? Something along the lines of, my sweet boy doing life?

Experienced in war zones, accomplished in adversity, she transited smoothly from ballet to blood pressure monitors, from satin bows to poultices for bedsores and within six months she was renowned and much in demand, her clients, whom time had ravaged, my cadavers, as she called them even to their faces while she fed or sprayed them with cologne, bribed her so she wouldn't leave them, with cheese pies and grape-must cookies from well meaning neighbors and disclosed their wills to her, some would only bequeath their good example of stoical endurance and others would sow seeds for future strife among the disappeared relatives, who'd be at each other's throats over the measly two-room apartment and the fake gold jewelry.

Sometimes in her nightly expedition to the center or north or south of the city for a change of catheter or to measure blood levels of sugar, she sat with them longer, what would she do alone in her decrepit little home, she sweet-talked them, you'll be fine by the time you get married, and, I'll kiss it where it hurts and, pain makes friends of enemies and, sickness brings out all the strength in us, she wheedled them for a bit of back and forth of compassionate mottos, to relieve their deranged loneliness, to lessen the abundance of silence that grips old mouths, especially just before the night's lead sets in.

Almost all of them knew just fine how to sum up the basics.

It's good being a child because at eight and at ten you've only a few things to remember, the one, despicable, to spend three hours trying to remember what you had for lunch, the next one is a one-liner, nobody in my family really cares what I want, they only allow me to wish for a peeled kiwifruit, the third, the fourth a variation on the same theme, they come to visit for one hour every Sunday and, instead of all of us having a talk, they sit on the couch and continue with where they left off, the fifth, from sixty onwards you need a quarter of an hour to iron your underwear, ten times the size it was twenty years ago, right from its start, life hangs on a cotton thread, the sixth, the seventh and much traveled, I've been to many countries but the world's nicest nation was my table with my family gathered around, may God give us passage for our way out, the eighth and so on and so forth.

One couple in Exarchia, married for sixty-five years, watched all the day's news bulletins fanatically, by nightfall they had memorized national and global news, everything a pulp in the husband's head, the fires in Attica, the tear gas at Clinton's reception, the stock market plunge, Cathy Freeman in Sydney, the protests for the insurance measures, the wife, with an elephant's memory and the wisdom of an owl, could listen to the initial phrase and finish the sentence by herself, she had lived through all versions of political, economic and diplomatic fiascos on the planet, a world that no longer surprised her on any count.

A second couple were mildly deranged and overweight, like hot air balloons still moored, unable to lift up to the skies, all day and night on two armchairs surrounded by their works, second-rate writers of children's books with seventy-odd little tomes and booklets, *The Nightingale with Mouth Sores, The Half-Burnt Pancake, My Heart's Sweetheart, The Tear that Secretly laughed, The Prayer of the Sandwich.* Their son, a family man and father of three in Salonika, had finally found the one and only way to keep them happy and perfectly well behaved, video porn. By necessity, he'd let the nurse in on the secret. So they would take their pills, a dozen each, and then would devote themselves to the night episodes of *Restless Youth*, as the son had told them, which they found infinitely more engaging than the day ones.

Another client, an eighty-minus one retired theologian, his one daughter married in Milan to a carabiniere, the second to a traffic cop in Frankfurt, himself recovering from a heavy stroke, his fourth, he'd get as far as death's door, find it closed and come back.

Next was a grandmother who suffered from a bit of everything, completely dependent on hair curlers and cream soaps. After her primary care, she commanded Viv to paint her nails and take out the hairs from her chin with the tweezers, all anxious about looking good at her life's last, great date.

Yet another, wearing on all occasions her favorite brooch, a tiny golden turtle, even on her flannel nightie, continually stroked the piece of jewelry she bore on her chest above her heart, where everything takes root, including her sorrow for her deceased mate, his Volvo now is my Volvo, his cat now is my cat, his dressing gown now is my dressing gown and his angina now is my angina.

Further down the line was the old Cretan, crooked like a crescent moon, who made up a different rhyme daily for his tombstone, alongside all the sayings which had provided him with comfort all his life though Viv, who listened to them, found no comfort: *Where the goat leaps, so does the kid, No seed out of a rotten pumpkin*, and, *A man's face is a sheer cliff*. It was as if they were handpicked to rekindle her own actions in her mind.

Another, born to the poverty of rural Thessaly, a hundred different bags with dried leaves hanging on the walls of his room, overwhelmed her with his botanical obsessions, the weed-killing thyme, the soporific poppy, nettle for anemia, rue for the lungs, tall mallow for the digestion, and asked her if and when she could venture to certain gorges and nature spots to unearth some bulbs that worked miracles with erections. Viv was watching out for his blood pressure, every so often banging some cortisone into him for his dilapidated knees, and she gave him her word that as soon as he got himself a girl-friend, she would bring him the bulbs and would personally go to the Public Health Fund to have them prescribe him some Viagra.

Injections affected the elderly like a truth serum, in the next fifteen minutes, before she was due to leave, they would come up with one or two secrets that weighed on them, that they'd cheated on their now deceased husband, they'd encroached on some poor neighbor's land in the village, they'd been unfair with their second daughter's dowry, they had unjustly accused their daughter-in-law to the son and their son had divorced her.

Viv Koleva, Sotiropoulos to all of them, was furtively rummaging through other people's sacks and, day by day, was building a goodly stock of others' trespasses, both petty and otherwise.

The number of clients would ebb and flow, every two months she led at least one departing ceremony, since as a rule she was hired at five minutes to the grave, death's sentinel and helper, hardworking, discreet, deft at hole-punching, cool-headed, brought them boiled greens in Tupperware, treated them to the odd cigarette.

Death, a habit really. Ever since Fotis died, she'd had the upper hand on death. She was polishing her pumps when the Highbrow called with news of the fatal heart attack of Eleftheria, a fellow student in the first year of Medicine, she thought of her for a while and went on shoe shining, she was

listening to a favorite program on the radio when the hairdresser from two doors down came in to say his sister had been
killed in a car accident, she knew her, relatively young, the
hairdresser left, she went straight back to the radio, she got a
letter from Germany about her godfather's death and went on
calmly breaking walnuts for the pie, she went to the funeral of
Aunt Zoe, the one she'd lived with during that first year in
Athens, but didn't stay for the coffee, she headed back home
because she was expecting the carpets from the cleaner's,
Linus told her about a girl at school dead from heroin and
within half an hour she was reading poetry, her father died and
immediately he was added in her head to the three thousand
dead in the Twin Towers, after three days Kazantzidis was gone
as well, the idol of Fotis's group, she was probably the only
Greek who didn't have a tear in her eye, whereas even her
coterie of old folks lamented bitterly, she went to the funeral of
Judy, the old English woman who turned her on to the lucrative Elizabeths, and clinched another ten orders on the spot,
because, although she was done with the shop, she was far
from done with the royal dolls, an untaxed bit of business,
especially under the current circumstances, she had an obligation to steal from the government and, as much as possible, she
did, she got paid for her work under the table, no receipts, and
one of the two offices was supposedly unrented, trifles, to be
sure, in comparison with the jackals of the ministries and big
business, going all out for stocks and Rolexes and big scale
scams.

Her house full of paramedical supplies, Pampers, gloves,
wet tissues, plastic kidney bowls, cottons, antiseptics, douches,
self-adhesive bandages, dressings, masks, gauzes, syringes, dis-
pensable aprons and slippers, under the gaze of the Elizabeths
from the high shelf, they'd now become the United Kingdom
of plasticized under-sheets and urinary bags.

Sometimes, late at night, at eleven and twelve, when she

trekked back to her place, exhausted by the hard labor and inflamed by other people's stories, she thought that virtually all people ached over one thing or another and that she would like to give them five million analgesic injections, one each and for free, so they could have a break, get a night's rest and have a dream, at last, deserving of the name, boats in calm seas or gardens and fragrant citrus flowers raining on smiling kids.

No kids to be found anywhere, in her sleep or in her waking. Only her relics. For twenty years she had lived off the young girls and the adolescents with the well trained physiques. Now she earned her living from the flabby and half-rotting carcasses of the aged, barely able to drag themselves to the toilet, who were shuffling in line in death's dance and one by one waved their handkerchiefs goodbye to this world.

Yet all these people, strange and ephemeral in her life were actually probably very useful. In some way, by force of their agony and the nonnegotiable ending, little by little, they asserted themselves over her, something which she hadn't known before, others having the upper hand, even briefly.

She did not despise them, was not bored with them, did not tell them off, did not charge an arm and a leg, she worked on a Bulgarian's wages, at times when work was scarce she even asked for less than did the Valentinas, Rummis and Stefkas. She was fond, too, of their outmoded blankets with the beige and brown leopards against a mustard backdrop, she shared in their shame when the deodorizer was finished and the room smelled bad, she respected their bony hands with the perishable skin.

Though they did work her to the bone, they strangely did not weigh her heart down, sometimes she even felt like the old folks were her respite, the wizards of a queer, if short-lived, muscle-relaxing harmony, her "break," like they said on TV.

In their good moments, they narrated their lives as if they

were a demotic song, whether from Crete or Hepeirus or Macedonia, with a sigh accentuating the pauses, a handsome old-fashioned word working its magic and resurrecting the old triumphs, which is to say, their small village, their first suit, their little garden with the now scarce crabapples and baby pears.

She would think of things they'd said, such as, for all life gives us we only owe it one death, and she almost envied them, no matter that some were stranded in the same position on a fold-up bed, or as good as forgotten inside their private worlds. They were edging toward the end and were accepting of that, leaning for comfort on the Old Testament, *A time for giving birth and a time for dying.*

If there was one thing on which Viv agreed with the Japanese, it was that the most beautiful trees are the old ones. At times, she even inwardly told herself that instead of the years passing her by at their ease, she would have liked to pass them by herself, decisively and swiftly, one stride for each decade.

– Viv, my lass, you do sometimes mangle your words, take marjoram if you have a headache or jasmine leaves as an over-all tonic, this from the old Thessalian.

– Viv, my child, I listen to you coming up with words that aren't right, lermon and coorkie and jarket. *The mind makes the body weary and the mind can give it rest*, this from the more specific old Cretan.

Because next to all of them and all of it roamed continu-ously, without giving her a moment's reprieve, the shadow of her son.

***

The prison house of Korydallos is inside the city, throngs of buildings and people around, yet it is at the end of the line, that is the address, and the monthly journey there, with a load of clean clothes inside the two plastic bags and the Tupperware with the beef in the third, was yet another odyssey of the mind.

During the visits, Viv spoke to Linus about far-fetched things, parrots that said Viva Maradona, monkeys that suckled orphan tigers, the antioxidant properties of olive oil and a Swiss pharmaceutical company which aimed at releasing to the market within three years, the new medicine for Parkinson's disease.

She fished the bits of news from papers she occasionally bought and magazines she thumbed at her clients' houses, evaluated them and jotted them down on a small pad to have them handy.

She prepared the subjects for days, so as not to spoil the final effect with artless words, to have them in order, which one will make a good start, that especially was very important so she could get a flow and deliver the rest with ease.

Almost always she was the only one talking and each time she found that the fifteen minutes allocated for the visit was too long, she was standing on tiptoe and trying hard to fill the time with no breaks. Behind the glass, he held the receiver and listened absentmindedly, only at the end did he look at her with an intense stare, filled with contempt for both of them.

On certain occasions, pretending to be relaxed, to be exclusively and earnestly interested in the world's oddities and the progress of medical science was impossible. The elections are easily skirted, the global petrol reserves likewise, what is there to say about armament programs, the Pope's visit and his apology for the Crusades weren't exactly appropriate for small talk behind the glass, the arrest of the members of the organization 17 November, in the same prison as he, brooked no commentary, how could it when the communist's grandson happens to be in for life and isn't even a political prisoner.

Beginning of September 2004 the fifteen minutes were taken up with the explosion of the school in Beslan. Viv referred to the three hundred and ninety-four victims, young kids mostly, to Vladimir Putin, to the negotiator Ruslan Aushev, to Chechnya's media representative Achmat Zakayiev, to the two Ossetias, Georgia and the whole of the riddled Caucasus. She was pale, spoke curtly and evocatively, she delivered the whole thing breathlessly and she only let slip one "r," hoorded men.

– Do you want me to think you are unhappy because of Beslan?

Her son rarely commented or interrupted her, if he talked, he did so straight away with his stare, faster than a gunshot. It was a good thing, then, that he put a question to her, but there was no point in replying to this specific one, Seneca had answered this already, *No one is unhappy only because of the present*, Yukaris mentioned him often.

– I have made up my mind, mother, about one thing, to be unhappy on your account for all my life.

How was she to cover the damned fifteen minutes with him? Only with monkeys, yaks, Marco Polo rams and assorted quadrupeds? Was she supposed to brag about her professional life, *Work is the sickle which reaps time*, Napoleon Bonaparte, again compliments of Yukaris, her gainful employment, in ordinary parlance, with folks who were fading away, some speedily and others not so fast? Was she supposed to tell him about the incontinence of the old Cretan who doused her with sayings and improvised verses? About her neighborhood which had become filled with banks and was looking for some more? About the entire city which had lost its stamina and was acquiring a look of permanent ugliness? Would he be interested in discussing where the Cyprus issue was and the enormous complications of the Annan proposal?

They had come to an arrangement regarding things dietary and monetary, as for family news, it was delivered telegraphically and not in its entirety. His grandfather's death had affected him, he had lost another ten pounds, and he'd had a petit mal as well, that autistic delirium with the zdoops. Grandma sent best regards and a knitted talisman against the evil eye, she came to Athens very rarely, had asked to see him, if only the once, he kept refusing.

The Canadians' arrival in 2003 was not mentioned as his aunt Xenia did not receive her husband's consent to visit him. Their little ones, Meg and Stavroula, didn't even know they had a cousin, but a time would come when they'd find out everything, *Time is the wisest of all, for it discloses all things*, this one by Thales, next to Yukaris, Viv also memorized things of that sort.

After the screeching of the media had died down, Aunt Kiki had also made an appearance, Fotis's unknown sister. She called the lawyer four times, asking to reestablish the connection. What she had in mind was half an hour with Viv, straight out. After much deliberation Viv consented, thinking that if something happened to her, there could at least be a third party on standby, those two old letters she'd found in Linus's room now took on a new meaning, maybe the old guilt could turn out for the good. She knew from Fotis about her and her husband, they were in with the Socialist Party since 1981, whenever it was to their interest they brought up the persecuted communist dad, when it wasn't, they played dead. Sole purpose of the meeting was the paying up of the sum of one hundred thousand drachmas, just the once, they would patch the hole in their conscience and things would be fine.

The present-day Kiki bore no relation to the old heart-rending letters. Viv heard her offer, listened patiently to the old compassionate clichés about the martyrdom and the social out-cry, discovered how her own children had studied, married and now had settled lives in London, she learned, without ask-ing, about the other sister, Melpo, in Texas somewhere for a number of years, also cut off, followed by news about places and people she hadn't the slightest interest in, not a word about any piece of property in Corfu, if such existed, she paid for the coffees and got rid of her with an "and now you can get lost, you and your money." Fine indeed was the offspring left behind by her heroic in-laws, their lives bedraggled from one place of exile to the next.

She said not a word to Linus, there was no reason to.

She did tell him about his godmother. Rhoda, who would put in a hurried call from Serres at Christmas and Easter, had sent a wedding invitation, after having erotically sucked dry a few legions of penniless and increasingly younger men, she would tie the knot with a car dealer, adding a new surname to her own and making up into the deal for her losses at the stockmarket of twenty-five million.

– Have you sent her the two hundred thousand back? Linus's question. She had indeed, in the new currency, six hundred euros, alongside her wedding gift, two silver picture frames and a cut-and-dried wish, may you be happy and prosper, and that was the end of the relationship of two women who for years had been vying over which of the two was the smarter.

She also told him about the Cretan brothers, they'd had her over for a meal in the yard of their house, a two-story in the western suburbs, one on each floor. They had invited others too, after some trouble she did remember them one by one, then fierce and all fired up about the revolution, now unstrung balalaikas, disillusioned and embittered, one of them, from up north, an unrepentant romantic, proud, moneyless and therefore divorced, his wife had split. The missus of the younger brother gave her two kinds of sweet cheese pastries for Linus, the prison administration did not allow them.

Once every so often, there was the milk pie by the same bearer always, the prison guards had tasted it and so had the other inmates, the latter a whole chapter unto themselves. Viv learned about the beings of Korydallos, sometimes from the relatives waiting long hours under the awning and fighting over the yellow priority tickets, gypsies with armfuls of babies and sad Pakistanis, sometimes from Yukaris or from the papers and the TV channels who remembered them whenever they came out onto the rooftop and burnt a mattress or two, rarely from Linus.

The most noteworthy thing, to her, was the hangings in the cells. How come her son hadn't made even a single suicide attempt? Shouldn't he have at least tried it, though he would have, of course, been found on time and the blood flow staunched from the cut veins? Something of the sort would offer his mother a bit of relief. But it seemed that Linus had great endurance when it came to unhappiness, he had no intention of saving himself, inimitable. She watched him head in a straight line for baldness and a hump.

Viv Koleva would leave the prison compound and start on her itineraries, faithful to the ad, *keep walking*, to stock up on eyedrops, ointments, yogurts and not forget the frankincense and the votive breads, drop in on a main hospital or two to see clients whose time had come to be hospitalized, go and check the bank account, send a bit of money to her mother, pay the money due for the bones at the charnel house, change the Fiat's oils.

If it was summertime, all the streets flowing like rivers to the sea, her gaze stabbed the mothers who were parading their half-naked nubile daughters as if expecting to get a good price.

If it was winter, the winds swooping wildly down and the cold cutting up her back, a saw on dead wood, there were other things to take note of, little children wrapped in thick coats in their fathers' arms.

In December's scenery, with the gold-and-red lanterns and the tiny lights on the bare trees, the lead role belonged unequivocally to the families, the whole town became an album with shiny postcards.

The Christmas trees stood near the windows so they could be seen from the outside, I saw all of you, one hundred, two hundred, I see you, and here's one more, Viv was thinking as she drove or walked alone in the streets at dusk or at night, scanning the ornaments and colored lights that blinked along the windows framing the Athens of the festive living rooms where friends and relatives came and went, well-wished and laughed, jostled children on their knee, put the old folks at the head of the table, surrendered themselves to the few days of release that reigned at that time of year, imposing a truce on all conflicts, a necessary respite until the vacuum cleaner sucks up the glitter and everything goes back to normal.

Usually every Christmas and New Year's Eve, after putting her old folks to sleep, she drifted under the awning of one of those taverns specializing in egg-and-lemon stew of lamb's intestines, watched the patrons inside, solitary like herself, and after some looking, made up her mind, walked in and celebrated bent over a plate of lamb stew and a glass of wine.

As was expected, she'd get the come-on from one of the single males present, Albanian cruising with the eyes, days like these, in a place like this, a woman on her own was probably looking for it.

Whether she was looking for it or wasn't, Viv Koleva went back home unaccompanied and the occasion, a year going out, a year coming in, invited her to sit and think of her son's holidays, again in prison, his life in the prison cell, her life in the successive cells of her apartments.

At the beginning of 2000 and in the middle of 2005 she'd changed neighborhoods, she kept stumbling on curious folk, possibly ready to blow her cover, she couldn't stand their attitude and she had run away with her cardboard boxes.

Always and everywhere same old, same old. Black seeds of peony that drive away nightmares, the black hellebore or Christmas rose, a plant against sadness according to the now deceased sage from Thessaly and where could she get these, to keep at bay, even artificially, even for a while, all the things that riddled her.

Nothing refined or delicate in her life, everything rough. And plenty of it. In her head a commotion. For there to be space for so much, it shouldn't be the size of other people's heads, a football, it should be one huge monolith as big as the rock of the Acropolis.

This was the rock that contributed to the idea with the antiquities.

During visiting hour, playacting the positive thinker, she tormented her son with proposals that might distract him from his predicament, with questionnaires about the protection of the arctic environment, with the biographies and lifeworks of philosophers from newspaper inserts, with treatises about Islam, so that he would be understanding towards his Muslim fellow inmates or with one hundred stamps, Linus, here's the beginning of your collection.

He, unfazed, had no wish to give in to any distraction, there was nothing worth diverting him from the truth.

Twice he had dressed her down, asking her not to set foot there again bringing training programs, his mind was fully occupied anyway.

– With what?

– With negating all pleas of innocence.

– Be more clear.

– I've no intention to.

Nevertheless, Viv Koleva did not give up. Apart from the son in jail for life, she, too, needed a goal. It was defined for her after much agonizing on nights full of delirium and a nerve pain in her neck, by the documentary on National Channel 3, besotted archaeologists, decrepit Indian workers and a magical atmosphere of excavations in the places of the Incas.

That's it, she decided, her own country would stand her in good stead with the multitudes of antique goodies.

White marbles make the world go round.

***

– We'll stand here first to catch our breath, to turn our gaze backwards and mentally enjoy the sight of the first ten votive offerings along the Sacred Way, a total of about one hundred bronze statues, elsewhere water sprouts at the base of the Iampia peak, *the best of all waters*, according to Pindar, and then there was the monument of the fleet commanders, and there was this, that and the other, a glut of masterpieces, always with the helpful booklet at hand. Antinoos, the Charioteer, the Castalia Spring, the Rock of Sibyl, Leto's Stone, all the ancient lures going to waste, the fish wasn't taking the bait.

Friday's guided tour in the midst of May's conflagration didn't have the anticipated result, Linus remained unmoved. His mother couldn't believe such impassivity, nothing getting through to him, his not reaching out for the chance after all those years in the dungeon where, besides, he was due again Monday night.

When even foreigners from the far reaches, Indians, Brazilians and what looked like Tartars, had been assailed by the ancient pulse and were roaming around bedazzled by the powerful vibration.

Viv Koleva, however, did not lose courage, with time those impressions might work in her son's head and two months later, or six, a year at the outside, Linus could see the light and ask her for, say, essays on the still undeciphered 242 symbols on the disc of Phaestos or even to organize a five-day expedition to Vergina, Alexander the Great was back in vogue,

Hollywood films, protest marches, Bucephalus was charging into Scopje, the hierophants of war were to be seen riding roughshod on all the TV channels.

She had another three days at her disposal and she meant to persist, it's not as if there was a plan B.

All these years she'd busted her ass examining the pros and cons of the sciences, arts and hobbies, Linus was not going to evolve into a mathematical mind, do decent paintings, give himself over to a passion for stamps, antiquities, specifically those surrounding them, which, on top of everything, washed of the miasma of spilt blood, had finally won the most points.

Not that she meant for him to make his name as an archaeologist, she'd be satisfied with making a dent, a small uplift, seeing him be less of a vegetable, that would be a welcome minimal gain of her mission.

***

Saturday morning at the small dining hall of Amphictyonia.

Thoughts about mentioning that in the seventh century BC, the confederacy of Amphictyonia transferred its home base from Anthili, a small town near Thermopylae, to Delphi, which it proclaimed an independent city. She might add that delegations were present from the ancient Hellenic tribes, the Achaeans, Aenians, Ionians, Dolops, Dorians, Maleans and a host of others, who escaped her just at the moment, and, certainly, saying all this sweetly and civilly, like a prize student, without yesterday's hysterics, dear Lord, thinking about it now, she was a runaway one-woman comedy skit.

Meanwhile, she was counting his bites of food and his swallows of drink, she would hate for the two-yolked eggs and the freshly squeezed juice to go to waste, part of her plan was to return him to his cell perked up.

To their left, three fifty-five-year-old German women were

picking up their strength, the little hump of fat at the back of their necks, Viv had it as well, to their right a rosy-cheeked Englishman was picking up his, bent closely over a poached egg, his glasses needed changing, so did hers, her presbyopia had gotten worse. She hadn't been to the ophthalmologist for three years and to the gynecologist for over ten.

– While you finish, I'll tell you about the dream I had, she began, she didn't know what on earth to say so that their silence wouldn't be noticed. She buttered his slice of bread and started describing, she was in Alonaki but it seemed to her mighty changed, the church dome was smaller, the belfry shorter, the houses were more distant one from the other, the graves had spread outside the cemetery fence, the mountains had retreated and the whole area was in motion, expanding and shrinking, the square, the plane tree, the coffee shop, the kiosk, the school and all the rest, in an irregular to and fro, blowing up and deflating.

Linus's response:

– Didn't you finally ask Yukaris about that thing?

He pushed away the half-eaten and the uneaten and lit a cigarette.

– I asked him.

Her reply was late in coming, it was clear she wanted to avoid discussing that particular subject.

– Didn't you find out?

– I did.

– You haven't told me.

– I haven't.

– Tell me now. The truth.

In his voice there was imperiousness combined with pleading.

His mother complied, bending her head and speaking in as low a voice as she could.

– One's married, she has two little kids. It's the second one I'm talking about.

– The other one?

– Not in a good frame of mind. She's in and out of clinics.

She lit up a cigarette as well and, determining it would be worse to give the news in installments, she went for the rest in one fell swoop, the father of the third one had a heart attack at forty-nine, off to meet his dead only daughter.

That was that, she'd said it. She only kept undisclosed that some nights, and without fail on the eve of St. Kyriaki's name day, the trial takes place again in her dreams, with herself in the role of Koula's mother, breaking through the circle, leaping like a lioness at the stand and strangling the rapist and killer of her girl.

After that, it was nigh impossible to keep dragging him by the ear to the statues, she saw him turn yellow, get up and go staggering up to his room.

Was it right of me to tell him? And why does Linus have to find out from his mother? Why couldn't he ask Yukaris himself, all this time? Couldn't he, at all events, imagine the consequences by himself? Why, what did he expect? And how did any of that fit in with this godforsaken outing?

Still, she did feel sorry for him, felt sorry for herself and, in the name of justice, felt sorry once more for the other folks, the unlucky girls and their people.

Where was all this heading to? She thought that, seeing they'd started, they might as well make a clean sweep of it, he was hiding things, she was hiding things, here at Delphi was their chance.

If their tongues loosened, if the unspoken things were said, if the poison inside of them fizzed out, she might even win her bet with the ancients, the gloriousness of the place was intact for three thousand years, everybody was stymied with shock and awe before beauty, before History, Linus ought not be the exception to the rule.

Transfixed, Viv Koleva noticed neither the foreigners who bade her a good morning, gathered their maps and video cameras and left, nor Sabine who tidied up the tables and settled with a book in the nearby living room, her husband was there, too, on the couch for the morning talk shows.

She was lost in her smoking and her thoughts.

Would Linus come down? Should she go and knock on his door? Instigate an all-out conversation in his room? Or did he maybe need some time on his own to digest the news? Was she, perhaps, afraid of him? But, as a bottom line, wasn't there every reason to be?

She would wait for him here, and play it by ear.

She turned her chair to face the TV.

Frau Sabine and Mr. Thanassis were commenting not on what the guest speakers on TV, ministers and parliamentarians, spoke about, the Sarkozy-Royal battle for votes or the local political hurly-burly, but the knots in their ties, one guy's was like a meatball, another's like a horse's bridle, a third's like a hankie with the wafer from the Sunday Eucharist, the Socialist Party members were all spick-and-span, the New Democrats dressed like country bumpkins and the lefties like goons.

Sabine called out to the only remaining customer in the small hall, Mrs. Xenia, I know what I'm talking about, in Cologne I worked in men's retail.

Viv was envious of both the couple and their light conversation, I wish I, too, was concerned with tie knots, she thought, she smiled politely, picked up her eternally frozen feet and went out into the yard for the morning sun, which she needed.

Off to one side, two Albanian handymen were shoveling sand and cement into a pile, putting together a mix for widening the paving. Very shy the both of them, very thin, very pale, probably recent arrivals, a new addition to the migrant labor force. Their committed shoveling the only sound in the laid-back Saturday morning, the time was barely something past nine.

The day pure blue, May already, the winter gone. From now on, a stretch of sunny daybreaks, the festival of blue skies would keep up till September and would meet with great success, the sun's clients would be most pleased, the unmitigated light would clear out their eyes, the breeze would clear their lungs, the holidays in the islands and ancestral villages would clear out their heads and rest their bodies. Viv and Linus were among the summer's few exceptions, him especially.

So, was he coming down or not? Didn't he think of his mother at all and what she was going through for his sake? She was wrong not to have spoken to him about Cleovis and Viton, the two youths of Argos who reined themselves to the chariot and carried their mother a distance of sixteen miles to the sanctum of Hera. Were they jackasses, now? But wait, he wouldn't have turned into a junkie, would he, and was upstairs shooting up right at that moment? You think? Had yet another disaster befallen them?

Her heart started beating. She immediately moved farther along and raised her eyes to his window. He was in there, standing up, his head touching the windowpane of the closed balcony door, his eyes huge, trained on the Albanians.

His day and her day would pass with a knot in the throat again, a knot that had nothing to do with ties. And which there was probably no way of undoing.

***

It had been consuming her for ten straight years, she weighed it up this way and that, should she tell him or should she not, when would it be the right moment, how much longer to put it off, or had she better take it to her grave? And carry this weight all her life? Could she stand never getting it out? Was she able to make a final decision and forget about it? How do you support that? How do you delete something of such significance? And if she mustered the courage to confess it, how would he react? What if it made things even worse?

Mythical peaks, rocks in the middle of nowhere, steep mountainsides, monotonous hills, distant plateaus. Flighty swallows and ivory skies, smell of dusk and universal reverie, the time when locals and visitors alike get immobilized on a chair facing the west and give themselves over to colors, fragrances and drawn-out cigarettes.

The Kolevas, mother and son, were smoking in the balcony of her room at the pension. They'd almost finished their coffee wordlessly. Time was passing slowly and purposelessly, the only concrete thing awaiting was the duty of dinner somewhere, anywhere.

– I turned you in to the police.

The phrase was uttered in a low but clear and decisive voice and put an end to the decade's prevarication.

Linus, unaffected, kept on smoking, following with his gaze the swallows' thick formations, as they were descending and distributing themselves to their nests.

– It was me who told the police, Viv repeated her disclosure, changing the words and increasing the volume of her voice by a couple of notches, the neighboring balconies were vacant, there was no risk of eavesdroppers.

Linus still attending to the swallows.

– Did you hear what I said?

– I've known all along.

It was something his mother did not expect, she'd had the cops' assurance of anonymity, at the trial her decisive contribution to her son's arrest hadn't come up, and in the intervening years there had never been any mention.

– Who told you?

– Nobody.

– Someone must have.

– There was no need.

– Since when have you known?

– Ever since then.

– How did you figure it out?

He turned and looked at her full in the face.

– Does it matter?

He was telling the truth, there are moments when you know there's no chance the other could be bluffing, there are certain issues on which, when the time comes, nobody is going to cheat or lie, it just isn't appropriate.

Viv could barely breathe, she was fairly prepared to stand up to his gaze, relentless over her betrayal, to listen to a thousand curses and complaints about being a snitch and heartless, to get spat at or punched out. None of any of that, though. Linus's eyes with no sparks of anger or lightning bolts of hatred, glued onto hers, were punishing her with their own disclosure that all these years he'd been meeting her behind the glass partition knowing it was her who'd put him inside.

– You took the shoelace to them, he said quietly, you'd been saving it wrapped around your arm.

He finished his cigarette, got up, my own mother snitched on me, he said to the swallows and jumped up and down a bit on the narrow balcony as if his knees had locked up, with Viv getting scared and pulling back, a crab into its shell.

– I'm going, he said, and she didn't stop him, let him go to his room alone, so she could also be alone to think, to carefully choose her dinnertime words, explain her position, tonight there was going to be a real conversation, things would be called by their name, with no detectivelike fishing around and baiting. A new beginning was ahead for the two of them, a new period with fewer secrets and hidden aces coming out from up their sleeves at sunset and blowing up the quarry of their lives.

She lit a cigarette, leaned her head against the balcony's lukewarm metal railing and looked inquisitively at her left arm. She couldn't get over the fact that her son knew, yet never let on, all those visits and never a squeak. She tried to recall if in their monthly meetings, especially at the beginning, any vague reference had been made to the circumstances of the arrest, the preliminary questioning, the interrogation, and she had dissimulated like a ham actor, while he knew the truth. Was it, perchance, her mistake, and a fatal one at that?

Who else was going to stop him before he did again what he had done and then some? She didn't want for the questions to start again parading in her mind, she gave them short shrift, nor could she trick herself into organizing dinner, choosing the menu and the venue.

To escape, she availed herself of her sense of duty, exemplary at her work, time to check up on her replacement. She called the Bulgarian woman, everything in order, still, she wanted to hear her cadavers with her own ears, she called the couple of Exarchia, she called the whiner downtown, the ex-army bachelor of the northern suburbs, the Cretan Methuselah who assured her he had no intention of dying in anyone else's arms, let alone those of a Bulgarian, and devoted to her for the occasion, a verse he'd been keeping at the tip of his tongue for two days, *God takes his time judging.*

So there's a long road ahead, Viv thought looking across the valley.

Mountains hunker down, peaks pull over to the side, Rotas, *And I when I lift the cup off the table, a hole of silence is underneath,* Ritsos, may our poets fare well seeing as she remembered them and their verses and the still uncut tome of Sikelianos in her bag.

She drained the last of her now cold coffee with her mind twisting and turning forward and backward, to the summer of '97 and the spring of 2007.

In the old days and now, in the old days and now, in the old days and now, the words were her old folks' bread and butter, just the thing for her case as well. She glanced at her watch, eight-thirty, took it off, went into the room and set it on the bedside table, time for a quick shower before going out. From the bedside table, isn't that where she'd left them? the car keys were missing. She had a good look, not in her pocket, not in her bag, not in the two plastic bags with the pine honey she had bought, she looked all around, lifted the pillows, bent under the bed in case they'd fallen out of sight, no keys.

She went out into the hallway and knocked on Linus's door, no answer. With her heart racing wildly, she went back in her room and called reception, asked Sabine if her nephew was waiting for her at the downstairs hall, no, her husband had asked him to join him for the basketball finals, but Mr. Takis had left in the car and since the young man was off having a drive, why didn't she fix them two drinks so the two women could sit and have a chat. Maybe later, said Viv, with the blood beating at her temples.

Now that she was at a complete loss, she was out of bloody cigarettes.

Where did he go? If he wanted just a ride, he would ask and she would happily agree and, of course, go with him, because Linus hadn't driven for ten years and his hands and feet mightn't manage so well, the steering, the accelerator, the brakes. But, after the stripping down, damned be the hour when she told him and he told her, there was no chance her son was in the mood for a relaxing ride in the car. What then? Did he decide to make a getaway, live the glorious life of a fugitive? Did he have enough gas? Had he any more money apart from the two fivers she'd given him, to have, a grown man, in his pocket? And in which direction would he go? Was this prearranged? Were there others waiting for him? And what should she do? Inform the police so they got him before he went a great distance and could no longer be traced?

She looked in her wallet, her money was there, but he must have surely pilfered her cell phone. She called her number from the room's phone, heard it beeping outside on the balcony, she had used it a while ago to call her clients. She replaced the receiver and lifted her hands to her head, my Lord, he must be heading for some precipice, pressing down on the accelerator to end his life. She thought some pretext or other to borrow the German woman's car. Would she catch up with him? Should she catch up with him?

Ah, Charioteer, Viv Koleva was bitterly regretting the five day outing, trapped in the lime-sticks of Amphictyonia, not knowing what her next step ought to be because she didn't know what his next step would be.

Suddenly she felt her insides knot up and the terrible suspicion took root in her mind. This was it, that is where his permanently much promising, dark gaze pointed to, her son had gone out hunting.

The small town already had several women tourists, some daydreamer was bound to be roaming on her own, relishing the May evening and the spring smells. Day before yesterday and yesterday and today, in the archaeological enclosure and at the museum and all over, there had been no shortage of pretty ones with pale blue eyes and pale blue shorts and golden bangs, an alarm kept sounding in Viv, she kept dragging her son away and occupying his attention with the things she'd memorized about pillars and statues, gods and demigods and all those who serially raped any virgin they took a fancy to without being expelled from Olympus and its environs.

– Mr. Menio?

She found him at a tavern by the sea, *en famille*.

She reported to him briefly, telegraphically, I told him I turned him in, he said he's known all the time, he stole my car keys. I realized twenty minutes later. He's either escaped or he's going to kill himself or he's possessed by the old evil and is looking for a woman. He's been gone one whole hour and, to be sure, doesn't have a driver's license, but that's the least of it.

Menios Yukaris said, fuck, we're done for, he went on with things he'd said before, at first I thought that he was mad, then

I thought you were, then both of you, you'd break all the psychiatrists' records, now I think I'm the mad one for not giving up on you. Finally, he asked her to give him five minutes to think.

How do five whole minutes pass? The first two and a half with a storm of sounds and images from the summer of '97, shaved skull, zdoop against the wall, isolated parks, telephone booths and police stations. The next two and a half with zooming in on the inch-high letters and screaming headlines from the press fiesta. A very crowded five minutes, with space for it all, it landed Viv facedown on the bed. She had an impulse to give up once and for all. To pay for the pension and leave immediately on a bus, if there was one at this time, or a taxi. She would go back to her work and she would stop taking an interest, protecting, getting scared and suffering over that merciless spawn of her belly. She might leave Athens, go to work in Salonika as a carer, to Komotini as a factory worker, to Heraklion as a maid.

She called Yukaris back, he was busy.

Tonight, however, Saturday, May 5, 2007, she herself was solely responsible for the fate of the poor soul who would be pounced upon by her son, the one sick soul she couldn't manage with an injection and some vitamins. In her waking, now, she again identified with the dead girl's white-haired mother and started beating her cheeks as if they were drum plates, just like the other one had at the trial.

She would go out to look for him in the darkened fields. The chances of catching up with him were infinitesimal but at least she wouldn't remain impassive, she would have done her duty.

She reached out to her bag, felt the heavy bulk at its bottom and stood up ready for everything.

At the same moment she heard his door open in the next room.

So he was back. She pictured him again dishevelled, his eyes caves again, his face again with nail-marks and dried up snot. Should she storm his room? With the pestle? Or maybe with the knife?

In split seconds there was his shadow at her door. His hair was still combed, his appearance was orderly and he was strangely calm. He was holding two packets of cigarettes, her brand, and the bag from a local store, Apollo, like the spaceship.

He put the cigarettes and the keys to the Fiat on the bedside table and then, immediately emptied the bag on his mother's bed.

Two black swimsuits, one a man's, one a woman's.

Viv collapsed on the edge of the bed and he sat on a chair, bent over and unspeaking.

When the cell phone rang, Yukaris, she praised the mellow evening, not chilly at all, a clear sky with a lot of stars, they were going out somewhere for chops, she wished him a quiet evening and a good night and she didn't mind at all that the lawyer rang off with something not terribly apt, by Khalil Gibran, about the ox that loves its yoke and considers the forest elk and deer to be mongrel creatures and mighty strange.

**

The nighttime breeze had molded the sand into pleats, unmoving little yellow waves that lay in the quiet morning. In places, pebbles, white, black and gray, the size of olive pips, created mosaics like the icons of a church wall that was shattered in a sea storm and was washed out on the shore in pieces.

A seagull was following a ridge in the shallow water. In the middle of the bay, a rock rose gurgling like a hippopotamus diving to wash and quench its thirst. On the horizon a sail, a nail on the flat stretch of blue. Only thing missing was a dolphin, they'd never seen a live one.

The water was very cold, but they felt obligated to have this swim, a forceful order still valid from the summer of '97, the first one for both after ten whole years. They walked in to the knee, stayed for a while to get used to it before wading further in, they got wet by degrees, reaching their hands out to the short choppy waves that came their way, limping slightly.

When they were in to the neck and washed out their mouths, it was impossible to not feel grateful.

They had the impression that the sea had been expecting them all this time and was now showing its best side for their sake, what with its teasing breeze, its translucency, its aquamarine blue, like a fairytale.

They had been up at dawn.

Mr. Takis, isn't it a shame you're leaving earlier? Didn't you enjoy my pension? Aren't you going to write something in the visitors' book, Sabine had said, who'd stayed up the night reading, as she was doing their bill and taking the money, to then go into a proper German assault, Mrs. Xenia, you do have something on your mind, now, don't you, thoughtful all the time, always under a cloud, one might go so far as to say grumpy, and if you can't enjoy life, then, why don't you smarten up and become a writer, that's what I say.

On the way, mother and son, on the lookout for a small beach which, at the beginning of May, would offer privacy, hadn't exchanged any words, the intensity of anticipating this haunted swim in the sea was keeping their mouths sealed.

Their eyes, too, were virtually sealed as, within breathing distance of each other, they undressed down to their swimsuits, she didn't want her son to see her scrutinizing and pitying his bony, gray carcass and he didn't want his mother seeing him notice her flabby arms and thighs, resigned and prematurely aged at barely fifty-two.

Immediately afterwards, Viv watched Linus draw farther away, place his hand over his eyes and gaze at a distance and westward, to the green mountains on the far side of the Corinthian gulf.

He must have been thinking of Alonaki.

In a short while, it would be about eight-thirty, they were swimming freestyle in opposite directions, not counting on how soaking in the numbing water can work miracles and inaugurate changes of its own accord. Within ten minutes, the opposite directions turned parallel and given that silence had had its run, Viv decided to abolish it.

– You could come out at some point. It's possible to put in a submission for clemency and sometimes they get accepted.

– I'm not meant for the outside.

– Your director says to both me and Yukaris that you're a model inmate, never get into any trouble.

– Yes. I don't hurt a fly. I'm being quiet again.

– He said you also read some.

– Two books, with no covers

– You mean poetry? I have Sikelianos in my bag. I have some at home I can bring, too. It's useful after all.

– It's a death toll.

You've said in the past it's all about repentance. People change, the young grow up and acknowledge their mistakes.

– They're no mistakes. They are crimes.

His phrase jarred in the peaceful setting, but was true. Only the two of them in the isolated bay, there was no one to hear them, yet they spoke softly like aged couples in their room of an evening who say everything whisperingly, as if they conspire about the taste of the chicken soup, the buying of one hundred grams of coffee and the changes in temperature.

A fairly good start to the conversation, the sea had unplugged his mouth, how well and rightly he does speak, Viv thought, his replies evidence that he's got his reasoning back, therefore sane, as sane as anyone, there is no way this man could have been crazy in his life for more than two months, his madness, like that of many others, had picked up and reached its peak only in the summer of '97, before even the psychiatrists got hold of him and correctly pronounced him compos mentis.

– You've got it together now, only the others don't see it because they're not looking at you anymore, you no longer interest them. But you need to believe that your bad self was a one-off, during those two months, so long ago now.

– I have been charged.

– And you are paying.

– I've done much harm.

– And were punished.

– To three people.

– And you're still being punished.

– I strangled a girl, Mom.

His voice shook, his hands did also. That phrase of his put things in their precise place and, woe! it seemed like it would spoil everything. The five-minute silence that ensued was unavoidable. With utmost effort, Viv Koleva gathered her thoughts and resumed control.

– You wouldn't hurt anyone now.

– Who knows that?

– I know it.

– I'm afraid.

– I am not anymore.

– Yes, you are. You have the pestle and a kitchen knife in your bag. While I am in my cell, you can have your peace of mind.

It came like a blow and she again lost control. The only thing she wanted at this moment would have been to take the two pieces of iron and, like a fakir, swallow them in front of him as if they were marshmallows. Before even wondering what her son felt when he'd found them, what she herself feels for having being caught red-handed and whenever it was agreed that she left her bag unattended, he helped her out, saying that yesterday, when he was after the car keys, he stuck his hand in her bag, it was the only time she wasn't clutching it to herself with suspicious persistence, she'd left it sitting on a chair in her room.

He doesn't miss a thing, he observes everything, his mother thought that the endless hours he sat isolated in his cell and shut off in himself had trained his antennae to peak, radar-like performance.

Right now, however, she needed some comeback, something impressive and to the point.

– Enough already with the old stories. With that shoelace you also tied up the top of your sack. Full to the hilt since you were twenty. There's no room for more.

He didn't even turn around to look at her, his gaze fixed steadily on the open horizon, again in the direction of Alonaki.

The talk moved along more slowly, more bitterly, with pauses.

– A day will come when you'll be ready to come out from there.

– They'll be waiting for me at the gate, she with her mother and father, and the others.

– Think other thoughts. Imagine different things. Don't you want for this to be over at some point in time?

– No. I've found my hell and I'm O.K.

– We'll go live far away.

– There is no far away. I won't be wanted by those on the outside, not anywhere.

He was right. People, almost all of them, are more or less punishers, whether voluntarily or not, whether courageously or cowardly, in secret or in the light of day, deluded or perfectly composed. But in cases like her son's, everyone was absolutely adamant. Viv had thought of this a long time ago, finally the hard cases and the life-timers, the prison's ancients, are the scum, they've sold tons of heroin, slaughtered people, they don't fit in with those outside, but they work things out fine in there, among themselves.

Linus was no star in the criminal underworld, hadn't killed a rival lover in a moment of rage, hadn't appropriated public funds, his actions were of the kind which forgetfulness doesn't include in its plans.

Was she able to change the subject urgently?

She had no lyricism to spare on Apollo or the masterful nature of Fokis. The water kept them bound to the subject at hand, they couldn't play at being flies flittering from one plate to the next with the leftovers of a mundane conversations cut short.

He took it up.

– A barber's razor is on the prowl outside, ten feet long, a spear-blade, and it shears to the root every good feeling that grows. The yards are strewn with rotting leaves and stems. That's why everyone's abandoned you.

He was stammering, both their lips blue, half an hour in the cold water, they were shivering.

They got out, dried themselves and sat, not too close, ten feet apart, with eyes fixed on the sea.

No dolphin on show. The waves lapped at their feet, the breeze tossed about dried lumps of weeds and the sun, increasingly hotter, danced around the shape of the rocks guarding the bay.

– Is there a planet for me and for you? A place where they'll have us?

His question dictated the answer too, negative.

Inwardly, Viv Koleva agreed with that as well, the mass rapes of thousands of women by deranged soldiers during wartime are silenced or erased or amnestied, world history both of the past and of today, look at Yugoslavia, look at Iraq, full of such feats, but a disturbed twenty-year-old in peacetime is worthy of stigma, not pity and forgiveness.

Do we always forgive someone and then love them or do we love them first and then forgiveness follows?

Viv pondered this for the hundredth time, a question that filled her increasingly with shame because it did not refer to some strangers in a general, abstract way, but to her own child, the one and only, no matter what he was. Her terrible a fate it was to struggle to love what everyone else abhorred. Hard if not impossible. It's not as if there were organizations of rapists' mothers with presiding members giving speeches at gatherings, ladies and gentlemen, we are fighting mothers, and suchlike, in truth she and the few like her were solitary duellers with no prize, no laurel wreath and no praise.

She breathed deeply or sighed, didn't know which of the two it was that came out of her. She turned and looked at him. The German woman's flattery would have him be handsome and a gentleman.

Eventually, the Delphi epic was about to end with the envious Apollo doing away with yet another Linus, after that mythical singer, her son, a relic at thirty, that's what she was seeing before her.

And if the regular relics, the Charioteer and the ancient treasures, had been too much for him, these days weren't lost, she thought, the news about the victims had been communicated, the snitching had been divulged, that's what outing permissions are for, you can't say things like that in front of the square of glass. Then, in addition, Linus remembered what the sky is, what is a mountain and the sea, at least he heard a thrush, smelled wild jasmine, touched a pine bark, observed lizards, saw dogs, sat in a bamboo armchair, had a meal on a tablecloth, felt the shovels of the Albanians, ever since he was a kid he had that thing about shovels. Moreover, he put on a pair of swim trunks, went in the water, saw a seabird.

Had he seen a crab? A seashell?

She looked around her, got up, kicked at some seaweed, walked on, overturned pebbles, no crab or seashell.

Then Linus struck again.

– Let's be off. We're going back. And forget about me, don't come anymore. Make me this gift of saying good-bye.

– I will not leave you, let me hope in something, even blindly.

– You have served your sentence enough. I pardon you.

His mother's chest was in an uproar, a tempest, her heart was apt to leap out.

Ah, Linus, if only, but it's not up to you.

***

Whether one is or isn't a lover of antiquity, the immortal marbles are unparalleled, whether one is or isn't a nature lover, one is taken with the cascades of roses and the philharmonics of the finches, surrenders to the siege of the red bush and the intoxication of the sage.

Sunday brought out into the countryside buses and private cars, scooters and racing bikes.

Steak houses, canteens, ancient temples, monasteries, rural churches, cypress groves, flatlands with silver-leafed olives, silken fields and beaches crowned by precipices, all these were targeted by the hordes of leisure.

May's crazed in action, all out to burn gas, sun themselves, lay siege, indiscriminately consume.

Mother and son with minimal right to beauty, and none whatsoever to carefreeness, felt like thieves laying hands on others' property.

They stopped at a parking spot with a view over half of Greece, our beauteous homeland, perfectly perfect, destined to live on into the ages, like Viv's theology teacher used to say in high school.

Time to throw out the milk pie and the spinach pie; forgotten in the back seat of the Fiat, they'd started to stink. Viv also shoved the kitchen knife and the pestle in the bag with the spoiled food, there was no chance she could drive with the weapons in the car now that her son had seen them and, to be sure, after what had been said earlier. With a couple of decisive motions and a couple of poisonous stares, Linus took the armaments out of the plastic bag and returned them to their previous place. He was as thin as a rake, had grown old and a hunchback, but the gaze ejected from the recesses of his eyes was perfectly intact, the good old rage there for all to see.

– Sunglasses, she told him, deftly putting hers on, waited for him to put his on, you never know what might come up, and got out. While approaching the bin, careful not to step on the surrounding refuge, mementos from visitors strewn around like votive offerings, two buses slowed down and coupled in the parking spot.

Middle-aged folks poured out into the bushes for a joyous pee or for group photos with a priest in the middle.

Viv recognized him and was taken aback. The prattling man of the cloth who had visited her then, at the apex of that frenzied summer, hardly believing his luck to get a shot at the choicest of choice sins. Then ten years had hardly made a difference for him, unlike her, because his eye did fall on her but with the extra pounds and the dark glasses she didn't remind him of anything and a good thing it was. If he went up to her, asked her questions, discreetly gossiped to his parishioners, it'd be the end. She gathered from their spirited chatter that the high point of their excursion would be a feisty pilgrimage to the monastery of the rocker monks, over towards Nafpaktos.

She went back to the Fiat in a hurry and started the engine.

What followed had on it the stamp of the end.

Last looks to the open sky, last shared meal, last trip together, last hours of mother and son sitting side by side. The Delphi migration was over, they were repatriating to familiar grounds.

The scarce words of the incomplete five-day outing gradually became scarcer still, almost none at all, a process of making ready for the son to go back to the listlessness of the cell, the deadliness of silence, the morose inaction.

What if the sea had freed them to have a flowing conversation, they again became what they were, veterans of wordlessness both, the old rule at the kitchen table or the living room had been nerves or grumpiness, sighs or dry coughing, lips pursing or eyebrows raising, the persistent silences of chastisement or intimidation or anger.

The silences of the present were different, they signified subjection.

The two intervening phone calls didn't count, Viv Koleva was purposefully repeating everything she was being told, an echoed conversation and the illusion of dialogue, if a brief one, inside the mute Fiat.

So, then, the old bird clad in black, with the turtle-jewel, thirty years a widow, was concerned that her deceased husband would have despaired waiting for her in the other world and would say of her, such indifference! And the mummies at Exarchia said that the Bulgarian had left them and gone away, the grandpa sounded lost and tearful.

It was almost seven, nature was turning to caramel, the sun was descending, Athens was coming ever closer and Viv, too, was rapidly approaching her familiar chores, tending to the abandoned churches of old age, her clients half-burnt candles on the stands, scorched and olive-soaked wicks in the oil lamps, but also, to be sure, a coffer for her expenses.

She didn't head straight to the jailhouse of Korydallos, making instead for her house. She wanted to get the keys to the old couple's apartment and the already purchased wedding bon-bons, she would drop by to check on them later, give them the honey and the bonbons from the alleged wedding at the village.

When she parked close to her building, she communicated with her son by means of a single look, she couldn't leave him alone in the car. He followed her in, a faithful dog.

Linus would see the layout for the first time. Viv raised her eyes to the apartment block, noticing in a second that the walls were covered in soot, three tents were derelict, the penthouse balcony with the grey perpendicular rails only had two pale blue ones at the end, someone left off painting, in old Tiger's balcony the Ukrainian had hung to dry two moth-eaten African carpets with embossed lions.

No one loitering around, they went up to the apartment at their leisure. In the ten minutes they stayed, just enough for Viv to drop off the terrible weapons and the dirty laundry of Delphi, wash the salt off her face and find the keychain and the rest, Linus was, after many years, again inside a private home, his mother's latest base, the household of the illegal carer of the elderly.

The narrow two-room apartment had no family photos, knickknacks or the paintings he had known, it was a stock-room with piles of Pampers, antiseptics, oxygen cylinders, chlorines, douches, a wheelchair folded behind the door, and the ironing board out with creased white robes, the white robe is good for the elderly, they feel reassured.

Viv read in Linus's look his impression from all this. She scanned the room with his eyes, this is where my unlived life is flowering, she thought. Was it the right thing, bringing him up? Would he by any chance think she got him up here to rub her decadence into his face?

He spoke to her in the car.

– Should you now maybe go to those old folks the Bulgarian left?

In ten minutes they had parked, he followed her obligingly, they went up to the third floor, she would introduce him as Takis again, a distant nephew, and nothing more said, she never did allow for too many personal questions.

She unlocked and immediately the fetid smell hit them.

Wallowing in shit, the two old people were soaked and paralyzed on the shitty bedclothes. They were more embarrassed than relieved by the unexpected visit, Death forgot about us and so has God, the grandpa stammered and, crushed, told them the whole story. The fruit yogurt had upset his bed-ridden missus and she'd had diarrhea all night long. She dirtied their bed and, so that she wouldn't feel bad, after he had smeared himself all the way to his neck in his failed attempts to move and clean her, he had stayed by her side, hadn't left for one minute, holding her in his arms and saying whatever thing he remembered, old-fashioned songs and the story of Tito and the atrocities of dictators the world over.

Their son was gone with his family to their in-laws in the Peloponnese, they hadn't called him so as not to piss off their daughter-in-law again, the couple were fed up with their longevity and their problems, now this, then the other, and were constantly fighting. The Bulgarian had come in the morning, sleepy and tired from her night shift, she saw the state of things, had said many things in Bulgarian and left slamming the door.

They spent all day unable to think of something practical to do, their will turned over to whatever the Good Lord had in store.

While she soaped them from head to toe, one by one, changed them, doused them with cologne, calmed them, made the beds, put the place in some order, aired it, washed the old man's shitty walking stick, rinsed the dirty linen three times and left it in the bathtub soaking in detergent, one whole bloody hour, Linus was sitting in the small hall. He went into their bedroom when his mother called him, come over here and let me introduce you to two collectors' items, Mrs. Maria, Mr. Marius, this is my nephew Takis, we were at the wedding in the village together.

Against the clean white sheets, I've turned them into angels, she said to him. The old woman sized up the newcomer thoroughly, asked him to come closer, she wanted to touch the young hand, hold it in her own for a bit.

– Your aunt is the angel, young man, not us, she told him, noticed his prematurely gray hair and shook her head with understanding for his troubles, she could imagine as far as being laid off from work or a love affair gone sour, there was no wedding ring on his finger.

She made the sign of the cross over him with her free hand and seeing Viv looking at her watch and nimbly collect her things, she let go of Linus's palm after handing him his tip in words.

– Bless you, my birdie, and when the time comes may you find someone to make you happy.

The old man seconded, good luck to you in life and a good heart, a good heart is a talent.

– All right, now, you need to eat something solid, no honey and bonbons tonight, some tea and dry toast, Viv called and with her bags in hand, she made for the kitchen.

– I think the toast bread's finished, says Grandpa.

– I'll go and get some. There's got to be a mini-market open.

– Not you, my girl, let your nephew pop out. Why don't you go, now there's a good boy. We've worn your aunt out with everything that's happened.

But Viv Koleva brooked no objection.

– Takis is staying here.

***

You dragged me through the streets with the swollen gums,

seeing and hearing shovels quake, pavements creak, the dead giving birth.

Why did you cut down the branch I tied the noose to?

Why did you get the Albanians to drag me out of the railway lines?

You've provoked a domino effect of crazed looks that weigh megatons and chase after me night and day, for years on end. You've shoved two tapes in my ears playing continuously the zdoop.

Bloody hell, turn the fucking tape recorders off, I'm buzzing inside and out. And get your machinery to work backwards, the dirt to lift off of my father, go back into the shovels, the shovelfuls go in reverse and the lumps end up on the pile to the side of the grave. And resurrect him, make him rub his eyes, sit up, then jump out niftily and call Linus, Buddy, we're off, and the three of us go for our long walk, and make that walk never end. Tell me, in what clothes did my mother bury him? I couldn't have asked. I rummaged inside the wardrobe secretly but it wasn't just the two suits missing, the trousers and shirts and jumpers were all gone, it had been some time and she'd given them away somewhere. I chose in my mind a grave uniform, a blue pair of shorts and a red top, same red as your cape.

Linus Kolevas was talking to the Virgin Mary in a low voice, under his breath. His mother had gone out for toast bread, locking the door behind her just in case. With no jailer, no handcuffs, he was free to do harm again or to split by jumping from one balcony to the next, but he, completely tamed by the miracle of the shit and the present delight of the old folks, considered them his own people, inmates in the cell of prolonged old age.

Outside the sky had disappeared, darkness, black walls.

Inside, in the yellow light of the table lamp, sitting quietly on a chair next to the mummified folks, he had noticed three shitty finger-marks on a small icon above the double iron bed. He took it down, looked for wet tissues, finally used two napkins from the pile on the bedside table to clean it. Then he spat at Mary, on her golden halo and on the palm upon her chest, polished the glass well with his T-shirt, holding it close to his face, looking for a while at her sweet, mild eyes, the Gioconda smile and the bright red drapes of her clothing, and he let loose, not out loud but with a torrent of whispers, he'd have spoken to her whisperingly even if it wasn't for the two witnesses, who, in a state of advanced deafness anyway, weren't in a position to make out the words. They were seeing the nephew Takis praying to Her Grace and were made to think about youth's unrequited passions and requests for the coming to pass of future plans.

They prayed along with him with their own steady requests, Virgin Mother, shelter under your care the world's poor and deprive us not of our daily bread and then, quiet and a little puzzled, they watched the visitor's lips chewing on a prayer with no end and spitting out cut up words and bitter syllables like pips.

You've singled me out since I was eight years old, Linus kept up his list of accusations at Mary, instead of uprooting every vineyard, striking down every winery and breaking all the bottles, you spend your time submitting folks to tortures, you took my father, my dog, my grandparents. You let the girls make fun of me. You let that slut my godmother suck my dick. You saw to it that I destroyed creatures I didn't know, in whose blond hair I saw and hurt myself, blond hair takes off years, it takes all the years off. Why did she have to say to me, I know you, I know who you are, you come and get cocoa milk and ice cream from the Alaska, you are the one who likes stracciatella gelato? Why did you have her ID me? She could live, at least she could have lived. You had me hiding in construction sites out in the suburbs. You didn't let my mother become a doctor, make a good living, you let her become a snitch. Did you enjoy it? You've lost your son but in none of your pictures do you look as broken as her, your cheeks all aglow. Do you get herpes and psoriasis? Do you froth at the mouth with too many r's? Don't you hurt my mother anymore, she's seen harm enough for ten lives.

Now you've arranged for them to send Bessos to the inland prison and Aziz off to the island, so I'm left on my own, not even someone to share a smoke with. Did you enjoy that, too? You're way out of our league, nobody can touch you. Your frankincense and your coals aren't smeared with shit. Do you want me to light them for you, to fall on my knees and thank you that at least I didn't reach the heights of a Hannibal Lecter?

You've stuck a bad bug in my mind. It's still there, I can feel it. I can understand myself hating, but you hating as well? Hating me since I was a child? How did you choose me? What's this experiment of yours? And you still haven't had enough? Hatred can be beneficial to everyone, provided it comes and goes, it lasts an hour or maybe a day or two, that's enough to discharge the spleen and for everything fear messes up to be put back to order. Mine cannot be undone. The long razor that's out and about can't reach it. It's left intact to rile me. I think everything is hatred, I call everything hatred and there are so many that I see looking with a vengeance for someone or something to hate, to hate a lot.

Even though the meaning in his words was burning, there was no wrath or complaint, nor the intensity of a reminder or the ache of an announcement of novel, all-important evidence, it was all a repetition for the umpteenth time, he'd often said it in his head, so he had it virtually ready for the Virgin Mother too, and he spoke to her as an equal, seeing she fell into his hands.

It was moreover a way of not staying entirely mute before the two immortals who, flat on their backs, didn't take their eyes off him, alternately making a hand gesture urging him to say more, his faith and devotion were unheard of in a young man of these times, they were a first-rate surprise and a blessing in their dour monotony, a private vespers in their home.

How could Linus Kolevas not oblige them? While his mother was away it was easier for him to go with the flow, to whisper those things and then some, thoughts, ripe already from long ago, carved out inch by inch, as solid as statues, one next to the other, a virtual antique bas-relief on the walls that surrounded him and closed in and in, year by year, day by day, night by night.

The numbers alone of victims and victimizers since the world's beginning were proof to Linus Kolevas that there is no God of mercy and compassion, kindness fell, falls and will fall from the sky as rare as an asteroid.

The granny who stroked my hand is more of a saint than you, who can't spend a single night where I'm going back to tonight. You're merchandise, a plastic fake image who wouldn't fetch more than five euros in the open-air market, these words accompanied the icon back to its place, on the nail above the two white heads.

If all of the above wasn't a prayer or a confession with or without a pardoning of sins, then what was it? Apology at the Court of Appeals, his retrial at last? And who the members of the court and who the audience?

Everyone in their places, the elderly couple and Nana Mouschouri who started her deposition from the apartment next door, *My love is somewhere*, a television applauding the Greek participation in the European basketball league, a cat mewing on the balcony across, two Albanians in the courtyard waiting for a relative, who were saving him the chicken breast, limes, "kracor" and "bremie," Linus half knew their language, he had picked up a smattering of others too, Arabic and Russian, at the language school of Korydallos.

– All the bakeries were closed, I had to run up all the way to the kiosk at the square, said Viv holding up two packets of dry toast bread and breadsticks.

She looked inquiringly at her son, the clients, the open window, the curtain, the coat hangers, everything under control, law, peace and order.

She was paid on the spot by the old man, the money for her services as in the drawer of the bedside table, under the health insurance booklets and the pack of old Christmas and Easter cards, old wedding invitations and death notices.

She remembered the thank you in the kitchen and called it out loudly like a cry so it would reach the half-useless old ears. She put on some water to heat and took down two cups, time was getting on.

They weren't expecting them at the prison tonight but Viv was now fearful of the moment of separation, so she might as well go through it earlier rather than later, get it off her in a jiffy, recoup herself for the return to the things she'd learned to manage.

***

The birdie, to the old woman, vulture, to the many others, with the plucked and battered wings, before its mother returned it to its nest, asked her for a little ride, a zigzag course through the western suburbs spreading seaward.

Leisurely idlers of the Sunday evening, the locals few, the migrants many, some walking, some sitting, young and old on doorsteps, crates of fruit and benches for people to eat, play, laugh, fight.

The drone of Balkan, Asian and African languages was rising shrill above every badly designed square and every badly lit alley, the migrant tribes in full evidence. Today's Athens bore no relation either to the city Viv Koleva, then Sotiropoulos, first saw at eighteen, or the one her son left behind at twenty. The foreign poverty had snuck in silently and with its sharp preeminence had asserted itself, block by block, street by street.

Linus had again leaned his head backwards, outward at an angle, he both wanted to see and hear and he didn't.

He acted likewise almost systematically the previous days, even without sunglasses, his eyes turned to smoky lenses, for his mother to not be able to see what the weather was deep down inside him. May his blond bangs of yesteryear be damned, their gold overshadowed everything else and who would search behind it in case a few tears gave a timely signal that there was something wrong. It's not like he was a girl, let alone a homely and spoiled daddy's girl, the kind who bawl with frequency. Actions talk, yes, but man is not his actions alone, he's also his thoughts, especially the ones that get stuck like oysters in the innermost recesses of his head and never stray from there to help fill in the puzzle.

Viv was driving and every so often cast sideways glances at the repulsive, brutal, ill-starred pariah, her son. He had half an hour left.

She wished she believed in God so she could ask for miracle here and now, to erase Linus's actions or, at least, replace them with other ones. Let him have been a legionnaire war criminal, she would seek expiation for him herself at the island of Tinos. Let him have been a hooligan, she would make a votive offering of his club to Her Grace. Now, what could she deliver to the icon of Christ's Mother? A shoelace?

Enough with the religious acrobatics prompted by despair, the gate loomed before them.

But there they were, having not only not taken a single photograph at Delphi, but she'd again forgotten to show him the four photographs. She turned the engine off, turned on the overhead light, rummaged through her bag, brought out the envelope, passed them to him one by one, all taken by Xenia in 2003, after her last visit to Greece. For four years she'd hesitated to show them to him, she brought them at visiting hours and took them with her again.

In the first, Meg and Stavroula in white dresses, lying in the yard of the village like cats, next to five newborn kittens who are sleeping tightly wrapped together in a bow.

In the second, the kids and Charidemos wearing the trial suit with his typewriter in his hands, the trio posing in the village square, next to the monument to the fallen.

In the third, his grandmother and Xenia in between the two large rosebushes that provided the rose petals for the conserve, planted by Soritopoulos at the birth of each of his daughters so there would be sweetness in their lives. The entire photograph drenched in pink, it was a great art which that plant had of adorning itself with a multitude of moist buds like tightly bunched children's hands and another as many widely unfurled roses like silk christening caps, a great art indeed, and, in their case, illusionary.

In the fourth, Grandfather's grave and the surrounding part of the village cemetery, lively little bushes everywhere, nature showing off. The path to his marble slab as straight as the crease in his trousers, and the cypress behind his cross dark green and thin like his old-fashioned best tie.

As Linus was looking at them she saw them through his eyes, which rested insistently on the last one as if puzzled by the unaccountable beauty and the peacefulness of death's landscape, everything laid out in perfect alignment, symmetrically and ecologically.

She took them off him posthaste.

– Well, well, look who's back.
At half past ten, the guards of Korydallos were surprised,

here was one convict impatient to get back to the slammer before the end of his five-day break.

At the last moment Viv Koleva outdid herself, pulled her son to her breast and enclosed him in her arms.

She hadn't hugged him like this since he was thirteen, seventeen whole years.

He didn't resist her, didn't say good night to her, he was going back to his cell with head bowed yet relieved, as if returning to his homeland after a long absence.

The makeshift awning where the visitors waited, across from it the gym facilities, the women's prisons, the Third High School and Lyceum, all dark and quiet at this hour. Viv Koleva had gazed on them many times while patiently waiting for her turn to visit with the clean laundry and the fried beef in bags. She would be gazing on them more, she knew well what was in store for her. The poem was long and all the verses with a cutting edge.

Twelve-hour spells of trekking the streets to counteract the ravages and the discontent of the old folks and then, parked in the two-room apartment, those sleepless nights jam-packed with energy, every night a noose, every thought a headlock, making it to dawn a triumph and, then, the same thing all over, sharpening her already sharp misery and then the guilt breaking through with a delay of fifteen, twenty, twenty-five years, about whether she had done all she could to save Fotis, and whether she herself pushed her son on the road to perdition, interpretations not worth a cent and remorse with no exchange value.

She drove towards the city, stopped by three clients for a while, the Mrs. with the little turtle who was still waiting for the Bulgarian, the miserly ex-army guy who couldn't offer you a glass of water without feeling deprived, Mr. Anthousis her most ancient, her bent and battered Parthenon who now, thoroughly destitute, was weaving together new couplets for his tombstone, *I was done in by swimming pools and models and fast cars, the Health Insurance paid for it all, and now is out of funds*, she left with them the bonbons and jars of honey, she took care of them, mollycoddled them and she pinched from them three five-euro bills as well.

On her way out she called Yukaris, we're back safe, not to worry, more details tomorrow.

She was looking forward to her chair at her house. She wouldn't turn the TV on, she had cut it down a lot, just fluorescent stage sets and screaming and witticisms, there wasn't a single companionable channel where they spoke slowly, in whispers if possible, like old poets on the CD with their collected works. A voice like that was what she needed tonight to give her courage and the strength for her wake of recapitulation.

Of course, the recapitulation would bear no relation to a novel, let Sabine write her life story, let anyone who wanted to write books of the kind where their childhood is wrapped up in one hundred pages and in another one or two hundred the rest of life is shrouded, describing in overstated detail a room of ten by fifteen as if it stretched for a hundred acres, a divorce as if it were the Hundred Years' War, distending a mere sunset into a long-winded treatise and a mystery to be accounted for.

No, absolutely not, and though Viv did hold on to the books the cruel-hearted cardiologist unloaded on her, whenever she opened one, she skipped those pages, concentrating always on the action and the strict lineage of basic events, the juice of each story is distilled in two, three pages at most and in her own, no matter if the writer embroidered to his heart's content, embellished and beguiled, there was no way to ameliorate the nitty-gritty of the plot, three rapes, one murder, turned in by the mother, in jail for life.

The synopsis of the book for the other side, three rape victims, one of these vilely murdered, her father's death, two graves for her mother.

She had entertained the thought, theoretically, several times, of going to see her, she imagined entering the house on her knees, with her sewing kit, that she sewed up the lining of her skirt, that she said, if you had killed my son at the trial I would have understood and better that he were in the grave rather than your child, but in reality, walking down the street she was always looking out for thin, white-haired women, so she had time to beat a retreat.

A life that was plainly insulting and there was more to follow.

Past midnight she called the Bulgarian, why, Stefka, why? Because she couldn't take any more, that's why.

Then she dusted the sand off the two Delphi books and the uncut tome of Sikelianos, a *Delphic Speech* here as well, she packed them off to the drawer, washed off the salt in the shower, the herpes had passed, that was something, she put on a load of washing, made some tea, rubbed her ankles a bit, they hurt, like a retired ballerina's.

Dance is the prayer of the feet, she recalled the pronouncements of the old Rhoda about dance floors and cruising young men doing their proud, solitary dances like Japanese shadow warriors. Herself at a distance from all that, a magnet for troubles. So, then, chair and a cigarette.

What is, finally, the zdoop? A code? A spell? An order to a dog? The growl of a prehistoric animal? The title of a comic book? A word from cartoons, like phew, yum-yum, yippee and wow? Why hadn't she asked her son, again?

Every story has blanks, some are common to all the participants in its plot. Each one, though, has a few that only he has noticed, that don't add up for him alone no matter how he tries, if he does, which he probably doesn't.

In certain cases, some are well served by such blanks, gray zones which they guard by tooth and claw, terrified at the possibility that, if they were to be filled, the truth might be intolerable.

Lighting another cigarette she thought about absolutely everyone she knew, most had their spells of fanatical gripping, one mishap was enough to knock them off balance.

Why, what's in your sacks, then? A bankruptcy, someone leaving for another country, coming to blows with the tax department, failure to qualify for a job, a mean mother-in-law, a neurotic boss, a Molotov-throwing kid, a fireplace that smokes out the living room, esophageal constriction, fear of heights, conjugal infidelity, stretch marks on the butt.

Drop in and have a look at mine, and you'll think yourselves lucky.

Third cigarette, at first she despised it, then she sweet-talked to it, my little smoke. That smoke, drag by drag, filled her with mercy for everyone, the variety of sacks was endless, a military satchel filled with the wreckage of war and of peace, a fishing net that only ever caught the endless tide of contempt. She praised them all, the promiscuous and the drunkards, the switchblade-wielding bullies, the office bearers of impoverishment and those made arrogant by injustice.

The world is a convoy of thousands of trucks loaded with sacks, people die and the sacks, virtually intact, are waiting to be shouldered by an unlucky descendant.

The blameless in life are few with a light, silken pouch, the many are porters, no way to be spared the lugging of their sacks, some made of canvas, some hessian, sometimes with holes, patches, sometimes with bits of embroidery here and there. And every sack, a mailman's bag full of letters with crimes indelibly inscribed, parcels stuffed with passions and little boxes with unwanted gifts.

Thinking of boxes, her eye fell on an empty pack of cigarettes on the arm of the wheelchair, next to the cat-shaped ashtray with a butt in it. Linus's brand, he must have finished them while she was briefly combing her hair in their previous short visit. She stood up to throw it out along with her cigarette butt but, one of those crazy things the night can put you up to, as soon as she touched it, she felt like speaking to it.

– Year before last I had an old girl, she bored me and I neglected her. I never said an extra word to her unless her blood pressure hit the roof. In one of those crises, while I was stroking her to calm her down until the pill took effect, she said something terrible to me, you don't love me when I'm all right. It seems that some people can only give their best then, when the going gets tough. Me, I am like that. Why don't you do the same. Be by his side, to soften the wildness in him, to make pretty smoke drawings on the ceiling. Keep him company there, in the stronghold of stench and ash. He struck and was wounded and will be wounded for every day of his life, with no cure, no redemption.

After saying this to the packet, she had an urge to kiss it. She hadn't been able to kiss her own kid, she would kiss his cigarettes. She did, and she kissed the cigarette butt that had touched his bitter mouth and then she derided herself.

She turned off the lamp next to her, she had no intention tonight of moving to either the bed or the couch, she'd try to make it through the night on the carved chair, her base. She stood up, took the pillow from the seat and placed it behind her back. The pillow with the burgundy velvet and the four golden tassels, single remnant of her father-in-law's craft, much traveled, from Corfu to the bachelor rooms of Fotis and his subsequent homes, was still there, something always persists in surviving, to connect and remind.

She got comfortable, she tuned in, too, to Tiger's scratching sounds from next door who was again manhandling the useless keys, a common musical accompaniment to her nights in the apartment building and during her teas.

She had a sip, other folks wallow in anemones and sweet peas, us Kolevas in the ditch with the nettle and the devil's weed. Somewhere, somehow, both he and I need to find a corner in life to fit in. We don't ask for more, just a corner. Let those other folks turn their backs and walk away. Let them go on their way, let them get busy with putting on and off the mantles of conscience and reputation, let them vote governments in and vote them back out, let them change the laws, travel to Brussels for Christmas and playact at being European and go to their village for Easter, and playact at being true country folks, let them build palaces or mud-brick outhouses, let them not care about what they pay for the spaghetti and lobster or buy their cheese and salami on credit, let them all rejoice in May evenings, every night a wedding in the sky, the moon a silver dowry and the stars for bonbons, and let them wake up a different person a hundred times in their lifetime, we'll always wake up the same and to the same, in the ditch, ditched.

A home requires infidelity. It needs you to pick up your bag and walk out. A piece of advice from Sabine, she brought her to mind with the incontestable necklaces upon her German neck, different ones in the morning and in the evening, the most impressive reserved for the moment of their checkout and good-byes, starfish and nautilus shells, seahorses and boats sinking into her shipwrecked bust.

If there's one thing I've missed, it's a boat and an open sea, Viv suddenly thought and sighed, though without complaint, the necklace's pale blue finery did a good job of covering over that cut-and-dried I strangled a girl, Ma, of gently slipping her back into the cool waters of the sea. This was the feeling she ought to start with every day from now on. Because she would go on, there were days upon days to be had.

She had no way of knowing if there would be a second leave granted or if her son would be pardoned some day, she couldn't form friendships or take up sports, nor did she have any say on the direction the world was heading in, the movements, like they say, and the leaders and the planetary chiefs could go where they pleased, she was off to one side, at her post, responsible for the fate of only two, alone. So, then, tomorrow morning first thing, she'd pick up her bag and go. She would kneel, yes, she would, in front of the first pregnant woman she came across, would stroke and kiss her belly. A child would come out from there who might even, might well, love the sea breeze like Linus did who, as a child, at seven, at ten, stood stock-still in drafts, turned his head to the east, closed his eyes and with pleasure let the wind blow his shirt and blond hair.

At one such moment, she had called him, my little pony. She might as well wring her memory to unbury such things, she needed to, so as to give the lie from time to time to the notion that all the past was one frightful shadow, an informant who would be on her trails forevermore, policing her days and nights.

Tonight her mind would stay turned on like a rubber hose running all night, watering the ridges of a thirsty garden.

And tomorrow, after she had kissed a belly in the street—the pregnant belly is the sack with the most precious contents—Viv Koleva would follow the road down to the sea, maybe all the way out to Sounion, and would stand and face the little waves that would be pummelling against the shore like those dancers in the white skirts she'd seen on a documentary on NET television.

There, quiet on a rock, she would remember one by one all the good moments and she wouldn't be able to have enough of the best one, when she and her son went at last back into the sea. Ah, those first minutes, when suddenly and mysteriously it was as if for the first time, the three hapless girls were erased from their minds, the poor neck of the third with the shoelace, her father who raised up her photograph at the trial and the lining that had come undone in her mother's skirt.

It was an unexpected miracle in one fell swoop, what they felt would not happen to them again, like finding their full span and being taken over, if for two or three minutes, no more, by a joy, such a joy, as if they weren't to blame for anything.

About the Author

Ioanna Karystiani was born on the island of Crete, Greece, and now lives in Athens. Her literary debut came with the collection of short stories, *I kyria Kataki* (*Ms. Kataki*). She has since written three novels, including *The Jasmine Isle* (Europa Editions, 2006) and *Swell* (Europa Editions, 2010).